CRITICS PRAISE CATHERINE SPANGLER AND *SHADOWER*!

"Catherine Spangler has a unique gift to create characters who linger in your mind long after you have closed the book."
—Christine Feehan, bestselling author of *Dark Challenge*

"Terrific! Catherine Spangler knows how to keep you at the edge of your seat! Fast-paced and sexy, *Shadower* is a winner from cover to cover."
—Susan Grant, bestselling author of *Once A Pirate*

"Catherine Spangler's *Shadower* delivers another riveting glimpse into exotic other worlds. Imaginative . . . sensual . . . a must read!"
—Kathy Baker, Waldenbooks, 1999 RWA Bookseller of the Year

A HEATED DEBATE

Moving like a striking serpent, he grabbed her and pulled her against him, so close, she felt every millimeter of his unyielding body; felt the heat emanating from him. He was fast—she'd give him that. Furious, she squirmed against him, and he inhaled sharply. She stilled immediately, alarmed by the physical evidence of his reaction to her.

"I *will* see you off this planet," he insisted, straddling his legs outside of hers.

"I'll see you in Hades first!"

"Sweetheart, we're already there." He framed her face with his hands, his thumb wiping away another patch of slime. "You know, you clean up pretty good. You need to work on the attitude, though."

"Men like you don't bring out my best side." A second wave of dizziness rushed over her, and she clutched the front of his flightsuit for support.

Desire flared in his midnight eyes, sparking an odd rush through her veins. He must have sensed her reaction, because his expression turned predatory. "I wonder if you taste as good as you look," he murmured.

Before she could react, he lowered his mouth to hers.

Other *Love Spell* books by Catherine Spangler:
SHIELDER

SHADOWER

Catherine Spangler

LOVE SPELL   ✦   NEW YORK CITY

A LOVE SPELL BOOK®

December 2000

Published by

Dorchester Publishing Co., Inc.
276 Fifth Avenue
New York, NY 10001

Cover art by John Ennis.
www.ennisart.com

ISBN 0-505-52424-4

The name "Love Spell" and its logo are trademarks of Dorchester Publishing Co., Inc.

Printed in the United States of America.

Visit us on the web at www.dorchesterpub.com.

For my mother, Jacquelyn, a class act all the way. Your compassion and gentleness were a guiding beacon to all who knew you. Much love always.

And for my father, Henry, who taught me the importance of humor and acceptance, and tutored all my friends in math when I was growing up. You're the best.

ACKNOWLEDGMENTS

So many people have guided and shaped my life and my writing, that I can't possibly name every one. But I'd like to give special thanks to Erick Bening, for his computer expertise and keeping the concepts simple; to David Gray, for his scientific expertise on weapons and space battles. As always, thanks to my incredible critique partners, Jennifer, Linda and Vickie. And to Roberta Brown, an extraordinary agent and good friend. Also, to Chris Keeslar, for his sound insights and suggestions. Thank you all for helping to make this book possible.

SHADOWER

Chapter One

He'd always figured he would end up in hell. He just hadn't planned on arriving there while he was still drawing air into his lungs.

Well, he had been wrong—once or twice—before. Dreary and rank smelling, Giza's was a hellhole all right. Hazy lighting combined with narcotic-laden smoke created a murky mist, shrouding those present in anonymity. The dimness was probably for the better, Sabin Travers thought, scowling as he stepped in some unidentifiable muck on the floor. Too bad the poor lighting couldn't mute the drunken bellows of the miscreants of the universe who congregated here, or the stench assaulting his nose.

If he didn't need the solace of some good Elysian liquor, he'd have killed the time watching Radd repair his ship. Just the thought of that cursed ship was enough to propel him toward the bar for a refill. Spirit, what a day! Galen had eluded him again—a reward of a thousand miterons blown to

Catherine Spangler

blazing hells. Then his ship had developed a problem with the stardrive, and he'd barely made it to
Calt. Thank Spirit he'd finally been able to commission a new ship, which would be ready within
the next lunar cycle.

Sabin set his mug on the counter. "Hey, Thorne,
give me a refill."

A small, gnomelike man scurried along the inside of the bar. His bald head, overly large for his
body, bobbed up and down. "S-sure thing, M-Mr.
Travers." Ducking an empty glass heaved at him
by a soused Antek and ignoring the raucous laughter from the rest of the drunks, Thorne poured
more golden Elysian elixir into Sabin's mug. He
deftly snatched the miteron Sabin tossed him before scooting back to his safe niche near an exit.

So *this* was the nucleus of his existence, Sabin
thought sardonically. Endless hours spent among
the dregs of humanity. He had no real home, nor
anyone to go home to, for that matter. Never
would. It was simpler that way, he reminded himself.

"Here's to the carefree life," he muttered.

Just as he lifted the drink to his lips, a flash of
color at the end of the bar caught his eye. A
woman leaned in at the counter, clasping a drink
between slender fingers. Her hair had drawn his
attention; hair a rich bronze color reflecting myriad highlights, even in the dim interior of Giza's.
It was gathered into a sleek twist on top of her
head, revealing a graceful neck.

Her profile didn't appear too bad either, although he couldn't see the lines clearly at this distance. The tawny cape she wore hid her figure, but
she held herself with an air of confidence. She emanated an elegance not seen among the worn-out

14

females who routinely serviced the degenerates frequenting this soulless planet.

She was as out of place in this den of iniquity as a baby kerani in a pit of Oderan sand vipers. And she would last about as long. Sabin felt drawn to her, despite the fact that he usually avoided entanglements with women, preferring the uninvolved physical release he could find at the Pleasure Domes. This wouldn't be anything more than an offer to see the lady safely out of this abyss, he told himself, striding to the end of the bar.

As he approached, sidestepping an unconscious Leor sprawled across the floor, she glanced up from her drink, making momentary eye contact with him. He stared into unique eyes, as golden as the Elysian liquor he'd been drinking. And as intoxicating. He felt as if he'd been poleaxed. Her face was equally striking. The angular bone structure created a perfect frame for mesmerizing eyes, a patrician nose, and a lush mouth suggestive of decadent possibilities. Heat surged through his body.

Her gaze shifted, coolly sweeping the length of him. Then, with an indifferent shrug, she returned her attention to her drink.

Sabin seldom cared if women were interested in him or not, but he wasn't used to being ignored. Placing his hand on the counter, he leaned toward the woman. She was tall, only a few inches shorter than his own six feet. Her scent, sweet and musky, launched a secondary assault on his senses.

He forced his focus back to the reason he'd approached her in the first place. "Don't you know it's dangerous for a lone female to be in Giza's, much less anywhere on Calt?"

She didn't even look up. "Go jump in the Fires."

Despite the sharpness of her words, her low

15

voice struck an even deeper chord. Further intrigued, Sabin took on the challenge. Shifting to lean back against the bar, he crossed his arms over his chest. "Tsk, tsk. Not very original. Talk like that certainly won't deter these lowlifes. You really should let me join you. You'll be safe with me."

Icy amber eyes met his. "I seriously doubt that. And I find my own company preferable to"—she paused to peruse him once again, a look of revulsion crossing her face—"riff-raff." Clearly, she found him about as inviting as a rabid desert krat.

Involuntarily, Sabin glanced down to his immaculate black flightsuit and boots that were shined to a high gloss. He'd showered today, and shaved, although with his heavy beard growth, his jaw no doubt sported its usual evening shadow. Still, most women found him attractive, and always had.

"I have it from very reliable sources that my company is *extremely* enjoyable."

Her generous mouth curved into a sneer. "I can't imagine why. Look, I don't want company, I don't want conversation. I don't want anything from you, not even the time of day. Just stay the blazing hells away from me! Is *that* clear enough?"

Obviously, she wasn't the friendly type. "Oh, yeah, lady, very clear. Be sure and tell that to some of the other characters in here. I'm sure they'll be glad to respect your royal wishes."

"I can take care of myself, I assure you. I certainly don't need any help from the likes of you."

The likes of me? Familiar feelings of unworthiness reared, but Sabin shoved them back. "Fine." Needing that Elysian liquor more than ever, he returned to the opposite end of the bar to finish his drink in peace. After that, he'd go see about his ship. He'd find better company with the taciturn

Radd than with this serpent-tongued female. By the Abyss! This day couldn't end soon enough.

Moriah breathed a sigh of relief when the man strode away, an angry set to his shoulders. Males were forever hitting on her, sickening her with their crude advances. And this man emanated danger, with those inscrutable midnight eyes glowing in his chiseled face, and his long, black hair tied at the nape of his neck. Dressed entirely in black, with two evil-looking blasters and a phaser slung from his utility belt, he'd seemed shaped of darkness.

She had taken on bigger men than him, certainly, but watching the lethal grace he displayed as he stalked along the counter, the ripple of muscles beneath his flightsuit, she suspected his lean body was superbly trained. He was surely the most dangerous one here. She could handle the rest of these drunken idiots.

She wouldn't be here much longer anyway—assuming her luck didn't get any worse.

Downing the rest of her drink, she cursed Turlock. He was an ugly, half-Antek scum, and she should never have gone in on that disastrous Ataran deal with him. She had thought she was far ahead of him. Obviously she'd been wrong, as he had helped himself to her ship while she met with Fletch. Not surprising, given she owed him several thousand miterons. That ship would be difficult, if not impossible, to replace. Ultra-fast starcraft equipped with nondetectable armaments and concealed storage compartments were scarce and costly. Damn Turlock to the Fires!

Now she had to come up with five hundred miterons to purchase her passage off this viper pit. Moriah shoved aside rising panic. She had faced far more perilous situations than being stranded, without a ship, in a hellhole. All she needed was money. She scanned the dim bar, confirming the fact that she was the only female present. In her business, most of her dealings were with males, and the majority of them surrendered their money for two things: sexual gratification and gaming.

The first option was unthinkable. A shudder wracked Moriah, and she clamped a mental lid on the dark images clamoring too close to the surface.

The second option terrified her almost as much as the first.

She hated games of chance. They were games with stakes higher than mere gold, or even entire ships; souls exchanged hands.

Wiping her palms down her cape, Moriah turned toward the gaming tables. She was well versed in most of the most popular ways to gamble—she'd had years of exposure. Yet, despite her competence, every time she approached a gaming table, she battled an army of demons. She'd long ago accepted that most of her life's memories were best forgotten, but that didn't make them go away, especially in situations like the one she now faced.

She chose a table where a new game of Fool's Quest was starting. Players had already taken three of the seats—a renegade Antek, a Shen, and a Jaccian; a highly unlikely combination anywhere in the quadrant but Calt. But then, the long reach of the Controllers—that evil race that ruled so much of the universe—didn't extend here. Their Antek henchmen couldn't patrol every sector of their huge domain.

Nor could the Controllers maintain mind domination on every planet, moon, or meteorite; which was why rebel groups, such as Shielders, had managed to survive, despite Controller determination to decimate all opposition. Calt, having no natural resources, no value whatsoever, held no interest for the Controllers. Over the years, it had become a hotbed of the lowest life forms in the universe.

Moriah stopped behind the empty chair at the gaming table. She tossed her pouch of miterons on the table. "I'm in."

The Antek grunted, his beady eyes glazed from too much drink. Good. He'd be easy to outmaneuver in the game. Moriah angled her face away to avoid inhaling his foul odor.

"Lookee, lookee, a lady!" the Jaccian chanted in his sing-song voice. He assessed her with a cunning, lascivious gaze, then waved a tentacle for her to sit. "Join us."

The Shen, his face shrouded by the deep hood attached to his tunic, reached out graceful, slender fingers to swoop up her pouch of miterons. He balanced them on his palm as if measuring their weight. "One hundred fifty miterons is the required wager, mistress," he said, his voice calm and melodic.

It was a standard wager, and one that would enable her to win the entire amount she needed in one match. And Moriah fully expected to win, having chosen a game that required intelligence and strategy rather than just pure chance. She would never again allow her life to be controlled by luck.

"There are one hundred and fifty miterons there," she answered.

The Shen returned the pouch to the table. "Have a seat, mistress."

Sliding into the chair, she drew a deep breath, mentally pushing her demons away. She pulled out the keypad and activated it, then rapidly selected from various choices the three components—power source, armaments, strategy—she wished to employ in the game. She made her choices carefully, basing them upon her experience with the beings with whom she was gaming. She hoped these gamers were like others of their kinds.

A hologram of the three-dimensional, five-tiered battle arena appeared at the center of the table, followed by images of the players, randomly placed. During the thirty-second countdown before the game began, Moriah studied the holographic arena, and her foes' strategies.

She had drawn fair positioning, with all three of her components on mid-levels below her. The Antek and Jaccian had chosen as she expected, and could be defeated. The Antek had gone for brute force, while the Jaccian had selected for mental control. She'd expected the Shen to go for power, but he surprised her, choosing a blend of game components that closely matched her own choices. He was the opponent to beat.

The game progressed rapidly, demanding all of Moriah's concentration and skill. As expected, she and the Shen hurriedly dispatched the Antek and Jaccian components, turning the game into a grueling two-way battle of wits. As Giza's patrons realized this was a truly challenging match, they gathered around the table, placing bets on the outcome and offering their own battle tactics. Moriah focused, tuning out the shouts.

At last she defeated the Shen—just barely. She sank back in her chair, some of her tension easing. Murmurs of disapproval swept through the crowd. They didn't see many women on Calt, and the vast majority of those earned their wages on

their backs, not at gaming tables. Most of the bets
had been against her.

The Shen nodded in acceptance. "Well played,"
was all he said, pushing back his chair. Taunts and
jeers followed him as he faded into the crowd.

Moriah wasted no time collecting her oppo-
nents' money pouches and stuffing them into her
cloak pocket. The sooner out of this pit, the better.
But as she turned to leave, an inexplicable feeling
of being watched drew her attention toward the
bar. The black-clad man leaned nonchalantly
against the counter. His dark gaze locked with
hers and an odd fission of awareness sizzled between them. He raised his drink in a mocking salute.

This was an arrogant, obnoxious man who obviously expected every female to swoon before
him. Narrowing her eyes, Moriah whirled and
strode toward the entrance. A loud bellow and a
jerk on her cloak brought her to a halt. She turned
to face the Antek she'd just defeated.

His face and snout were blotched red from too
much liquor, and drool oozed from his mouth.
"No female beat me," he growled. "You cheat."

She tried unsuccessfully to yank her cloak free.
"Let me go."

He snarled, showing razor-sharp teeth. "You
cheat, female. Give back money."

Moriah employed a quick chop of her hand to
the Antek's arm. She followed up with a solid kick
to his solar plexus. Staggering back, the creature
smashed into a table. He slid to the floor, too
drunk to get up. The patrons cheered, hoping for
more. No one could expect help here, only bloodlust.

Disgusted, she turned back toward the entry.
She'd only gone a meter when a tentacle wrapped

around her waist and spun her around. She found herself face to chest with the seven-foot Jaccian. "Lady, lady! Cheat, cheat!" he sing-songed.

Great, just great. Jaccians were even stupider than Anteks. And tougher.

"Get your hands off me, alien!" Moriah snarled, shoving hard against the creature's chest and kicking one spindly leg from under it.

He crashed to his knees as she reached for her phaser. He reached out a second tentacle to stop her, but her weapon was already drawn. Two quick blasts amputated the tentacles in a spray of slime. She was free.

She spun to dash for the entry, but more tentacles wrapped around her, squeezing the breath out of her. Caught off guard, she dropped her phaser. How could the Jaccian have recovered so quickly? "No do that," sing-songed a different voice. By the Abyss! Two of them! She could readily handle one, but two—Moriah kicked and thrashed, battling for breath as the tentacles tightened even more.

"Let me go!" she gasped, crunching her boot heel into her assailant's shin. He jerked, his hold loosening momentarily. Sucking air into her lungs, she rammed her elbow into his abdomen. He squealed, and she slid free of two of his tentacles.

The first Jaccian staggered to his feet, waving his two remaining tentacles. He ripped off her cape. Moriah aimed a high kick at his midriff, and he stumbled back again.

"Need some help?"

She looked up to see the black-clad man standing two meters away. While most of Giza's patrons were busy betting on the outcome of the fight, *he* wanted to play hero. She could just guess what he'd expect in payment. "I already told you to stay away from me," she snarled, wrestling with a tentacle. "I can take care of myself."

The first Jaccian approached again. The man raised sleek black brows. "Appears to me you're outmatched."

She didn't need this distraction. Twisting sideways, trying to free herself, she gasped, "I can . . . handle . . . this. Go away."

"Think I'll hang around, just in case."

Obnoxious *and* obstinate. "If you really want to help, get me my phaser." Moriah heaved herself backward, crashing the second Jaccian into a table. He grunted. She jolted forward and bumped the creature again. One more time, and she'd be—

The first Jaccian lunged against her, pinning her between him and his friend. "Money and weapons good," he chanted, ripping at the seam of her flightsuit. "Having woman good, too."

Black, insidious fear flooded through her, robbing her of coherent thought. "Let me go!" she shrieked, frantically slugging at her assailant.

The Jaccian dug the jagged edge of his tentacle into her shoulder. She felt blood welling. Another tentacle wrapped around her breast and the familiar terror threatened to overcome her. A scraping noise drew her back from the edge of hysteria. Looking down, she saw her phaser sliding toward her feet.

Her gaze shot to the dark-haired man. Even through the panicked, nightmarish haze, she noted the shift in his bearing. His eyes glittered dangerously as his gloved hands moved to rest on his blasters. "Let the lady go." Steel edged his voice.

The Jaccian in front of her let loose a string of

obscenities. "Female is mine," he insisted shrilly. "I keep."

"Let her go. *Now*."

"No!" the Jaccian screeched. "I mate with her!"

"This is your final warning. Release her."

"You die!" shrilled the Jaccian, jerking her toward him and drawing his weapon.

If he thought to use her body for a shield, he was sadly mistaken. Moriah made herself go limp. Falling back against the one behind her, she wrestled the first Jaccian against his partner. The tentacles loosened enough for her to slide down prickly legs to the relative safety of the floor. She grabbed her phaser.

Blaster explosions filled the room. She managed to shoot a tentacle and disrupter from one Jaccian. Slime splattered the top of her head. Then, before she could move, a heavy weight collapsed on her, slamming her back against the floor and forcing the air from her lungs. More slime oozed over her face and chest. She tried to claw her way free of the heavy Jaccians—or what was left of them.

She heard a thud, and the weight suffocating her eased. Then the weight was gone completely, as a strong hand clasped hers and pulled her to her feet. Chest heaving, legs wobbling, Moriah stared at the carnage around her.

The large amount of smoke clogging the room, and the charred chairs on each side of the black-clad man attested to the firepower which had been loosed. She noticed blood on the man's upper left arm, although it appeared to be a surface wound. He'd survive.

His dark gaze met hers, and he shrugged. "Fortunately, they had poor aim."

It galled her that she'd needed his help to extri-

cate herself. "If you're expecting some sort of reward, you can forget it," she snapped, heart still
pounding. "In fact, you should be thanking *me*.
They missed disintegrating you only because of
my quick action. Which, by the way, probably
saved my life as well, since you showed no reluctance about firing with me trapped between those
two brutes. You could have hit me!"

His eyes narrowing, he slid his blasters back
into their holsters. "Maybe I should have. It would
have simplified things considerably." He probed
his wounded arm and winced.

"I didn't ask you to get involved. All I needed was
my phaser. I had the situation under control. You
didn't have to get hurt."

His gaze snapped back to hers, his eyes sparking. "Oh, right. You were only pinned between two
seven-foot Jaccians, had three tentacles wrapped
around you, no weapons, and your clothing being
torn off. You didn't need any help. Pardon my interference, but I love getting phaser burns. I live
for them."

Opening her mouth to retort, Moriah inhaled
smoke and went into a paroxysm of coughing. A
momentary wave of dizziness washed over her.
She grabbed a table for support.

"Hey, you okay?"

"Yes," she choked out, just as her legs buckled.

He caught her before she hit the ground, his
arms encircling her and pulling her flush against
his hard body. "Sure you are."

Alarm resurfaced, lending strength to her legs.
She'd sworn no man would ever hold her like this
again. "I told you I'm fine. Let go of me!" More
coughing interrupted her protest.

He eased her onto a chair. "Take shallow
breaths."

Moriah gasped and wheezed, her eyes stinging. The man seemed unaffected by the smoke from the smoldering chairs. He retrieved her cape from where the Jaccian had thrown it. Prying her phaser from her hand, he shoved it through his utility belt. Then he tossed her cape around her.

"You need some air. Let's get out of here." Taking her arm firmly, he pulled her out of the chair and to the entry. All those who had gathered to watch the action stepped back, giving them a wide berth. Hoots and lewd suggestions followed them to the exit.

Shivering violently, Moriah stumbled after the man. She didn't know if her physical reaction was shock from the narrow escape, or from the ugly memories that surfaced every time a man touched her.

Outside, the humid, stale air offered little relief to her burning lungs. Twin full moons illuminated the barren surroundings and the litter scattered on the hard-packed sand.

"Ugh. There's nothing worse than Jaccian slime." The man removed his blast gloves, then helped himself to the edge of Moriah's cape to wipe his flightsuit.

"Hey! That's mine." She snatched the cape away, but he immediately retrieved it and raised it to her face.

Strangely lightheaded, she made no protest as he wiped the ooze from her cheeks and chin with surprising gentleness. It felt so good, she closed her eyes, swaying a little, forgetting for a moment that a man was touching her. Until his ministrations moved to the front of her flightsuit, jolting her to full alert.

She smacked his arm away. "Stop that!"

"Just trying to help." He flashed her a devilish

26

grin, and her heart missed a beat. She'd spared him only a cursory glance when he'd approached her inside Giza's. Now the moonlight illuminated a face most women would call devastating: high cheekbones, deep-set black eyes, an arrogant nose, a sensual mouth. The shadow of a beard only served to emphasize a stubborn jaw, to enhance his overwhelming masculinity.

He was just the type of man Moriah found the most threatening.

Needing to put some space between them, she stumbled away and headed back toward the settlement, ignoring the shakiness in her legs and the throbbing in her shoulder. The footfalls behind her told her this man wouldn't be so easily brushed off.

"Wrong way, lady." He took her arm again and turned her toward the landing strip. "Where's your ship? You should get off Calt—now."

"I have business to take care of first."

"Haven't you learned? There are a lot safer places than Calt to support a gambling habit. Unless offering that luscious body of yours to any lusting male is your business. Even that would be safer elsewhere."

Outrage and disgust shot through her. "Why, you sleazy scourge of the universe!" She raised her arm to strike him, only to find her wrist caught in the magnasteel vise of his hand.

"Temper, temper," he said with a laugh. "Now is this any way to thank a man who risked his life saving your honor?"

She wondered if he was ever serious. Jerking her arm free, she snapped, "All right then, you overgrown desert krat. *Thank you!* Now, as I said, I have unfinished business. Then I'll be all too glad to leave."

"Care to tell me what that business is? Perhaps I can help."

She wanted to tell him she'd never accept assistance from him—or any other man—except that she just had. But that was as far as it went. "Arius could go nova, and I wouldn't need any more help from you."

All playfulness vanished from his face, and a glittering determination filled his eyes. "Then forget it. Calt is far too dangerous for you to hang around, especially since most of the beings at Giza's just lost a lot of money betting against you. You're leaving now, if I have to strap you into your ship and set the pilot for automatic."

Oh! She'd love to blast that overbearing expression off his face. One small problem—he had possession of her weapon. "Give me back my phaser."

"You really don't believe in saying *please*, do you? Someone needs to teach you some manners."

"I don't need you or anyone else to tell me what to do. Go burn in the Abyss."

Moving like a striking serpent, he grabbed her and pulled her against him, so close, she felt every millimeter of his unyielding body; felt the heat emanating from him. He was fast—she'd give him that. Furious, she squirmed against him, and he inhaled sharply. She stilled immediately, alarmed by the physical evidence of his reaction to her.

"I *will* see you off this planet," he insisted, clamping her legs inside his own.

"I'll see you in Hades first!"

"Sweetheart, we're already there." He framed her face with his hands, his thumb wiping away another patch of slime. "You know, you clean up pretty good. You need to work on the attitude, though."

"Men like you don't bring out my best side." A

second wave of dizziness rushed over her, and she clutched the front of his flightsuit for support.

Desire flared in his dark eyes, sparking an odd rush through her veins. He must have sensed her reaction, because his expression turned predatory. "I wonder if you taste as good as you look," he murmured.

Before she could react, he lowered his mouth to hers. Her body felt sluggish, like she'd been drugged, but her senses went into overdrive, making her acutely aware of the rock-hard pressure of his legs hemming her in. Of the searing solidity of his body pressed against her; the startling feel of his lips molding to hers, taking confident possession. Of the heady taste of liquor as his tongue invaded her mouth.

Her thoughts scattered like marbles in a vortex, leaving her oddly disoriented. For one mad moment, she almost savored the unique experience; the comfort and security of this man's embrace . . . the absurd feeling of finding a haven.

Then the black talons of horror and revulsion descended. Panic resurged; adrenaline pounded through her body. Another surge of dizziness sent her reeling. She tried to push away, but her legs collapsed.

Darkness engulfed her. . . .

Chapter Two

Well, blazing hells, Sabin thought wryly. He knew he was good, but he'd never made a woman faint before. *Yeah, right, Travers. You're such a lady killer.* He had no idea what had possessed him to kiss her, given her obvious aversion to him. But her lush, tempting mouth had lured him into a fool's game. That, and something in her eyes, a vulnerability contradictory to her fierce bravado.

Sabin shook away that last thought. It was lust, pure and simple; one of those inexplicable attractions that just happened sometimes. No big deal. As for her fainting, the shock from the just finished brawl was the likely culprit.

He eased her to the ground, gritting his teeth against the pain in his arm. He was bleeding, but not heavily. He'd take care of the injury later, after he dealt with the woman. She should come around quickly. But the dark stain seeping from her left shoulder gave him cause to reconsider. He pulled her cape back and saw ugly, raised welts through her torn flightsuit, blood oozing from them. He wanted to kick himself.

He should have blown those two goons to smithereens as soon as the woman had been compromised. He'd known no one else at Giza's would come to her aid. Bar fights, and betting on who would win them, were a favorite pastime there. Sabin would have stepped in sooner, but she had displayed an impressive ability to hold her own, readily dispatching the Antek. She hadn't done too badly against two seven-foot Jaccians, either.

But if he had intervened sooner, she might not have been injured. A wound from a Jaccian tentacle could be serious, especially if the victim reacted unfavorably to the mild poison stored in the barbs. Even without a high sensitivity, the poison left the victim sluggish and disoriented for a few hours; not to mention there was also a risk of infection.

So now he had to play healer to an overbearing female who showed no gratitude whatsoever to him for saving her hide. Hell, he didn't even know her name. Since he had no idea where her ship was and had no intention of taking her back to the settlement, his own craft was the only option. Just what he needed—an unwelcome intrusion into what had already been a miserable day.

He hefted her into his arms, staggering slightly and trying the keep the weight off his injured arm. She obviously didn't miss any meals, although from what he'd seen, her body was in top condition. The woman was tall and statuesque, nicely curved in all the right places.

Don't go there, he warned himself. He didn't need any distractions, not with so much gold on the line for Galen's capture. And not with the horrifying rumors of a deadly virus the Controllers

Catherine Spangler

had unleashed in their struggle against the Shielders. He prayed to Spirit those rumors weren't true.

Shifting his burden more securely in his arms, he trekked across the hard-packed sand to where his ship sat on a landing pad. It was a battered piece of junk, but it had seen him through many a scrape. He punched the hatch control with his elbow and carried her up the ramp. The cockpit was on the right. He could see Radd's legs protruding from the open stardrive casing.

"How are the repairs coming?" he called out.

"Huh?" Radd slid out and sat up, a far-away expression on his face. He was always like that when he was deeply involved in the complexities of stardrives and stabilizers and thrusters. He looked like a youth, with his mussed, dark-blond hair, and a smattering of freckles across his round face. But Sabin knew he was older than he looked, a lot more astute than he acted, and one of the best star-class ship mechanics in the quadrant.

"How are the repairs coming?" Sabin repeated.

"Uh, just fine. The new stardrive is almost in, then I have to run diagnostics. Should be done in about three hours." Radd stared at the woman in Sabin's arms. "Who's that?"

Sabin didn't feel like going through lengthy explanations, especially since he didn't know very much himself. "A woman."

Radd blinked his owlish eyes. "You're bringing a woman on board? D'ya want me to leave?"

"She's unconscious, in case you didn't notice."

"Uh, there's only one kinda woman on this planet, far's I know. And some guys don't seem to be too picky about whether a female is conscious or not."

Outside technical ship jargon, that was the most Radd had ever uttered at one time. Sabin stared at him, bemused. "Yeah, well, I don't go in for that one-sided stuff. I like my partners more active. This lady tangled with some Jaccians and needs medical attention."

"Oh. Looks like you need some treatin' yourself."

Sabin's arm was throbbing painfully, but he'd suffered worse. "It's just a phaser burn. No big deal."

Radd started back inside the casing. "By the way," he called out, his voice muffled, "your subspace transceiver sounded twice while you were gone."

It had probably been his partner, McKnight, since Sabin hadn't checked in at the prearranged time. He'd just have to wait. Sabin carried the woman into his cabin and lowered her onto the bunk, shaking out his cramped arms.

He slipped off her cape. Her deep, even breathing reassured him she wasn't suffering an acute reaction to the poison. But her smooth skin was pale, her full lips bloodless. Despite that, despite the blotches of slime, her classic beauty took his breath away. Her lustrous hair had come partly undone from its twist, and he couldn't resist sliding his fingers beneath her head to loosen the rest of the strands and smooth them out. Her hair flowed like rivers of burnished copper over her shoulders and generous breasts.

Who was this woman? And what business could she possibly have on Calt, outside prostitution? Although, as Radd pointed out, that would be the obvious assumption, Sabin would be willing to bet a lot of miterons she wasn't a prostitute.

She could be a professional gamer, although that didn't feel right, either. She knew how to fight. One unpleasant possibility reared its head: she was a Controller agent. Maybe even a shadower, although Sabin had never heard of any female bounty hunters.

He hoped both those possibilities were wrong. He rifled through her cloak and the pouches of miterons, until he found what he sought—her identification disk. He would check it after he took care of the woman's wound.

She stirred, and he realized he'd better hurry and treat her wound, as well as his own. Unfortunately, he had only the most basic medical supplies on board. While he knew rudimentary first-aid, a necessity for those in his profession, he wasn't willing to spare the funds to stock his ship with such sophisticated equipment as infrared sterilizers and suture units. Not when others had needs more pressing than his own. His partner had a well-equipped medical lab on his ship, but McKnight was on the other side of the quadrant, tracking down a lead.

Sabin did have something to sterilize the wound, though—sulfo nitrate, a harsh but effective treatment. It wasn't the ideal cure, but it was all he had, and it would have to do. Stuffing the woman's ID disk into his pocket, he retrieved the antiseptic and some bandages from his supply vault. Realizing her phaser was still stuck inside his belt, he tossed it inside the vault, then returned to his cabin.

He quickly peeled away the top of his flightsuit and slapped a bandage over his wound. He'd clean it later. Right now the woman's needs were more pressing. He turned to the bunk. She hadn't moved. He thought about cutting her suit away, but decided instead to undo the front seam and slide it off her shoulder. The suit was ruined, but she needed something to wear back to her ship.

She moaned as he eased her arm out of the sleeve, letting the fabric rest against her chest. The shoulder looked bad, puffy and black, but the bleeding had stopped. He cleaned the wound with water and soap first. She stirred and protested, unconsciously trying to knock his hand away. He hoped she didn't wake up too soon.

He slid a folded towel under her shoulder, then opened the flask of sulfo nitrate. Holding it over the wound, he took a deep breath. "Here goes," he muttered, and poured.

She didn't react for a few milliseconds, then the nitrate hit home. With a shriek, she came off the bunk. Prepared for that, Sabin pushed her back down. He wasn't prepared, however, for the right hook that smashed into his cheek.

"Ouch!" He stumbled back, and she rolled to her feet. She was halfway through the entry before he regained his senses and caught her, looping his arm around her waist and snagging her.

Her dash had apparently sapped her strength, because he pulled her back to the bunk easily enough, evading her feeble kicks. As a precaution, though, he leaned over her, capturing and trapping her hands against the mat.

She twisted and heaved beneath him, her golden eyes burning with fury. "Spirit, that hurts! Are you trying to kill me?"

"I would say it was the other way around," he responded, resisting the strong urge to rub his throbbing cheek. "You have a pretty bad Jaccian wound on your shoulder, and I had to put sulfo nitrate on it. I know it stings. Let me blow on it and—"

"I don't want your breath on me. Don't do another thing," she gritted out between clenched teeth. She tossed her head to the side, her shimmering hair fanning out like Saija silk over her injured shoulder and across her chest. Feeling the tension in her arms, her fingers digging into the mat, he knew the nitrate must sting like crazy.

"This will help, I promise." He released one hand and drew her hair away from her shoulder. He froze at the sight of her breast poised on the verge of overflowing her flightsuit, which had slipped perilously low.

Abundantly rounded and firm, it swelled temptingly above the torn fabric. His body reacted immediately, the blood pounding to his lower extremities. By the Fires!

He was no untried, inexperienced youth, and he'd long ago learned to control his desires. Yet the overwhelming urge to feel the weight of that fullness in his hand, to explore its texture and taste, battled with reason. Somehow, this woman had managed to have this unwelcome effect on his libido not once—but twice, even though she had obviously despised him on sight.

Under different circumstances, he might have shown her what she was capable of *really* feeling, at least physically. But the ugly shoulder wound reminded him now was not the time to satisfy ego or physical lust. He took a deep breath, willing his overheated body to cool. He did have to do one thing, though—remove temptation.

He reached toward her.

The man's fingers brushed against her breast, and Moriah tensed, forgetting the burning agony in her shoulder. She squeezed her eyes shut. A band of darkness tightened around her heart, robbing her of breath. Dread surged through her body. She'd seen the expression on his face; she knew what would happen now. She was far too weak to fight it. Deep inside, a wrenching keening sliced upward, but she refused to utter a sound.

It took her a moment to realize she was shaking uncontrollably, then another to comprehend he'd tugged her flightsuit higher over her breast. She felt his hand gently lifting her hair as the cadence of his deep voice washed over her. "It's okay. It will stop hurting soon, I promise. See if this makes it better."

Then his warm breath wafted over her shoulder, and the stinging receded. Dazed, she perceived his actions held no direct threat, only an odd sort of comfort. His breath drifted over the wound again, and she allowed herself to relax, while she tried to gather her wits. She felt the loss of heat when he moved back.

"How does it feel now?"

She opened her eyes to find him sitting on the edge of the bunk, watching her. The sight of his bare, powerful chest rekindled her apprehensions, and she quickly averted her gaze to his face. He had the darkest eyes she'd ever seen, bottomless ebony pits. But she saw nothing threatening in their depths—for now. Finding her hands free, she flexed her fingers.

He held up a hand in warning. "No more right hooks."

Moriah scrutinized the small room. "Where am I?"

"My cabin. I brought you here after you passed out."

His cabin? She struggled to clear the fog from her brain. How long had she been here? "What time is it?"

He glanced as his chronometer. "2300 hours standard."

Panic evaporated the fog. She was supposed to have met Fletch an hour ago. She pushed herself up and tried to swing her legs off the bunk. "I have to get out of here."

Planted dead center on the edge of the bunk, he didn't budge. She tried to scoot around him, but she was as shaky as a loose solar tile. He pushed her back against the pillow. "You're not going anywhere for a while. You're still disoriented and weak. You will be for a few more hours."

She didn't have a few more hours. It might already be too late. Besides, who did this man think he was, telling her what to do? "I didn't ask for your help, or to be carried aboard your ship. I can take care of myself."

"Yeah, just like you did in Giza's."

His comment rankled Moriah. She *had* lost control of that situation, and she hated not being in control at all times. She could take care of herself perfectly well; she'd been doing so since she was eight seasons old. She'd taken care of Celie, too. *Celie!* By the Spirit! She had to get to Fletch.

She took more deep breaths. Her mind was clearer now, although her body was still weak. She knew this arrogant male probably wouldn't let her off his ship until he thought she was recovered. She didn't know where her weapon was, and she couldn't overpower him in her current condition. She'd have to outsmart him.

She smiled at him, something she knew motivated most men to do her bidding. "Perhaps you're right. I am really tired. If I can just rest awhile, I'm sure I'll be able to function again."

He stared at her as if he could see right through her ploy. "You're welcome to stay here as long as necessary. Besides, I need to bandage your shoulder."

She found the thought of him touching her again very disconcerting. Her fingers slid beneath her hair, moving protectively to her breast and tugging the flightsuit up again. "I can do that myself."

"No, you can't. It requires two steady hands, and mine are perfectly capable, I assure you."

She stared at his hands, resting against his muscular thighs. Strong, lean, bronzed from the sun, with long, square fingers. She'd long ago learned what men's hands were capable of: pain and killing.

She'd survived by being able to read people, and she knew this man would have his way. The sooner she let him tend her shoulder, the sooner she could make her escape. Anxiety twisted inside her. She could only hope Fletch would wait. Five hundred miterons was a strong incentive. Reluctantly, she nodded.

"I need you to sit up," he instructed. "Here, let me help you." He slid one arm beneath Moriah's upper back, ignoring her protests that she could do it by herself, and eased her up, propping the pillow behind her. The dizziness her upright position produced warned she needed this extra time to recuperate before she went in search of her ride off this spiritforsaken rock.

She didn't realize she was still clutching the top of her flightsuit until her host placed his hand over hers, flattening it against her chest. "Just keep that right there, and we won't have to worry about show-and-tell."

She supposed that some women would find the deep timbre of his voice, along with his impressive chest, appealing, but it only spurred her determination to leave him behind as quickly as possible.

As he folded a piece of gauze, her attention

shifted to the bandage angled haphazardly over his powerful right bicep. She'd forgotten about his injury—incurred on her behalf. She wondered if it hurt as badly as her shoulder did. An unwelcome twinge of guilt nagged her conscience. He *had* gotten her out of a bad situation. Damn him! She hated being obligated to any man. Yet her resentment couldn't override the fact he had put his life on the line for her.

Reaching out, she lightly touched the swell of muscle just below his bandage. Spirit, his arm was as hard as magnasteel and his skin incredibly warm. She jerked back, feeling singed all the way to her boots.

"Does it hurt very much?"

He shrugged. "Not too bad, as phaser burns go. I've had my share of them." An impish glint danced into his eyes. "But if you'd like to kiss it and make it better, sweetheart, you're more than welcome."

A hot rush, which she chose to believe was anger, heated her face and she jerked away. She'd forgotten how obnoxious he was. "No thanks," she muttered. "I'd rather take on a regiment of Jaccians."

"Testy," he chided. "If you don't want to play healer, then I guess we'd better take care of your shoulder."

Moriah steeled herself for the procedure to be painful. He was infinitely gentle, however, as he gathered her hair into his hand and brushed it behind her neck, draping it over her uninjured shoulder.

"Your hair is beautiful," he commented.

When she didn't reply, he grasped her chin, bringing her face up and forcing eye contact. "We definitely have to do something about your manners. And I'd like to know your name, considering I saved your life and all."

Her manners? He was absolutely boorish. "You didn't save my life, and my manners are a lot better than yours."

His mouth quirked into a smile. "My manners are flawless, and I did save your life. In some cultures, you'd be indebted to me for life. That's an intriguing thought. I always collect on my debts—sooner or later."

Disappointment cut through her. He was like every other male she'd ever met. Out for what he could get, regardless of the pain or cost to others. She twisted her face away.

"I still don't know your name."

Her name. She had lots of names, one for every occasion; one for every role she chose to play. She started to give him the alias on the identification she had with her, but for some reason, her real birth name slipped out. "Moriah."

"Moriah. Nice. I don't suppose you have a last name."

"No."

He threw back his head and laughed, his black hair whipping between his shoulder blades. "I suspected as much. *Moriah* probably isn't even your real name."

She noticed for the second time the white flash of his teeth, the gleam of amusement in his black-as-sin eyes. "So, what's your name?" Her question slipped out impulsively, surprising her.

"My *real* and *full* name is Sabin Travers. At your service, Moriah No-Last-Name."

She looked away again, and he placed some gauze over her shoulder. She gritted her teeth to keep from reacting to the spears of pain shooting down her arm.

He paused. "Does that hurt?"

Not trusting her voice, she shook her head.

"That's odd. Never heard of a Jaccian wound that didn't hurt. I'm sorry I don't have any deadening spray. I'll try to make this as painless as possible." He proceeded to bandage her shoulder quite efficiently. When he finished, he said, "Here, let me help you get your arm back in the sleeve of your flightsuit."

He'd touched her enough. "I can do that myself." She stared at him pointedly. "If you don't mind, I'd like some privacy."

"That can be arranged." He rose and strode to a recessed dresser to retrieve a shirt. Shrugging into it, he moved to the entry. The door slid open, but he paused, turning back. "Just remember, nothing has changed. It's far too dangerous for you to be wandering around Calt. When you feel recovered, I'll escort you to your ship and personally supervise your departure." He stood in a nonchalant slouch, but the hard expression in his eyes warned her he fully meant what he said.

Over your dead body. She smiled sweetly. "Of course."

His eyebrows arched, and he started to say something, but a sandy-haired young man leaned around the frame and cleared his throat. "Uh, Sabin, I need your help with the diagnostic scan."

Sabin's intense gaze never left her. "Be right there. But I'll be checking on you, Moriah."

She got the implied message, loud and clear. He didn't believe her compliant act for one millisecond, and he planned to keep a watchful eye on her. She'd have to move fast. She nodded and sighed, closing her eyes as if she were going to sleep. She heard him leave and the panel close behind him.

Immediately, she looked to be sure he was gone,

then scooted to the edge of the bunk. Her movement sent the cabin spinning, and pain ricocheted
down her arm. Wincing, she grasped the edge of
the bunk with her good hand and dragged air into
her lungs. The spinning slowed, and she gingerly
tried to work her arm into her flightsuit. Spirit!
Her shoulder hurt worse than a blast wound.

Apprehension that Sabin would return seemed
to make her even more inept. It took several agonizing moments to get the suit on, then another
few while she clumsily closed the front seam. Obviously, she couldn't count on much use from that
arm for several cycles. It was a good thing her left
arm had been the one injured.

She stood on unsteady legs, balancing herself
against the wall until the renewed spinning
slowed. Seeing her cape at the foot of the bunk,
she snatched it up and checked it, heaving a sigh
of relief. The miterons were still there, thank
Spirit. She draped the cape around her shoulders.
Then she worked her way to the only cabinets in
the room, embracing the wall for support. By the
Abyss, she was weak. No wonder Sabin seemed
unconcerned that she might slip away.

Only the urgency of her situation, the knowledge that other lives depended on her, lent her the
strength to push forward. She searched the cabinets, cursing her feeble movements. No sign of her
phaser, or anything else which could be a useful
weapon. Blazing hells! She'd have to return to
Giza's without protection, but there was no help
for it. She struggled to the entry, and the panel
whispered open.

She peeked into the corridor, finding it empty.
The main hatch lay to her right. Staying against
the corridor wall, she inched toward the hatch,
pausing when she saw the cockpit just beyond.

Great. Why couldn't the hatch be at the rear of this stupid ship? But there should be an airlock. She looked down the corridor, noting several panels, indicating either storage areas or more cabins.

At the very end of the corridor, she found what she sought, an airlock with a secondary hatch. She listened and heard voices coming from the cockpit. Sabin and the other man must be there, but she needed to be sure. She edged along until she was almost to the cockpit.

"So where ya going after you leave Calt?" a youthful male voice asked.

"I'm making a stop at Star Base Intrepid," came Sabin's deeper voice. "Hoping to find some space scum there."

Reassured of the whereabouts of both men, Moriah changed direction and moved quietly to the rear. She slipped into the airlock, then paused, her hand hovering over the control panel. Hoping it wouldn't send a signal to the cockpit when she opened it, she activated the mechanism and stepped out onto the hard Calt sand. So far, so good.

She staggered quickly away from the ship, taking cover behind a nearby outcropping of rock. Sagging against the rough surface, she rested, trying to recover some strength. The heavy, humid air made it difficult to draw a full breath, but after a few moments, Moriah felt stronger. She saw no signs of anyone leaving the ship. Encouraged, knowing the Jaccian poison would work its way out of her system as time passed, she left the shelter of the rocks.

Nightfall lent much-needed cover. The twin full moons guided her. She remained in the shadows of ships and then buildings, stopping to rest and gather her hair into a bun. Her luck held, as no one came after her and she finally made it back to Giza's without running into any lowlifes on the way.

Once there, luck abandoned her. Rather than risk going back inside, she went to the bar's rear entrance. Since Thorne never gave information freely, she pulled out some miterons. It was then that she discovered her ID disk was gone. Her eyes narrowed in fury. She knew who had it. Sabin Travers—if that was his real name, which she seriously doubted. Well, no matter. She had other ID disks on Risa.

When the agitated little Thorne popped his oversized head out the back door, she enticed information from him with two miterons. But the news was devastating.

"Fletch wa-s-ss here er-er-earlier," Thorne stammered. "But he s-s-seemed real nervous and l-left."

"He left?" Moriah's heart sank. "How long ago?"

"About an h-hour." Thorne scampered back inside.

Her thoughts spun through several possibilities. Fletch often had money lenders after him; plus there was a bounty on his head, so he had to avoid shadowers. He was probably lying low.

Hopefully, he'd be waiting for her at his ship. She'd go to his landing pad. She would be all too glad to leave Calt, which ought to make Sabin Travers very happy.

Unbidden memories of his kiss slid into her thoughts. No man had ever kissed her like that. The kiss blazed in her mind, as if it had been branded there by its very intensity. She could still feel Sabin's hard body dominating hers, feel the heat and texture and taste of him. And most shocking of all, how she had responded to him—

at least momentarily—before the familiar feelings of disgust interceded.

She wouldn't have allowed the kiss if she hadn't been weakened by that damn Jaccian wound, she told herself. Absolutely not allowed it. Curse Sabin Travers anyway. If he hadn't dragged her out of Giza's, she might have found Fletch before she'd passed out.

Shaking away the memory, Moriah headed toward the landing strip. Her progress was slow, for by now, she was physically depleted. She again stayed in the shadows to avoid running into trouble. Relief pumped through her as she neared the landing pad. She couldn't get off this planet fast enough. When she did, she would— Moriah stopped dead in her tracks.

Fletch's ship was gone.

She stared at the empty pad, hoping against hope she'd taken a wrong turn in the shadows, that it was the wrong landing pad. But she knew it wasn't. The odd cryptic figures someone had scratched in the sand were still there, and Fletch's pad number was etched into her memory.

She sank to the sand, the last dregs of hope and energy gone. She had no ship, no weapons, and no identification. And no way off Calt, thanks to Sabin Travers.

She could approach one of the miscreants passing through and ask for a ride. But she couldn't trust any of them—not like Fletch, at least. Although no prize, Fletch was an androgynous being already mated to another androgyne, and had posed no masculine threat to her.

Moriah battled back rising hysteria. She had to find a way to the iridon auction, then back to Risa. And she had to talk to Celie, who would soon worry something terrible had happened to her.

She dug her fingers into her palms, forcing herself to think clearly. She needed to get a communiqué to the group, so one of them could pick her up. Only it would be far too dangerous for her to stay on Calt, especially after the fiasco at Giza's. She had to stick with her original plan to travel to a star base.

An elusive thought nagged at the back of her mind. Star base . . . where had she just heard that? Moriah bolted to her feet as the answer came to her. Intrepid. She'd heard Sabin tell the other man he was headed to Star Base Intrepid.

She spun around and started walking. Her luck had just turned. Sabin Travers didn't know it, but he was about to provide her transportation to Star Base Intrepid. She certainly had no desire to see him again. He was arrogant, obnoxious, and dangerous. But if she had any luck at all, they wouldn't cross paths.

Because he'd never know he had an extra passenger.

Chapter Three

Wedged inside the stardrive casing, Sabin made adjustments as Radd provided specs and monitored the readouts. Sabin couldn't hear the hatch tones from there, but he figured he had at least half an hour before Moriah was strong enough to attempt to slip out.

He fully expected her to try. Having spent his life adapting to every possible existence imaginable, he'd learned to land on his feet by whatever means necessary. He was a survivor, first and foremost. He recognized that same trait in Moriah. It would be very difficult to bend her to any will except her own.

The beep of the subspace transceiver interrupted his musings. "Hey, Sabin, communicator's beeping."

"I hear it, Radd." He squirmed from the tight confines of the casing. "It's probably McKnight. Answer and tell him to hold on."

He wasn't at all concerned about Radd answering the transceiver or knowing the identity of the caller. The mechanic was known for his discretion, as well as being a person of very few words.

Sabin squeezed out in time to hear Radd saying, "Naw, he's fine, Chase. He just didn't call ya back because he was taking care of a woman he brought on board. Here he comes now."

Great. Just great. So much for discretion. Sabin glared at the young man who, outside discussions of propulsion systems and fuel replenishment, had never uttered more than three words at a time. He'd sure turned into a talking echobird all of a sudden.

"Gee thanks, Radd," Sabin snapped, coming around the console.

"No prob." Radd stepped back with his usual guileless expression, although his eyes held a mischievous glint.

"Travers here," Sabin barked at the intercom. He didn't bother with the videoviewer. Chase never used them.

"Where are you? Did you catch Galen?"

"Not that lucky, old man. He got away, and my stardrive went out. I'm on Calt. Radd's working on the drive right now."

"So who is this woman you brought on board?" McKnight questioned. "A felon?"

"Not exactly."

"She's not a prisoner, then?"

Sabin hesitated. "No."

"I've never known you to be desperate enough to approach a Calt female. Have the Pleasure Domes begun making ship calls?"

"Very funny. For your information, the lady had a Jaccian tentacle wound. I was just helping out."

"Is she all right?"

"Yeah. She came around pretty quickly."

"You need to sterilize the wound, and if it's deep, apply sutures—"

"Whoa! Hold it right there, partner," Sabin interrupted. "I don't happen to have a fancy ship like you do, with that high-tech lab you're always so secretive about. I don't have a whole lot of medical aids, either. So I did the best I could with what I have."

He could almost hear the disapproval in McKnight's long silence. His partner could be such an old man at times. "And what was that?" McKnight finally asked.

"Sulfo nitrate."

"Blazing hells! Remind me to stock your ship with some medical supplies."

"Hey, it woke her up! And it should take care of any risk of infection."

McKnight released a frustrated breath. "Assuming the patient survived the treatment."

"She did just fine. She appears to be of sturdy stock." Sabin decided to move the discussion away from Moriah. "How did it go on your end?"

"Another false alarm. But I did hear some interesting rumors about an illegal shipment of iridon up for grabs. Seems it was hijacked while leaving a mine in the Verante constellation."

Sabin let his breath out in a low whistle. "Do you think Dansan's behind it?"

"Wouldn't surprise me. But I also heard Galen might be after the shipment. Could be a way to track him down."

"Thanks for the lead," Sabin said, already mentally sorting through his list of informants. Someone should be able to secure information on where the shipment was last seen, and where it was headed.

He glanced at his chronometer and tensed, realizing almost three-quarters of an hour had elapsed since he'd left Moriah alone. "Look, I've got to go take care of some business."

"You might give the lady a chance to recuperate first."

Even his partner had to insert sexual innuendos into the situation. "I'm real amused, old man. I'll contact you in two ship cycles, usual time." Sabin disconnected and headed for the corridor. "Be right back, Radd. I've got to check on the lady."

"Uh, Sabin, she's gone."

He whirled to face Radd, whose round, innocent-looking eyes stared back. "What?"

"I heard the hatch tone about half an hour ago, while you were inside the casing."

"Why in the blazing hells didn't you tell me?"

"Well, I didn't know she was a prisoner. Ya didn't lock her in the brig, like ya usually do with criminals."

"This whole day has been wonderful," Sabin muttered, whirling back toward the corridor. "I'll be back."

He should just let Moriah go. She wasn't wanted anywhere, and it wasn't illegal for a lone female to traipse around Calt, so he couldn't detain her. But, as he thought about her resilient spirit and phaser-sharp intelligence, he knew he couldn't allow her to be devoured by Calt's degenerates.

He'd put her weapon in his vault, so she had no defense. She might know how to fight, but without a phaser she didn't stand a chance on a planet where no shred of decency existed. He couldn't let such beauty and vitality be destroyed. After checking his cabin and verifying she had indeed slipped away, he strapped on extra weapons and headed back to Giza's. Maybe she'd returned there.

He came up empty-handed. He didn't see her

anywhere between his ship and the bar, and Thorne informed him she'd only returned long enough to learn the person she'd been waiting for had come and gone. Sabin checked the rest of the settlement without success. He searched though the landing pads, but knew he had little chance of finding her without knowing which pad her ship was on.

Concern and regret accompanied him as he headed back to his ship. He hoped Moriah had escaped the planet safely, although he would have enjoyed more mental sparring with her. He wouldn't have minded exploring the sensual side of her nature, either—a thought he quickly pushed aside. It was time to get back to business—to catching Galen.

Radd was outside adjusting the ship thrusters when Sabin returned. "Did ya find her?"

"No. She must have left the planet."

"Sorry about that." Radd lifted a thruster flap and scowled. "Awful lot of rust under here."

"The whole damn ship's nothing but rust on rust. At least I'll have my new one inside of a lunar cycle." Sabin thought about the ship he'd finally been able to commission, after seasons of hunting down wanted felons, transporting them to Alta, and collecting the rewards. It would be the closest thing he'd ever have to a home.

"Yeah," Radd said reverently. "A Skymaster SC-8400 long-range cruiser, fully loaded. The same thing McKnight has. Boy, I can't wait to work on that baby."

"I hope you won't have to for a long time. And I can't say I'll be sorry to see this heap of junk go to scrap."

Radd closed the flap. "Okay, then, she's ready to go." He took the credit disk Sabin offered him, slid it into his portable collection unit, and entered the charges.

Moments later, Radd was gone, fading into the shadows, either off to his own ship or to another lucrative repair job.

Nothing more here for Sabin. Besides, he had an important delivery to make. But as he took off a short while later, it wasn't the upcoming mission he was thinking about. Instead, visions of remarkable golden eyes and a wealth of burnished hair haunted him.

Forget her, he told himself. He had no place in his life for a woman. The Pleasure Domes could provide the physical release he needed, without the danger of involvement. He would never have a real home, or the commitment of a mate and a family. If nothing else, his wretched past had shown him that. Yet, even over his brutal self-reminders, thoughts of Moriah, the image of her hair fanning over her skin, persisted.

"Get a grip, Travers," he muttered to himself. The chance he would ever cross paths with her again were about as good as the sun going nova.

On impulse, he pulled her ID disk from his pocket and inserted it into the computer, punching in access to IAR's Universal Citizen Registry. The Registry scanned the code on the disk, then Moriah's picture flashed onto the screen, along with her stats. "Mara Carlen" the name read, with the information that she was licensed to deliver medical supplies, replicator food suspensions, and clothing to star and Controller bases.

Like hell. No legitimate supplier would give a different name from the one on their identification. And no legitimate supplier would be caught dead on Calt. It was far too dangerous. Only the lowest riffraff of the universe came to this planet.

The exchange of goods here was usually illegal, with exorbitant prices paid without argument.

Mara/Moriah wasn't who she claimed to be. She wasn't a Controller agent or a shadower either, as he had first suspected, or her identification would have indicated that fact. No, without a doubt, she had to be involved in illegal activities. If that was the case, sooner or later she would be caught. If she was on the Controllers' long list of wanted deviants and criminals, then it was only a matter of time before a shadower tracked her down and turned her in for the bounty.

A shadower such as himself.

Moriah awoke with a start. She noticed immediately that the rhythm of the ship had changed. They must be going into orbit. Again she wished, as she had numerous times since she'd stowed away on Sabin Travers's ship, that her chronometer hadn't been broken by the Jaccians. She had no idea how long she'd been holed up in the lav of this extra cabin, but it seemed she'd been there longer than the three cycles it should have taken to get to Star Base Intrepid. She couldn't afford any more delays.

Luck had been with her the last hour on Calt. From the shadows of the rocks, she'd seen Sabin head for the settlement. The young man working on the thrusters of Sabin's ship had appeared oblivious to everything around him, and she'd slipped aboard undetected.

Behind the first panel she checked, she discovered a cabin apparently being used for storage, as it was filled with stacked-up crates. Reluctant to take the time to explore the ship further, she'd hidden in the tiny lav, hoping Sabin wouldn't venture there. She had remained there through takeoff and the long ensuing hours.

She was stiff and sore from being in such restricted quarters, although she'd tried to stretch as much as possible. Starving, too. She'd gone longer than this without food, she reminded herself. A lot longer. A father's drinking addiction didn't leave much money for necessities.

Automatically, she pushed the nightmarish memories away. Instead, she focused her thoughts on Risa, and on Celie, resorting to the mental diversion she'd used since childhood.

When her father had been on one of his drunken rampages, Moriah would hide with Celie, and try desperately to recall their mother's loving face, a memory fast fading with each passing season. "Don't think about what's happening now," she would tell Celie. "Think about good things, and nothing can hurt you." How wrong she had been. Yet the silly habit had remained with her all these seasons.

The increasing vibration and sudden sharp angling of the ship jolted Moriah back to the present. They were descending to land—finally! She grabbed the handle of the shower stall and wedged her feet against the opposite wall to keep from sliding around. Once she was on Star Base Intrepid, she'd be able to contact someone from the group. She steeled herself to remain patient as the ship connected to the pad with only a small jolt. Not a bad landing for such a decrepit craft.

At least Travers had one. The loss of her own spacecraft would have serious repercussions on the group operations. Moriah heaved herself to her feet, determination filling her. Nothing she could do about it now. She'd find another ship, even if she had to confiscate one.

She was quite skilled at breaking into security systems, thanks to her father—another line of thought she didn't care to follow. Drawing a deep breath, she stretched her cramped muscles and waited.

Sudden voices came from nearby. She froze by the lav panel, listening intently.

"All these crates in here go, too," Travers said, just on the other side of the panel.

She heard shuffling noises, and assumed the crates were being lifted. She waited, while the voices and footsteps returned several times. Finally, silence prevailed. Moriah waited a while longer, then emerged cautiously. The cabin was empty, but she didn't know if Travers had left the ship. Surely he would take advantage of being on a major star base to restock supplies and avail himself of the entertainments offered there.

She opened the cabin panel enough to peer down the corridor. Seeing no one, she slipped to the airlock, then cracked the portal cover and looked out. Sabin stood a few meters away, talking to a ragged group of people. He faced away from her, but she knew it could only be him.

The arrogant way he braced his legs apart, his phaser-laden belt riding low on his lean hips, the broad expanse of back, his midnight hair tied with a leather thong—he stood out like a towering Yarton tree on a desolate plain. The people around him looked out of place for being on a sophisticated star base. Moriah's keen senses went on alert.

She studied the ragtag group, noticing the leather bracelets worn by several of them. Where had she seen bracelets like that before? Recognition nagged the edges of her memory, until the answer came to her in a startling jolt. *Shielders!*

The persecuted race was known to wear custom-tooled leather bracelets, tracing their ancestry. Moriah had seen such bracelets on Shielder children being sold as slaves. But they didn't usually wear items so blatantly declaring their race outside the safety of their settlements. They'd never wear the bracelets on a star base, where they would be identified and arrested. Then this group of people couldn't possibly be Shielders, unless . . .

Moriah shifted her gaze to the outside terrain. Instead of being inside one of the well-engineered landing bays found on Star Base Intrepid, the ship sat on a dirt pad, obviously outdoors. Bare mountains rose in the distance, no trees or greenery to soften their starkness. Star Base Intrepid boasted no mountains. Shock speared through her.

Where were they? Moriah strode to the cockpit, determined to learn their coordinates. Travers's computer system was as archaic as the rest of the ship, and she readily accessed his navigational pod. But the displayed coordinates, placing their location in a little-traveled sector of the quadrant, were unfamiliar to her. The screen didn't even list a name for the planet they were on.

This must be a Shielder settlement.

Apprehension clawed at her. Damn Sabin Travers to the Fires. Not only was she not on a star base, but she was in the hostile territory of a race known for their barbaric lifestyle and warlike fierceness. Not that she blamed them.

The Controllers had been trying to wipe out the Shielders for decades, and had managed to drive them to the far reaches of the quadrant. But the Shielders persisted in surviving, living on barren moons and planets no one else would inhabit. They even fought back with surprising tenacity—

attacking Controller ships and bases, then escaping into the myriad wormholes and vast expanses of the quadrant.

Moriah had no quarrel with Shielders, but she certainly didn't want to be at their mercy. The Controllers paid very well for information leading them to Shielder bases, and many beings were only too glad to provide such information for gold. Her knowledge of this Shielder colony's existence could well be her death knell.

She must hide in the lav again and hope that Travers took them out of there soon. Quickly, she made her way back to the cabin. Just as she punched the panel pad, two strong hands grabbed her and spun her around. Heart pounding, she looked up at Sabin Travers.

He stared back in disbelief. "What in the Abyss are *you* doing here?"

"I—I—" she stammered, willing her muddled thoughts to clear.

His eyes narrowed, fury replacing disbelief. He took a step closer, crowding her against the panel, intimidating her with his sheer presence. "Answer me!"

She could feel the heat from his body, feel the waves of anger radiating from him. Panicked memories sent her thoughts swirling like dust devils. *Think, Moriah!*

"I never got off your ship before you left. I must have wandered into this cabin, delirious from the Jaccian poison."

He pressed his hands against the panel, on each side of her head. "Cut the lies, Moriah, or is that Mara? I know you went back to Giza's after I treated your wound."

He was too close, too threatening. Moriah battled feelings of being trapped and smothered. If she showed any weakness, she would be power-less. She forced herself to concentrate on what Sa-bin had just said. Since he knew her name, he must have her identification disk. He also knew she'd gone back to Giza's. Damn.

"Well, then, I must have gotten lost in the dark on Calt and boarded your ship by accident."

"Yeah, right. And you've been inside this cabin the entire trip?"

"Sleeping off the effects of the poison," she of-fered lamely.

He snorted, obviously not falling for that. "Where have you been while I was planet-side?"

"I had just come out of the cabin when I saw you and tried to duck back in."

"Likely story." He grabbed her arm and dragged her back down the corridor, stopping to look out the hatch. Scowling, he dragged her the rest of the way into the cockpit. His eagle gaze settled on the navigational screen. Moriah realized that she'd stupidly neglected to clear it. There, the incrimi-nating evidence of their coordinates glared back at them.

He raised narrowed eyes to her. "You're a liar. I'm tempted to dump you out and leave you here."

"You can't do that! They'll kill—" Moriah froze, realizing she was only incriminating herself fur-ther. What was wrong with her? Normally, she was quick on her feet. Lack of food must be dull-ing her wits.

The murderous expression on Travers's face sent another realization careening through her. One she should have fathomed earlier. *He was a Shielder.* That was the only way he could possibly know about this colony; the only way the inhabi-tants would have welcomed him.

The Controllers had declared every Shielder a

criminal, an enemy of the government. It was every citizen's duty to turn in any member of the race, a duty bearing a financial reward. Shadowers made the majority of their bounties hunting down Shielders. If Sabin was a Shielder, every time he ventured out into the quadrant, he risked discovery and certain death. There was no way he could allow Moriah to live, given what she had learned.

"So you know, then," he said softly, the quiet surety in his voice just as terrifying as if he had yelled. "You know exactly what type of colony this is, and you also know the coordinates."

He would kill her now. Adrenaline surged. Moriah looked around the cockpit, hoping to find something—anything—she could use for a weapon. She spotted the phaser hooked to his utility belt. Desperation spurring her to attack, she lunged toward him.

She intended to hit him in the solar plexus with her shoulder, then confiscate his phaser. But he sidestepped with surprising agility, forcing her to swerve around the console. Before she could regain her balance, he spun her toward him. Grabbing her shoulders, he jerked her forward. She hooked a leg behind his, shoving against his chest as she kicked his legs toward her.

Caught off balance, his own momentum working against him, he toppled down. But he kept a tight grip on her, taking her with him. Her plan to knee him in the groin as she went down was thwarted as he rolled when they hit, pinning her beneath him. Pain shot through her shoulder, reminding her it had not yet healed.

"Get off me!" she demanded, slugging at him with her good fist.

He grabbed her arm and pressed it to the floor.

"I don't think you're in any position to bargain, lady."

He might be right, but Moriah had long ago learned not to show any vulnerability.

"I can help you more than you might think," she replied, trying to come up with something—anything.

"Oh, yeah?" His gaze raked contemptuously over her breasts. "Seems to me I can find that lots of places."

His fury was still evident, as was the blatant reminder he was just like any other man. His weight pressing on her made it hard to breathe, much less think clearly. Desperate, she made an offer she wouldn't make under normal circumstances—at least not before payment.

"You can't find supplies being delivered to a place like this with no questions asked. I'd be willing to do that."

"And just what type of place is this?"

She hedged her answer. "Apparently someplace no one else knows about."

He grunted, bringing her arms to rest on the floor above her head. Shifting both her wrists to one hand, he reached down and unsnapped a pair of electronic shackles from his belt. Panic resurged. She heaved against him, trying to throw him off.

"Be still!" he ordered, straddling her with his legs. This brought him fully pressed against her. She felt suffocated by his weight and heat. She battled his attempts to get the shackles on her wrists, without success. He didn't hurt her, but his sheer strength dominated her resistance. He snapped the shackles on her. Then he grabbed her arms and rose, lifting her with him.

Spinning her around, he tore away her cloak

and pushed her against the console. "Spread them," he ordered.

Old fears pressed in on her, sharp and jagged. Staggering pain, a paralyzing reminder of the strength men could wield over women. Blindly, Moriah shook her head. "No."

His grip tightened. Pain speared through her left shoulder, and she winced. He must have noticed, because his hold loosened. "I said spread 'em."

"Why? I have no weapons. You have my belt and phaser."

"Afraid I can't take your word on that. I didn't search you when I brought you on board my ship. But then, I didn't know what kind of woman you were."

His insulting tone sent heat rushing to her cheeks. "What kind of woman is that?"

"One who lies about her identity, for starters. Put your hands on the console and spread your legs. *Now.*"

She had no choice but to go along until she had an opening to catch him off guard. Drawing in a deep breath, trying to stop her shaking, Moriah placed her palms on the console, the shackle links clinking. She noticed Sabin hadn't activated the shock mechanism, which surprised her. She had no idea why he didn't just kill her. Was he planning to torture her—or worse—before he did?

"What are you going to do with me?"

"I'll have to think about it—after I check you for weapons." He fumbled around behind her for a moment, and she heard several clicks. "Damn piece of junk," he muttered, and there was a clatter as he apparently threw something down. He paused another moment, then his hands slid slowly over her arms, causing her to start.

He meant to search her *by hand*. "There are scanners for detecting weapons," she bit out.

"Yeah, well, mine seems to have malfunctioned, like everything else on this junk freighter."

He continued the downward slide of his hands. The warmth of his touch penetrated the fabric of her suit, only intensifying the chill Moriah felt inside. Her arms trembled, much to her chagrin. He paused a moment, his fingers circling her wrists, brushing over the magnasteel bracelet she wore. She held her breath, praying he wouldn't examine it too closely.

When he moved back up her arms, she almost sagged with relief. But then his hands slipped beneath her arms, and his fingers flattened over her chest. They came in contact with bare skin on the left side, where her torn flightsuit sagged alarmingly low.

Images of a leering face, of hands groping against her, tearing her clothing, hammered at her. Her breath froze again, tension ricocheting through her body. She struggled to shake away the memories.

"Your heart is pounding," he said. "It's good to know I haven't lost my touch."

Anger at being in this man's power flared, overriding her apprehension. What she wouldn't give to have a fully charged blaster in her hand right now.

"Arrogant bastard," she hissed. "Just finish this."

"We still need to work on those manners." He slid his hands over her ribs, brushing the side of her breasts, then across the front of her midriff and abdomen. He seemed nonchalant about the excruciating intimacy.

Moriah forced herself to stand completely still,

as he moved from there to run his hands slowly down the outside of her legs. He stopped long enough to raise each leg and remove her boots, then he continued slowly up the inside of her legs. He took his time, applying firm pressure, forcing her to tense her muscles to keep her balance. By the time he stopped within a millimeter of the juncture of her legs, it took all her self-control to remain still. She gritted her teeth, refusing to give him any further pleasure from her humiliation.

He was just as thorough on her backside. If she had a phaser, she'd set the charge on low, she decided. She'd kill him very slowly.

A sense of victory raced through her when he stepped back, seemingly satisfied. Her bracelet had not caught his attention, so he hadn't realized she actually did have a weapon—lethean patches.

The tiny patches, which contained a powerful sedative, were affixed on her bracelet. They looked like tiny decorative medallions, rather than four highly effective ways to incapacitate an opponent long enough to get away. All she needed was an opportunity to use them.

She shook the hair from her face. "I told you I didn't have any weapons."

"And I'm supposed to believe everything you tell me." Taking her arm, Sabin maneuvered her to a chair. "Sit." He pushed her down. Then he leaned against the console, crossing his feet at the ankles. "What am I going to do with you?"

Killing her would be the logical choice, she knew. Then Celie would have no one. Panic edging her desperation, she quickly suggested, "Take me to the nearest star base. I've already forgotten this place."

He shook his head. "No can do. I can't trust you as far as Astra's orbit around Vilana."

"I give you my word of honor I won't reveal the location of this settlement to anyone."

"Your word of *honor?* What would that be, exactly, Moriah/Mara? The honor of thieves? Somehow I find it very hard to accept the word of someone who lies about her identity."

His words stung her pride. Despite the fact that she had operated under numerous false aliases, Moriah never went back on her word once she gave it. Of course, if semantics colored what she was promising a little differently from what the other party believed the agreement to be, that was their problem. But, unlike her father, and creeps like Turlock and Pax—shadowers, the scum of the galaxy—she did have a code of honor. Which was probably a lot more than she could say for Sabin Travers.

Noticing his attention had wandered below her face, she raised her manacled hands to jerk her sagging flightsuit up over her breast. "The name is Moriah. Moriah Cameron. My word is good. And *you* owe *me*. It's your fault I'm here. If you hadn't interfered in Giza's—"

His gaze snapped back up to meet hers. "Interfered? I saved your hide, as I recall."

"I was holding my own. Then you detained me on your ship, and my ride left without me. That was my only way off Calt, since my ship has been stolen."

"Your ship stolen? Now that's very interesting." His eyes gleamed as he considered this information. Moriah suspected his annoying nonchalance hid a light-speed intelligence, making him a dangerous opponent.

"Of course," he continued, "if you hadn't been on Calt, that wouldn't have happened. You take your chances, lady. So why did you choose to stow away on my ship? You had no idea where I might be headed."

She considered how much to tell him. She had learned giving as much of the truth as possible was better than offering lies. The impression of honesty gave her credibility. The trick was determining what information she could leave out.

"I overheard you talking to that other man on your ship. You told him you were headed to Star Base Intrepid. I figured I could find transport from there." She looked around the antiquated interior of the cockpit. "Although I must have been under the influence of the poison. It's amazing this clunker could make it anywhere."

"You wound me," he mocked. "This clunker, as you call it, has been trustworthy, which is more than I can say for you."

"I've given my word," she insisted. "I won't reveal this settlement's location. If necessary to buy my freedom, I'll agree to deliver supplies here—for a modest fee, of course."

He snorted at that. "Yeah, I'll just bet your fees are modest. I'm sure *exorbitant* would be more accurate." His gaze raked over her again. "So, what to do with you?"

Moriah watched him, anxiety mounting inside her.

He appeared to come to a sudden decision. Striding forward, he took her arm and pulled her out of the chair. "Come on." He pushed her into the corridor.

Stumbling ahead of him, she sifted through offensive strategies. If she could turn and trip him, and land a few well-placed kicks to groin, solar plexus, and head . . .

"Don't even think about trying anything," he warned. Looking over her shoulder, she saw him hold up a small object. "I have a remote activation unit which can send a lot of voltage through those shackles you're wearing. I can—and will—put you out before you can blink an eye."

She almost groaned in frustration. Obviously, physical force wasn't going to work. She'd have to depend on a more covert method. Her plotting came to a stop as he turned her back into the cabin she'd just vacated and guided her to the lav entry.

He stepped around and reached for the seam of her flightsuit. "This is coming off."

Her heart slammed against her rib cage, ugly memories crowding in. *He's a man! What did you expect?* she told herself. She lurched back. "I'll burn in the Abyss before I give you the pleasure."

Sabin rolled his eyes. "Sex, sex, sex! Is that all you women ever think about? Forget it. This once, I'd like you to obey a simple order, lady. I want you out of that suit and in the shower."

"The shower?" Moriah stared at him, totally confused. No doubt about it—the man was a loose fusion cannon.

"Of course the shower. Look at you!" He gestured toward her again, a look of revulsion on his face. "Your hair and flightsuit are covered with dried blood and slime. I'm going to have to clean the ship as it is."

Who cared if this rust bucket was clean? The man definitely had a gear out of orbit. Moriah wasn't immune to her unclean state, although it seemed a ludicrous concern in view of the situation. Then it occurred to her that he wouldn't want her clean if he planned to kill her right away. Relief eased some of the terrible tension gripping her body. This might present an opportunity to gain the upper hand—especially if she could get rid of the shackles.

She held out her arms. "Release me, and I'll clean up."

A speculative gleam lit his eyes. "Hmmm. The shackles are waterproof. I can leave them on and just cut the suit off of you. Scrub you down myself."

Her elevated adrenaline levels surged even higher. "No!" She didn't realize she had backed away until she hit the lav panel. It slid open, and she almost fell backward, but Sabin caught her arms and pulled her upright.

"Let me go!"

He ignored her. "You're trembling. That makes me wonder what you're hiding beneath that suit."

"Nothing you're not already aware of!" she snapped. "Unless you want to lose a few body parts, let me go!"

He cocked his head, his eyes glittering. "Which ones?"

"What?"

"Which body parts? I like to know my options."

His mockery fueled her agitation. "*Crucial* ones," she assured him.

He didn't seem too concerned as he considered. "Okay, I'll take off the shackles, and leave you to shower—under two conditions. First, you give me your promise you won't try to attack or injure me. Second, you do exactly what I say, as long as you're on board this ship."

He released his hold, and Moriah rubbed her upper arms sullenly. "I thought you didn't trust my word."

"I don't. The first time you step the least bit out of line, I'll not only shackle your hands, but your feet as well. *And* I'll activate the shock mechanism."

Damn him to the Fires. Yet she had no choice

out to agree. "All right, I give you my word. I won't attack you." *Just render you unconscious at the first opportunity.*

"And you'll obey orders?"

She could imagine what some of his orders would be. Moriah pushed back the darkness, focusing on survival. She'd have to find a way to circumvent such orders. As long as Celie needed her, she would survive. "Yes."

"Hold out your hands." Pulling a sequencer from his pocket, Sabin snapped it over the lock. The shackles clicked open, and he removed them. "Toss that torn suit out after you take it off. I'll leave a clean flightsuit for you on the bunk."

"Wait," she said as he started to turn away.

He looked at her, his brows raised. "What now?"

She forced herself to swallow. "What are you planning to do with me?"

"That's a good question. I would say what happens next depends entirely on you." He left the cabin without a backward glance.

It did depend on her, Moriah thought, fingering her bracelet. She had a weapon he didn't know about. One she planned to use at the first opportunity.

Chapter Four

He had definitely lost it, agreeing to take the shackles off Moriah. Sabin didn't trust the woman for one instant. But she desperately needed a shower, and the stark fear in her eyes made him think twice about washing her himself.

Not that he needed to be tempted any further by her lush curves. Searching her had not only been torture, but provided proof the lady did indeed feel as good as she looked. As a matter of fact, being in close proximity to Moriah seemed to disintegrate any good sense he possessed. His body, on the other hand, came to full alert.

This unusual lack of control over his physical reactions did not sit well with him. It was time for a visit to the Pleasure Domes at the next opportunity. But first, he had to deal with Moriah.

She was intelligent and a skilled fighter, but he wouldn't give her an opportunity to get the upper hand. He had only promised to remove her shackles. That didn't mean he'd give her free reign on

he ship. When she finished showering, she was
joing in the brig. Then he wouldn't have to worry
bout her until they reached their destination.
And where would that be? he wondered.

Wearily, he leaned against the wall and pinched
he bridge of his nose. He could put Moriah out
on the planet, and that would solve the problem
of her knowing too much. Of course, it would also
be her death warrant. Too much lay at stake for a
colony of Shielders to allow an outsider to know
their location and live to tell about it. Technically,
he himself was obligated to shut her up perma-
nently, but he had no stomach for killing inno-
cents.

Ugly images reared in his mind; screaming
Shielder children, fleeing for their lives, while
their parents, waging a futile stand against hordes
of Anteks, were cut down like morini grass.

He shook his head to force the images away, but
newer ones took their place: graves. Growing in
number almost daily. He'd seen the profusion of
new burial sites at the Shielder colony today. According to the colonists, the virus engineered by
the Controllers was no idle rumor, but a very real
threat. Called Orana, it was rapidly spreading
among Shielder settlements. Highly contagious, it
was devastating and merciless.

All the more reason that he deal with Moriah as
quickly as possible. He needed to start checking
with other colonies and to see if anyone had for-
mulated an antidote to the deadly Orana. Unfortunately, he couldn't just turn her loose. If only
there were some way he could turn back time,
undo what she had seen.

He froze halfway to his cabin as the answer torpedoed him. Undo what she had seen—of course!
All he had to do was have part of her memory

71

erased. A skilled healer could do that with a hypno-trance procedure. And he knew just the healer—Darya, on Elysia.

Unfortunately, Elysia was four ship cycles away even with hyperspace. Then they would be there a cycle while the procedure was performed. All of which meant he would be out five ship cycles and Spirit knows how much revenue. Not to mention losing Galen's trail. And, more importantly, the time lost finding a way to deal with the Orana virus. His situation was getting worse and worse by the millisecond.

Muttering a curse under his breath, Sabin retrieved a clean flightsuit from his cabin. As soon as he had Moriah safely in the brig, he would take off, and set the ship's coordinates for Elysia.

He was waiting in the corridor when she emerged from the cabin, wearing the flightsuit he'd left on her bunk. She was almost as tall as him, but his flightsuit hung on her smaller frame. She'd rolled the sleeves and the pant legs up, and the loose fabric managed to drape provocatively across her breasts. Her coppery hair, still damp, fell in glorious waves down her back. Sabin wondered fleetingly if he could order her to keep it down at all times.

She walked toward him slowly, her eyes wary. For the first time, he noticed the dark circles beneath them, the hollows of her cheeks. He realized she must be exhausted and hungry. He'd seen no evidence she'd had any food with her, and she'd been on his ship four cycles. Okay, so he would put her in the brig, then fix her something to eat after he took off for Elysia.

He stepped aside, gesturing for her to walk ahead of him, alert to any false move on her part. "Go to the next panel down," he instructed. After a barely perceptible pause, she complied.

"Get inside," he ordered when they reached the open entry. She stepped in, then turned, her expression an odd blend of defiance and uncertainty. As far as she knew, her life hung in the balance, yet she held herself proudly and with admirable poise.

Sabin punched the outside pad to activate the brig force field. Nothing. He punched the pad again. No hum indicating the presence of a charged field. Blazing hells. The field had been working a few cycles ago. What more could go wrong on this damnable ship before he got his new one? Clenching his hands into fists, he resisted the urge to kick the wall.

Moriah raised her brows questioningly.

Blowing out his pent-up breath, Sabin gritted out, "Cursed panel won't work."

He didn't see the sense in telling her this cabin had been redesigned to act as a brig, so the actual panel had been removed and a force field unit installed in its place. He didn't make it a habit of advertising the fact that he was a shadower, even though in this case, a healthy dose of fear might help keep Moriah in line.

On the other hand, considering that she appeared to be involved in illegal activities and probably had a bounty on her head, knowing he was a bounty hunter might make her more desperate to escape him.

He'd keep quiet about his shadower status for the time being, even though he had no intention of turning her in. The Controllers had so many damn ordinances that virtually every citizen committed an infraction sooner or later. Probably half of the population in this wretched quadrant had bounties on their heads. Moriah might willingly be on the wrong side of the ordinances, but it was obvious she wasn't in the same league as vicious criminals like Galen.

Sabin refused to participate in persecuting every citizen who broke the law, especially those who did so in order to survive or best the Controllers. He couldn't accept that kind of blood money. He saved his energies for the criminals who preyed on the innocent, the ones who truly deserved to be punished.

Except now he had to decide what to do with Moriah. He couldn't restrain her with a force field, which meant he either had to keep her shackled or give her free reign of his ship. By the Spirit!

Moriah stared at him silently. Probably plotting her escape. Great. He absolutely didn't trust her, so the shackles might be best. Still, she hadn't done anything to him, except for being in the wrong place at the wrong time. He decided to hold off on the shackles—for now.

"Come on," he muttered, stepping back and gesturing for her to walk ahead of him. "To the cockpit."

"But you just told me to come in here."

He clamped a tight reign on his temper. "I changed my mind. I'd rather keep you in sight. Get to the cockpit."

She flashed him a look of disdain. Tossing her hair over her shoulders, she strolled past him and down the corridor. The sway of her nicely rounded hips only fueled Sabin's agitation further. Taking a deep breath, he forced himself to focus on the back of her head. When they reached the cockpit, he ordered her to strap in while he began takeoff procedures and notified the colonists of his departure.

Moments later, they broke free from the planet's

gravity field and headed away. After setting the co-ordinates for Elysia, Sabin leaned back in his chair and drummed his fingers on the armrests. Unsnapping her harness, Moriah rose and leaned to the navigational screen. He switched it off. "Oh, no, you don't."

Straightening, she leveled a golden glare at him. "Where are we going?"

He rose. "You don't need to worry about that."

She chewed her bottom lip, a surprisingly vulnerable gesture. She probably didn't even know she did it, Sabin reflected, his attention drawn to her lush mouth. He thought of the kiss he'd commandeered on Calt, the feel of her lips, the taste . . . Hell, why did the force field have to shut down *now?*

"I need to know our destination," she insisted.

"All you need to worry about is keeping your word not to give me any trouble."

"But we're obviously headed *somewhere*. I want to know what you have planned!"

"We're going to take care of a little business." He again noted the circles beneath her eyes and remembered she needed to eat. "Come on. Let's go to the galley. The least you can do is make yourself useful while you're on board."

She drew a deep breath, and he could almost see her composure slip back into place, like a shield against him. But the wariness remained in her eyes. "How so, Travers?"

Her refusal to use his first name or the proper title of *captain* amused him. "By replicating our meals, *Cameron*. At least I assume that's your real last name, and we do seem to be on a last-name basis here. Lack of manners, and all. I hate to cook, so you can have that duty now."

She gave a small shrug and headed for the corridor. "I don't know how to operate a replicator. Where is the galley?"

"Second panel on the left. What do you mean, you don't know how to operate a replicator?"

"Never learned."

Sabin's eyes narrowed in disbelief as he followed her to the galley. "Every ship that's less than fifty seasons old has a replicator. How do you fix your meals?"

"I don't. I eat prepackaged food." Moriah turned and smiled tauntingly. "So I guess you get to cook."

Several choice words came to mind, but Sabin decided he'd cursed enough for one cycle. "I should have known," he grumbled. "But you get clean-up duty. And you can get out the dishes. Except the utensils. I'll handle those."

Silently she began opening cabinets and looking for the plates. Sabin punched the pads on the replicator panel. "How do protein sticks and amar-grain sound? I might even throw in some of my special bread, if you ask nicely."

"Fix whatever you want," she answered indifferently.

But when they sat down a short while later, she dug into her food without hesitation. She ate like she hadn't eaten in cycles—and she probably hadn't. There was nothing dainty about her at the table. Sabin leaned back to watch as she rapidly diminished the food on her plate.

Here was evidence that her graceful poise and modulated voice hadn't always been part of her persona. When she ate, a more basic woman emerged—fascinating. A sudden flash of insight told Sabin that perhaps she had learned to eat so fast out of necessity, such as a lack of food and having to battle for what was available. He knew what that was like.

"Whoa! Don't you think you should slow down? If you haven't eaten in a few cycles, you should give your body time to adjust to solid food," he cautioned. "I'll give you more later, I promise."

She paused, her fork heaped with food halfway to her mouth. Still chewing, she lowered the utensil. She swallowed before raising her eyes to his. "How do I know this isn't my last meal?"

Her tension was palpable. She appeared to be strung tighter than a miserly Shen. Yet Sabin was reluctant to tell her much. She was too clever and resourceful, and any knowledge in her hands could be dangerous.

"Look, you'll just have to trust—"

"Forget it," she cut in. "I've heard that line before, especially from men like you, and I know how meaningless it is." She shoved back from the table and rose swiftly, picking up her plate. Sabin tensed, halfway expecting the plate to be hurled at him, but she turned toward the wall unit. "Is this the refuse chute?"

Without waiting for an answer, she began scraping the food into the chute, her movements jerky. *Men like him?* What did that mean? Damn, but she appeared madder than a wounded Antek. Sabin rose and approached her. He placed his hand on her shoulder, his fingers tangling in her hair. "Listen—"

"No!" Tossing her head, she jerked away from his hand and turned to glare at him. "I don't want any empty promises from you, Travers."

The flash of fear in her eyes tugged at Sabin's heart. He reached toward her, but she brushed past him to pick up his plate. He reached out again. "Moriah—"

She whirled, knocking his arm away. "What are you *really* going to do with me?"

She didn't trust him, and he couldn't blame her. She didn't know him from a Trion cave dweller. She probably assumed he was going to kill her to keep her quiet about the Shielder colony. He understood her fear.

He understood fear all too well.

For a brief moment, the present faded, and the black void opened around him, obscuring everything but the screams of anguish, the explosion of blasters, the stench of burning flesh. The fleeing, the hiding, the darkness, but most of all—the fear. The all-consuming fear which dominated every sense . . .

Wrenching himself back from the void, Sabin knew he had to tell Moriah his plans. He had thought to keep her in the dark, to use her uncertainty to control her. He couldn't do that. He couldn't endure seeing in her face that which was etched in his soul for eternity.

"I'm going to have part of your memory erased," he answered. "Then I'll let you go."

She froze, staring at him, astonishment in her eyes. In a world where survival depended on staying one step ahead of the Controllers, or their Antek henchmen, or shadowers; where it was frequently a matter of kill or be killed, an act of compassion was as rare as a warming cycle on Atara. She obviously had not expected mercy from him.

"I can see that surprises you," he said. "It just so happens I don't believe in killing innocent people. It was an accident that you turned up at the wrong time."

She considered a moment. Then, instead of showing relief as he had expected, she shoved him. "How long?"

He stumbled back. "How long what?"

"How long will your plan take? Did it ever occur to you, Travers, that I might have places to go, business to take care of?"

A little gratitude would have been nice. His anger boiled over. "*You* have business to take care of? What about *me*? My life has been completely disrupted ever since I met you, lady. No, make that miserable. I had to play healer to you, then I spent hours traipsing around that hellhole Calt trying to be sure you were okay. Now I have to take five cycles out of my time to get your memory erased and—"

"Five cycles!" she screeched, stomping toward him, a fork clutched in her hand. "Where the blazing hells are we going?"

He didn't know if she intended to use that utensil, but he wasn't taking any chances. He lunged forward, grabbed her wrist, and pried the fork from her fingers.

Tossing it into the sterilizer, he growled, "Don't ever approach me with anything that could be used as a weapon. And don't ask me again where we're going. All that matters is that I'll release you after your memory is altered. You'll be alive, which is more than anyone else would have done. Now, finish cleaning up the galley."

She glared at him, her chest heaving, but she didn't say anything further. Finally, she turned and began loading the sterilizer. Sabin slouched against the wall, watching her alertly. When the galley was clean, he insisted on patting her down to be sure she hadn't pocketed a potential weapon. She remained silent, although he could tell the brief search didn't sit well with her.

When he was satisfied she was unarmed, he stepped back and stretched. "Time to turn in."

"Where am I going to sleep?"

Where indeed? He certainly wouldn't mind having that lithe body curled around him. The images unfurling in his mind sent shafts of heat through his body. It would be insanity to indulge in the fantasy. He didn't get involved with women. Besides, he didn't think his guest shared the attraction.

Still, he couldn't resist saying, "You're welcome to bunk with me."

She stood stiffly, her hands clenched against her thighs. "Do I have a choice?"

He should be relieved the attraction wasn't mutual, Sabin told himself. Involvement with Moriah could bring nothing but trouble. Yet her obvious reluctance stung his male pride.

"Don't try to resist too hard," he retorted. "Of course it's a choice. While you may think I'm no better than an Antek, I assure you I can control my baser urges."

Her expression clearly showed she didn't believe him, which rankled even further. "Then I choose to have my own cabin."

He'd been thinking about that and believed he had a way to contain her—with the intruder alert. He would set the alarms for the entire ship, including the motion detectors in the corridor. That way, if Moriah tried to leave her cabin during the sleep shift, he would know immediately. With her in her own cabin, he wouldn't have to worry about her while he slept. A good, albeit chaste, solution.

He wouldn't tell her about the alert. It provided the perfect opportunity to see if she would try to pull anything during the shift. He motioned toward the cabin she'd stowed away in. "You can sleep in your old hiding place—that last cabin."

Escorting her to the cabin, he showed her how

the intercom worked, in case she needed anything during the shift. That done, he left her and returned to his cabin. After setting the alert, he crawled into his bunk. It had been a long cycle, and he was exhausted. Yet visions of fiery hair and golden eyes inundated his thoughts, and sleep was a long time coming.

Moriah saw the small light begin flashing on the cabin's control panel. She suspected Sabin had activated a security program, and most probably, the corridor was wired with motion detectors. She hadn't expected him to trust her, but it was better than being shackled. Oddly enough, she was beginning to believe he didn't intend to kill her, although she wasn't sure why. She'd never known any man who kept his word if it didn't suit his purposes.

Yet Sabin had spared her life, when it would have been simpler to rid himself of her immediately. He could even have left her to the Shielders if he didn't want to handle the deed himself. He didn't appear to be keeping her alive to satisfy his sexual needs, either.

She didn't know what to think of any of this—except maybe he really meant to have her memory erased and then release her. Although grateful his intentions appeared benign, she wasn't inclined to let anyone alter her memory. Besides, she couldn't afford to lose any more time.

She stretched out on the bunk, fingering her magnasteel bracelet. The bracelet looked common enough, like a thousand other adornments worn throughout this quadrant of the galaxy. But its contents were highly valuable, in more ways than one. More than just the four lethean patches lent the bracelet value, although each of those little

81

patches cost at least a hundred miterons on the black market.

Even more valuable was the Leor credit disk hidden inside the bracelet—especially considering her life would be forfeit if she lost that disk. It would also be forfeit if she failed to appear in time to bid on the iridon shipment, which was why she had to act quickly.

According to her information, the auction would be held in eight cycles, giving bidders time to travel to the event. But she still had to find transportation, then travel to the auction site. With no time to waste, she had to use one of the lethean patches on Sabin at the first opportunity.

She'd held off this cycle, giving herself a chance to get her bearings and recover from fatigue and hunger. But tomorrow, she'd wait until Sabin's guard was down and then she'd place a patch on him. Within a minute, he'd be out cold, and his ship would be hers. A twinge of remorse pierced her. She'd just had her own ship stolen, so she knew how he might feel.

Surely this heap of rust couldn't be that great a loss for him, she argued to herself. Besides, she suspected Sabin Travers always managed to land on his feet. And her survival, along with that of Celie and the group members, hinged on getting to the iridon auction. She'd do whatever was necessary to ensure that.

With thoughts of Celie drifting through her mind, she finally fell asleep.

Chapter Five

The next morning, Moriah was awake long before Sabin deactivated the security program and came for her. She even had time to do her stretches and work through her fighting katas. Her kicks were a little stiff, but then she'd been in a cramped lav for several cycles. Her full range of motion would be restored with a few more workouts.

"Sorry to be so late." Sabin strolled into the cabin with his usual casual air. "I worked out this morning."

Inadvertently, Moriah's gaze went to his biceps, bulging arrogantly through the sleeves of his black flightsuit, then wandered to his impressive chest. He'd left the suit partway open, revealing a hint of dark hair. Forcing herself to glance up from his chest, she realized he'd showered. His dark hair, still damp, hung loose and silky around his shoulders. He'd shaved, too, the temporary lack of beard stubble lending a cleaner edge to his features.

He was six feet of pure, rugged male. Her mouth grew dry, and her pulse sped up. Shocked at the unusual reaction, she reprimanded herself mentally. She knew better. She'd learned the hard way that good looks could cover a rotten soul.

Besides, she needed to focus on placing a patch and escaping. The patch had to be positioned on bare skin, and required a full minute to take effect, which meant she had to place it without Travers being aware of it. She'd have to time it very carefully.

"I trust you slept well?" he broke into her thoughts, his intense perusal of her edging her pulse upward again.

"Like a baby kerani," she assured him, willing her heart rate to slow.

He paused, his gaze hovering right above her shoulders. "You put it up." He sounded disappointed.

She stared at him, uncomprehending. "Put what up?"

"Never mind. Ready for the morning meal?"

Sabin stood back, and Moriah led the way to the galley. She wondered if she should try to place the patch in the galley or wait until later.

"What would you like?" he asked as they stepped inside. "Amargrain, or protein sticks?"

"We had that last night."

"I like protein sticks and amargrain."

Noting the overly nonchalant look on his face, Moriah placed her hands on her hips. "I'll bet that's all you know how to replicate."

He shrugged. "So what if it is? *You* don't know how to replicate *anything*."

She had refused to learn. During the nightmarish time she'd been in Pax's clutches, he had tried to force her, but Moriah had been pushed enough.

84

She'd been determined to defy him in this one thing, even if it was small. As if it really mattered—Pax had already taken everything else.

But now she was condemned to a diet of protein sticks and amargrain. She threw up her hands. "Got any prepackaged foods?"

"If that's what you want. Look behind that panel there."

So he wasn't going to turn his back to her for any reason. His caution would make planting a patch difficult. But Moriah had learned the value of patience. She'd wait for the right opportunity.

After they ate, Sabin took her into the cockpit, so he could check and send messages, and conduct his business—whatever that was. He set his secondary computer on read-only access to IAR—Information and Retrieval—so Moriah would have something to do while he worked.

She half-heartedly scanned through data, covertly observing her captor. He downloaded a very large file and read it intently. She'd have liked to know what the file contained. But for the time being, she simply watched him. Strange, but now that she was reasonably certain Sabin wouldn't kill her or force his attentions upon her, she felt more relaxed around him. She began to wonder what made him tick.

"So, what do you do?" she asked casually.

He looked up, shaking away an expression of deep concentration. "You mean, when I'm not dealing with troublesome stowaways?" Clicking off his screen, he leaned back in his chair. "That's a good question." He steepled his fingers together thoughtfully. "I guess you could say I'm a trader—a merchant of sorts."

She looked around the cockpit incredulously. "With this refuse crate? Where is your cargo?"

"I unloaded the cargo just before I discovered you stowed away on my ship. I have to pick up more goods—after I deal with you. Those five cycles are really going to cost me, lady."

More than you think, Moriah thought. Although she didn't see how he could consider his ship being confiscated such a great loss. She might even be doing him a favor. Not only that, Shielders certainly couldn't afford to pay him much for delivering supplies. Most of them were reputed to be destitute. Sabin must have other sources of income.

"If you only deliver cargo to—to people like we just left, then I don't see how you can survive," she pointed out.

His dark eyebrows arched. "People like we just left, eh? What sort of people are those?"

Back to the lanrax-and-krat game again. "I certainly have no idea. But delivering supplies to small colonies can't be very profitable."

"I do well enough."

Which meant his activities were probably as illegal as hers were. "What kind of supplies do you deliver?"

"Not supplies, necessarily. Merchandise is more like it. I deliver . . . certain goods. Naturally, I get paid for those goods."

"Always on the proper side of the Ordinances, of course."

"Absolutely. As a matter of fact, the Controllers approve heartily of the merchandise I deliver."

A shudder ran through Moriah at the mention of the Controllers. A more heinous group of beings had never existed. For some strange reason, it bothered her that Sabin had sold his soul in a pact with the evil rulers of the quadrant. Especially since he was a Shielder, which meant he dealt with the same beings who wanted to destroy his entire race.

"I should have guessed you'd be in cahoots with them," she said.

He stiffened, his relaxed demeanor changing to one of cold anger, his eyes icing over like one of Atara's glaciers. "I'm not. Don't ever make the mistake of thinking that. As I said, I deliver certain goods to them, but that's as far as it goes. We've discussed this enough."

He clicked his screen back on, signaling the end of the conversation. Moriah still didn't know much about the man. Not that she needed to know anything except how to get a lethean patch on him without his knowledge.

She studied him as he read, trying to decide where to place the patch. He'd pulled his hair behind his neck, securing it with a leather strap, so she couldn't use the back of his neck. He'd also zipped his flightsuit up fully. Only his face, the front of his neck, and his hands offered any bare areas of skin. Not very good odds of succeeding, since she needed a full minute without him realizing the patch was there. Blowing her breath out in frustration, Moriah knew she had to bide her time a while longer.

After Sabin finished reading his downloads, they returned to the galley for lunch—more protein sticks and amargrain. Then they went back to the cockpit, where he worked more until the evening meal.

Used to long forays into space, Moriah didn't find anything unusual about his routine. Outside of exercising and performing basic ship maintenance, there wasn't much to occupy the time. Every space traveler relied heavily on computers to fill the long hours—for navigation, communications, information, entertainment.

As she and Sabin finished the evening meal, Moriah wondered how he filled what most spacers considered the loneliest hours of all, the evening shift. She got an idea when he settled into his chair in the cockpit and reached beneath the console to produce a bottle of liquor and two glasses.

"Care to join me?" he asked, opening the bottle.

She stared at the liquor. "I don't think so."

He cocked his head, his dark eyes inquisitive. "What's the matter? You drank in Giza's."

She could govern her own reaction to alcohol, but she couldn't predict the results of it in Sabin or any other male. She knew from bitter experience how drink had a way of changing a man's behavior. Sometimes to the point where he got out of control, like her father, or Pax. . . .

Shuddering, Moriah took a deep breath. Alcohol fogged a person's thinking, she argued to herself. Then she realized that this could be an opportunity to place a patch, especially if Sabin drank too much. He might drink more if he had company.

"All right. I'll join you."

He poured two modest portions and handed her one. Then, much to her surprise, he put the bottle away. He took a draught, then leaned back with a sigh.

She sipped her drink. Warmth immediately spread from her throat into her abdomen. It was good liquor, and very strong. She'd have to drink sparingly.

They sat in silence for a time, staring toward the large portal. Lulled by the mesmerizing spacescape, Moriah felt herself relaxing, but only for the moment. Her precarious situation as Sabin's hostage was never far from her thoughts.

She took another sip. "What will it take to convince you to disclose our destination?"

Sabin lounged back in his chair. Her heart lurched as she belatedly realized the potential innuendo he might have read in her request. How could she keep forgetting the inherent danger all men posed?

"Tell you what," he finally answered. "I'll let you see the destination screen if you'll take down your hair."

He'd surprised her again. His request raised her suspicions. It sounded innocuous, but there could always be hidden intention. "Take down my hair—that's all?"

"If I were asking for more, I would have said so." He shrugged. "Of course, if you don't care to know where we're going . . ."

Part of her wanted to demand why he would make such a request; at the same time, she didn't want to know. Didn't want to see Sabin's darker side. He knew she'd do as he asked, damn him. Slowly, she raised her hands and released the pins holding her hair. It fell against her shoulders in soft tangles.

"Shake it out," he ordered, his voice smooth and dark as ebony Saija silk.

Surprised to find her fingers trembling, she combed them through the tangles. Curious little tremors ran through her body. She shook her head, and strangely, for the first time, the weight of her hair against her chest felt almost sensuous. No more liquor for her, she decided. The small amount she had sipped was affecting her more than she had realized.

"Very nice," he murmured.

Oddly disconcerted, Moriah tried to ignore the way he stared at her. Spirit, Pax used to look at her like that, just before he— She clenched the arms of her chair, forcing away the memory.

Sabin reached over, punching pads until the navigational screen came on. She rose and leaned across the console to see the screen, which read: DESTINATION: ELYSIA.

"Elysia? Surely you can find someplace closer to have my memory altered."

He turned off the screen. "I suppose. But I'd rather take you to someone I trust. Darya is a good healer. She knows how to do a memory procedure safely."

Safely? Was he really concerned about her welfare? Or was it more likely Darya wouldn't ask any questions? Baffled, Moriah retreated to the portal. Sabin confused her. Honorable behavior was not something she'd witnessed in many men. She felt a twinge of regret about her plans for drugging him. The least she could do was express gratitude for his leniency.

She turned from the portal. "Thank you for sparing my life."

Sabin rose and joined her. He stood so close, she could smell his scent—clean, woodsy, male. His near proximity unsettled her, but she resisted the urge to move away. She would not retreat.

He stared out the portal. "A life," he murmured. "Just a life. So fragile, so temporary. So dispensable, it seems. At least, in this universe."

Idly, he reached out and captured a strand of her hair, rubbing it between his fingers. "So much ugliness, yet so much beauty."

Moriah's heart skittered into a rapid beat. The cockpit suddenly seemed much smaller, and a sizzling energy charged the air. She stared at Sabin's fingers tangled in her hair and tried to draw air into her lungs. Looking up, she found his gaze, burning hotter than a nova, fixed on her.

"So much beauty," he repeated hoarsely. He moved closer, cupping her shoulders. She couldn't breathe, couldn't think of anything but the feel of his hands, warm, possessive. Not sure whether to fight or flee, she froze, like a creature caught in a snare. Unconsciously, she chewed her bottom lip. His intense gaze latched there.

"Damn," he muttered. "Curse me for a fool, but I've been wanting to do this again."

His fingers tunneled up through her hair, cradling the sides of her head. He tilted her face up. Belatedly, she realized his intent. Before she could react, his mouth claimed hers. His lips settled over hers, gentle persuasion edged with inexorable determination. His tongue teased her lips, demanding entry. The strong need for self-preservation spurred her resistance.

He slid one hand down the side of her face. Drawing back, he hovered an atom's breadth from her mouth. "Open for me," he commanded huskily.

He placed his thumb against her chin, using it as leverage to coax open her mouth. His tongue slipped inside, stroking slowly, thoroughly. Electricity arched between them. Shocking, unfamiliar sensations stampeded through her body.

Stunned, she grabbed his shoulders to steady her reeling equilibrium. She thought briefly of retreating, but he moved one hand to her waist and pressed her against him, while the other hand captured the back of her head.

He tasted like liquor, the texture of his lips and tongue oddly stimulating. Heightened awareness imprinted the sensation of his body against hers—the feel of hard muscles molded to her softer curves, the heat of a thousand suns scorching her through the fabric.

Warmth spiraled through her, into her chest, and pooling much lower. She felt weak, pliant . . . what was happening to her? Sudden dread surfaced through the lethargy, washing over her in cold waves of reason. Forcing her hands between them, she pushed hard and pulled her mouth from his. He released her. Gasping, she backed away.

Sabin stared at her, chest heaving, his face harsh with the familiar, inflamed expression she had learned brought only pain. "So what's wrong with me?" he demanded.

Moriah pressed her fingers against her mouth, taking another step back. She was no virgin, yet Sabin was the first man who had ever kissed her. She'd refused to let Pax do that, turning her face away from his foul breath, even as he had forced himself on her. She knew such contact with Pax would only have been repulsive, while with Sabin, it was overwhelming, intense.

Damn him. She'd never let him know how a simple kiss had thrown her off kilter. Nor would it happen again. "I've had better," she countered. "A lot better."

He stiffened as if she'd phasered him. "Great. Just great. Now you're a judge of technique." Looking for all the universe like a sulking child, he stalked to the console and began switching the systems to auto mode.

"Time to call it a night."

The shrill beep of the subspace transceiver invaded the tension. "Who the hell is that?" Sabin snarled, whirling and punching the pad. "Travers here."

"Hello friend," drawled a male voice. "Somehow I knew I'd find you there."

Sabin went deathly still. "Who is this?"

"Don't you recognize me, Travers? I'm devastated. After all we've been through together. At least, all *you* have been through. I've found your pathetic efforts to catch me a mere inconvenience."

Sabin's face hardened. "Galen," he gritted out.

"Oh, you do know me. That's better."

Sinking into his chair, Sabin turned on the videoviewer. Curious, Moriah moved closer. The screen remained blank. "Show yourself, damn you!" Sabin hissed.

"Always so impatient. Always wanting your way. Time you learned respect, boy."

Sabin's eyes narrowed to slits. "How did you get this frequency?"

"I got it from a friend of yours. Actually, I came into possession of his ship, and I got it from his communications log. What was his name? Oh, yes. Aron, I believe. Too bad about his *accident*."

"You sorry son of an Antek! You're lying."

"Why would I do that, Travers? Besides, I'm contacting you. How could I know this frequency if Aron hadn't . . . bequeathed it to me?"

Sabin rapidly entered commands on his keyboard, apparently trying to lock onto Galen's location. "So why *are* you contacting me, you bastard?"

"Now is that any way to talk to an old acquaintance? After all, I'm going out of my way to tell you about Aron and offer my condolences. Besides, I thought you might like to meet my new partner."

The videoviewer flashed on, showing two figures. Moriah gasped in surprise. She'd never seen the gray-haired, bearded man with pale, malevolent eyes before, but she would know Turlock anywhere. Half-Antek, he had a large head with a partial snout and greedy, beaded eyes. She stepped back quickly so he wouldn't see her. They might even be calling from her ship, which Turlock had stolen on Calt.

"Greetings, Travers," Turlock snorted. "Sorry about your buddy. He died like a coward."

"You know you'll never get away with this, Galen," Sabin growled. "You'll pay for your crimes. You'll die a slow, torturous death."

"My, my. You're as bloodthirsty as my new partner here. You won't ever catch me, Travers. Now I've added two more ships to my fleet—Aron's long-range cruiser and another newly acquired spacecraft, which is a real beauty. How will you ever know which ship I'm using? And you can't track what you don't recognize. Even if you could, you'd never catch up with me. Not with that junk heap of yours," Galen leered. "Anyway, I just wanted say hello. Enjoy your evening, Travers."

The videoviewer went blank. "Damn!" Sabin roared, pounding the console. "I couldn't get a fix."

Moriah held her silence, inwardly seething. Those two cretins had *her* ship. If she ever got her hands on Turlock, he'd pay. And Galen . . . the man radiated evil, so very much like Pax. She shuddered.

Gripping the edges of the console, Sabin stared at the blank screen. "Blazing hells." He dropped his head, his shoulders sagging. "Aron was a good man."

"I'm sorry," Moriah offered, moved by his obvious misery. "Did you know him well?"

"I've known him since I was a boy. We learned to fly together. He was a good friend." He blew out his breath and pushed to his feet. "Well, that's life.

Never know when your time will be up. Galen's time is a lot shorter than the bastard realizes."

He gestured toward the entry. "Come on. Let's call it a night."

As she walked down the corridor ahead of him, Moriah realized she'd let not one, but two, golden opportunities to place a lethean patch, pass her by. If she'd had her wits about her when Sabin kissed her, she could have positioned the patch then. Or while Galen had his attention. But both times, she'd been distracted.

By the Abyss! What was wrong with her? It was unlike her to lose focus. Sabin Travers seemed to have the ability to shake her up and cloud her reason. She couldn't allow that to happen again. She had to grab the next opportunity that presented itself.

Unfortunately, finding the right opportunity might prove difficult. She needed two conditions to succeed. Sabin would have to bare more skin and his attention would have to be diverted. With startling clarity, the solution leaped into her mind—the one sure way to create the necessary scenario.

Seduce him.

Almost stumbling, she pressed a hand against the wall to steady herself. *No.* The very idea sent a surge of weakness through her body. Her heart pounded, her breathing grew ragged. After Pax, she had sworn she would never again barter her body. She couldn't do it.

Could not do it.

Stop it! she told herself, willing herself to calm. She *had* to do it, pride be damned and nightmare memories cast aside. Because if she didn't, if she failed, everything she'd worked so hard for could fall through. The others were depending on her.

She had survived such degradation before—she could again.

She had to seduce Sabin.

But she would be the one in control of the situation this time. Not the man. And it wouldn't be too hard to entice him. She knew how easily male lust could be incited. Sabin wanted her. The way he looked at her, the way he kissed her, clearly indicated his interest. He would be easily convinced.

She didn't have much time left, so she'd have to act quickly.

She would have to seduce him tonight.

Chapter Six

The panel slid open. Sabin stood in the doorway, silhouetted in the dim corridor lighting. He had removed his shirt, and his hair was loose. Framed by the narrow entry, he appeared taller, his powerful shoulders broader.

"What is it?" he asked, stepping into the cabin. Moriah stared at his bare chest and flat belly, her throat going dry.

You can do this. She gripped the cover tighter, keeping her right hand out of sight. One of the lethean patches was poised on her right index finger, a special adhesive holding it there. She'd have to peel off the protective plastic layer on top before placing it on Sabin. She didn't dare do that too early, or she'd risk drugging herself.

"You said on the intercom you were sick." He moved to the bunk. "What's wrong?"

"I—I have a fever." She tried to pitch her voice to a provocative whisper, but it came out a nervous rasp.

Catherine Spangler

Concern etched his face. "A fever? I hope it's not a secondary infection from that Jaccian wound. Let me feel your forehead." He reached toward her.

Tossing back her hair, she took the plunge. "It's not that. Your kiss raised a mating fever inside me. Join with me."

He tensed, his hand dropping by his side. "What?" He backed away, his distrust obvious.

She licked her parched lips and dropped the cover, exposing her bare breasts. "Mate with me."

His gaze flicked downward, his eyes widening, then narrowing. "What in blazing hells are you up to?"

"I told you. I want to mate with you." She slid from under the cover and stood. "I have no weapons on me. You can search me if you wish. You seemed to enjoy having your hands on me before."

His gaze drifted over her naked body, his dark eyes firing like a nova. But he quickly banked his reaction and took another step back. "You don't even like the way I kiss. You made your feelings about me very clear. This is not a good idea." He held out his hand as if to ward her off. "Get back in your bunk—now."

Now what? Moriah was woefully ignorant of the tactics of seduction. Her only experience consisted of male domination. Thinking of Pax was enough to make her tremble, panic rising like a tidal wave. She swallowed. One thing she did remember—how a simple touch had inflamed her tormentor.

Stepping around Sabin's outstretched hand, she pressed herself against the length of his hard body. The heat of his flesh seared into her. She heard his heart thundering, felt his sharp intake of breath. She slid her hands around his neck.

She only needed to peel the plastic and— He grasped both her wrists and tugged them away. "Moriah—"

Her wrists had to be free. Acting solely on instinct, she lowered her head, kissing one flat nipple. He shuddered, but kept his grip on her arms, lowering them to her sides.

"Moriah—" He gasped again, this time less forcefully.

She pressed closer, pushing her pelvis against his, feeling the proof of his response. "Don't you want me?"

"Sweet Spirit, I'd be crazy not to," he responded, his voice hoarse. "But—"

She rubbed against his arousal. "Don't talk. Just do it!" she whispered desperately.

She knew she'd won when he released her wrists with a groan. She'd have to wait for just the right moment to ready the patch; she'd only get one chance. So she steeled herself for what would come next; the lust-driven, painful possession of her body, the violation of her soul. It was a price she had to pay. When Travers was in the throes of his own greedy desire, oblivious to all else, she'd have her opportunity.

He grasped her chin, forcing her to meet his gaze. "Do it? Sweetheart, you have no idea of the things I'd like to do with you. Hang on for the ride, lady." He startled her by swinging her into his arms and pivoting toward the bunk.

Instead of immediately dumping her there to take his pleasure, however, he captured her lips with his. Her gasp of surprise granted his tongue access to her mouth. She started to draw back, but stopped herself, lest she raise his suspicions. Besides . . . he tasted good and . . . she was beginning to like the way his tongue stroked inside her mouth.

For a moment, she allowed herself to savor the experience. Oh, Sabin was very good at this kissing business. He employed several techniques, boldly exploring her mouth and dueling with her tongue one moment, then withdrawing to tease her lips with tantalizing nips and just a sweet pressure against them. Then he'd plunder the sensitive inside of her mouth again, stealing her breath. He lowered her to the bunk, breaking the contact. She murmured a protest.

"Just a moment, sweetheart," he promised. "In the meantime, hold that thought."

He stood back. With his midnight hair flowing around his shoulders, his eyes glowing like black embers, he looked like a cave dweller, primitive and wild. His molten gaze caressing her body, he opened his pants and peeled them down his muscular thighs and off.

About to thumb the plastic off the patch, Moriah froze at the sight of his nude body, her attention riveted to the evidence of his desire. He was so big, so throbbing, so threatening.

Hysteria, spurred by dark remembrance, bubbled up. She tried to bolt, but he was over her, pushing her back onto the bunk. He twined his fingers with hers and pressed them into the mat above her head. She felt suffocated, trapped. Not again! She twisted and writhed beneath him. She couldn't do this.

"Whoa! Slow down, lady. What's your hurry?" He eased to his side, turning her to face him. "We'll get to it soon enough. I prefer to take my time. To savor the experience."

With his weight off her, the frenzy receded somewhat. She forced herself to draw a deep breath. *It's all right. This is not Pax*, she reminded herself. *Think of Celie, of the iridon shipment. You have to do this.*

She willed herself to relax, lulled by Sabin's sweeping caresses over her shoulders and arms. He trailed his fingers back up her arms and beneath the curve of her breasts. The breath hissed from her lungs. She never realized her body could be so sensitive, that a man's touch could be so . . . potent.

"Beautiful," he murmured, cupping one breast and rubbing the nipple. His touch was gentle, not the painful plundering she'd expected. Her skin tingled, and she experienced the wild urge to press against his hand. Caught up in her body's response, she was only vaguely aware of him shifting their positions.

Somehow, she was on her back then, with him leaning over her, both hands inflicting exquisite torture on her breasts. But she no longer felt panic. Instead, an amazing surge of pleasure sizzled through her when he leaned down and took a nipple into his mouth.

Coherent thought fled. Pure sensation flooded through her as he suckled her breast, his fingers teasing the other one. She could only lie there, her plans momentarily delayed.

"Spirit, you taste good," he murmured, finally lifting his head. "But I want to see the rest of you."

Rising up, he slid both hands down her breasts, her abdomen, her thighs. He parted her legs wide, stroking partway up the inside, his intense gaze fixed between her thighs. His hand followed his gaze, trailing fire. Surely he wasn't going there— *Oh, Spirit!* He claimed her most private flesh, caressing with a sure touch. She couldn't help herself—she moaned at the onslaught of pleasure.

"Hot and ready," he muttered hoarsely, sliding a finger inside her. Desire jolted through her with the force of a blaster. She gasped and arched, opening her legs even wider.

"Spirit, sweetheart, you're so incredibly responsive." He kissed her abdomen, then pressed kisses upward until he reached her breasts. His mouth again claimed a throbbing nipple.

Sensations inundated her from two directions now, although they seemed to flow together: from where his mouth teased her breast to where his finger moved inside her, stroking, stroking. The patch, she remembered, trying to focus. She needed to peel the cover off the patch. . . .

But . . . she couldn't . . . think straight. She had to gain control of this situation. "Sabin, don't," she protested, her voice sounding weak and distant.

He raised his head from her breast, his glittering gaze capturing hers. "Don't ask me to stop now, sweetheart. There's something I want to see."

She tossed her head restlessly on the pillow, torn between his darkly seductive voice and the burning need between her legs. "What?"

He pushed his finger deeper inside her, and she moaned again. "That's it," he whispered huskily. "Come for me."

She had no idea what he was talking about, or why he watched her so intently. Or how the relentless movement of his hand could render her so helpless, so incapable of anything other than pressing closer. Or give such pleasure. The patch . . . she needed to place the patch. . . .

Then he slid a second finger inside her and stroked deeper . . . faster. All logical thought disintegrated. She could focus only on the incredible sensations, the intense need to reach some unknown pinnacle. Of its own accord, her body arched upward.

"That's it," he urged. "Let go, Moriah."

Something shattered inside her. A wall of restraint which had held her in check crumbled beneath the assault of his sensual words, of his knowing touch.

She did let go, pitching into a vortex of light and sensation. Pleasure exploded through her like a nova, and colors sparked behind her clenched eyelids. She was faintly aware of her hips lifting from the mat, of crying out, as wave after wave of shimmering tremors slammed through her body.

Finally, the swells subsided, and she sagged against the mat, nearly witless. Awareness returned gradually. She heard Sabin's low voice crooning to her as he swung himself above her. Reality lurched back into focus.

How could she have let him touch her like that? How could she have *enjoyed* it?

The patch! Was it still there? She felt her right index finger. Thank Spirit! It was still on the tip of her finger. Sabin rested over her, obviously ready to take his own pleasure.

"Wait!" she cried.

He drew back. "What's wrong? Are you okay?"

Moriah stared at him, amazed. He was concerned about her? The idea was beyond comprehension. Not that it mattered—she needed his attention diverted, and she needed to plant the patch once and for all.

"I'm—it's okay," she told him.

He leaned down and kissed her, sliding a hand up to caress her breast. "You're trembling," he murmured.

That was just on the outside. Inside, she was smoldering ruins. This man had just hurled her

103

into a maelstrom of such sensual magnitude, there was no telling how long it might take her to recover. And yet, he acted as if what had just happened was the most natural thing in the universe. But she didn't have time to analyze what had occurred.

Taking a deep breath, she urged him closer. "Please, just kiss me a little longer," she whispered.

"I think I can handle that." He lowered his mouth to hers. She looped her arms around him and peeled off the patch's cover. With a quick, firm push, and a twist of her finger, she transferred the sedative to his shoulder.

All that was left to do was wait. She tried to relax, to stay focused, which was difficult. Sabin knew how to kiss, and she found the sensual strokes of his tongue against hers highly distracting. He touched her, too, caressing her hips and thighs, sliding his hands between them. When his fingers delved between her legs, she gasped and jolted against him.

He raised his head and looked down at her. "Are you sure you're okay?"

Just a few seconds more. "Give me a minute to, um, recover from . . . you know . . ."

He stared at her, his eyes glazing slightly. He shook his head as if to clear it. "That's funny," he said, his voice slurring. "But you look . . . so . . ."

His head fell forward, painfully hitting her chin. At the same time, his body went completely limp, crushing her beneath its dead weight. She could barely breathe. To make matters worse, the male part of him had not gone limp and was now pressed into her abdomen.

With great effort, she extricated herself, heaving until Sabin fell to one side. She managed to sit halfway up and roll him the rest of the way off. He slid over the edge of the bunk and landed on the floor with a loud thud. Moriah stared at him lying there, a prime male specimen, even if his mouth was open and his eyelids only partially closed.

Guilt gnawed at her, feelings of regret that she had to do this. Sabin had treated her decently. He'd bandaged her wounded shoulder, prepared food for her. He had shown her a glimpse of her own sensual nature. At least she was beginning to understand why some people actually claimed to enjoy mating.

But as she remembered how it felt to have him lying on top of her, pinning her down, she shuddered. It reminded her far too closely of her experience with Pax, even though Sabin had not tried to force her. And even though some of it had been . . . enjoyable. Perhaps one day— No. Mating would never be for her.

She leaned down and dragged Sabin into a more comfortable position, then covered him with a blanket. He would have a terrible headache when he woke up. And he'd no doubt be furious at the loss of his ship.

Fortunately, after she left him on the next habitable planet, their paths would never cross again.

A malfunctioning thruster hammered somewhere nearby. Pounding, pounding, pounding . . . Spirit, but his head hurt! Sabin clapped his hands over his ears, trying to shut out the infernal noise. His movements blasted shards of pain through his head. He groaned, forcing himself to lie still, and the pounding receded—just slightly. His mouth . . . that taste . . . like rocket fuel. What the—

"Oh, Sabin . . . Sabin, sweetness, are you

awake?" a high-pitched, feminine voice trilled. A wisp of sensation brushed across his face. "I have on my feathers!"

Feathers? Oh, no! *Don't sneeze.* He'd die if he sneezed. The pain would kill him for sure. Maybe he *was* dead. Pounding, pounding, pounding . . . No, he needed to pray to die.

"Sabin, honey, you're moving. You must be awake."

He squinted one eye open to gaze at a sea of deep blue Saija silk. The glare zapped him like a lightning bolt, and he quickly closed the eye again. *Saija silk?* Where the blazing hells was he?

"Sabin?"

He heard a rustling noise, then the surface beneath him dipped. Everything careened wildly inside him and pain exploded through his head. He dug his fingers into the silk.

"Don't move! Not a single millimeter," he growled.

"Does your head hurt? Want me to rub it for you?"

Sabin flinched. That voice, that high, grating voice. Where had he heard it before? A memory nagged at him, and he braved opening an eye. The figure before him blurred, then came into partial focus. Feathers. Lots and lots of blue feathers, covering a small body with big—assets. A feathered headdress rested atop fluffed blue hair which flowed over the woman's shoulders and the aforementioned assets.

"Lani? Is that you?"

"It is!" she squealed, shimmying the bed. "Oh, Sabin, you have such a good memory."

He waited until the room stopped spinning. "Lani, be still and tell me something. Where are we?"

"Why, we're in the Pleasure Dome. In our usual room. Don't you remember?"

Pleasure Dome? Sabin struggled to focus his thoughts. Lani. Where had he last seen her? As the answer came to him, he started to bolt up, then thought better of it. Sinking back with a groan, he rubbed his face. He ached all over. "What planet are we on?"

"Oh, Sabin, you are too funny! Saron, of course."

Saron? The last thing he remembered, he'd been on his ship . . . with Moriah . . . in her cabin. That brought him more alert, as he tried to piece together his last conscious memory. Moriah, warm and incredibly sensuous, spreading shapely thighs for him, responding wantonly to his touch . . . was that real? What in the Abyss was going on?

Drawing a deep breath into his lungs, he forced both eyes open. The room settled after a moment, and he turned his attention to Lani's gamine face. "Lani, I want you to tell me exactly how I got here."

She giggled. "You should know better than to drink so much, sweetness. Some woman left you here. Came to the Dome and said you'd had a little too much Elysian liquor, but that your last—how did she put it?—oh, yes, your last conscious request was to leave you at the Dome. She even gave us your credit disk and said to charge everything to it."

His credit disk? Before Sabin could assimilate all this information, Lani cooed, "By the moons of Alta, you are the most generous man."

He thought he might throw up. Drawing another breath to settle his heaving stomach, Sabin gritted out, "What did this woman look like?"

Lani's bright blue lips rounded into a pout. "Oh,

she was tall, with red-brown hair." She arched back, jutting her generous breasts forward. "Not very well endowed."

That's not exactly how he remembered it, but Moriah's actual measurements weren't important right now. "How did I get *here*?"

She tsked and shook her head, feathers swaying. "You don't remember anything, do you? That's not at all like you, sweetness. We had the slaves carry you here."

Sabin closed his eyes, trying to figure out what had happened. He slid his hands over the Saija sheets, feeling their coolness against his skin. Bare skin. Opening his eyes, he glanced down at his naked chest. Lifting the sheet, he saw he had on . . . nothing.

"Where the hell are my clothes?"

"I don't know. You didn't have any when the slaves brought you. You were just sprawled out on that blanket, as naked as the day you were born." She sighed, running her fingers along his side. "It was a sight to behold."

Sabin grabbed her hand to keep it from wandering any further. There was only one way he could have a major memory lapse and end up on Saron without his knowledge. He had seen enough narcotics used for controlling prisoners to recognize the symptoms. He'd been drugged—and he could guess who was responsible.

Moriah was going to pay.

Much later, after he'd revived enough to drink some broth and take a shower, he borrowed clothing and went looking for his ship. Nowhere in sight—and neither was Moriah. He limped back to the Pleasure Dome, his head still throbbing, but refused to let Lani lay a hand on him. He didn't want a female anywhere near him.

Oh, yes, the clever, thieving Moriah was going to pay for this, all right.

If he didn't kill her first.

Moriah punched on the video transmitter. An image formed, then sharpened into focus. Her breath hitched, as it did whenever she came face to face with a Leor. In spite of the fact she'd had numerous contacts with members of the militant race, in spite of the distance of a galaxy quadrant between her and this particular Leor, his powerful presence jolted her. Reminding her that, at best, her position in this professional relationship was tenuous. At worst, life-threatening.

As Leor propriety dictated, Moriah made direct eye contact, staring into impassive obsidian eyes. Leor eyes had no pupils; no expression or emotion. Instead, the black, bottomless pools had the ability to mesmerize a victim, either to probe the truth from a weaker mind or move in for the kill. Fortunately, that power didn't extend over great expanses of space.

Again following the strict procedure mandated by the Leors, Moriah waited for her contact to speak first. "Captain Cameron," he rasped in his guttural voice. "Greetings."

"Your Lordship, Commander Gunnar," she responded. "May a thousand suns shine favorably upon you."

"You attended the iridon auction?"

As if she would dare admit otherwise. "Yes, your Lordship. The negotiations were successfully completed."

"When will the transfer take place?"

"In about twenty-five standard cycles. The iridon is not stored in this quadrant. It must be shipped in, then brought to Saron."

If this information displeased Commander Gunnar, he gave no indication. Since the Leors didn't want the Controllers to know of their desperate need for iridon, nor did they wish to pay the excessive tariffs on shipping the iridon out of the quadrant, they had to depend on smugglers such as Moriah to obtain it for them. Like a serpent lying in wait for an unsuspecting krat, the Leors were methodical and patient. They would achieve their goal.

The commander inclined his bald head, the light glinting off it. Leors, male and female alike, had no hair anywhere on their bodies. Because their bodies drew in heat from outside sources, they wore little clothing, to better absorb warmth from their environment. Moriah found her attention shifting to Gunnar's powerful, bare chest.

But it was another chest she was thinking of, one which had been warm and tantalizing beneath her lips. The unbidden recollection of how Sabin had felt pressed against her, how his mouth had taken possession of hers, sent surprising tremors through her. She struggled to shake away the memories.

"Captain! Did you hear me?"

"Uh— Pardon me, your Lordship. I didn't hear your last statement."

His unreadable gaze bored through her. "I asked if you would be switching ships again. I remind you that our agreement allows us to track you at all times."

Moriah wasn't concerned about the Leors tracking her, not even to Risa. They already knew about it, having given land on the planet to her as payment for an earlier deal.

She looked around the antiquated cockpit in disgust. She would have to replace the ship Turlock had taken as soon as possible. "I'm sorry about that, Commander. As I explained, the homing device is out of order on this ship." *I had to disconnect it so Travers couldn't track me.*

"But I don't plan on picking up the iridon in this ship," she continued. "I'll be trading this in shortly, and I'll notify you of the homing frequency of the ship I'll be using."

"See that you do. We'll contact you in a few cycles with instructions on where to deliver the iridon. Signing off."

Gunnar was gone without further ado, but Moriah had grown used to the curt Leor ways. At least Leors meant what they said. They stood behind their word—and their threats.

But any threats pertained only to her. At the very beginning of their business dealings, she had procured Gunnar's vow that, should she fail the Leors, she alone would face the consequences— most likely death. They would not seek revenge against her sister or anyone close to her.

Releasing her breath, Moriah set the coordinates to drop into Risa's orbit. Spirit, it was good to return to the only place she had ever considered home. This little corner of Risa she owned might be barren and bleak, with only rude structures for shelter, but it belonged solely to Moriah and Celie, and the odd assortment of women who made up their extended family. Even the outcasts of the quadrant needed a home.

Her unruly thoughts flashed to Sabin again, and guilt gnawed at her that she might have taken away his only refuge when she had stolen his ship. He'd land on his feet, she told herself. Besides, she'd left him the one credit disk he possessed that wasn't charged to the maximum . . . and he'd get more clothing.

A sudden vision of Sabin lying magnificently naked on the blanket sent unwelcome heat coursing through her. With it came even more intimate memories. Memories of his wicked touch between her legs; his earthy, sexual whispers; of ensuing pleasure more intense than anything she'd ever experienced.

No! No, no, no. She did *not* want to remember those things—had willed herself to forget them. It didn't matter that Sabin had not used force to mate with her, that he had shown her pleasure instead of pain.

She could never depend on any man, certainly never trust one. Not with her experiences.

Why, then, couldn't she get him out of her mind? Why had she tossed and turned every sleep shift since she'd left him on Saron, seeing midnight eyes and a sensuous mouth, remembering the feel of his soft hair brushing against her bare skin. . . . By the Spirit! She would banish all thoughts of Sabin Travers. She would! She must.

Too many other matters cried out for her attention. The iridon delivery to the Leors, finding a new spacecraft, picking up several other shipments of contraband which had already been scheduled. And then, moving forward with plans to irrigate the land on Risa, build permanent structures, and invest the remaining miterons in ventures that would provide a stable income for seasons to come. She didn't want to depend on her small band of dispossessed smugglers forever.

Her life was finally starting to turn around. She didn't need interference from Sabin Travers, or any other man. Willing her breathing to level out, she opened communications with Risa, letting the sentinel know she was back, albeit in a strange ship.

Moments later, Moriah brought the ship to rest on the hard-packed dirt pad that served as their main landing strip. She was out before the dust settled, arms outstretched as her younger sister raced up the strip. "Celie!"

"Moriah!" Celie charged into her, almost sending them both to the ground. "You're back! We were so worried when you disappeared from Calt, and then we didn't hear from you."

Laughing, Moriah staggered backward. "Silly rax! I contacted you nine cycles ago. You knew I was all right."

Celie hugged her tightly. "But we hadn't heard anything for over four cycles, and we couldn't pick up your homing signal. I knew something terrible must have happened to you."

Moriah pulled back and looked into her beloved sister's brown eyes. "I'm fine, as you can see. I'm sure Turlock altered the beacon, sweetness, which was why you couldn't pick it up. By the Fires! I hated losing that ship."

"You should," came a gravelly voice. "I don't know how we're going to replace the best ship in our fleet."

Moriah released Celie, meeting Tyna's disapproving gaze. She didn't need to be reminded that her carelessness, and the ensuing loss of the ship, would have a negative impact on the welfare of this entire group.

"I don't know how we'll replace it, either." Moriah looked past Tyna to Roanne and Lionia standing beyond her, and to Janaye, who was making her way slowly down the strip, leaning on a thick Yarton branch for support. "I'm sorry Turlock got a jump on me. But we'll think of something. At least I obtained another ship."

Tyna's mouth curled in contempt as she eyed Sabin's craft. "Hmmph! Can't say as I'd call this a ship. Garbage scow is more like it."

Middle-aged and stout, Tyna had led a tough life, as had most of the women in the group. She'd been trapped on Odera, serving drinks to lowlifes at a bar there, unable to purchase passage off the planet, when Moriah had offered her a chance at a new life. Her rough, bitter exterior hid a kind heart, and the other women had learned to tolerate her acrid comments.

"It's just as bad on the inside." Moriah slipped her arm around Celie and started toward the small group of huts.

"Wh-what h-happened to y-your s-suit?" Roanne stammered. Her stutter was worse when she was excited or agitated. Small and quiet, Roanne had been a slave until Moriah spirited her away from her abusive owner. Speaking little, she was the most observant of the group.

"It got ruined in an altercation with some Jaccians. The flightsuit I'm wearing belonged to the previous owner of our new ship."

"Jaccians! Oh, Moriah, you take far too many risks," Celie protested.

"Nothing but scum," Lionia scoffed. Statuesque and well over six feet, she was a Zarian, a race as warlike as the Leors. Few could match her battle skills or bravery. "I hope you blasted them into the next galaxy," she added.

Smoke and slime everywhere. Sabin, self-assured, cocky, and undeniably handsome as he holstered his phasers. His kiss—her first one—beneath the twin full moons. Moriah shook the images away. She'd been far too sedentary these last cycles—

114

that was part of the problem. It was time for action.

"Those Jaccians will never bother anyone again," she assured Lionia. "Janaye, how's that leg of yours?"

Janaye stopped, her breathing labored. "It's been better." She raised gnarled fingers and pushed her snowy hair from her face. Her clear, gray eyes focused on Moriah. "So, what's his name?"

Moriah hated it when Janaye looked at her with those discerning eyes. "Who are you talking about?"

"The man." Janaye lifted her stick toward Sabin's ship. "The one who loaned you that flight-suit." She paused, her gaze sharpening, seemingly fixated over Moriah's shoulder. "The one who disrupted your energy field."

With a collective gasp, everyone looked from Janaye to Moriah, whose chest tightened. The last time Janaye had spewed gibberish about disrupted energy, Rayna, the object of the conversation, had been pregnant. The time before that, Janaye had targeted Kasinda, who, it turned out, was secretly in love with an Elysian merchant and planning to elope.

The old woman was becoming senile, Moriah told herself. Neither of those cases applied to her, and she would never see Sabin Travers again, so he couldn't possibly unsettle her life any further.

"I would say I disrupted *his* force field, not the other way around. After all, I ended up with his ship."

Tyna cackled and Lionia nodded approvingly. "End of story," Moriah stated firmly. "We don't have to worry about Sabin Travers any further."

Janaye's gaze settled on Moriah's face with unwavering intensity. "You haven't seen the last of him."

Her words sent Moriah's heart pounding, but only because she was fatigued and hungry—that had to be it. "Enough talk about something that's finished." She turned back toward the camp. "What's cooking? I swear I could eat an entire kerani. And we need to make plans."

As she sat near the fire, eating a simple meal, Moriah gazed at the faces of the women seated around the flames. They looked to her for leadership and guidance, and the weight of that responsibility lay heavily on her. She had let them down by allowing Turlock to catch up with her and take the ship, as well as the loss of those cycles spent trapped with Sabin Travers. She vowed to be more careful in the future. These women depended on her. She wouldn't fail them again.

After the meal, she told the group about the large shipment of Saija silk, liquor, and engine parts she'd purchased at a cost way below market value, while on her way back to Risa. She had located her credit disks stored in a vault on Sabin's ship, so she'd had the necessary funds.

"Unfortunately, there are several catches on the deal," Moriah explained. "The seller wants the goods picked up on Star Base Intrepid, within the next seven cycles. We'll need three ships to hold the entire shipment."

"Th-three sh-ships?" Roanne gasped. "We only have t-two here r-right now."

"That can't be right," Moriah argued. "We had seven before Turlock took mine."

"Kiah and Marna are delivering those supplies in the Verante Constellation. They won't be back for another ten cycles," Lionia explained. "And two of our ships are down."

"Two of our ships aren't functioning?" Moriah questioned, not at all pleased with this news. "What's wrong with them?"

"Junk heaps!" Tyna sniffed. "As bad as that clunker you brought back."

Lionia shrugged. "I only know weapons, not engines."

"I looked them over, but I couldn't find the problem," Celie said. She had the most mechanical knowledge of anyone in the group, but it was limited to basics. Distress filled her eyes. "You won't let me pilot on pickups or deliveries, and I can't even do ship repairs. Sometimes I feel so useless."

Moriah slipped an arm around her sister's shoulders. "You're only sixteen seasons, sweetness. Already you know more about ship engines than the rest of us do. Give it time. You'll be flying your own ship one day."

"All this talk doesn't change anything," Tyna pointed out. "We're still one ship short."

"Actually, we have three functioning craft," Moriah countered. "We'll be able to make the pickup on time, if we leave tomorrow."

"S-surely you w-won't take th-that ship!" Roanne pointed to Sabin's, and Tyna added an uncomplimentary opinion.

Moriah sighed. "I don't see that we have much choice. I've already paid for the goods, and we can make a huge profit with them on Calt. That ship got me home. I'm sure it can make it there and back." *If we're lucky.*

"Star Base Intrepid is not the safest place to make a pickup," Tyna observed. "Too many of them cursed Anteks are crawling all over the place."

And Sabin had probably reported his ship stolen, a fact Moriah declined to mention. She didn't like the added risk of going to Intrepid, either, but they couldn't afford to pass up the potential profit. It would cost a lot to replace the craft she'd lost.

"We'll just have to be more cautious than usual," she replied.

"We'll take extra weapons." Lionia's eyes gleamed. "I wouldn't mind ridding the quadrant of some Anteks."

"We don't want to draw unnecessary attention to ourselves," Moriah warned. "No fighting unless absolutely necessary. Clear, Lionia?"

The warrior woman nodded reluctantly. Knowing Lionia's word was good, Moriah relaxed, sinking back against a large rock. Spirit, she was tired, but she still had a lot to do before she could rest. Stock the ships and plot the course to Intrepid. They'd have to rise early tomorrow to get a good start.

Then there was the matter of the malfunctioning ships. Those spacecraft were their lifeblood. No way around it. They needed a good mechanic, and soon.

Janaye painstakingly slid next to Moriah, grunting at the exertion. She patted Moriah's hand. "Tired?"

"Exhausted," Moriah admitted.

Concern filled Janaye's translucent eyes. "You need to stay here and rest. Let the others go to Intrepid tomorrow."

"You know I can't do that. I have to be there."

"You need to stay here," Janaye insisted. "I have a premonition about Star Base Intrepid, and I sense it concerns you. Something bad will happen if you go. Let Lionia, Roanne, and Tyna handle this. They're all good pilots."

Whenever possible, Moriah oversaw the transfer of goods onto her ships. She made the deals, and she wanted to be sure everything was in order. Once the ships were loaded, the other women made the bulk of the deliveries, except for the most dangerous ones. Moriah handled those.

This time would be no exception. The arrangement involved a huge inventory, with a lot of gold at stake. Plus it was the first time Moriah had done business with this particular seller. She had to be sure he held up his end of the bargain.

She shook her head, and Janaye sighed. "You won't be swayed into staying here."

"Of course not."

"Then Spirit go with you," the old woman whispered, squeezing Moriah's hand. "Be careful, child. Be very, very careful."

Unease slithered through Moriah. Janaye had never voiced such warnings before. She shook off a feeling of impending doom, attributing her reaction to fatigue. This would be a routine pickup, like dozens of others that had gone flawlessly. Nothing would go wrong.

Absolutely nothing.

Chapter Seven

Sabin paced the cockpit, Chase's larger flightsuit flapping around him. "Not one more word about how I look," he snarled when Chase started to say something. The man had enjoyed enough entertainment at Sabin's expense. Seeing the expression on McKnight's face when Lani fluttered her feathers at him, Sabin had wished he'd had someone else—*anyone else*—to contact besides his partner.

Ever since they had become partners a season ago, Sabin ribbed Chase whenever the opportunity arose. Now payback rebounded with a vengeance. Who'd have thought a guy who acted like such an old man could dish out abuse—and with such relish?

Chase shrugged, punching on his view-screen. "Just thought I saw a blue feather sticking to your flightsuit."

"Very funny," Sabin muttered, throwing himself into the opposite chair. He drummed his fingers on the console, wishing, as he had every one of the last fifteen cycles, that his new ship was ready. But the manufacturer needed at least seven more cycles. Sabin didn't know if he could tolerate his smirking partner that long.

He'd thought the three cycles waiting for Chase's arrival at Saron had been bad, having to put up with Lani's overzealous concern; having to convince her he didn't need, or want, physical release with her—or any other female. Leaving with Chase had appeared a welcome reprieve. For about two milliseconds.

The last twelve cycles cooped up with McKnight had been like a stay in the Abyss. It wasn't the ribbing from his partner; Sabin could give as good as he got. It was the numerous urgent matters weighing on his mind. His inability to act only increased the sense of urgency.

Galen was still on the loose, roaming the quadrant and committing atrocities against innocent citizens. And Aron's death was a blood debt crying out to be paid.

Money was also a major consideration. The bounties Sabin collected went mainly to Shielder colonies, whose resources provided their inhabitants with the barest existence at best. They depended on his monetary donations, as well as his deliveries of supplies and weapons. Also, he was funding the purchase of his new ship with bounties.

Perhaps it was wrong to earn money from tracking criminals, especially when turning them over to the Controllers meant certain death. The Controllers were evil, but he had to admit they had a swift and efficient method of handling criminals. Sabin had grappled over the questions of morality many times during the long lonely hours of space travel. But that was why he only hunted the really vicious criminals—those with no remorse for their crimes. Still, who he was, what he was forced to do to ensure the survival of his people, weighed heavy on his soul. To work for one's enemies to further the cause of right . . .

He'd continue to do what he had to; he had no alternative. Though, right now, for the next seven cycles, he was out of commission, unable to do anything. Unless Moriah turned up and he got his old ship back.

At the mere thought of the golden-eyed vixen, his blood pressure shot off the chart. What he wouldn't give to have his hands on her—literally. He could think of myriad ways he'd like to demonstrate his seething anger, starting with blistering her shapely bottom, then throwing her in the brig for a few hundred cycles.

The vision in his mind shifted, as his body joined the fray, casting a vote for what it would like to do with Moriah. Fragmented images of her lying naked beneath him swirled through his mind. Fantasy or fact? He honestly couldn't say, because he'd lost a chunk of time between his last concrete recollection of Galen's taunting disclosure of Aron's death and waking up to blue feathers.

It hadn't been a fantasy in the cockpit, however, when he'd foolishly given in to temptation and kissed Moriah again. He could still remember the texture of her hair tangled in his fingers, the taste of her, the feel of her pressed against him . . . her vehement withdrawal and taunting retort. The lady had a way of shredding his ego. So she'd had better, had she? He'd just have to prove her wrong.

Damn! He leaped from the chair and paced.

"Are you still scanning for my ship's homing signal?"

"Of course," Chase replied. "But I think we'd have picked it up by now if that woman was still in the quadrant. Unless she's disconnected it."

She was certainly clever enough to do that. She had disappeared, seemingly without a trace. It should have been difficult, if not impossible, to elude the net Sabin had cast. He'd notified the authorities at every Controller facility and star base; every shadower, every Shielder scout—everyone he knew. No one had reported seeing his ship. Moriah had either left the quadrant or gone to ground somewhere.

Sabin wasn't just determined to find her because of the blow to his pride, or the loss of his ship, although those rankled him plenty. Of even more concern was Moriah's potentially disastrous knowledge of a Shielder colony's location. In the wrong hands, that information could precipitate the loss of dozens, even hundreds, of innocent lives.

He knew firsthand how the Anteks operated, moving into Shielder colonies and slaughtering men, women, and children. And when he managed to block the memories for a cycle or two, the nightmares always returned to remind him.

The subspace transceiver beeped, jolting him back to the present. He pivoted as Chase punched the pad. "McKnight here."

"Hey, McKnight," came a familiar voice. "Radd here. Got Sabin with ya?"

"Right here." Sabin strode toward the console. "What's going on?"

"So's your new ship ready yet?"

Sabin shifted impatiently. "Not for seven more cycles. Is that why you're contacting me?"

"Naw. I thought if you still need it, you might want to come get your old ship."

That got his attention. "Are you saying you know where my ship is?"

"Yep. Just been working on it, matter of fact. Starboard thruster went out. Whole thing had to be replac—"

"Cut the commentary, Radd. Where the hell are you?"

"Oh, uh, Star Base Intrepid."

"And my ship is there?"

"Yep."

Sabin waited, but no information appeared forthcoming. "Care to elaborate?"

"I'm on Star Base Intrepid, your ship's on Star Base Intrepid. What's there to know?"

Gripping the console, Sabin groaned in utter frustration. Chase leaned back in his chair, grinning broadly. Glaring at his partner, Sabin gritted out, "I want to know details, Radd. *Details!* Where on Star Base Intrepid are you, how did you find my ship, and have you seen the woman who hijacked it? She's the same one who was on the ship at Calt."

"Yep, she's with the ship. Her and three other women."

Obviously, Sabin was going to have to ferret out the information. "And you just happened to see my ship on Intrepid," he prompted.

"Actually, one of the women approached me, 'cause the ship broke down. Asked me to work on it."

For once, Sabin was grateful his ship broke down at regular intervals. Then panic raced through him, as another thought occurred. "You haven't finished the repairs, have you? Is the ship operational yet?"

"Nope. Figured you might not appreciate your ship gettin' away again. I told the ladies I had some parts ordered, that it would be another cycle or two."

Thank Spirit Radd was more intelligent than he acted. Sabin released his pent-up breath, noting Chase entering new coordinates on the navigation screen. "What did Moriah have to say about that?"

"I haven't dealt with her too much. More with the tall, belligerent one. But none of 'em were pleased. They don't have much choice, though. All the other mechanics refuse to work on your junker. Say it's cursed."

Chase snickered, but Sabin ignored him. "That's great, Radd. You handled the situation well. Now, listen, I need you to keep that ship from being operational until we get there. You can do most of the repairs, just don't do all the wiring or diagnostics. We're two cycles out, so stall Moriah and the others as long as you can."

"Okay."

Another thought occurred to Sabin. "Oh, and Radd, install another homing beacon while you're at it. Make sure it's hidden, and fix it so it can't be disconnected without a security code. And the force field on my brig needs to be repaired, if you can find a way to get inside the ship."

"Can do."

Sabin got the location of the landing bay and the dock number where the ship was, and agreed to meet Radd there in two cycles. Then he signed off. Jubilation shot through him. He was going to get his ship back—and deal with Moriah. He sank into his chair, already thinking about the reunion. Any exchanges with her promised to be very interesting.

And most satisfying.

Catherine Spangler

Chase eyed him quizzically. "So, partner, aren't you going to contact the authorities on Intrepid?"

Sabin hadn't considered that. With a quick communiqué, Moriah and her accomplices could be thrown into prison and held until he got there. The idea offered an appeal, but he quickly discarded it. They'd be at the mercy of guards known for their debauchery; plus, they might be sent to Alta before he arrived at the star base. As a shadower, he could claim bounty rights and obtain their release on Intrepid, but once they reached Alta, he couldn't help them.

He didn't want Moriah to be tortured and executed, no matter how furious he was with her. She was a liar and a thief, but she wasn't a vicious criminal deserving of the horrendous punishments doled out by the Controllers and their henchmen. Besides, it would be so much more rewarding to deal with her himself.

"No, I'm not going to call the authorities," he answered Chase. "I'll handle the matter personally."

"Lucky lady," Chase murmured.

Sabin shot him a sharp glance, but McKnight's expression was impassive.

Sabin didn't care now if his partner harassed him all the way to Intrepid. Things were suddenly looking up. He'd get his ship back. Although he hated to admit it, even to himself, he had a soft spot for that decrepit piece of junk. It had been the first thing that ever really belonged to him. For the last twelve seasons, it had been his home.

Even if those seasons had been lonely, at least they'd been profitable, allowing him a freedom he'd never known until then. He'd been dependent on no one, and he swore he never would be again.

His thoughts returned to Moriah, and his pulse

quickened. Anticipation heated his blood at the thought of seeing her again and making certain she got her just reward. He could hardly wait.

"Aren't those repairs done yet?" Moriah demanded as Lionia entered the cockpit.

"No!" Lionia snarled. "The little serpent claims he needs at least another cycle. I don't trust him." She pulled her magnasteel dagger from the sheath at her trim waist. The light glinted off its laser-sharp edge. "I say we use *kamta* to speed him up."

"No," Moriah said firmly. "Carving Zarian war patterns on the mechanic's body won't speed up anything, and would only draw attention to us. But I don't trust this guy either. He looks so familiar, I know I've seen him somewhere. Celie, has he ever worked on any of our ships before? Celie!"

Celie glanced up from the computer screen, a faraway look in her eyes. "What?"

Moriah looked at her affectionately. Her sister, the dreamer. Despite the hardships they'd endured, Celie maintained an innate innocence, and a fascination with learning. She had the ability to lose herself in the wealth of information in the computer, something Moriah had always been too restless to do.

"Sweetness," Moriah prompted, "have we ever used this mechanic on any of our ships before?"

Celie pushed her golden hair from her face, her dark eyes thoughtful. "Not that I recall."

Moriah tapped her foot. She knew Radd from somewhere. . . . Why couldn't she remember? Usually she had a holographic memory. She did know he was a legitimate mechanic, and a good one, because they'd made inquiries before commissioning him. Besides, he was the only one willing to take the job.

Catherine Spangler

Curse Sabin Travers and his ship to the Fires. What should have been a routine deal was becoming riskier by the millisecond. The longer they remained on Intrepid, the greater the risk of drawing attention to themselves. *And* the greater the danger of Sabin or Turlock or Pax or any number of others catching up with them.

She'd asked the question before, but she was short on options, so Moriah asked again. "Celie, you're sure this mechanic is performing the correct repairs on the ship?"

"As best as I can tell. I've checked his work every time he takes a break. The new thruster looks good and appears to be installed correctly. The wiring still has to be done, though, and he says he's waiting on an adaptor kit. He can't get parts for this ship any longer, so he's using parts from a newer model that's similar."

"Naturally none of the parts we're carrying will work on this junker." Moriah whirled around. "Lionia, I want you and Roanne to take the other ships back to Risa. The longer we stay on Intrepid like sitting echobirds, the greater the danger. Celie is to go with you."

"But I want to stay with you!" Celie protested, jumping up from her chair.

"I don't want to leave you alone," Lionia argued, stroking the hilt of her dagger. "You might need assistance."

"I can handle anything that comes up. I don't want to risk losing this shipment. We've got the majority of it on the other two ships. We have to consider the good of the group, and get the merchandise to Risa. As soon as this ship is repaired, I'll be right behind you."

"If that is your order," Lionia conceded grudgingly. "Then I shall honor it."

128

"It is," Moriah answered, eternally grateful that she had once saved Lionia's life. The fierce warrior woman had sworn loyalty and obedience because of the life debt; otherwise, Moriah would have had a battle on her hands.

She turned to her sister. "Celie, you'll go with her. I can't finish up here and get away quickly if I have to worry about your safety as well as my own."

Celie's large brown eyes filled with distress. "But Moriah—"

"Do this for me. Please, sweetness."

Lionia stepped forward and took Celie's arm. "Your sister is right, little one. She can work much better alone. Come, get ready to leave."

Celie looked like she might argue further, but shrugged in resignation. "All right, Mori. If you think it's best, I'll go with Lionia."

"I know it's best," Moriah reassured her. "Go change into your rhapha first."

Celie made a face. "Do I have to? I hate that thing. It fits so tightly across my chest and pushes my breasts up. I feel half-naked!"

Moriah glanced down at her own rhapha, the dress of choice for all female courtesans from Intrepid's Pleasure Domes. It identified them as members of a unique, elite group which, oddly enough, commanded a considerable amount of respect.

Moriah and most of her women wore a variety of disguises when they were planet-side, from the religious robes of Shens or other pilgrims, to Trion tunics. The rhapha was their favorite disguise on star bases because it afforded a large degree of protection. The Pleasure Domes brought in a lot of revenue, as well as keeping the soldiers stationed there content.

Catherine Spangler

Skilled courtesans were highly sought after, and every effort was made to guarantee their protection. No one would dare harm a courtesan, for the legal retribution was shipment to the Controller prison base on Alta, and certain death.

Lionia, of course, scorned such a feminine disguise; but then, tall and fierce and obviously Zarian, she didn't need the protection of a costume. Sweet and innocent Celie did.

"You need to put on your rhapha," Moriah insisted. "Just be sure and drape your scarf across your chest. No one need see any more than necessary."

"I'll warm my ship up for takeoff and tell Roanne to do the same." Lionia headed for the hatch.

"I'll walk out with you." Moriah turned toward her sister. "I have to go check on some things, so this is good-bye for now. As soon as you've changed, go straight to Lionia's ship. I'll feel better once I know you're safely away."

Celie nodded and hugged her tightly. "Be careful, Mori. Contact me every cycle, okay?"

Moriah stroked Celie's face. "I will, I promise. Now get ready. I'll see you on Risa in a few cycles."

She left the ship with Lionia, giving last-minute instructions in a low voice. "Don't unload any of the cargo when you reach Risa. As soon as I arrive, we'll head for Calt. Hopefully Kiah and Marna will have returned, so ready one of their ships to transfer the cargo from this pile of kerani manure."

Lionia nodded. "A good plan. I'll see to it."

"Thanks. Give my instructions to Roanne and have her get ready for takeoff. Leave as soon as Celie is on board, then contact me."

"It will be done." Lionia turned and strode regally toward the other end of the huge bay.

130

Moriah watched a moment, then circled the ship. The thruster being repaired was on the starboard side. She came around, her attention focused on the young man leaning into the thruster casing.

Reputed to be one of the best mechanics in the quadrant, he worked with a quiet confidence. She could only hope the repairs would be completed soon. Otherwise, she might have to hijack another ship. She started forward to question him, but a magnasteel grip on her upper arm brought her up short.

"Well, well. If it isn't Mara/Moriah, liar and thief extraordinaire."

Adrenaline flooded her at the sound of that deep, familiar voice. She whirled partway around, impeded by the relentless fingers digging into her flesh. Her gaze locked with blazing midnight eyes. Sabin Travers glared back at her, his mouth thinned to an ominous line. He looked bigger and darker than she remembered, the shadow of beard growth accentuating the danger he radiated.

"And, let me add, a drug trafficker." He spoke slowly and softly, barely checked fury echoing in every deliberate word.

"Let me go!" She jerked back in an unsuccessful attempt to break his grasp.

He pulled her forward. "Do you know what the Controllers do to those who carry illegal drugs, Mara/Moriah?"

She shuddered, well aware of the Controller methods of punishment. She had to dump the bracelet on her arm before Sabin called the authorities. But first, she needed to come up with a story to placate him. Various scenarios flashed through her mind, none of them very convincing.

"I can explain everything."

"Don't even try."

"But you must listen to—" She paused midsentence, alarmed by the change in his expression as his gaze drifted lower.

"What's this you're wearing?"

Glancing down, she realized her scarf had slipped off one shoulder, exposing the generous swell of her breasts above an immodestly low neckline.

"So you've changed professions," he drawled, his free hand pushing the scarf off her shoulders. "Or perhaps you were a prostitute all along." He brushed his fingers along the emerald Saija silk barely covering her breast. "Nice. I'll have to tell Lani she was wrong about your endowments."

She swung her free fist as hard as she could. His hand shot up, catching it millimeters from his face. "We'll get to the shackles in just a minute," he promised.

He pushed her back against the ship, trapping her arms behind her, holding them in an unbreakable vise with his left hand. His body pressed blatantly against hers, preventing her from levering free. "But first, I have a few questions."

"I told you I can explain—"

"What's this?"

His attention had moved downward again. Damn the revealing rhapha, and damn all men! He cupped her right breast, the heat of his touch searing. "So . . ." he murmured. "I didn't imagine it."

She stared down stupidly as his thumb rubbed across the distinctive mole on the upper slope of her breast. Her body reacted immediately, her breast swelling to his touch, the nipple pebbling. Frissons of pleasure skittered along her nerve endings.

Trying not to gasp, she swallowed hard. "Didn't imagine what?"

"That night in your cabin."

Her gaze snapped up to meet his, and her heart bolted in her chest at the heated intensity she saw there. Images swirled through her mind—Sabin lowering his mouth to her breast, his hand moving along her leg. Spirit, no! She forced the vision away. She refused to be affected by him, by his touch.

"No, I didn't imagine this intriguing mole." He continued to stroke her bare skin. She shivered, battling her body's traitorous reaction. "Which also means I didn't imagine you lying naked on your bunk, spreading your legs for me. Playing the whore to draw me into a trap I should have seen coming light-years away."

His crude words sent heat flaming through her face. But it was the truth behind those words that seared her to the core. *Whore*. Pax had dragged her to the dredges of the Abyss and back, leaving her forever tainted. She had sworn she'd never again barter her body—and ultimately, her soul. *Never again*.

And yet, with Sabin, she'd done just that. She'd had no choice, she told herself fiercely. If she had to trade her soul in order to ensure the well-being of Celie and the others, then so be it.

"Tell me, did you enjoy it?"

Sabin's taunt pulled her thoughts back to the present. Apparently his memories of being in her cabin were fragmented, a very likely possibility with the drug she had used. If she could convince him otherwise, she might diffuse some of his anger.

"Nothing happened between us," she argued.

"You must have dreamed it. You probably saw the mole when you treated my wound."

"I think not." He grasped her chin, forcing her to meet his scathing gaze. "It was your left shoulder that was wounded. I never bared your right side. Don't try to deny it."

She stared at his furious face, knowing he wouldn't be swayed. By the Fires! She had left her phaser inside. She had to find some way to—

"Halt there, citizen! Release the lady and put your hands up."

Still gripping her wrists, Sabin glanced over his shoulder. Standing behind him were three Anteks, two armed with disrupters, the third holding an electrolyzer rod. Their rank smell permeated the air.

With a frustrated sigh, he jerked away from her, raising his hands and slowly turning around. She hastily slipped past him, retrieving her scarf off the ground and flinging it around her bare shoulders.

Her actions drew the soldiers' notice momentarily, but as soon as they saw her rhapha, their attention returned to Sabin. She wanted nothing more than to slip away, but knew she would draw far more suspicion if she did. One Antek, apparently the leader, lumbered forward and took Sabin's phasers and identification. The other two circled behind him.

"What goes on here?" the leader demanded in a guttural voice. "Who is the owner of this ship?"

"I am," Sabin answered.

The Antek grunted, showing a row of sharp teeth. "Odd. This ship happens to match the description of one that's been reported stolen."

"It's my ship," Sabin insisted. "I'm the one who

reported it stolen, and I just caught up with the thief."

He pointed toward Moriah, and she decided it was time for a distraction. "This man was trying to force himself on me," she informed the one in charge.

His dull eyes narrowed into slits. "Harming courtesan very serious."

"She's lying!" Sabin protested, taking a step forward. "I didn't hurt her. Besides, she's a fake. She's not even a—"

The Antek behind him shocked him with the electrolyzer rod. Sabin jerked and staggered, and for a moment, Moriah thought he might fall, but he regained his balance. She winced, knowing how painful an electrolyzer jolt could be.

"You're foolish, citizen," the leader snapped. "Accosting a courtesan and stealing a ship are high-level crimes."

"Check my identification," Sabin gritted out, "and then check the ship registration. You'll see I'm telling the truth. This ship belongs to me."

"I intend to do that," the leader growled. "And to search the ship as well."

Searching any questionable ship was standard operating procedure. There went Moriah's inventory. Goods she couldn't afford to lose. Damn Sabin Travers! But there was nothing she could do about it now. This was her cue to cut out as quickly as possible.

She stepped close to the team leader, trying not to gag at his smell, and gave him her brightest smile. "Thank you for coming to my assistance, Commander. If you don't mind, I have a rendezvous with an important client at the Dome. I really must be leaving."

"You can't let her go!" Sabin roared. "She's the one who stole the ship."

He got another shock for his outburst, this one almost sending him to his knees. A second, surprising wave of concern swept through Moriah.

"You will present charges against this citizen?" the head Antek asked.

She tore her gaze away from Sabin's accusing glare. "Uh, no, I don't think so. He didn't hurt me. Just got a little excited."

"Why don't you check *her* identification?" Sabin pressed. "I'm telling you, she's not a courtesan. She's a fraud."

Shaking her head as if Sabin were crazy, Moriah slipped her ID from her pouch and offered it to the Antek. "The poor man. Go ahead, Commander. Feel free to check it."

He glanced briefly at the picture, but didn't run the disk through the unit at his waist. "It looks okay, lady. You free to go."

"She's lying, I tell you!" Sabin endured another shock, while Moriah tried not to cringe. She wished he'd just be quiet and let them check his registration. He'd prove his ownership soon enough—and she'd be long gone by then.

She smiled once more at the leader, playfully flipping one end of her scarf against his barreled chest. "Thank you again for rescuing me, Commander," she purred. "You come see me at the Dome and you'll get special treatment—at no additional charge."

The Antek snorted, drool slipping down his jowl. "I will, lady. I come see you."

Moriah tried not to shudder. She gestured toward Sabin. "Go easy on him, as a personal favor to me. He's not really dangerous, just a little deranged."

136

Ignoring Sabin's blistering glare, which clearly broadcast an unspoken promise of retribution if he ever caught up with her, she turned and gracefully swept away.

Once she was completely out of sight, she lifted her skirt and ran to the other side of the huge bay. She hoped it wasn't too late, that Lionia and Roanne hadn't taken off yet. If they had, she'd have to take cover until someone could come back for her. She knew she'd better not let Sabin catch up with her.

Guilt twinged through her—guilt at leaving him in the hands of three Anteks. But there was nothing she could have done, and he should be able to prove he was the legal owner of the ship. There was also the matter of the contraband on the ship, but he could get out of that, if he knew who to bribe.

She really didn't know much about Sabin Travers, although she knew he was involved in illegal activities, as were more than half the citizens in this quadrant. He'd land on his feet.

If the ship wasn't legally his, that was another matter, because stolen ships fell under interstellar authority. Moriah hoped, for his sake, that it did belong to him. Otherwise, he'd be on the next prison transport to Alta—a thought that bothered her more than she cared to admit. Just guilt, she told herself, nothing more. After all, he'd treated her reasonably well, and she'd repaid him by drugging him and stealing his ship.

She'd done it out of necessity, though, and personal feelings didn't enter into her actions. Not that she had any personal feelings for Sabin Travers. Absolutely not.

Relief swept through her when she saw Lionia's ship still on the pad. At least one thing had gone right today. She punched in the hatch code. As she entered, Lionia strode from the cockpit. When she saw Moriah, a surprised expression crossed her face.

"Moriah! What are you doing here? I thought you were Celie."

Moriah stared back, a sick feeling in the pit of her stomach. "You mean Celie's not here yet?"

Lionia shook her head.

"She should have been here by now," Moriah said, trepidation vibrating through her. "Either she's still on the other ship, or something happened to her on the way here." She recalled the scenario she'd just left: Anteks about to search Sabin's ship. Panic raced through her.

Celie!

Where in the blazing hells was her sister?

Chapter Eight

He was definitely going to kill Moriah. Painfully, slowly—dismemberment came to mind—but only after he tortured her first. Seething, Sabin stood under the guard of the Antek leader, while the other two soldiers searched his ship. His identification, along with his ship's registration number, were being run through Intrepid's central computer system. He knew he'd check out, like he always did. He would get his ship back. Then there would be hell to pay.

The lumbering tread of a returning Antek drew his attention. Startled, he saw the soldier escorting a strange woman from his ship. Tall and slender, she was clad in a generic tan flightsuit. The Antek had a firm grip on her arm, and his electrolyzer rod was at the ready in case she ran. Sabin couldn't see the woman clearly because her head was down, a wealth of golden hair shielding her face from view.

She stumbled as the Antek jerked her to a halt

139

before Sabin and the team leader. Regaining her balance, she kept her head down. Tremors shook her body.

"We found woman on board, trying to escape out back hatch," the Antek grunted.

"Show yourself," his captain commanded.

Slowly, she raised her head, wisps of silky hair clinging to her cheeks. She was young, much younger than Sabin's initial impression. Stark, utter terror shone in her brown eyes, and all color had drained from her face.

She looked familiar, yet Sabin didn't recall seeing her before. Since she'd been on his ship, he felt certain she must be one of the three women Radd had said were with Moriah. The realization kindled his interest. This woman might be key in tracking Moriah down.

"Present your name and identification," the leader barked.

The girl's eyes widened and her chest heaved. "My-my name is Celie. And I-I left my identification on another ship."

The leader's eyes narrowed. "Ordinances state citizens will carry identification at all times. You under arrest." He jerked his head at the other Antek, who stepped forward to put shackles on the girl's slender wrists. She shook so badly, Sabin thought she might faint. But she rallied, drawing a deep breath and fixing her gaze on her shackled arms.

Sabin glanced at the bonds on his own wrists, courtesy of the Anteks and Moriah's deviousness. "Welcome to the club," he muttered.

She glanced sideways at him, her dark eyes flaring in alarm before she looked down again. She appeared as frightened of him as she was of the Anteks. She also appeared very innocent, a state which wouldn't last long in a Controller prison. Sabin shook his head, disgusted with a system so permeated with evil, any spark of decency was quickly and irrevocably snuffed out.

Hell, why was he entertaining sympathy for this young woman? She was most likely one of Moriah's minions . . . and as such, a potential tool for revenge. Yes, the more he thought about it, the more he liked the idea. She'd make a useful hostage.

Of course, at the moment, he was in no position to be taking hostages.

The second Antek stomped from the ship. "Commander!" he barked. "I have found some unusual items. You come see."

Sabin pivoted toward the ship, perplexed. Unusual items?

The leader gestured toward Sabin and the woman. "Guard them."

The two Antek lackeys flanked them as their leader entered the ship. Celie remained silent, her gaze on the ground, while Sabin mentally catalogued everything stored on board. He had nothing out of the ordinary, unless—

"You there!" the leader growled, pointing at Sabin as he stepped through the hatch. "You have a certified bill of lading for the goods on your ship?"

Goods? What goods? Sabin stared at the leader, an unpleasant premonition stirring inside him.

"Or a receipt for payment of tariffs for transporting Class III commodities within the quadrant?" the head Antek persisted.

Class III commodities? Sabin rarely carried such, couldn't imagine how . . . Yeah, he could. Would it be possible to kill Moriah more than once?

"I have no idea what you're talking about," he

answered, although he had a very strong suspicion.

The leader moved closer, getting in Sabin's face and baring sharp teeth in a feral grin. "Saija silk, bolts of it. Ship engines and parts. Crates of Elysian liquor—the best of all, eh? So, you have tariff receipt?"

"Of course not," Sabin gritted out, trying avoid inhaling the horrible odor of Antek. "I didn't put that stuff on the ship. It was stolen, remember? But I can certainly tell you who's responsible. A woman who goes by the name of Moriah Cameron."

A soft gasp escaped the young woman beside him. He turned to find her staring at him, her dark eyes huge with fear. She shook her head. "No," she whispered. "That's not true."

"Oh, really? I happen to know that it is. Moriah Cameron drugged me, then hijacked my ship. She was here just moments ago." He turned a blistering glare on the Antek commander. "And you let her get away."

"No!" Celie cried.

The leader snorted. "Don't try to blame the courtesan. Her identification was in good order." He turned a crafty gaze on Celie. "*She* was on ship. Maybe she's responsible."

Biting her lips together, she lowered her gaze, offering no reply. "No," Sabin objected sharply. "She's an accomplice to part of this, but I'm positive she's not the one who stole my ship."

The commander glanced at the readout on his portable computer unit. "Your identification checks out, Sabin Travers. This ship is registered to you." He raised beady eyes to Sabin. "But no thief around, no tariff papers. You under arrest." He gestured at the other two Anteks. "Take them."

142

Realizing resistance would be futile—and dangerous—Sabin went along calmly, although he was raging inside. He knew McKnight would figure out what had happened soon enough and provide proof of his whereabouts for the past fifteen cycles.

But maybe this huge inconvenience wouldn't be for nothing. Now, Sabin had a connection to Moriah—the young woman sitting in front of him on the tram taking them to Control Headquarters. He wouldn't allow this opportunity to slip through his fingers.

From his hiding place behind the thruster casing, Radd watched the Anteks unload the crates from the ship and haul them away. Idly, he wondered if he should deduct the time he'd been stranded behind the casing from his charges. Naw, he decided. It wasn't his fault Sabin had gotten himself arrested. Business was business and time was money.

Radd shrugged, not the least bit concerned about Sabin. He'd seen the shadower get out of far worse predicaments than being thrown into prison.

Humming to himself, he headed inside the ship. He had already installed the hidden homing device Sabin had requested, and the thruster repairs were completed. All that was left was to repair the force field on the brig.

Inside, he pried the plate off the brig control panel and studied the circuit boards. Joy flowed through him as he plunged into checking the circuits and their connections. He loved the challenge of unraveling difficult problems, then using his considerable skill to restore a complex system or engine to working order. And Sabin's junk heap offered plenty of challenges. Radd would be kinda sorry to see it go to scrap.

One moment, he was sliding out a circuit board from the panel; the next, he was hauled backward against a firm body and the razor-sharp edge of a dagger was pressed against his throat. Odd, he hadn't heard the hatch tone, or any footsteps.

"Where is the girl who was on board?" a voice hissed.

Radd remained relaxed. Working around the quadrant as he did, he came into frequent contact with lowlifes and their violent behavior. He didn't even pretend ignorance to the question. "She was arrested."

The arm across his chest tightened and the blade edged closer, nicking his skin. "You lie, serpent. I ought to perform *kamta* on you."

Ah, a Zarian. It had to be the tall, arrogant blonde—Moriah's sidekick. Her body was almost as hard as a man's, except for the lush breasts now pillowing his jaw. He could think of worse ways to die. "If ya cut my throat, I can't give any information," he pointed out.

She eased the blade back slightly, and he felt blood trickle down his neck. "I can do *kamta* without killing you," she growled.

"Whatcha wanna know?"

"Where is the girl?" The voice came from behind him. Moriah, now dressed in a brown flightsuit, stepped into his field of vision.

"I already told ya. She was arrested."

Her eyes narrowed. Stalking forward, she shoved an activated phaser against his chest. "That tells me nothing. Explain, in full detail. Tell me everything that happened, or I'll let Lionia carve you up before I disintegrate your puny body."

Radd sighed. Everyone always wanted *details*. They wanted to turn simple facts into complicated scenarios. "After ya left, the Anteks searched the ship. They found the girl and some unauthorized goods on board. They arrested Sabin and the girl and took them away."

Panic flashed across Moriah's face, and the phaser pressing against his chest shook. Radd drew a sharp breath, wondering if this would be it for him. But she stepped back, the weapon still aimed at him. "Where did they take her?" she asked hoarsely.

"There's only one place they woulda gone," Radd answered. "The prison." Reason had to tell her that, but he suspected clear thinking had momentarily evaded her.

As she dropped her arm to her side and turned away, the other woman's dagger pressed against Radd's throat again. "Should I finish off this serpent?" the Zarian asked.

"Hey!" he protested. "I told ya the truth. It's not like I'm responsible for this."

Standing ramrod-stiff, Moriah sighed. "No. Don't harm him." She turned and stared at him speculatively. "We need a mechanic. He's coming with us. After we get Celie back."

At headquarters, the two lower-ranking Anteks marched Celie and Sabin to a cell. One shoved Celie inside. Sabin started to follow, but an electrolyzer rod blocked his path.

"You go to another cell," the Antek rumbled.

Both soldiers were eyeing Celie, practically salivating. Sabin knew they planned a return visit in the near future. He had no intention of being separated from her. "What about your orders?" he asked.

Catherine Spangler

"Commander issued orders," one answered woodenly.

Thank Spirit Anteks were inherently stupid, Sabin thought. So dumb, in fact, that those in positions of authority were always mixed-breeds, because only they had a modicum of sense. "I heard those orders," he told the soldier. "Your commanding officer specifically requested that I be placed in the same cell with the female. He plans to question us together."

The Anteks looked at each other uncertainly. "I not remember that," the first soldier said.

Sabin shrugged. "Your commander will be very displeased that you forgot his orders. Better put me in this cell while you go check with him."

The soldiers shuffled their feet uneasily. It was not a good idea to admit to forgetting orders. Harsh discipline would be dispensed for sure.

"All right," one Antek finally conceded. "You go in, too."

Tamping down a triumphant smirk, Sabin entered the cell. His elation quickly evaporated as a foul odor assailed his nose. The sludge squishing beneath his feet added the finishing touch to the infamous Controller prison ambience. The Anteks activated the force field and lumbered away.

Moriah's accomplice edged her way to the wall nearest the entrance. Determined to find out more about this opportune link, Sabin settled next to her.

"Looks like we're cell mates," he commented.

She jolted away, slipping and almost falling. "Leave me alone."

He reached out his shackled hands and grabbed her arm, tightening his grip to steady her. "Careful, or you'll be facedown in this stuff."

She struggled against his grasp, almost pulling

146

both of them down. "Get away from me, or I'll scream. I swear it!"

He jerked her around and against the stone wall. "Try it and I'll have to silence you. I have no desire to be visited further by our Antek comrades. And if you're smart, you'll avoid that too. Whatever you fear I might be thinking of doing to you, they'll do ten times over. And it won't be just one soldier. Whoever's in the vicinity will want to participate in the fun."

He paused to see if his message was sinking in. Ordinarily women didn't view him with abject horror. But Celie looked at him like he was a demon from the Abyss—right before she screamed.

He clamped his hand over her mouth. "Little fool! Didn't you hear a word I just said? No female, human or otherwise, young or old, is safe in a Controller prison. Just imagine your worst nightmares, sweetheart. They can come true right here. I promise you."

She stared at him, her eyes huge, her slim body trembling. "I mean you no harm," he continued. "Look, we're together in this cell, whether you like it or not. You're going to have to trust me. I'll try to protect you from those goons out there, but you have to cooperate with me. I'll release you if you agree not to fight me, and not to scream. Deal?"

After a moment, she nodded. He removed his hand cautiously, waiting for her to renege. But she held her silence. She lowered her head again, a habit that was beginning to irritate him.

"Don't," he said, grasping her chin and raising her face toward him. "Always keep eye contact with people you don't trust. And never show your fear."

She didn't resist his hand, and he took the opportunity to study her. Dark brown eyes domi-

Catherine Spangler

nated a classic, angular face. She had a patrician nose and a lush, full mouth. A haunting familiarity nagged at Sabin—then it came to him.

Moriah. That was it! Except for her coloring, this girl strongly resembled Moriah. She was almost as tall, too, although slighter in build. But then, she was young and had not yet blossomed into full womanhood. The similarities were so striking, Sabin realized the two must be related.

"So, Moriah is your sister," he speculated, gauging her reaction. He got his answer in her soft gasp, the surprised look in her eyes. She was too young to hide her feelings, too easy to read. "How did you know? I mean, you couldn't possibly— Moriah's never talked about you."

He snorted. Not surprising. Moriah would be too shrewd to talk freely about drugging a man then hijacking his ship. *Not to mention seducing him senseless first.* Heat blasted through him, along with the return of the fragmented memories of Moriah lying warm and compliant beneath him.

Today she'd been dressed in that rhapha which had caressed every curve, its low bodice pushing her breasts to nearly overflowing. The emerald color had set off her blazing hair and golden eyes to perfection. Sabin had been hard-pressed— mentally and physically—to keep his wits about him.

Blazing hells. He needed to get control of his libido, and fast. He would not allow Moriah to cloud his thinking from now on. And he'd use her sister, innocent or not, to obtain as much useful information as possible to lead him to Moriah.

"Your sister may not have mentioned me, but I know her quite well. I rescued her from two Jaccians, and treated her injury. I gave her a lift because her ship was stolen. She repaid me by stealing mine."

All color drained from Celie's face. "She didn't tell us she'd been hurt," she murmured.

"Ah! So she did tell you something, then?"

"She—she said that she'd been in an altercation with some Jaccians, but she never mentioned being injured," Celie replied slowly, her eyes troubled. "I'm sorry about your ship. She must have been pretty desperate to take it from you."

Sabin refrained from airing his opinions on Moriah's motivations. Celie obviously had a strong bond with her sister, and he didn't want to alienate her. He pondered the best way to get her to trust him enough to open up and give him information. The opportunity presented itself a moment later when the heavy tread of boots approached their cell.

"Quick! Sink down against the wall," he ordered, pushing her onto the floor. "Cross your arms over your chest and groan. Act like you're sick and in pain." When she just sat there, he leaned down and tugged her arms across her breasts. The chain from the shackles dangled between her wrists.

"Groan," he demanded. "Make them think you're dying."

She apparently caught on to his ploy, because she moaned loudly just as the force field was switched off. The two Anteks who had arrested them earlier lumbered in, hitching up their pants, slobber hanging from their snouts. They approached Celie, their small eyes glinting lewdly. One began to unfasten his uniform, while the other shoved his electrolyzer rod at Sabin. "Get in other corner," he ordered.

149

Celie shuddered and groaned again, gaining the attention of both Anteks.

"I wouldn't touch her if I were you," Sabin said. "She's extremely ill."

Taking his cue, Celie slid down further, crying out. "I'm so sick," she gasped. "The pain . . . oh, it hurts! Please help me!" She thrashed her legs wildly, flinging up muck.

So the little actress was more like Moriah than Sabin had realized. "I told you," he said, moving to the opposite corner. "She started acting like this right after you left. Must have some terrible disease. Maybe Alberian flu, or maybe . . . Raxis." Just then Celie tossed her head to the side and groaned some more.

"I think I'm dying. Help . . ."

Raxis was a disease Anteks were particularly susceptible to, and it made them deathly ill. The two soldiers backed away uneasily, and Sabin pressed his advantage. "Yep, all the signs of Raxis, all right. You've got to get me out of here. You can't leave me with her." He knew they wouldn't care what happened to him, nor would they cross their commander's supposed orders.

Ignoring his request, both Anteks scrambled for the entry. As they reactivated the force field and beat a hasty retreat, looking for a healthier victim, Sabin chuckled softly. He strode to Celie and offered her a hand up. "Good job. You're quite an actress. Must have learned it from your sister."

She struggled to her feet, looking down at her slime-covered legs with distaste, "Ugh! What is this stuff?"

"You don't want to know." He leaned against the wall. "Well, all that's left to do is wait."

He felt her stiffen next to him. "Wait for what?"

"For my partner to realize I'm missing and figure out where I am. Then he'll offer proof my ship really was stolen and that I couldn't possibly have been around to load contraband on it. Spread a few bribes, if necessary. In the meantime, you're safe with me. I give you my word."

She looked askance at him, her dark eyes wide. "How will your partner know where you are? Do you get arrested often?"

"I avoid it as much as possible," Sabin muttered. "But where I'm concerned, McKnight usually expects the worst."

"Will he be able to gain your freedom?"

He couldn't miss the tremor in her voice. Like a trapped baby kerani, she radiated fear. He turned to face her, leaning his shoulder against the wall. "McKnight has a lot of credibility and a fair amount of gold. It should be sufficient. What do you suppose will happen to you?"

She chewed her lower lip—apparently a family trait. "Moriah will think of some way to get me out."

Knowing how resourceful Moriah could be, Sabin didn't doubt that for a millisecond. It would be interesting to see what her next move would be. Regardless, he wouldn't leave Celie behind in this hellhole, even if he had to evoke bounty rights.

"Don't worry, little one. I won't leave you here. I can get you out."

She sighed, leaning her head back, her golden tresses spilling over onto her chest. "I hope someone can. How long do you think we'll be here?"

"No more than a cycle, I shouldn't think."

"Oh."

She sounded so despondent, Sabin smiled inwardly. In many ways, she was still a young girl, although poised on the brink of adulthood. Hoping to put her at ease, to draw information from her, he began to talk. He conversed about many things; the interesting places he'd visited, some of the natural wonders of the quadrant, some of the different races he'd encountered.

She listened, her face radiant with wonder and curiosity, her questions and replies indicating a surprising amount of knowledge. She obviously spent a lot of time delving into IAR computer files. As he sensed her relaxing, developing a tenuous trust of him, he gradually brought the conversation around to more personal matters.

"How old are you, Celie?"

"Sixteen seasons."

"You're very mature for your age. How old is Moriah?"

"Twenty-four seasons," Celie answered readily enough. "She raised me."

"What happened to your parents?"

A shadow crossed her face. "My mother died shortly after I was born, and my father . . ." She hesitated, clenching her hands against her thighs.

"It's okay," Sabin soothed, his curiosity kindled. "Tell me. Please."

She stared upward, drawing a deep breath. "Not much to tell. He was a worthless father—drunk most of the time. What money he managed to earn as a shadower, he usually gambled away."

A shadower as a father? What kind of life was that for his children? "Did you travel with him when he was tracking criminals?"

"Of course. He could barely afford a ship, much less another place for us to stay. Besides, we usually had to take care of him."

Pain and bitterness resonated in her voice. It didn't take much for Sabin to fill in the blanks. He'd seen a lot of drunks in his travels and the patterns were pretty much universal. Buying liquor took precedence over everything—even eating.

"Tough childhood, huh?" he asked quietly.

She released a shaky breath. "Moriah made it bearable. She took care of me, made me eat most of the food she hoarded. She protected me, keeping me away from our father when he was drinking. She would step in front of me when he tried to hit me and take the blows instead."

Rage boiled inside Sabin. Children were defenseless, at the complete mercy of adults. He'd spent his own childhood dependent on the benevolent inclinations of his elders. The thought of Moriah having to become Celie's parent, having to go hungry, then taking care of her drunken father—her abusive father—only fueled his rage further.

"Where is your father now?"

"I have no idea. He gambled us away in a game of chance when I was ten."

For a moment, Sabin wasn't sure he had heard correctly. *"He gambled you away?"*

She nodded. "To another shadower. My father thought he could win the man's ship, so he put Moriah and me up as a bet. But he lost. We haven't seen him since."

Sabin stared at her incredulously. "So you became the property of this other shadower? Basically slaves?"

"Not slaves, exactly. Indentured servers—" Her voice breaking, she turned away.

He battled the urge to pound his fist into something. "How long—"

"I don't want to talk about it anymore."

The agitation in her voice halted his interrogation. He cursed the shackles on his wrists, which prevented him from offering comfort.

"I'm sorry. We won't talk of it further," he promised.

She seemed to calm in the ensuing silence, but Sabin's tension didn't abate. Celie's story explained a lot of things about Moriah. Her hard-edged grittiness, her independence, her smuggling activities. She'd had to learn to take care of herself at a very early age. After living in what had to be near poverty with a father who gambled away everything from food money to his own daughters, it wasn't surprising she didn't trust men. Since she'd lived a life of deprivation, the gold to be made smuggling would hold great appeal.

A grudging respect edged its way in, diffusing the rage toward Moriah he'd been hoarding. He tried to shove it back, tried to hold on to his anger by reminding himself of her transgressions—and there were a lot. Yet admiration for her determination to survive and her resourcefulness further weakened his outrage.

She'd managed to raise a pretty likable sister, too. A familiar sense of regret stirred inside him. He'd had a sister once, an older sister, and they'd been very close. Until the ravaging Anteks had attacked their colony, and she—and everything else in his young world—had been destroyed.

Shaking away the grim memories, Sabin forced his thoughts back to Moriah. The fact remained she had cheated him. He could accept her lying about her true identity; no one in their right mind would confess to smuggling illegal goods. He might even be able to accept being drugged, as she must have been desperate to escape him.

But taking his ship—his home, his security—that was far beyond the limits of his toleration. Then to load it with contraband! Sabin's anger rekindled and leaped to life. Maybe he wouldn't be quite as tough as he'd originally planned when he caught up with her. But he would deal with her, and now he had the bait for the trap.

Celie might even give him more information. Casually, he asked, "So where were the goods on my ship being taken?"

"To Calt. But it was a fairly small deal, only to tide us over until Moriah delivers the iridon to the Leors—" She stopped abruptly, mortification filling her eyes. "Oh, Spirit! What's the matter with me?"

Shock torpedoed through Sabin. *"The Leors?"* he stormed. "Does your sister have any common sense in that pretty head of hers? Does she have any idea how dangerous the—" The alarm on Celie's face stopped his tirade midstream. "Blazing hells," he muttered, disgusted.

The Leors! The most dangerous, warlike species in the quadrant, and highly unpredictable. And Moriah was not only doing business with them, but she was delivering *iridon*. That was only the most sought-after compound in the quadrant, with a black market industry more volatile, more cutthroat, than any drugs or weapons combined.

He had just answered his own question. The lady didn't have a gram of sense. She needed someone to put her in her place, to make her understand the deadly nature of the game she was playing. And he was just the man to do it, Sabin decided, his plan forming. Once he had her at his mercy . . .

Celie's shackles clinked as she turned away from him. Great. He'd upset her. "I'm sorry. I shouldn't have exploded like that," he said awkwardly. "It's just that I can't—that you . . . Hell, Moriah shouldn't be involved with the Leors!"

"I know," Celie replied, her voice muffled. "I

shouldn't have told you what I did. I know better, but I worry all the time about Moriah's safety. No one can tell her what to do. She's as stubborn as a bonded lanrax." She turned to face him, her eyes pleading. "Maybe you could talk to her, after we get out of here. She might listen to you."

Oh, he was going to talk, all right—among other things. "I'll do that," he promised grimly.

"Thank you." Celie smiled, stealing Sabin's breath. Damn, but her smile was every bit as dazzling as Moriah's.

"Think nothing of it," he muttered, then froze when he heard the force field being deactivated. "Get down and act sick!" he ordered. She quickly complied.

In stepped a tall guard, too lean to be an Antek. He wore an armored vest and a helmet with a half-visor, and held an activated electrolyzer rod. All Sabin could see above the visor were two piercing aqua eyes. The soldier was most likely a Zarian mercenary, known for their ruthlessness and lack of mercy. They sometimes hired out as prison guards.

Celie groaned, drawing the guard's attention.

"What do you want?" Sabin demanded.

The soldier ignored him, taking a step toward Celie. Sabin moved to intervene and got an electrolyzer shock for his efforts. The jolt almost stopped his heart. Pain radiated through nerve endings he didn't know he had. Staggering back, he found his breath.

"She's sick, in case you hadn't noticed. Why don't you find a healthy female?"

The guard gestured toward Celie. "This female is to come with me." Celie's eyes widened and she fell silent.

"Now wait a minute," Sabin protested. "I claim bounty rights on her."

The guard sneered, "Sure, prisoner. Many seasons will pass before you see sunlight again."

Sabin started forward, and the guard raised the electrolyzer rod.

"Wait!" Celie interceded, struggling to her feet. "It's all right, Sabin. I'll go."

"You won't," he growled, but took a step back as the electrolyzer rod swung at him.

"It's okay," Celie insisted, and something in her tone caught his attention. "I want to go."

He finally glanced at her face, noting the excitement in her expression. His eyes narrowed. Something wasn't meshing here. Celie and the guard stared at each other as if sharing a silent communication. They *were* communicating, Sabin realized with astonishment. They knew each other!

This was one of Moriah's cohorts, trying to get Celie free. He found himself grinning at their audacity and cleverness. Breaching a Controller facility's security was no easy feat—and she'd done it in an amazingly short length of time. But he wasn't about to let his only link to her get away. Spinning quickly, he grabbed Celie and pulled her in front of him. A calculated risk, if he were wrong, but he'd bet five hundred miterons he wasn't.

"Sorry. She's not going anywhere. Your weapon is worthless, because if you shock me, you shock her."

The guard raised the electrolyzer rod, then hesitated, confirming Sabin's hunch. "You will release her to me now, and I'll go easy on you," the guard offered. "If not, I'll call more guards."

"Go ahead," he challenged. "Call away." The guard glared at him, but didn't act.

Celie tried to strain away from him. "But Sabin! You don't understand. I want to go."

"No. I'm not letting you go with this impersonator. The real guards would soon discover your escape and hunt you down. And I would miss the opportunity to visit with your sister, which I'm *really* looking forward to."

"Release her!" the guard hissed, trying to edge around them. He pulled Celie closer and backed up.

"You have to let me go!" Celie cried.

"I will, I promise. My partner will get both of us out of here in a short time."

Sabin gestured to the guard. "I have a message for you to deliver."

"What?" the guard growled, gripping the rod. Sabin knew he'd be in a galaxy of pain right now if they were alone.

"Tell Moriah that her sister and I will soon be out of this hellhole. If she wants Celie's freedom, then she can purchase it, at the cost of her own. She's to be at my ship at 1200 hours tomorrow, alone and with no weapons. We'll discuss my terms then. Oh, and do tell her that I expect her to be wearing the attire of her newest profession."

The Zarian's glare intensified, radiating hatred. Footsteps approached the cell. Milliseconds later, the prison commander appeared, Chase McKnight behind him. Sabin blew out a relieved breath.

"About time you got here," he told McKnight.

His partner raised golden eyebrows. "Arrogant rax. I should have left you another cycle."

The commander surveyed the cell, his beady eyes narrowed. "What goes on here?" he demanded.

The guard hastily backed away, lowering the

rod. "Nothing, Commander. I thought I heard the female prisoner cry out, so I came to check on her."

"Of course," the commander agreed, his lecherous gaze sweeping Celie. "Too bad for the interruption." He jerked his head toward the entry. "Return to your duties."

"Yes, Commander," the guard muttered, backing away. He—or was it she?—shot Sabin another damning glare and left.

Sabin felt certain his message would be delivered. And at 1200 hours tomorrow, Moriah would once again be at his mercy.

Chapter Nine

Moriah slowly mounted the ramp to Sabin's ship. She stared at the hatch, her heart pounding and every instinct screaming at her to run.

He has Celie.

The fury she'd experienced when Lionia returned with Sabin's message resurfaced. Damn him to the Abyss. How dare he hold her sister hostage? Celie was young and innocent. She deserved no part in his underhanded schemes. What Moriah wouldn't give to have an activated disrupter in her hands right now, to see the look on his arrogant face when the hatch opened and she took aim.

No weapons. His message had been clear, and as long as Celie was his hostage, he called the shots. Wiping her hands against her rhapha, Moriah drew a deep breath. Tremors, reverberating from the darkest memories of her soul, warred with anger. But she pushed all emotions aside. Her sister was on board this ship, and nothing, not the past, nor the urge to maim Sabin Travers, would distract her from getting the girl to safety.

She raised her hand toward the control pad, but the hatch slid open before she could sound the tone. Sabin shadowed the entryway, his overwhelming presence eroding any thoughts of escape. His ebony hair flowed loose around his broad shoulders; his black flightsuit clung to his lean, powerful frame. He looked sleek and wild, more like a primitive Trion savage than the Controller agent he claimed to be.

The triumphant smirk on his face, the anticipation in his black-hole eyes, shot adrenaline through her veins. In a flash of déjà vu, she was back with Pax, experiencing the same sense of inevitability. She battled conflicting urges to either flee or destroy. She had to stay calm, focused. Celie needed her.

Sabin stepped forward, his strong fingers wrapping around her wrist. "Second thoughts so quickly?" he sneered. "But you just got here. And I've been looking forward to this." He drew her inside the ship and closed the hatch. His gaze traced down the length of her body and back up. "I see you followed my directive, at least with your clothing."

"Where's Celie?"

"On board, safe and sound."

"I want to see her—now."

"You'll see her after you and I come to terms." Keeping a firm grip on her wrist, he raised his other hand and grasped the silk scarf she had wrapped around her shoulders and chest.

"Now this won't do at all. I much prefer the rhapha without the scarf. I want to see what I'm getting for my miterons." He unwound the scarf, tossing it to the side.

"Much better," he murmured, his gaze roaming over her again.

She felt exposed, vulnerable to his intense scrutiny. Her breathing became labored, her breasts heaving against the skintight rhapha. Heat, trapped beneath the Saija silk fabric, flooded her body. "If you're through—"

His gaze snapped up, the promise of retribution in his eyes. "Oh, no, I'm not through. I've hardly begun. Turn around."

Her breath suspended completely. She should have known he would search her. The determined look on his face told her he would brook no resistance. He wouldn't allow her to see Celie until she cooperated with his little game. She turned, brushing against him.

"Place your hands against the hatch, and spread 'em."

She resisted the urge to punch him. "Haven't we already done this?"

"Obviously, I wasn't thorough enough last time. A mistake I don't intend to make again." He squatted down and raised her right foot, slipping off her boot, discovering the bottom of the flightsuit pants she wore beneath her rhapha.

"Moriah, Moriah," he sighed. "You disappoint me. I gave specific instructions about your clothing."

"You ordered me to wear this," she retorted, pulling at the silk rhapha. "You didn't tell me I couldn't wear anything else." She would have worn the top of the flightsuit, too, if the rhapha hadn't fit her chest so snugly. Instead, she had folded the top into a narrow strip and tied it across her hips, to wear later.

"I didn't realize you felt the need to protect yourself from me."

Not just him, but any man. Yet she'd never admit feeling vulnerable to him. Moriah gritted her teeth as he kneaded her foot and toes, repeating the procedure with her left foot. Then he ran his hands beneath the rhapha and slid them up her legs. If she had thought the flightsuit would offer some protection, she'd been mistaken. Even through the fabric, the heat of his touch seared her, jolting every nerve ending in her body. She stiffened, refusing to react.

But when he reached her thighs, sliding his palms along the outside, then inside, pressing against the resilient muscle, his touch ignited tremors of sensation—and conflicting memories. The black images of Pax's unwelcome groping and painful invasion were there; but somehow the memories of Sabin, touching her with startling intimacy, eclipsed the ugliness. She trembled, trying to force the images away.

Sabin rose, bunching up her skirt. His fingers slid along the waistline of the flightsuit, then he splayed one hand over her abdomen.

"Want me to go lower, Moriah? Make you cry out in passion? Or were you just pretending to come apart that night in your cabin?"

Even now, the heat of his hand invaded her senses. Shame followed. How could she react to his touch like this? He was trying to humiliate her, yet her body resonated to the inexplicable energy that had sizzled between them from the very beginning. She wasn't repulsed by Sabin, as she had been by Pax. And that represented the most danger of all.

She was attracted to this man. Irrationally drawn to him, especially considering that men had caused nothing but pain in her life. But she would control her reaction to Sabin Travers, by the Spirit! She'd never give him the satisfaction—the power—of knowing she was drawn to him.

"What I would like," she gritted out, "is for you to take your clumsy hands off me."

Surprisingly, he obliged, releasing the skirt of the rhapha. The fabric whispered back down her legs. Resuming his search over the thin fabric, he placed his hands on her midriff, sliding them up to cover her breasts.

Again, sensation skittered through her nerve endings, and her heart hammered like a rocket coil. She wanted to jerk away and fight him, but concern for Celie held her in check. She stood stiff and unyielding, trying desperately to ignore the internal clamoring.

"You may claim you don't like this," Sabin whispered in her ear, "but I think you do."

"It's disgusting," she hissed. "Hurry up."

Despite her protest, her body *did* enjoy his touch, if the swelling of her breasts and the painful hardening of her nipples were any indication.

Damn him to the Fires for a thousand lifetimes. He might have shown her physical pleasures of the body; he might have undermined her control over her body's reactions, but that was as far as it went. She'd be free of him at the first possible opportunity. Until then, she had to endure the humiliations he obviously planned to dish out.

He took his time as he continued the search, molding his hands to her rear before moving on. Since the rhapha left her back and arms bare, there was no need to check them, but he did, skimming his hands over her shoulders and down her bare arms. His fingers briefly encircled her wrists, then stroked her palms and fingers. Even that felt strangely erotic, and she cursed under her breath.

"No bracelet this time," he commented. "I assume that's where the lethean patch was hidden during your last visit."

Moriah held her silence until she felt a tug on her hair. The neat twist came undone and her hair tumbled down her back.

"What in Hades are you doing?" she demanded.

Sabin combed his fingers through the strands, sending another sensual shiver through her. "Have to be sure you have nothing hidden here," he answered, spreading the tresses over her back. "And while you're on board my ship, you'll wear your hair down. That's an order."

An order? She'd tell him what to do with his blazing orders as soon as Celie was safe. "I want to see my sister now."

"Not so fast. You and I have to come to an understanding first." He took her arm and pulled her into the cockpit. Dumping her unceremoniously into a chair, he slid into the opposite one.

"I'm going to tell you what I expect—no, *demand*—from you. You will agree to my terms, will give your word of honor, for what it's worth, on your sister's life. In return, I'll release Celie, and she'll be free to go wherever she wants. That clear?"

Moriah bristled with anger that he questioned her honor, even though she'd given him every reason to believe the worst of her. But she forced herself to reply calmly. "Very clear."

"Have you told anyone about the Shielder colony?"

The question caught her off guard, because she hadn't given it another thought. She had no quarrel with the Shielders, and she would never sell information leading to innocent people's deaths, no matter how lucrative. She wouldn't turn in Sabin, either, although she felt certain he was a Shielder. She didn't expect him to believe that, but now was not the time to alienate him.

"No," she answered. "I haven't told anyone, and I have no plans to do so."

His eyes hardened. "You'd better be telling the truth," he warned. "Because I'll find out soon enough if you've lied. Even if you are being honest, I can't allow you to retain such information. So you will agree to travel with me to Elysia, where a healer will erase your memory of the colony. That's the first condition."

Elysia? Incredulity knifed through her. "What? That will take at least six cycles!"

He inclined his head insolently. "At least."

Why was she so surprised? She should have expected this. Sabin was the quintessential male, obstinately inflexible. Once he fixated on an idea, he refused to let go.

She calculated the time remaining before the iridon shipment arrived. She'd lose the six cycles from Star Base Intrepid to Elysia, then some downtime on Elysia for the procedure and waiting for someone to pick her up. That would leave only eight cycles to pick up the iridon. Still, she could do that directly from Elysia. The other women could deliver the goods they'd received on Calt.

What choice did she have? Besides, if it got Sabin Travers out of her life for good, it was well worth it.

"All right," she agreed. "I'll go with you and submit to having my memory altered."

His eyes gleamed. "*Submit.* Now I like that word. And that is what you'll do, Moriah. You will comply with my every order, immediately. That's condition number two."

Outrage rolled through her. Drawing a deep breath, she ignored the longing to ensure he would never father children while at the same time pushing back encroaching images of Pax's leering face. Sabin did not display the cruel tendencies that Pax had shown, she reminded herself.

"All right. I agree."

He leaned back smugly. "I knew you would. Condition three—you will not attempt to injure me in any way. Nor will you attempt to commandeer this ship or escape."

"Afraid of me?" she taunted, anger overcoming good sense.

"Cautious. Do I need to remind you what's at stake?"

Since the man had Celie in his possession, he had Moriah right where he wanted her, and there wasn't a damn thing she could do about it. She blew out her breath, frustrated at her ineffectiveness and his power. She'd sworn she'd never again allow herself to be under a man's control, yet here she was.

"I agree to that condition as well. Any more?"

He smiled, looking for all the world like a lanrax cornering a krat. "I think that's enough, for now. Any infractions, and you make the trip in shackles. Do I have your word?"

Realizing she was clenching the arms of the chair, Moriah forced her hands to relax. *Celie*, she reminded herself. "You have my word of honor, Captain Travers. I swear on the life of my sister that I will follow all your directives."

"Then we have a deal." Sabin flipped a switch on the console. "Celie, your sister is here. Please come to the cockpit."

"Be right there!" Celie answered, her youthful

voice jubilant. Moriah rose and faced the entry, anticipation lightening her spirits.

A moment later, Celie bounded into the cockpit. "Mori!" she cried, flying into her sister's arms.

Moriah held the girl tightly, trembling with relief. Celie was her joy, her light, her life. She was all Moriah had, and every shipment Moriah delivered, every miteron she banked, every plan she made for developing Risa, she did for Celie.

When she'd learned the girl had been taken to a Controller prison, Moriah had suffered a thousand agonies, imagined innumerable hideous scenarios. And when Lionia had returned emptyhanded, with only Sabin's ominous ultimatum, Moriah's anxiety had escalated tenfold—until now. Gently, she set Celie at arm's length.

"Let me look at you, rax," she said, her voice uncharacteristically shaky. She studied her sibling, noting Celie was freshly scrubbed and her flightsuit clean. She looked rested and happy. No bruises marred her soft skin, no shadows lurked in her dark eyes.

Hesitantly, Moriah asked, "Did anyone . . . hurt you while you were in the prison?"

Celie shook her head, but a look of revulsion crossed her face. "It was horrible, Mori. This . . . slime covered the floor of the cell and it had the worst smell. These Anteks wanted to—" She paused, color staining her cheeks. "You know, force themselves on me. But Sabin was too clever for them."

Moriah's stomach clenched at the thought. "Celie, the Anteks, did they—did they do anything to you?"

Celie flashed Sabin a smile. "Nope. Sabin had me pretend to be sick, and they left me alone. I was afraid, but he kept talking to me and then his partner, Chase, got us out. Chase was really nice, too. Then we came back here and cleaned up, and Sabin fixed us amargrain and protein sticks on the replicator. He knows how to use one, Mori. Isn't that neat?"

Moriah stared at her sister, amazed. After their experiences with their father and Pax, Celie kept her distance from men. *All men.* Yet here she was, looking at Sabin like he kept the planets in orbit, and chattering away in front of him like an echo-bird. Well, it appeared he hadn't mistreated her. Indeed, he now appeared to be her champion.

"How did you get arrested?" Moriah finally asked.

Celie's expression clouded, and she shifted her eyes away from Moriah's probing gaze. "I guess I lost track of time after you left the ship, and stayed on the computer longer than I should have. Then I couldn't find my rhapha. I must have left it on Roanne's ship. I was getting ready to leave for Lionia's ship when these Anteks came on board." She raised her eyes to Moriah's. "I'm sorry, Mori, I really am. I'll try to do better."

How could Moriah be mad when Celie looked so guilty, and when she was obviously unscathed from her experience? Even if her slipup now put Moriah in an untenable situation. She sighed, hugging Celie again.

"I'm not mad, sweetness. I know you didn't do it intentionally. We'll talk about it more when I get back to—" she paused, remembering Sabin's alert presence. "When I return to the base."

Celie pulled away, confusion clouding her face. "Aren't you coming back now?"

Feeling Sabin stand up behind her, Moriah knew time had run out. She struggled to keep her

voice even. "No, sweetness. Sabin and I are working on a—a business deal. I'm going with him for
about six cycles. But I'll be in touch and keep you
updated on my plans."

"Oh." Concern filled Celie's eyes. "But what—"

"We need to get going," Sabin interrupted.

"What—" Celie started again, but Moriah cut
her off with a final hug.

"Please don't worry," she told Celie. "Just go
with Lionia. She's waiting back at the ship for you.
I'll be fine."

She released Celie, her gaze roaming over her
sister's face.

"Help take care of Janaye, okay? I won't be gone
very long."

Sabin patted the girl on the shoulder. "Good-
bye, Celie."

She whirled, hurling herself against him and
hugging him tightly. "Good-bye, Sabin. Thank you
for watching out for me."

Her impetuous action stunned Moriah. Sabin
appeared surprised as well, hesitating a moment
before hugging Celie back. "My pleasure, sweetheart. Take care of yourself and stay out of trouble, okay?"

"Okay." Celie turned and smiled tremulously at
Moriah. "Bye, Mori."

Moriah's throat tightened, and she wanted to
hold on to her sister for dear life. Why was she
reacting this way? She spent many cycles away
from Celie and the base. This time was no different, she told herself—even if Sabin Travers did
think he had complete control over her for the
next six or seven cycles.

"Good-bye, silly rax. See you soon," she said,
managing to keep her voice steady. "I'll contact
Lionia shortly to be sure you're safely on board."

Then Celie was gone. Moriah was alone with Sabin. She faced him across the cockpit, her heart rate accelerating.

He slouched against the console, his arms crossed over his chest. He seemed relaxed, but she wasn't fooled by his casual stance. He was angry. His glittering eyes and compressed lips told her that.

He'd been restraining his temper, waiting until he had her firmly in hand, perhaps waiting for Celie to leave. Now there was no reason to contain it. At least he'd demonstrated self-control on more than one occasion, unlike her father.

She'd shown admirable control over her own anger, for that matter. Sabin had held Celie ransom, damn his black soul. He could confront Moriah all he wanted; she could handle it, but no one took advantage of her sister.

"I've been looking forward to this moment," he said, his voice deceptively soft. "Been dreaming of it, as a matter of fact. Planning down to the last detail how I'm going to extract revenge for everything you've done to me. And you did a lot, lady. Let's see . . . first, you stowed away on my ship, gaining access to highly confidential information. Data which should have cost you your beautiful hide. Next, you plied your wiles and drew me into a trap older than the universe. Then you drugged me, dumped me naked at a pleasure dome, and hijacked my ship."

His anger, already primed, appeared to be building with every offense he listed. Moriah swallowed hard. Sabin shoved away from the console. "As you can see, the list is quite long. But I'm not through yet." He stalked toward her, his body poised for the kill.

"It wasn't enough for you to hijack my ship. Oh,

171

no. You had to load it with illegal goods. When you got caught, you managed to pawn it off on me. I'm the one who went to prison. Ever been to prison, Moriah? Ever been strip-searched? Thrown on a slime-covered, vermin-infested floor and left without food?"

She backed away as he advanced, but the navigator screen halted her progress. His hand shot out, gripping her arm painfully. "Have you?"

"No," she murmured. She hadn't ever been in a Controller prison. But she'd been in a different type of prison—one just as degrading. And now it seemed she had returned to a similar entrapment.

"I've been debating what would be an appropriate punishment. I could lock you up, except I don't have a working brig." He shook his head. "You know, there's really nothing which would do the situation justice. But . . . you can work off some of your debt."

"Work it off?" *Like Pax had demanded?* Dread spread icy fingers through her chest.

"Yep." He released her and returned to his chair, propping his feet on the console. "For starters, you can scrub this ship from top to bottom, the good old-fashioned way—on your hands and knees, with a bucket and brush."

The ice melted, thawed by anger. "You want me to clean this worthless scow? It won't do any good."

"I'll really enjoy watching you on your hands and knees, especially in that rhapha," he continued, as though she hadn't spoken. Heaving an exaggerated sigh, he leaned back in the chair, lacing his fingers behind his head. "Then there are my personal needs."

Moriah's hands clenched against her thighs. *"Personal needs?"*

"Yeah. You can clean my cabin and lav, do my laundry." He paused to leisurely inspect his feet. "And my boots need to be polished."

Clean his cabin? Polish his boots? She had spent the first eighteen seasons of her life taking orders from men. First her father, then Pax; waiting on them as if she were no better than a slave. Her temper exploded. No, by the Spirit! She was through playing slave to anyone.

Rage pumped through her, so fast and furious, she couldn't breathe. It was so uncontrollable, she didn't even think about her next action. She marched over to Sabin and said sweetly, "So your boots need polishing? Well, let's get started on those this millisecond!"

Grabbing one of his feet, she lifted his leg and yanked at the boot, tilting him further back. She noticed three of the four bolts attaching the chair to the deck were gone. If he weighed enough . . . She depressed the pedal controlling a magnetic lock which was the chair's secondary anchor.

Pressing her leg firmly against the seat, she heaved it upward. Sabin's weight did the rest, toppling the chair backward. He thudded resoundingly, his head hitting the floor with a very satisfying crack.

Moriah smirked down at him, enjoying the momentary confusion on his face. Then his eyes narrowed, and anger darkened his face.

"Oh, I am *so* sorry," she cooed. "I was just trying to obey orders and get your boo—"

With a roar, he came up from the floor, exhibiting light-speed agility. "You demon! That's it! I've had it. It's time you got what's coming to you, lady, and I'm going to make certain you get it."

He charged her like a rabid tri-horn bull. She

hadn't expected him to react this strongly. Taking flight, Moriah darted behind the other chair. Sabin reached across to grab her. She sent the chair spinning, and the high back smacked his chest. He staggered back, and she raced to the entry panel.

Before she could open it, though, he caught her arm in a magnasteel grip. Pivoting, she broke his hold with a chop from her free hand. She leaped back and landed a high kick to his midriff, throwing him off balance. Whirling back to the entry, she reached for the control pad.

Sabin grabbed her wrist before she could open it. Pressing her against the panel, he held her spread-eagled with his body. He rapidly punched a sequence on the control pad.

"Now you *can't* open the panel," he said grimly. "You can't escape me—or your punishment."

Punishment? Oh, Spirit, he was going to hit her—or worse. Panic rushed through her like a nuclear meltdown. "What are you going to do?" she demanded, struggling to free herself from his grip as he pulled her away from the exit.

"What I should have done as soon as I caught up with you," he growled, dragging her to the other chair. He dropped into it, pulling her toward him, despite her frantic resistance. "And I'm going to enjoy every millisecond of it."

"You're primordial slime, lower than an Antek!" she spat, managing to get one arm free.

He lunged forward and grabbed the arm again, pulling her over his legs. Adrenaline spurred her on and she kicked him. He gave a grunt of pain and changed tactics. Grasping her waist with both hands, he twirled her facing away from him, then jerked her into his lap.

"Let . . . me . . . go!" she gasped, trying to squirm away.

"And miss the pleasure of teaching you this lesson? I think not." Reaching diagonally across her chest, he flipped her like she was a miteron, face down, across his lap.

She realized his intent. "You can't do this!" she screamed, kicking and bucking. He flung one leg over hers to hold them still.

"Just watch me," he grunted. His other arm pressed against her back, forcing her upper body downward. She lay draped over his lap in an inverted angle, her squirming rear in the air. He planned to hit her, and she couldn't stop him.

She shouldn't be surprised. She'd had enough experience with her father and Pax to witness the violence that apparently lay at the core of every man. Why had she even foolishly thought Sabin any different?

Disappointment left an acrid taste in her throat, followed by apprehension at the thought of what Sabin would do after he hit her. Violence had always sexually excited Pax. After he was in a fight or had pounded some poor prisoner into a pulp, he had always turned his attentions to Moriah. Memories, like spreading poison, held her paralyzed in their grip.

Sabin Travers was about to prove he was no better than any other man.

Sabin raised his arm, his hand itching to mold itself to the shapely target dead center on his lap. Outrage ricocheted through him, intensified by the throbbing at the back of his head. Yet his hand stalled midair.

"Go ahead," she spat. "Just get it over with."

"You've got this coming." He paused again.

Blazing hells! He'd never hit a woman before,

hadn't intended things to progress this far. But no one challenged his authority—or ridiculed him. He'd had enough of that in his life. He was going to put Moriah in her place once and for all.

"Maybe I just want to hear you beg for mercy," he muttered. Yeah, that would be highly gratifying.

She went deathly still. "Never," she whispered.

He flexed his fingers, finding her sudden silence more unsettling than her firing insults like missiles. Resolute, he prepared to see this farce to the end. But his hand stopped midair once more.

Why wasn't she fighting him? Damn her uncharacteristic submissiveness! It was almost as if she had accepted her fate.

Hell. She'd drugged him, dumped him in a brothel—naked—and stolen his ship. He should be furious, should make her regret crossing him. Yet she had an effect on him he'd never experienced with any other woman. And he didn't like it.

But he didn't like violence either. He couldn't do it. He lowered his hand . . . and howled in pain.

Sharp teeth imbedded firmly in his thigh sent agony shooting all the way to his groin.

"You bit me!"

His leg jerked up reflexively. Moriah rolled off his lap, her upper body hitting the floor. Wresting her lower body free, she scrambled away.

Fury and pain rapidly amended Sabin's aversion to violence. By the Spirit, he could finish what he'd started! He lunged after her, determined to seek retribution.

"Come back here!" he roared. Catching the back of her rhapha, he yanked her toward him. The delicate silk gave way, rending to her waist.

"No!" she screamed, twisting. Sabin lost his grip on the shredding fabric.

Moriah quickly crawled away before pushing to her feet. Her chest heaving, she shook the wild mass of her tangled hair back from her face. The front of the rhapha sagged perilously low and she yanked it up.

"I won't let you!" she cried. "Nobody, ever again, is going to lay a hand on me. I'll kill you first! Just like I should have killed Pax."

Her words froze Sabin in midstride. *Pax?* The name blasted him with the force of a fusion cannon. He knew of only one person who went by that name. He was a man who embodied the most evil traits a shadower—or any being—could possess.

Pax was depraved and inhuman, and he didn't care if the beings he tracked were guilty or innocent, as long as he got the bounty. It was common knowledge his female prisoners bore the brunt of his voracious sexual appetite—willing or otherwise.

If Moriah had been at Pax's mercy, that must mean—Sabin expelled his breath, reaching for rational control. Spirit, he didn't even want to think about it—about what she had been through. First her father, then Pax.

And here he'd been all too ready to inflict his own brand of abuse. He felt lower than an Oderian viper. He stepped toward her. "Moriah—"

She flattened herself against the entry panel and crossed her arms protectively across her chest. Her face was pale; shadows hollowed her cheeks and traced circles beneath her eyes. But it was the dread in those eyes that torpedoed his heart. She looked at him as if she *expected* him to hurt her, like it was the natural order of things.

He took a step closer. "Moriah, I'm sorry. I . . . I got a little crazy. Hell, you make me crazy! But I'm in control now. I'm not going to hurt you."

She fled his advance, leaping over the fallen chair.

Sabin halted and held up his hands in surrender. "Okay! Okay. I'm not coming after you, all right? Just answer a question for me."

She clutched the rhapha higher. "What?"

"Are you talking about Pax Blacklock?"

She nodded, her gaze hardening. "One and the same."

Blazing hells. Sabin suddenly made the connection with what Celie had told him. "Is he the one who won you and Celie in a game of chance?"

Her eyes narrowed. "How did you find out about that?"

That meant Moriah had been in Pax's clutches for some time. He drew a fortifying breath, wondering at the full extent of the bastard's brutality. "How I know doesn't matter. Did he hit you?"

Her bitter laugh jarred him. "Oh, no, Pax didn't use his fists as punishment. At least not on me."

She pressed her lips together, not offering any more information. But the torment in her eyes clearly said what she hadn't voiced, what Sabin already knew.

Pax doesn't punish women with his fists. He rapes them.

Sabin had his answer. The realization of what Moriah had suffered at the brutal bounty hunter's hands sickened him. The rage he'd felt toward her earlier couldn't compare to the nuclear blast that now rampaged through him—only it was aimed at a fellow shadower. He'd give a thousand miterons to have Pax here right now, and to give the bastard a slow, painful death.

178

He also wanted to kick himself, because he should have seen the signs. Looking back, he recalled Moriah's skittishness whenever he tried to touch her. By the Abyss, thinking of the times he had searched her so intimately, the times he'd kissed her, the sexual innuendos he'd thrown out, he was surprised she hadn't knocked his teeth down his throat.

Now, after threatening to hit her and practically tearing off her clothes, he was faced with convincing her he wasn't like her father or Pax. He ventured another step forward.

"Moriah, I won't hurt you. I swear it."

She sidled away, her expression stark. She was withdrawing, mentally and physically, probably the only way she'd survived the horrendous circumstances she had endured.

An overwhelming compassion penetrated Sabin's emotional armor. He understood growing up in traumatic circumstances. Still, not being a woman, it was difficult to comprehend how Moriah must have felt, a helpless possession in Pax's ruthless grasp.

All things considered, Sabin was amazed that she had actually tried to seduce him in order to drug him. She must have been desperate to put herself in such a situation. Unfortunately, he couldn't recall enough about that night in her cabin to know how far the seduction had gone. Had she really experienced pleasure, as his blurry memory suggested?

Suddenly, he wanted to find out. He wanted both of them in that situation again; a second chance for him to convince Moriah mating didn't have to be sordid. He thrust his fingers through his hair.

Spirit, how had this happened? One moment, he'd been ready to pound out his anger on Moriah. Now, he wanted only to show her not all men caused pain.

Warning alerts clamored inside his head. This was not a good idea. After the trauma of losing everyone he loved when he was only six seasons old, Sabin had avoided relationships which even hinted at permanence.

It had been an easy enough feat as he'd been passed from household to household, settlement to settlement. Just another set of hands to claw out the survival of a race marked for genocide. Just another mouth to feed in Shielder colonies where there was never enough to eat.

He had finally escaped that indifferent acceptance when he'd gotten his ship from the leaders of one colony—in return for promising to deliver supplies on a regular basis. Now, he had no one to answer to, no one to disrupt his safe, noninvolved existence. He had no need to let himself care about the fate of one troublesome smuggler, no matter how beautiful, no matter how spirited . . . no matter how unloved.

Don't get involved! his inner alarm cautioned.

But, as Sabin looked at Moriah's closed expression, at the pain mirrored in her golden eyes, he knew he was dangerously close to an emotional black hole. Close to being bombarded with feelings he didn't want to acknowledge. He felt anger at how Moriah had been treated. Empathy for her pain. And, as always when dealing with her, the thrill of challenge—a thrill as old as creation.

But no. This was a trap, not a challenge, and one he couldn't—wouldn't—risk.

He could, however, show Moriah that not all men were brutes. He could give her the respect and consideration she deserved. He knew better than to ever let her get the upper hand, but he didn't have to be overbearing or militant, either.

He took another step. "I acted like an Antek. I'm truly sorry. I swear I won't ever raise a hand to you again. Let's call a truce, okay?"

She drew a deep breath, the tops of her breasts rising above the torn silk. He sensed her hostility easing, although she wasn't willing to trust him. Not that he blamed her.

He offered his hand. "Truce?"

She stared disdainfully at his outstretched hand. "That depends on what you're planning to do next."

Delighted to see some spark returning, Sabin grinned. "I'm going to get us off this star base and headed toward Elysia. Then I'll replicate the evening meal."

Surprise flashed in her eyes. Apparently, she'd expected him to do something else, such as shackle her. But force and intimidation would no longer be key components in handling Moriah.

He was bound and determined to disprove her perception of men—one way or another.

Chapter Ten

Moriah lay on her bunk, exhausted, but too keyed up to sleep. Images of Pax, intertwined with images of Sabin, swirled through her mind. She saw again the rage on Sabin's face as he came after her in the cockpit, heard the horrifying rip of her rhapha. Why had she ever thought she could handle him? She'd become too self-assured in her independence, too certain she could never fall prey to a man again.

Yet . . . Sabin had halted his own rampage. He hadn't hit her, hadn't forced himself on her. He'd even apologized, sounding sincere. She shrugged that off. Her father had always been sorry, too. After the liquor wore off and he sobered up, he would be contrite about the bruises he didn't even remember inflicting. Words and promises didn't always depict the true nature of a person.

The shifting of the ship told her they were taking off. Glancing at the chronometer, she wondered why Sabin had waited so long. It had been at least two hours since they had called an uneasy truce in the cockpit. She had even had time to make certain Celie was safely aboard Lionia's ship and to give Lionia some instructions. Afterwards, refusing the evening meal, she'd fled to her cabin.

Her stomach growled. She had not eaten since Celie had been arrested. Now she questioned her wisdom at turning down a meal. Hunger was a minor consideration, she told herself. As was brooding over Sabin Travers and his erratic behavior.

Delivering the iridon shipment to the Leors within the promised time frame was far more crucial. Funds for Risa, her group's survival—her own survival—depended upon her completing that transaction. But she had given her word she would accompany Sabin to Elysia, and she had to keep it, if for no other reason than honor and pride.

She turned on her side, her gaze falling on the ruined rhapha draped over her cabin's single chair. In his rage, Sabin could have done anything he wanted. She'd been trapped in the cockpit with no weapon. She was a skilled fighter, but he had the advantages of greater mass and strength.

Yet he hadn't hurt her.

Heaving a disgusted sigh, Moriah flopped onto her back, draping her arm over her eyes. How easily she'd slipped back into thinking about Sabin when she should have been planning her next course of action. What was it about the man that managed to diffuse her normally single-minded concentration? Perhaps fatigue and hunger were affecting her ability to stay focused. A few hours' rest should sharpen her wits.

She closed her eyes. As she was drifting into an uneasy doze, her panel tone sounded. Moriah bolted up. Pax had never used the chime. He just barged in and took what he wanted.

The tone sounded again.

"Moriah! Are you all right?" Sabin demanded.

She swung herself off the bunk. "What do you want?"

"Permission to enter."

Her heart skipped a beat. She was too tired to deal with him. "Why don't you go away instead?"

"Not an option. I am coming in. I'm just giving you the courtesy of advance notice. Are you decent?"

As decent as a long-sleeved flightsuit, zipped up to her chin, could make her. "No. Go away."

A low chuckle reverberated on the other side of the entry. "Indecent is good." The panel slid open, and Sabin entered, carrying a tray in one hand and a box in the other. He halted inside the doorway, his gaze roaming over her.

She drew a deep breath. "What do you want?"

He flashed her his devilish grin, again exuding his usual arrogance. "Manners, manners. I can see I have my work cut out for me. I brought you the evening meal."

He stepped forward, she stepped back. "I'm not hungry," she insisted, just as her stomach rumbled.

Ebony brows rose. "Liar."

"Don't believe everything you hear, Travers," she retorted, irritated that her own body had betrayed her—again.

"I don't. But I already knew you were hungry and tired."

"How in the universe could you know that?"

"You're pale and have circles under your eyes. You looked like that after you stowed away on my ship for four cycles without food."

Janaye, her mentor, had made the same obser-they vations on occasion. But she knew Moriah much better than this arrogant man. Sabin was far too perceptive, a fact which made Moriah distinctly uncomfortable.

His gaze never leaving her face, he leaned over and placed the tray on the bunk. "Why don't you sit down and eat?"

She finally looked at the tray. Next to the plate of amargrain and protein sticks sat a stunning scarlet Thermaplant in a crystal planter. Thermaplants were so rare, she had seen them only twice in all her travels.

"Where did this come from?" she asked in wonder, reaching down to touch the crystal pot.

"Intrepid's cultural center." Sabin tossed the package onto the bunk. Lifting the plant, he took her hand and curled her fingers around the cool crystal.

She stared at the vivid scarlet leaves. Thermaplants needed not only heat, but also the electromagnetic energy radiating from all living things, to survive. They seemed to thrive best on the energy emitted by humans.

"It's beautiful," she murmured.

"It's for you."

Shocked, she tore her gaze away from the lovely blooms and stared at him. "You're giving this to me?"

He watched her gravely. "It's yours."

She couldn't comprehend such an action. No one had ever given her a gift. "But—but why?"

"Because I acted like an idiot earlier today, and I want to say I'm sorry." Taking her other hand, he pressed it around the opposite side of the planter. "Do you know how to care for a Thermaplant?"

185

Gazing at the plant in fascination, she shook her head.

"The vendor who sold it to me said you must wrap your hands around it for several minutes in the morning and several minutes at night, although you can do it as often as you like. Your heat and energy will provide sustenance for the plant. It will reward you with its scent. Let's see if she's right."

Moriah clasped the crystal pot tightly, unable to believe Sabin had given the gift to her, or that he had again apologized. Would she ever understand him? She stood silently, willing her life force into the plant.

The crystal pot began to glow, taking on a rosy hue. A moment later, an exquisite fragrance wafted from the plant's velvety leaves. Delighted, she inhaled deeply. She'd never owned anything this special. At a loss for what to say, she raised her gaze to Sabin. "Thank you."

He took a step back, clearing his throat. "No big deal. Now eat."

Unprotesting, she slid onto the bunk. Carefully setting Sabin's gift on the tray, she picked up a protein stick. Sabin strode to the chair, eyeing the torn rhapha. He flicked it off and pulled the chair closer to her bunk. Sinking down with a tired sigh, he closed his eyes, pinching the bridge of his nose.

"It's hot in here," he complained. "I need to check the climate controls again." He gestured toward the box he'd tossed onto her bed. "I replaced your rhapha."

Moriah paused, protein stick halfway to her mouth, ugly suspicions rearing. "Why?"

"I destroyed yours, so I owed you one."

All appetite fled. He'd had ulterior motives for

his actions. His kindness was just a front, and should have set off alarms. She stared at the Thermaplant, bitterness pooling in her throat.

"Then you're ordering me to wear the rhapha?"

"Wear what you wish." Sabin gestured to the tray. "But I *am* ordering you to eat."

He had her totally confused again. Frustrated, she bit off the end of the protein stick. "Why are we departing so late?" she asked after chewing and swallowing.

"I went to purchase a few things, and then I searched for my ship mechanic. He seems to have left Intrepid rather suddenly."

"Mechanics move around a lot," Moriah pointed out.

Sabin leaned back in the chair. "That's true. Radd probably got a lucrative offer he couldn't refuse. He's the best in the quadrant, so he's in demand."

Radd? Radd was Sabin's mechanic? The pieces fell into place. That's why Radd had looked so familiar. She'd seen him on Sabin's ship right after she was injured. It seemed pretty ironic that she had kidnapped Sabin's ship mechanic.

"So is he really the best mechanic in the quadrant?" she asked.

"The absolute best. Sure wish I could find him."

It pleased her to know she had kidnapped the right mechanic, at least. She took a bite of amargrain.

Sabin steepled his fingers and stared at them thoughtfully. "Moriah, as much as I regret my behavior earlier, we still have to get some things straight. I'm the captain of this ship. You will obey my orders."

They were back to that. She laid down her utensil. "I already gave my word on that, *Captain*."

"So you did. But in case you've forgotten, you broke our agreement by trying to injure me."

"I did not. I wasn't trying to hurt you when I tipped your chair over. Just expressing my opinion of your chauvinist demands."

"I'm not talking about the chair, although I still have a knot on the back of my head from that. I'm talking about that damn plug you took out of my leg." Sabin rubbed his thigh with an injured air. "If you'd bitten any higher, I'd probably be talking in a falsetto right now. *That* would be a serious matter."

His light tone surprised her. She had expected him to be furious, to seek retribution. Testing his mood, she retorted, "I wouldn't think of that as a big deal."

"No? Tell you what, sweetheart. There are some women who would disagree with your assessment there."

"Really? Well, *Lani* might find it a big deal. But what can you expect from a woman who wears *blue feathers?*"

Laughter flashed in his eyes. He shook his head, smiling. "Lani has nothing to do with this discussion. We're talking about your resistance to authority."

The smile disappeared and he leaned forward, serious. "I *am* the authority on this ship. I must have total compliance. It's only fair to warn you that I've taken some precautions. I've locked in the coordinates to Elysia. They can't be altered without the correct code. I've also contacted my partner, Chase McKnight, and informed him of the situation. I'll be communicating with him several times each cycle. He'll become suspicious if he doesn't hear from me."

So, he was going back to the Controller tactics.

Sabin might have good reason not to trust her, but anger knotted in Moriah's chest anyway. "What's this, Captain? You feel the need to protect yourself from a mere woman?"

"You're no mere woman. I could keep you in shackles, but I don't want to do that. Especially considering the treatment you've endured from your father and P—"

"I don't want to talk about it," she broke in, her heart racing at the reminder. She hated the compassion she saw in his eyes. She'd far rather deal with his anger than his pity. She shoved her tray of food away. "I'm tired. Please leave now."

Her gaze locked with his, silently defying him to push the issue. "All right," he said, his easy acquiescence another surprise. He seemed full of them tonight. "Just remember what we discussed. I trust there will be no defiance."

He rose and started toward the entry, then stumbled and almost fell. He caught his balance, grabbing the panel frame. "That's odd," he muttered.

"What is?"

"Oh, nothing. . . . I'm just clumsy tonight."

Moriah had never known Sabin to be clumsy. He always moved with a lethal, fluid agility. But this entire cycle had been tumultuous, so perhaps he was tired. She certainly was. She'd be glad when her obligation to him was fulfilled and all this was over.

"I'll be setting the motion detectors in the corridor. Use the intercom if you need anything. Good night, Moriah."

She nodded stiffly. Then he was gone, and she breathed a sigh of relief. Until she realized his presence still lingered, in the faint, clean scent of sandalwood. That, along with a whiff of the enticing fragrance from the Thermaplant, teased her senses.

She stared at the plant. No one had ever given her a present.

Her heart warmed and softened dangerously. She clamped down on the perilous emotions. She wouldn't be sidetracked.

She picked up the Thermaplant, held it between her hands. It was much harder to deal with Sabin when he was being nice.

Damn him!

Moriah paced her cabin, wondering what in the Abyss was taking Sabin so long. She had assumed he would give her the all clear after he deactivated the motion alerts, like he'd done before, but she had been awake for several hours, and it was long past time for the morning meal. She'd done her stretches and martial arts katas, showered, and even straightened the cabin.

Stacking the dishes on the tray Sabin had brought last night, she was startled to discover he'd left the fork behind. That wasn't at all like him. Either he had started trusting her, which she seriously doubted, or he must have been exceptionally tired.

His oversight was to her advantage though, she decided, slipping the fork beneath her bunk pad. She'd given her word not to attack him, but she could resort to using the utensil as a weapon in self-defense.

Defense against what? she had to honestly ask herself. Sabin didn't appear to pose a threat. At least, not a physical one. Instead, he threatened her more on a sensual level. Images flashed into her mind of Sabin, surrendering to her plea to mate, lowering his mouth to hers.

"Sweetheart, you have no idea of the things I'd like to do with you."

His words from that night in her cabin torpedoed through her, a shower of unwanted heat sizzling in their wake. Why couldn't she forget that near-disastrous seduction? Whirling, Moriah paced the cabin, willing her thoughts to safer avenues.

She forced herself to think about Risa and the others. By now, Lionia and Celie, along with their reluctant hostage, were well on their way home. Hopefully, Kiah and Marna had returned and would get the Intrepid shipment ready to deliver to Calt. When Lionia arrived with the mechanic, he would be able to fix the two ships which were down.

For the first time, Moriah had second thoughts about sending Radd to Risa. All of the women in the group either hated or distrusted males, and with good cause. She hoped Radd's presence wouldn't unsettle them. Still, he seemed to be a quiet, dull little man. If anyone could keep him in line, Lionia could.

Chafing at her confinement, Moriah checked the chronometer again. Sabin Travers might like to lounge the day away, but she didn't. She punched the com button to his cabin.

"Sabin." Nothing. "Sabin, are you in there?" No answer. She paused, wondering if he'd already gone to the cockpit. Perhaps he meant to keep her a prisoner in her cabin the entire trip—six long cycles. Not if she could help it.

She was about to break the link and com the cockpit, when she heard a groan. Startled, she listened intently. "Sabin? Are you all right?" Another groan was her only answer. Concerned, Moriah headed for the entry panel.

Shrill alarms blasted her eardrums when she started through the corridor. Clapping her hands over her ears in a futile effort to block the piercing shrieks, she ran to Sabin's cabin. She didn't bother with the panel chime. If the alarms hadn't brought him running, the tone certainly wouldn't. His panel wasn't secured; it slid open when she punched the pad.

He lay sprawled facedown on his bunk, the cover tangled around his hips. He apparently slept nude, a fact she forced herself to ignore as she approached the bunk.

"Sabin!" she yelled in an attempt to be heard over the relentless alarms.

He shifted restlessly, clamping his hands over his ears. He didn't appear to be conscious, although she thought he muttered something. She wasn't sure, because her ears were going numb. She whirled and crossed to his control panel. It took several tries before she found the correct switch and finally shut the howling torment off.

Returning to the bunk, she grabbed his shoulder and shook him. "Wake up!" Spirit, but his skin was hot to the touch. She shook him again.

He flopped onto his back, his cover slipping off completely. Her throat went dry at the sight of his body, skin stretched taunt over smooth muscles, dark hair forging a trail from his chest down to his . . . She jerked her gaze away. No sense in reiterating what she already knew—that Sabin Travers didn't need to wear one of the highly fashionable codpieces to enhance his assets.

She pulled the cover over him. Grabbing his shoulders, she shook him insistently, alarmed by the heated skin beneath her fingertips. "Sabin!"

He finally opened his eyes, but they were glazed

and unfocused as he stared at her. Panic speared through her. He appeared to be deathly ill. But in a moment, his eyes focused somewhat and recognition flared.

"What are you doing here? Why did you set off the alarms?"

"I came to check on you when you didn't get up. It's not my fault you insist on setting those stupid alarms."

He groaned and closed his eyes again. "Damn, but I feel like I've been run over by an ore freighter." He opened one eye to glare at her. "What the hell did you do to me?"

She stared at him, outraged. "What did I do to you? You idiot. More likely, the question is, how much did you drink?" But even as she hurled the accusation, she knew alcohol wasn't the problem. He was burning with fever.

"I didn't drink a drop." Fumbling the cover away, he sat up and swung his legs over the side of the bunk.

"Something is wrong with you."

He rose shakily to his feet, totally unconcerned with his nudity, and staggered toward the lav. Moriah forced her gaze away from his heavily muscled legs and taut backside.

"Maybe you should stay in your bunk," she suggested.

He waved her suggestion away, swaying and catching his balance against the lav entry. "It's just a little virus. I'll be fine as soon as I stretch the kinks out of my muscles."

Fine muscles they were, too, she thought, watching the ripples across his back as he opened the lav panel. She had never seen a nude man. Pax hadn't undressed when he'd forced himself on her. She had found him so repulsive, that if he had stripped, she wouldn't have looked. She had no problem looking at Sabin, however.

She caught herself. No more of those thoughts. She pivoted toward the exit.

"I'll leave, then."

"Meet me—" he paused and coughed, a dry hacking cough. "Meet me in the galley in a quarter hour."

She didn't like the sound of that cough, but knew he was too stubborn to listen to any suggestions from her. He certainly wouldn't trust her with his ship. But that was his choice. Shrugging, she left his cabin.

He looked worse when he joined her in the galley. He had showered, but he hadn't shaved, and his beard growth accentuated his washed-out pallor. Shadows ringed his eyes, dulled from fever. He coughed frequently as he replicated the meal, despite her suggestion they eat prepackaged food. Then he ignored the protein sticks and amargrain on his plate, taking only Kava tea.

Moriah was becoming genuinely alarmed, both for Sabin and herself. If whatever he had was contagious, then she could get it, and neither one of them would be able to function. If it were a long-lasting virus or infection, it might hamper her pickup of the iridon. No, it wouldn't, she told herself. Elysia had a large population of healers, and she could seek treatment from one. Besides, she was amazingly healthy. She had never been sick, even after nursing Celie through childhood illnesses.

After the meal, Sabin rose unsteadily and headed for the cockpit. He didn't even insist she walk ahead of him.

"Don't you think you should go to your cabin

and rest?" she suggested, following him down the corridor.

"You'd like that, wouldn't you?" He collapsed into the pilot's chair. "Sorry, but I'm not about to let you have free reign of the ship."

She shook her head at his stubbornness. Typical male, refusing to admit to any weakness, however temporary. "Fine."

Silence fell over the cockpit, punctuated by Sabin pounding on his keyboard, muttering beneath his breath, and coughing. Exploring IAR files for the best routes out of Elysia, Moriah kept a covert watch on him. More than once, he just stared blankly at the screen as if he didn't see it; or he appeared on the verge of dozing off. But then he'd shake himself awake and pound the keyboard some more.

At last, the beep of the subspace transceiver shrilled through the cockpit. Sabin lurched forward in his chair, punched the receive button, and snapped, "What?"

"Sounds like you're having a bad day, partner."

"I've had better," Sabin growled. "What do you want, McKnight?"

"Just checking in. Wanted to see if you were still in possession of your ship, or if I needed to put out a blue-feather alert."

Sabin audibly ground his teeth. "Very funny, old man. As you can see, I'm still here."

"Then I take it everything is under control. No problems?"

Sabin's partner didn't have to be specific. Moriah knew he was referring to her, checking to be sure she hadn't caused any trouble—or any harm to Sabin.

"Everything's f—" A coughing spasm halted his

words. Finally catching his breath, he finished, "Everything's fine."

"Sounds like a bad cough you have there."

"Yeah, well, it's just a bug. Don't worry about it, old man."

"Do you have any—"

"No! I don't, whatever the hell it is. I said, don't worry."

McKnight sighed. "You inspire worry, Travers. You still headed for Elysia?"

"Coordinates locked in and secured," Sabin sent a meaningful glance to Moriah. She got his message loud and clear. She couldn't alter the course without the code. Narrowing her eyes, she tossed her hair over her shoulder and turned her attention back to her own screen. She refused to be concerned about it, because she'd given her word, and she was going to Elysia.

"I'll check in later," McKnight said, then static filled the airwaves.

Sabin didn't talk after that. Moriah suspected it might be too much effort to speak between the episodes of coughing. A while later, he pushed to his feet and turned his bloodshot gaze on her.

"I'm going to the lav. Don't even think about touching the controls while I'm gone."

She was tempted to shoot back a scathing retort, but the way he swayed as he turned toward the entry halted her. She rose to her feet, afraid he'd fall. He managed to stumble down the corridor and into his cabin.

Moriah returned to her chair, concern gnawing at her. She halfheartedly studied sixth-sector shipping routes, but her thoughts kept wandering back to Sabin. When he didn't return after half an hour, she decided to check on him. There came no answer to the tone, so she entered his cabin.

He was sprawled face down on his bunk, apparently unconscious. Alarmed, she rushed to his side. She pressed her hand against his stubbled cheek, feeling the scorching heat even before she made contact. He stirred and moaned, then stilled again. She straightened, her brow furrowing in worry. Celie had contracted all the usual childhood diseases, but she had never been incapacitated this way.

Sabin needed something to bring down the fever, but Moriah knew he didn't have medical supplies, outside of sulfo nitrate. She had thoroughly searched his ship while it had been in her possession. She knew where everything was, including the weapons vault, and the code for accessing it. But that didn't help when he didn't have the supplies.

She went into the lav and wet a cloth in cool water. Returning to the bunk, she sat on its edge and stroked the cloth over Sabin's face. Other than turning his head from side to side, he didn't respond, and the cloth quickly became warm from the contact.

Moriah rinsed the cloth out and repeated the procedure several more times. He felt a little cooler after that, and she decided to wait and see how he did. This was a golden opportunity for her to do some business, and she needed to take full advantage of it.

Hurrying to the cockpit, she opened communications to Lionia. Fortunately, Sabin had not blocked outgoing messages. But his com system was old and very slow.

"Hail comrade." The Zarian's image flashed on the videoviewer moments later. "You are well?"

It had been a standard Zarian greeting, but Moriah heard the underlying concern in Lionia's voice. Having lost her father in a raid when she was only three seasons of age, Lionia had been raised by her mother. At thirteen seasons, she'd witnessed the murder of her mother and older sister by men of an enemy clan.

Warfare among the clans of her world was common enough, but Lionia had been deeply affected by the experience. Since that time, she'd harbored an intense hatred and distrust for males of all species. She wasn't at all happy about Moriah traveling with Sabin.

"I'm fine," Moriah assured her. "Not a bit of trouble from Travers. As a matter of fact, he's passed out in his cabin."

"Ha!" Lionia snorted. "Weakling can't hold his liquor? Here's your chance to slit his throat and return to Risa."

Moriah didn't share Lionia's bloodthirsty tendencies, preferring subterfuge to killing—although she wouldn't be averse to witnessing Pax's slow and painful death. As much as Sabin irritated her, as much as he threatened her on several levels, she certainly didn't want to end his life.

While it was very tempting to dump him at another Pleasure Dome—she'd just bet he'd be known at every one in the quadrant—and return to the pressing business matters at hand, she had made a promise.

"I gave my word of honor I would travel to Elysia with him," she told Lionia.

The woman narrowed her eyes in disgust, but she didn't argue. Like the Leors, Zarians placed great value on honor. "Then I will continue as planned, unless you have other orders."

"No. Have you contacted Risa?"

"As soon as we left Intrepid's air space."

"Have Kiah and Marna returned there yet?"

"Yes. They reported completing the Verante delivery without any problems."

Moriah blew out her breath in relief. At least *something* had gone right. "Good. Okay, as soon as you return to Risa, have Kiah and Marna take the two shipments of cargo to Calt. I'll contact Thorne and have him arrange a deal."

"I need to go with them," Lionia argued. "I am the most capable of handling the cretins on Calt."

"You are the best fighter, but Kiah and Marna can take care of themselves. I need you to watch over our mechanic and see that he does the repairs on the ships. Make sure he doesn't bother any of the women."

Lionia's expression turned mutinous. She hadn't wanted to take Radd back to Risa and had clearly expressed her opinion of male mechanics. Moriah's refusal to let her keep Radd shackled for the four-cycle trip hadn't pleased her, either.

"He won't bother them, or he'll be carved into a thousand pieces."

"No mutilation or torture," Moriah ordered. "If he gets out of line, lock him up. I'll decide what to do with him when I return. Has he given you any trouble so far?"

"As if he could," Lionia retorted, her warrior pride obviously stung. "I could strangle the muckworm with one hand. But he insists on skulking around the ship, fixing *everything*. I find the sight of him disgusting. Unfortunately, your sister does not share that opinion."

"Celie? What do you mean?" Moriah asked, alarm clamoring through her. It hadn't occurred to her that Radd might be a threat to Celie. The girl was very naive. If the mechanic made one improper advance toward her sister, she'd let Lionia carve out his miserable heart.

"She follows him like a shadow," Lionia growled. "Asking him questions about everything he does."

Some of Moriah's tension eased. "So she's interested in the repairs. How does he react?"

"He answers her questions," Lionia admitted grudgingly. "He even allows her to do some of the work. I keep telling her to stay away from him, but she sneaks off to watch him every chance she gets."

"Anything Celie can learn from him will be helpful," Moriah pointed out, her fears allayed. Lengthy space runs could be very boring, and Celie had always been fascinated with mechanical matters. Moriah couldn't see any harm in her watching Radd, especially under Lionia's suspicious scrutiny.

"I trust you'll keep Radd in line. Just get that shipment off to Calt. I'll be working on the iridon pickup. Which reminds me—as soon as you get to Risa, send Roanne to meet me at Elysia. I'll probably go directly from there to meet the iridon shipment. I'll update you on the status as often as I can. Any questions?"

Lionia hesitated. Moriah suspected she wanted to object to being left on Risa with the mechanic, but she didn't. "No," she said after a moment, "I'll take care of everything."

"I know you will. Can I speak to Celie now?"

Moriah chatted a few moments with her sister, who glowed with excitement over all the neat things she was learning from Radd. She also asked about Sabin.

"Oh, he's elsewhere on the ship right now," Moriah hedged, still bemused by Celie's apparent bond with the man. "Listen, I need to go, sweetness. I have other calls to make. I'll talk to you soon."

She signed off, then contacted Eark. The Shen always wore a deep hood which shrouded his face in darkness, and Moriah had never seen his features clearly. Just shadows and angles. Even his voice, an odd, hissing whisper, was mysterious. But his information had always been accurate and his discretion unquestionable. He was one of her most dependable contacts.

"Greetings," he whispered. "I have been waiting to hear from you."

"I've had a few unexpected delays, Eark."

His head bowed toward his console, a dark oval of shadow all she could see in the hood's interior. "This is not your usual ship."

Sabin must have reactivated his homing device, she realized. Eark had noted the different frequency. Not that it mattered. She wasn't hiding from anyone right now.

"Calling it a ship is debatable," she replied. "But I will be on board for about six more cycles, then I'll be back on one of my regular craft. In the meantime, please don't contact me. Let me contact you."

The hooded visage lifted toward her again. "I'm always compliant for you, Moriah. What is your wish?"

"What's the current status of the iridon? When will it arrive?"

"The shipment is still on schedule. I expect its arrival in approximately sixteen cycles."

Thank Spirit it wouldn't be there any sooner. "Is the delivery point still in the sixth sector?"

"Yes."

So far, so good. "All right. I'll stay in touch. We can arrange the actual coordinates for delivery when the shipment enters the quadrant."

"I shall await your call." Eark's whisper faded into static.

Moriah's next communiqué was to Commander Gunnar's flagship. The Leor officer happened to be on board, and flashed onto the screen with his usual intimidating effect. Stiffening, she locked gazes with him. Dark, glassy orbs returned her perusal, probing her soul.

He's light-years away, she reassured herself.

"Captain," he rasped. "I've been waiting to hear from you."

"My apologies, Commander Gunnar. I was delayed on Star Base Intrepid."

His expression hardened. "You seem to be experiencing an unusual amount of difficulties, Captain. I would hate to question your competency."

She certainly wanted to avoid that. Moriah took a calming breath. "The problems have been related to ship repairs, Commander. I have corrected the situation by adding a qualified mechanic to my crew."

"Then I trust there will be no more lapses in communication."

It was a command, not a question, and underlaid with a not-so-subtle threat. She would have to find a way to circumvent Sabin and stay in contact with Gunnar. "No, Commander. I will be in this ship temporarily, for six or seven cycles. Then I'll be on my regular ship. You already have that homing frequency."

"And now I have one for your current craft."

Surely it would be virtually impossible for Sabin to discover the Leors were tracking his ship. Why would he even check? Moriah took another breath. "The arrival of the iridon is on schedule, Commander. It should be in this quadrant within sixteen cycles, and will be delivered to the sixth sector. I'll have exact coordinates several cycles ahead."

His stared at her impassively. "Very well. I'll be awaiting our next contact."

The videoviewer went blank. Moriah sank back in her chair, suddenly shaky. Nothing had gone right from the start on this deal and failure would end her life.

She caught herself. *She would not fail!* The deal was worth the risk. It would bring a lot of miterons, enough to finish irrigating Risa and begin construction of permanent structures. She could pull it off. And she would.

As soon as she got free of Sabin Travers.

Chapter Eleven

Sabin! How long had she left him alone? Moriah looked at the chronometer. Less than an hour had elapsed, but she remembered how he'd burned with fever. Guilt and concern cut through her. She hurried to his cabin.

He lay very still on his bunk, but she heard his labored breath from the entry. At least he was breathing. He thrashed when she touched him, but he didn't wake up. Spirit, he felt hotter, if that were possible. She rewet the cloth and wiped his face. The water seemed to evaporate as soon as it touched his skin.

Panic elevated her heart rate. He was burning up. Surely he wouldn't die. She knew nothing about illness, only that this was serious—enough to incapacitate him.

This would be the perfect opportunity to escape. No. She couldn't do that. Sabin had treated her wound from the Jaccians. He had spared her life when she discovered the Shielder colony, and he had protected Celie. Every shred of honor within her demanded that she help him now. That—and an emotional pull she didn't dare want to admit or recognize.

But what to do? Stroking his hair back from his damp skin, Moriah stared at his flushed face. If she only knew of a nearby healer—or someone to call for help. . . . There *was* someone she could call. Chase McKnight, Sabin's partner. He might know where to find a healer.

Returning to the cockpit, she tried to access Sabin's communication log. Like the navigation pod, it was secured by code. Frustrated, she clenched her teeth and began typing furiously. She breathed a sigh of relief when she found what she sought—the decoding program she'd created when she had hijacked the ship. Sabin obviously hadn't had the time to determine she'd accessed his PWL file, which gave master access to everything on the ship.

She wasn't a computer genius by any stretch— Celie had much more ability in that area. Their father had been a liar and a thief, but he'd taught them early on how to do his dirty work for him. That had included stealing ships.

She reactivated the decoding program, and the codes appeared on the screen in proper alphanumeric sequences. There they were—the override codes for both the communication log and the navigation system. Now she could access the subspace frequencies for all Sabin's contacts, erase the records for her own unauthorized communications—and set the ship's course for wherever she desired. Not that she intended to change course, unless it was necessary to find a healer.

She found Chase McKnight's frequency and connected, wondering how much time had been lost while she overrode Sabin's lockouts. It seemed to take forever for the hailing signal packet to reach a satellite, then locate Chase's ship.

"McKnight here," finally came the gruff voice.

"Moriah Cameron here. I'm with Sabin Travers, on his ship."

"I know who you are. Turn on the videoviewer."

Blowing out her breath, she complied. McKnight's image flashed on the screen. Dark blond hair framed a harsh, chiseled face, dominated by cold gray eyes which pinned her to the spot. She felt as if the man were probing her deepest thoughts.

"Why in the blazing hells are you contacting me? Where is Travers?"

Obviously, McKnight didn't believe in standing on formality. "He's very ill, and I was hoping you might know of a—"

"Ill? What's wrong with him?"

"He's burning up with fever, and he's not coherent. Actually, he's not really conscious."

"Not conscious? How high is the fever? Has he had any seizures?" McKnight snapped out the questions rapid-fire.

"I have no way of taking his temperature. I haven't seen any seizures. But he doesn't seem to know where he is. He thrashes around when I try to help him and I need to find—"

"Transmit your coordinates."

"But what I really need is to contact a healer—"

"Transmit them *now*."

She did the calculations and pressed the send button.

206

After a slight pause, McKnight said, "Damn, I can't be there for eight hours. If only you could head my direction, we'd be able to cut the time."

"I can, but how's that going to help Sabin? He needs a healer."

"Are you telling me you can override his lockout code?"

Moriah sighed. No sense denying it. "I already have. That's the only way I was able to access your communication frequency."

"You'd better not be thinking of running," McKnight warned. "If you do, and he dies, I'll hunt you down and turn you over to the Controllers."

"Would I have contacted you if those were my plans?" she retorted, thoroughly irritated with overbearing males, not to mention her integrity being questioned. "I certainly wouldn't have admitted to having control of the ship."

A moment of silence ensued before he answered. "Your logic is sound. Just be forewarned that I'll be tracking every move that ship makes."

You and everybody else. "I won't take the ship off course, except to find a healer," Moriah answered. "Now, about Sab—"

"I'm transmitting the coordinates you need," McKnight interjected. "Use them to reset your course, and put the ship on maximum speed. We should rendezvous in four or five hours. In the meantime, try to get the fever down. Start by sponging Travers in cool water. If that doesn't work, use ice water. If he gets chilled, stop the process and cover him. Try to get him to take liquids. Contact me immediately if he gets worse. Understand?"

"Yes, but—" The connection went dead. Moriah threw up her hands. McKnight was more hardheaded than Sabin. And what could he do?

But she had no other choice. She didn't know anyone else to contact. Resigned, she studied the incoming coordinates from McKnight. Naturally they were the opposite direction of Elysia. Great. Half a day lost, at least, and she couldn't see the benefit of it. Sabin needed a healer, not a Controller agent.

However, McKnight's advice made sense. Moriah had bathed Celie in cool water when she'd had high fevers as a small child. Maybe McKnight would know what to do for Sabin. She reset the ship's coordinates, then headed for Sabin's cabin.

He was hotter than the sands of Calt. He opened his eyes when she felt his face, but they were glazed, with no sign of cognizance. Sweat beaded his forehead and dampened his hair, but he didn't appear chilled. Moriah opened the top of his flightsuit and eased his arms from the sleeves. He tossed his head and mumbled incoherently. Spirit, but he was so ill, so helpless.

A surge of emotion constricted her chest, and she tried to ignore it. She couldn't, wouldn't, allow herself to care for any man. If she felt anything at all, she told herself fiercely, it was compassion. Maybe a little gratitude.

She sponged his face and chest with cool water, trying not to notice the swell of muscles beneath smooth, glistening skin. Beautifully delineated biceps and pectorals indicated he kept himself in prime condition.

He'd been naked the night Moriah had seduced him, but the cabin had been dark. Today had been her first real look, and she had to admit he was magnificent. She froze, the cloth clutched in her fist. She'd found Pax repulsive in every way, although many women found him very attractive. How strange she didn't feel revolted by Sabin.

How strange she could stroke his bare skin, could experience an attraction toward him, without hideous memories of Pax rearing up. Instead, other images, sensual images of Sabin entwined with her, swirled through her mind; a kaleidoscope of intimacies they had shared.

By the Spirit! Her breath was almost as ragged as Sabin's, Moriah forced the disconcerting images away. She fled to the relative safety of the lav and splashed water on her hot face, telling herself her reaction was simply the stress of the past few cycles.

She owed Sabin Travers gratitude, nothing more. She was just unsettled right now, out of her element. In a few short cycles, he would be gone from her life and she would continue as before.

Fortified by these thoughts, she returned to him. Over and over, she sponged him. Her arms ached, but she continued. As his skin cooled a little, he became more vocal, tossing and calling out names. She soothed him, persuaded him to sip a little water.

Once he opened his eyes and stared straight at her. "You!" he rasped. "I should have known you'd be here."

"Where else would I be?" she muttered, although she wasn't sure he recognized her.

Finally, the alert went off in the corridor, warning of an approaching ship. She covered Sabin with a thin sheet so he wouldn't chill, then returned to the cockpit. The subspace transceiver was hailing, and she answered.

"I'm approaching," McKnight said. "Bring the ship to a standstill and await my boarding."

"Will do." Moriah entered the commands, slowing the ship until it was barely drifting. She went to the airlock to meet Sabin's partner, bracing herself for the docking jolt.

McKnight stepped through the airlock, his size overwhelming. Half a head taller than Sabin, he was broader through the chest, more massive. And while Sabin moved with lethal grace, this man radiated a grim power which reminded her of Commander Gunnar.

Tilting her head to meet his penetrating gaze, Moriah took a deep breath. She refused to let him intimidate her. "Captain McKnight."

"Captain Cameron. Shall we dispense with formalities? Where is Travers?"

She led him to Sabin's cabin. He'd thrown off the cover and rolled to his stomach. McKnight set down the black case he was carrying and snapped it open. He rolled his partner onto his back.

"Keep away from me," Sabin muttered, slapping at McKnight. "Don't look at me like that. I won't be tempted by you."

McKnight glanced at Moriah, his golden eyebrows raised. "He's been delirious," she offered lamely.

Pulling what appeared to be some sort of scanner from the case, McKnight sat on the edge of the bunk and ran it over Sabin, his face impassive. He lowered the scanner. "Alberian flu," he pronounced.

"That's what he has?"

McKnight nodded. "He probably got it at the prison on Intrepid."

Panic swirled through her. "The prison? Then Celie was exposed, too. She had it once when she was fourteen." At least Janaye had called it the Alberian flu, and the woman knew a lot about illness. Celie had been very sick for more than a

210

week. Moriah stared at McKnight anxiously. "Is it worse the second time?"

"You can only get it once."

"That's a relief."

"Have you had it, Moriah?" McKnight picked up the scanner and strode toward her.

Spirit, he was big. "I've never been ill," she answered, taking a step back. "I'm very healthy."

He grabbed her arm, halting her retreat. "Be still." He ran the scanner over her. She heard the faint hum of the instrument. "Ever had any inoculations?" he asked, studying the readouts.

"No." With her father's drinking, they hadn't had enough money for food, much less frivolous things like preventative medicine.

He looked up from the scanner, his steely gaze pinning her to the spot. "We're going to take care of that right now. You do have the flu incubating. But not for long."

Spirit, she couldn't afford to be sick for more than a week. "Then you can give me something to stop it?"

"Dead in its tracks. I can also give Travers something to speed his recovery. I need to get the serums from my lab."

McKnight went back to his ship, returning a short time later with a second case. Sitting next to Sabin, he took out a medical hypochamber and a vial. He filled the cylinder with the liquid, his movements sure and efficient, and injected the medication into Sabin's neck.

Moriah was fascinated. She'd never been to a healer, or seen any medical procedures. Obviously, Sabin's partner had received some medical training.

"Your turn." McKnight pulled out several vials of medicine and two more hypochambers. "I'm

---

Catherine Spangler

going to give you the antidote for the AF, as well as inoculations for all common illnesses."

Apprehensive, Moriah watched him fill the cylinders. She had no idea what to expect. He gestured her closer, and she moved forward slowly.

"Have you ever had an injection?" he asked.

"No." She wondered what one felt like, but pride kept her silent.

A small smile tugged at his generous lips and, for a moment, he didn't look quite so formidable. "It's only a small sting," he said, his deep voice laced with amusement. "Come on."

Moriah didn't know this man from the Exalted Controller, but her instincts told her she could trust him. Besides, she didn't want to risk becoming as sick as Sabin was. Halting before McKnight, she pulled her hair away from her neck.

She stood stiffly, jumping a little at the low buzz the first hypochamber made when it discharged into her neck. It did sting, but the discomfort was minor, just as he had told her. She was more relaxed for the second one.

She watched McKnight repack his case, puzzling over his actions. She could draw only one conclusion. "You're a healer, aren't you?" she asked.

The small amount of warmth on his face evaporated into a frigid mask. "No."

"But you have medical supplies and you know how to diagnose illness."

He picked up the case and swung toward her. "*I said no*. I am *not* a healer." Some unreadable emotion blazed in his eyes. "You will not tell Travers I was here, or that I treated him," he demanded fiercely. "You won't tell anyone about this. You'll regret it if you do. Understood?"

She didn't understand at all. McKnight was ly-

212

ing. He was obviously a competent healer, but for reasons of his own, wanted no one to know. Not that it mattered. She had secrets of her own to hide. "I understand. I won't tell anyone about this."

"Then I'll be off." McKnight strode toward the entry. At the panel, he turned. "Travers will be recovered in about two cycles. Be sure he drinks plenty of fluids. Replicate some plain broth for his first few meals."

"I don't know how to use a replicator."

McKnight rolled his eyes. "Then I hope you like amargrain and protein sticks."

"I'm starting to get sick of them," Moriah admitted.

"Come on, then." He gestured toward the galley. "I'll show you how to replicate some broth."

She let him lead her into the room and demonstrate. Afterward, he prepared to return to his ship. Stopping beside the airlock, he fixed Moriah with his mesmerizing stare. "I would follow you to make sure you reach Elysia, but I must catch up with someone who's reportedly at Odera. I expect you to head directly to Elysia. I'll be tracking your progress."

Despite his words, she sensed McKnight now trusted her word. "I'll set course for Elysia immediately," she promised. "And I'll take care of Sabin, as undeserving as he is."

A brief smile touched McKnight's lips. "That should prove interesting. Contact me if there are any problems."

Then he was gone. Musing over the oddness of Sabin's partner, Moriah went to check on their patient. Already, he was resting easier and his skin was cooler. She pulled the blanket over him, telling herself it was natural to feel relieved that he was better.

She just wanted to fulfill her promise and put all this behind her. That was all she cared about.

"What are you doing, muckworm?"

Radd turned from the airlock control plate he was tightening and faced the Zarian female. Brandishing her ever-present dagger, she radiated hatred and distrust. The woman was definitely too uptight. She needed to loosen up, starting with the golden hair pulled back tightly from her face.

He didn't mind her form-hugging leather bustier, though, or the leather leggings. They only served to emphasize her magnificent figure. Too bad she appeared to loathe all men in general—him in particular.

Radd didn't take it personally. In a universe cruelly dominated by the Controllers, he met many beings who had been adversely shaped by horrendous events. While most of his acquaintances might attribute Lionia's hostility toward him to the fact that he wasn't particularly attractive, and to the mistaken assumption he had little experience with females, Radd knew better.

He understood more about a woman's psyche than the vast majority of the males in the quadrant. He'd learned much from his father, a renowned paramour of Elysia's Pleasure Domes; and from his sister, who was a courtesan on Saron.

Besides, he was *very* good with his hands.

"Stop staring at me, muckworm. I asked what you're doing."

Radd ignored the blade hovering near his throat. "Adjustin' your airlock to the proper pressurization."

Breath hissed from her tightened lips. "You presume too much, serpent. This airlock has been functioning well. I will tell you what needs to be repaired and when the work will be done. Return to your cabin."

She glowed with anger and arrogance. Radd imagined all that passion being channeled into something infinitely more pleasurable than verbal sparring.

He felt certain a sensual encounter would be a new experience for her, because she wore a Zarian virtue chain draped loosely around her slender waist. Despite her apparent aversion to men, she chose to honor the Zarian tradition proclaiming her status of chastity for all to see. Intriguing. He'd have to give the matter some thought.

Shrugging, he snapped his tools onto his belt. "Whatever ya want, Lionia. It's your ship."

Her eyes narrowed and the blade whipped within a hairsbreadth of Radd's throat. "How dare you address me so insolently? I am the captain of this ship, while you are a prisoner, lower than scum. You will address me with the proper respect or suffer the consequences."

Yep, she was capable of a major meltdown all right.

Radd's calm gaze met her brilliant glare. "As ya command, *Captain*. I'm here to serve." He turned toward his cabin, unconcerned by her weapon. If she had planned to use it, he'd be carved up with intricate Zarian designs by now.

Strolling down the corridor, he hummed to himself. His original assessment of the situation had been correct. The lady was way too tense and uptight. His personal recommendation: a complete overhaul. Tough job, but he *was* the best in the quadrant.

And . . . he was very good with his hands.

*   *   *

Sabin finished off the food on his plate. "Never thought I'd enjoy amargrain or protein sticks so much, but after that liquified prison slime you forced on me, they taste pretty damn good."

"That so-called slime was broth, and it was intended to help your recovery," Moriah retorted, thoroughly irritated.

He had been a horrible patient, demanding, petulant, and downright cantankerous. He'd endured her care for only one cycle before he'd rallied and asserted his authority. But though he appeared completely recovered after only three cycles, he was still in a bad mood.

"Help my recovery!" he snorted. "I'm surprised it didn't kill me. I have to tell you, if that refuse is all you know how to replicate, then I understand why you don't cook."

Her eyes narrowing, Moriah considered dumping her half-full plate over Sabin's thick skull, then decided against it. In his current mood, he was likely to do anything. She held her silence as he rose and smoothed down his flightsuit.

"Do the clean-up," he ordered, striding through the entry.

She grabbed the edge of the table to keep from hurling something after him. He was the most arrogant, obnoxious son of an Antek—oh! Jolting up, she began tossing dishes into the sterilizer. Angry thoughts tumbled over one another, finally slowing. An unwelcome reminder of how concerned she'd been when Sabin was so ill slid in, diffusing her anger.

It hadn't meant anything, by the Spirit! It had only been concern for a fellow being. She'd have been better off taking advantage of the situation and dumping Sabin like she had before. But she'd given her word. She refused to consider the notion that there might be more to her actions than honoring their agreement.

She finished cleaning the galley, then headed for the cockpit. Sabin was hunched over the navigation console, a frown on his face. He looked up when she entered.

"What is this?" He motioned toward the screen.

"What?" she asked, moving to the console.

He jabbed a finger against the screen. "This."

Moriah leaned closer and studied the monitor. The screen was split, with the Onboard Timebase on one side and the Location Verifier Sensor on the other. Her chest tightened.

She had altered the records of detouring to meet Chase, but she hadn't possessed the technical expertise to adjust the computer's internal time base. As soon as Sabin was on his feet, he verified that the ship was on course to Elysia. She had hoped he wouldn't check further.

"I don't know what's got you concerned," she hedged.

"According to this, we're almost half a cycle behind where we should be." Sabin paused, his mouth set in a grim line. "Perhaps you can explain this inconsistency."

Any answer she gave, no matter how vague or neutral, would alert him to the fact that she'd been able to override his security codes. "I have no idea. I didn't notice any ship dysfunctions."

Suspicion sparking his eyes, Sabin stared at her. "I hope you're telling the truth."

"Why would I lie about problems with the ship? I certainly couldn't have altered anything, not with all your security measures."

He considered her words, then pivoted toward his chair. "Then the damn navigation module is messed up again. I need to find Radd."

Good luck, Moriah thought with gloating satisfaction as she slid into her seat. She accessed IAR and pulled up her files on the sixth sector.

Moments later, Sabin said in a deceptively soft voice, "You couldn't explain the time lapse, but perhaps you can explain this."

Moriah looked up, an ominous premonition slithering through her. "What?"

"Five communications sent from this ship, all on the two cycles I was too sick to move. Is it possible I was so delirious I don't remember making them? Hmmm, I don't think so. Most of these subspace encryption frequencies don't look familiar. No, wait, one of them does . . . it's McKnight's!"

Sabin rose from his seat and strode over. "Who gave you permission to use my communications system? And how in the blazing hells did you access McKnight's frequency? That was security coded!"

Rising to face him, Moriah damned herself to the fires of the Abyss and back. In the flurry of Chase's arrival and taking care of Sabin, she'd forgotten to erase her communications. She'd fixed the navigation records when she reset course for Elysia, but then she'd gone to care for Sabin, and had never given the calls another thought.

She realized trying to lie her way out wouldn't placate him. It would only provoke him further. It made no difference now whether or not he knew she'd breached his security.

"I overrode your security codes."

"How in the Fires did you do that?"

"It's an old system, easy to breach."

He clenched his teeth so hard, she thought his jaw might crack. "Then you contacted my partner?"

No way around admitting to that. She simply wouldn't reveal the entire story. Sabin would never know McKnight had actually traveled to the ship. "You were very sick. I thought he might know—"

"You contacted McKnight to tell him I was sick?"

"Well, yes—"

"Great, just great!" The ungrateful wretch threw his hands up in disgust.

"I thought you might die!"

"Yeah, right. So you called my partner. The old man probably had a fit. I'm surprised he didn't come and try to doctor me himself."

Spirit, he was way too close to the truth. "He told me to make the broth and feed it to you," Moriah said quickly.

Sabin regarded her, his expression skeptical. "That's all he said? No ranting about medical supplies and how I really needed this medicine or that?"

She shook her head. "No. Guess he knew you wouldn't have anything. He told me how to make the broth. Said it would help your recovery."

"Just proves McKnight secretly hates me," Sabin muttered, running his hand through his hair. He fixed her with a midnight glower. "And it makes me wonder if you can be trusted."

After all she'd done for him! Fury welled up in waves. Drawing back her fist, Moriah punched him in the chest as hard as she could.

He reeled back, a stunned expression on his face. "Damn! That hurt!"

"Good." She punched him again for good measure, then danced back before he could grab her. "You sorry son of an Antek!" she hissed. "You've got debris instead of brains in your head. You were helpless for two cycles—helpless! I could have taken this ship anywhere. I could have dumped you or killed you. But I didn't. I took care of you. Kept your fever down, fixed you broth. Not once have you thanked me. No. Instead, you yell at me."

She paused, heaving for breath, then plunged back into her tirade. "Notice where we're headed? Elysia, that's where! Just as I agreed. I gave my word to go there and I intend to honor it. Even if you are a kerani's rear!"

Sabin rubbed his chest. "A kerani's rear? Surely you can do better than that."

"A lot of descriptions come to mind. But I refuse to lower myself to that level."

"Thank you."

"I—what?"

"You're right. I never thanked you properly for everything you did while I was ill. No one has ever done anything like that for me before. You could have taken my ship or escaped. I'm grateful you didn't."

His sincere tone took the heat out of Moriah's anger. She hesitated, at a loss for words.

"Listen, I overreacted," he admitted. "I hate not being in control. When I was sick, I felt totally helpless. I've been taking it out on you. I'm sorry."

Another apology. At least he was willing to admit he was wrong. "It's no big deal," she muttered.

He studied her a moment, then a smile flirted around his lips. "I didn't realize you cared about me."

Electricity jolted her heart. He was far too handsome when he smiled, far too self-assured. "I don't," she clarified. "I wouldn't leave a wounded lanrax by the wayside to die."

"Right." The smirk on his face and the gleam in

his eyes indicated he didn't believe her for a millisecond.

The problem was, she was having trouble believing it herself.

Chapter Twelve

Moriah studied the screen, chewing her bottom lip. As always, the innocent gesture did wicked things to Sabin's libido. Unwelcome heat rushed through his body, settling in the lower extremities. Damn. He cursed her for affecting him this way; cursed himself for not having better control over his body.

As much as he desired Moriah, he could not—would not—make sexual overtures toward her. She had survived the unthinkable. After her past experiences with men, she deserved someone special, someone who would cherish her, help her overcome the past.

Sabin was not that man, never would be. He had no interest in emotional entanglement, no aptitude for it. He knew where it led. To pain.

The subspace transceiver beeped. Sabin punched the pad. "Travers here."

"Ranul here."

Sabin sat up straighter, tension spiraling. He

rarely heard from fellow Shielders—and even rarer was his communication with their leaders—unless they needed supplies or something was wrong. He activated the videoviewer. "It's been a while."

Jarek san Ranul's image flashed on the screen. "It has. I'm afraid I might have bad news. Are you alone?"

Trepidation slithered through Sabin. Spirit, he didn't want to hear Jarek's news, whatever it was.

His gaze went to Moriah, who watched with open interest. She already knew far too much, already posed a threat to a Shielder colony, and to Sabin himself. Yet, oddly, he was beginning to trust her . . . which was crazy, considering the lady had drugged him and stolen his ship.

Yet, although she had breached his security measures, she hadn't taken advantage of him while he'd been delirious with fever. She had remained by his side during his illness, keeping the course for Elysia. Still, regardless of her surprising actions, he couldn't take the chance of her learning any further information about his people.

"Give me a moment," he answered, his gaze still on her. He muted the contact. "I need to take this alone."

She stood, flipping her hair over her shoulder. The motion stretched her bronze flightsuit over her lithe form. For once, he was unaffected, too apprehensive about this communication to react to Moriah's allure.

He waited until the panel slid shut behind Moriah, then he released the mute. "What is it?"

"We believe the Nissar colony has been attacked by Anteks."

The news hit Sabin like firing blasters. He went rigid, frozen with dread, trapped inside an avalanche of dark demons. Adrenaline surged as an all-too-familiar kaleidoscope of hideous scenes flashed through his mind. Terror. Screaming. Death.

He finally found the strength to speak. "What—what information do you have?"

Jarek's features remained stiff, but torment burned in his eyes. "One of my men doing surveillance on Calt overhead a Neanderthal by the name of Turlock boasting that he and his partner had discovered the colony. Claimed he sold the information to the Controllers. He apparently had a lot of money to spread around. When we tried to contact Nissar, we got no answer. I fear the worst. I'm headed there right now. Where are you?"

Turlock. Just as Sabin wondered where he'd heard that name before, the answer came to him. Turlock was Galen's latest cohort. Coldhearted, greedy bastard that he was, Galen would be more than willing to sacrifice an entire colony for gold.

A tidal wave of fury broadsided Sabin. He knew with every cell in his body Galen was behind this senseless massacre. Because of the bounty on his head, Galen couldn't approach the Controllers with the information. But Turlock, his so-called partner, could.

Galen was a dead man. Reward or no.

"Sabin? Did you hear me?"

He forced himself to think. "I'm two cycles from Elysia, traveling from Intrepid."

Jarek punched up some data. "Then you're less than two cycles from the colony. You're the closest one. I need you to meet me there."

Sabin understood the request all too well. Traveling to Nissar would be dangerous enough for two Shielder ships, much less one. There might be

Anteks still loitering at the colony, or scavengers out for plunder, or slave traders searching for Shielder survivors to sell at Slaver's Square on Elysia.

But worse—far worse—would be the total, absolute destruction: of people, animals, buildings. Nothing remaining but charred bodies and smoldering rubble. The echoes of screaming terror. The stench of death.

He remembered them all too clearly.

Clenching the console, he willed air into his constricted lungs, willed himself to stay focused on the present. On what had to be done. No matter how horrifying. *It's been over twenty-four seasons*, he told himself. *Put it behind you and do your duty.* He was a Shielder, first and foremost. His obligations lay with his people.

Exhaling forcefully, Sabin met Jarek's watchful gaze. "I'll get there as fast as I can."

"You have my gratitude. I'm a little over two cycles away myself. I'll keep trying to contact them while I'm en route. When you arrive, orbit at a safe distance until I get there. We'll go planet-side together."

Sabin thought of Moriah. Her presence made the situation even more precarious. He could be putting her in grave danger. At the very least, this detour would become a major source of conflict. But duty to his people came before all else.

"All right," he told Jarek. "I'll wait for you to arrive. But contact me via computer rather than through the transceiver when you make orbit."

After Jarek signed off, Sabin stared at the blank screen, battling the nightmares of the past. The fear, the pain, the stark reality that hundreds of lives could be extinguished in the cold blink of an eye. Death that claimed its victims mercilessly, while leaving those who did survive dead inside.

Finally, he set course for Nissar. And steeled himself to endure the horror to come.

"Strap in and prepare for landing," Sabin ordered.

Moriah looked up from her computer. "We've arrived at Elysia?"

He'd been wondering how to handle this moment. He had kept quiet about their change in course, choosing to give her as little information as possible. He hadn't talked about much of anything, for that matter. He had no words, only memories that clawed at his gut.

Moriah had eventually quit trying to instigate conversation. The silence was fine with him. He'd needed the distance from her. She was entirely too enticing and distracting. He could never take the risk of caring for anyone—never. If anything, the situation he and Jarek were about to face should reinforce that fact.

"We're not at Elysia," he said gruffly. "I had to make another stop first. We'll be on track again within a cycle."

Disbelief filled her golden eyes. "Where are we?"

"Better you don't know. But we're going to Elysia after I finish here."

The color of her eyes turned bronze as anger replaced disbelief. "I have every right to know where we are. How far are we from Elysia?"

"Three cycles. Trust me, you don't need to know anything about this side-trip. It has nothing to do with you."

She rose slowly from her chair, radiating fury. "Trust you? I gave you my word, and I've kept my end of the bargain. For some idiotic reason, I expected you to do the same. Now you're telling me we've travelled two cycles out of our way, costing me five—*five*—cycles of precious time. And it's none of my business? You can go to the Fires!"

He regretted what he had to do next, but he had little choice. Reaching into a cabinet, he pulled out some shackles. "I'd hoped you'd be reasonable." He rose to face her. "I apologize for the loss of your time. I'll make it up to you if I can. But make no mistake—I have to do this. You can cooperate and agree to wait for me on the ship, or I'll be forced to restrain you. Your choice."

Her hands clenched against her things, she glared at him, shaking with anger. "You *bastard*."

He really felt like a bastard, especially since she had honored her end of the bargain. "Agreed. But I'm bigger and stronger, and you have no choice in the matter. Which will it be? Cooperation or coercion?"

She glared at him a moment longer, her eyes a blur of gold sparks, her hair tumbling around her shoulders. Finally, she tossed her head with a frustrated sigh. "I'll cooperate. I'll wait on the ship."

His bluff had worked. Relief swept through him. He had absolutely no intention of shackling her. If something went wrong—if anyone was plundering the colony remains, if an Antek patrol returned, if anything happened to him, Moriah would be on her own. She might have to defend herself. Or she might have to pilot the ship to safety.

"Your word that you won't try to escape—that you'll continue on to Elysia with me afterwards. Not that it would do you any good to leave the ship." He steeled himself against the suffocating coldness permeating him. "There's no one here who can help you."

"My word is good," she bit out. "I think I've proven that. How long will you be gone?"

How long? How long did it take to view total carnage? To determine there were no survivors? And then . . . how long to forget?

"No more than a few hours." Sabin turned and strode into the corridor. Going to the weapons vault, he opened it. He pulled out two blasters and snapped them onto his utility belt. Looking up, he saw Moriah behind him. He took out two phasers and a blast helmet.

"I take it this isn't a social call," she commented.

"No." He added one phaser to his belt, then checked the charge on the second.

"Here." He held out the weapon. "Just in case."

Her brows rose as she took the phaser. "In case what?"

So much evil in the universe. So many heinous possibilities.

A great heaviness in his gut, he answered, "You might need to defend yourself."

Frowning, she stared at him. "What's going on?"

He wanted her to have a life. A future. She needed an avenue of escape if one became necessary.

"Nothing that concerns you. But if I haven't returned in two hours or contacted you on the com link, fire up the engines and get out of here."

He paused. She still knew the location of a Shielder settlement. Similar knowledge had just destroyed innocent people. He went to the hatch and opened the portal. No one should ever see such a heinous sight, but desperation spurred his decision.

"Look out there."

Her expression perplexed, she walked over and stared out the portal.

"What do you see, Moriah?"

"I'm not sure. Everything is a distance away. There's smoke, and piles of refuse."

"See any signs of life?"

"No. No people, or animals." She turned back to him, curiosity sparked in her eyes. "What is this place?"

"I guess you've never seen a colony that's been razed by Anteks."

Her eyes widened in horror. Her skin paled. "Oh, Spirit, no!" She whirled back to the portal, clutching the frame. "Oh . . . no."

Oh, yes. And she couldn't begin to imagine the terror of experiencing it firsthand. Grasping her shoulders, Sabin turned her toward him. "That was a Shielder settlement, Moriah. Someone reported its location to the Controllers. At least two hundred men, women, and children are dead."

She stared at him, emotion churning in her eyes.

"Swear to me," he demanded fiercely. "Promise me you'll never tell anyone about the colony we landed at after we left Calt. *Swear it!*"

A tremor ran through her body, but her gaze remained steady. "I swear," she choked out. "On my honor and my life, I give you my word I will never tell anyone about that colony." She looked toward the portal. "How horrible."

"Yeah." He released her before she could feel his own trembling, and fumbled with his gloves.

"Sabin." Her hand on his arm reverberated through him. He looked up. The compassion in her eyes wrapped around his soul. "I'm sorry," she whispered.

He felt an inexplicable need to touch her. Reaching out, he cupped his hand against her cheek, watched her surprise. Her skin was warm and soft, but the woman beneath was solid. She had endured terrible life circumstances, yet emerged strong and sure.

He had the sudden urge to crush her to him, to absorb her unwavering strength. Instead, he murmured, "Just stay safe, okay?"

Drawing back, he yanked on his gloves and put on his helmet. He strode to the hatch and punched the pad. "Secure the entry behind me and don't admit anyone else. Contact me on the com link if you need me."

The hatch opened. "Sabin."

He turned. Moriah's golden gaze locked with his. He was amazed to see worry flickering there.

"Spirit be with you," she said quietly.

The blessing washed over him like a warm tide. Her unexpected concern gave him a kernel of strength he desperately needed. He nodded brusquely and stepped though the hatch . . .

. . . into Hades.

He'd landed a few hundred meters from the colony, but even from here, the unmistakable reek of burned bodies assaulted his senses. A gray haze, created by smoldering piles of debris, drifted over the settlement.

The past raced up to engulf him. His heart pounded against his chest. The blood rushed in his ears. He couldn't think. Couldn't breathe. *Have to breathe* . . .

"Sabin!"

The shout shattered his paralysis. He whirled, bringing up his disrupter, ready to discharge.

"Whoa!" Jarek san Ranul held up a gloved hand.

It took a moment for Sabin to free himself from the maelstrom. His arm dropped to his side. "Sorry."

Jarek released his breath. "Didn't mean to trigger your battle stance. Didn't you hear me calling? Feel my presence?"

Normally Sabin was acutely sensitive to the innate awareness all Shielders possessed for identifying other Shielders. That very ability, along with a natural mind shield which prevented Controller mental indoctrination, had thus far prevented the wholesale destruction of their race. But seeing the carnage of Nissar numbed him to all awareness.

"Guess I was distracted by this—" He gestured toward what had been a functioning Shielder colony, at a loss for words. Not sure he could have forced them past his constricted throat.

"Yeah," Jarek said, his expression as sickened as Sabin felt. "This . . . abomination." He stared at the remains, then pulled out a terrain scanner. "Let's get this over with."

Neither Jarek nor Sabin had picked up any signals from Antek or slaver ships; nor had they seen any scavenger ships while orbiting. There could be hidden ships, though, so they remained on alert. Barring that, they had only one goal.

Look for survivors.

Like Sabin had been. A young boy of six seasons, huddled beneath the bloodied body of his mother, eluding slavers. Cold, terrified.

Lurching forward, Sabin forced back the images, battling to keep his focus in the present.

Weapons drawn, the two men walked across the blackened ground. The smell worsened as they approached the remains of the colony, forcing them to lower the visors on their helmets. But even that couldn't obliterate the stench of decomposing bodies.

Nor could they close their eyes to the massacre. To the sightless eyes staring up, or the expressions of terror on half-destroyed faces. Nor to the absolute destruction. Broken bodies, broken household items, broken toys. Nothing spared. Men, women, children, babies, animals.

The Anteks had been thorough.

Don't think. Don't feel. Sabin willed himself not to look directly at the bodies, but rather at the peripherals. It seemed like he was in a tunnel, the only light a patch of gray far, far, at the end. A great weight bore down on him, making it increasingly difficult to go forward.

Keep walking. Get through this.

He shifted his attention to the energy all living Shielders exuded, trying to pick up another life presence. Jarek's infrared scanner would pick up anything that might be moving. Nissar was a small moon, and it wouldn't take long to search.

They both sensed it at the same time. A faint vibration from a living Shielder. Weak, but alive, it was coming from a pile of rubble about ten meters ahead. They quickened their pace, hoping to find a survivor.

A sound behind them had both men whirling, weapons primed. Moriah stood there, holding the phaser. Sabin raised a restraining hand toward Jarek. "Don't fire! She's with me."

"Blazing hells!" Jarek snapped. "You should have warned me, man. I almost killed her."

"I expected her to follow orders." Sabin lowered his shaking arm. Adrenaline still rushing through him, he turned his ire on Moriah. "What the hell are you doing out here? I told you to stay on the ship."

She stiffened, her chin lifting. "I thought you might need backup." She swallowed, her gaze drifting over the devastation. She quickly looked back to Sabin. "In case there were any Antek patrols around."

She looked so pale, he feared she might faint. "Get back to the ship," he ordered. "I don't have time to deal with this and you at the same time."

Her eyes narrowed. "I don't need any support. I came to offer assistance. But from the looks of things . . ." Her gaze drifted again, and she drew a shuddering breath. "It appears we're too late to help anyone."

Despite her harsh life, despite living with shadowers, she'd probably never seen much death, especially bodies so horribly massacred. Sabin wished he could claim the same.

"We need to investigate that pile, and quickly," Jarek interjected. "And she's not—" He hesitated, then finished telepathically, *She's not a Shielder.*

A small number of Shielders had telepathic abilities, which were linked to their ability to sense one another. Those lucky few were the ones usually groomed for the dangerous assignments, such as reconnaissance or smuggling weapons and supplies. Jarek, next in line to become the Council head of his colony on Liron, had strong powers, as did Sabin.

It's okay, he transmitted to Jarek. *She won't tell anyone about what she saw here, or about either of us.*

Suspicion glinted in Jarek's dark brown eyes, but he apparently decided not to challenge Sabin's judgment. Besides, what was the sense of trying to protect the identity of this colony now?

Sabin took a blaster off his belt and handed it to Moriah. "If you won't return to the ship, then keep an eye out while we look for survivors."

She nodded, and he and Jarek headed toward the life force. Nothing moved as they approached the rubble, but the vibration grew in strength. They knelt by the mound and quickly shifted debris aside.

"Don't be afraid," Jarek called out. "We're here to help you. Come out if you can."

They saw movement, the pile heaving. They pulled back a large rock, uncovering a depression in the ground. Huddled there, covered with cuts and filth, lay a shivering young boy.

The sight of the terrified child hit Sabin like a fist to the gut. It had been over twenty-four seasons, but he remembered every detail as if it were yesterday. Shaking almost as badly as the boy, he reached out. "It's okay. You're safe."

The boy shrank back. "No!" he screamed. "No, no! Mommy! Mommy, where are you? Mommy, Mommy, Mommy!"

He tried to scramble away, but Jarek cut him off. He whirled around, and Sabin snagged him, pulling him close. "It's okay. We won't hurt you. We're here to help you."

The boy struggled and kicked, despite their reassurances. Finally, he went limp, quivering like a trapped kerani.

"Mommy. Mommy," was all he would say.

Sabin closed his eyes, battling déjà vu. No one deserved to face this.

Moriah rocked the boy against her, cooing soft, nonsensical words of reassurance, while Sabin and the man called Jarek searched for more survivors. The child clung to her so tightly she could barely breathe. She moved him to a flat rock away from the carnage, but close enough to keep watch. The phaser and blaster lay beside her.

Horror pushed down on her. She'd never seen such destruction. Those bodies—the twisted faces, the stench. And the little ones. Oh, Spirit, the little ones. Children and babies. The images would be forever imprinted on her mind. No wonder Shielders guarded their settlement locations with their lives—and with the lives of those who discovered them.

Moriah hugged the boy closer, waves of emotion rolling through her. She felt nausea, horror, unadulterated fury toward the Controllers. They were the ones who propagated the destruction of Shielders; who paid large rewards for information on Shielder colonies, then sent Anteks to do their dirty work.

Then there were the shadowers, those despicable beings who hunted Shielders and numerous other wanted "felons" and turned them over to the Controllers in exchange for gold. It didn't matter that many so-called criminals were innocent, or had done nothing other than being born to an unlucky race. Nor did it matter that they suffered agonizing torture before they were executed.

All that mattered to shadowers was the gold.

Moriah knew all too well how shadowers operated, her father and Pax prime examples. As far as she was concerned, they were lower than Anteks, because Anteks were stupid brutes who didn't know right from wrong. Most shadowers were intelligent, crafty trackers. They knew what they were doing. They just didn't care, as long as they got their gold.

She hated them all. If she ever saw her own father again, she'd phaser him dead on the spot. And Pax—well, she'd turn the bastard over to Lionia for a slow, painful death by flaying.

Sabin and Jarek appeared from the other end of the settlement and headed toward the rock. Their grim faces and empty hands indicated the outcome of their search: no more survivors. There was only the one lone boy, now orphaned and emotionally scarred for life.

They stopped at the rock, snapping their weapons to their belts. Sabin appeared remote, withdrawn, his face like granite. His bleak gaze rested on Moriah and the boy, but he didn't seem to see them.

Jarek blew out a breath as he shook his head. "Nothing more to do here." He held out his arms. "I'll take the boy with me."

The child clutched Moriah tighter, burrowing his head against her chest. "What will you do with him?" she asked, her protective instincts on full alert.

"I'll take him to my colony. He'll live with one of the families there."

"A Shielder colony," she stated bluntly.

Jarek paused, then nodded.

Another Shielder settlement, another target for the Controllers' hatred. "It won't be safe," she protested, loath to send this frail child to face further danger.

Jarek's face hardened as he looked at the destruction around them. "Is anywhere safe for us?" he asked harshly. "Would the boy be better off among those who want him dead?"

Moriah bit her lip. What could she say?

"It's all he knows. It's *what* he is," Jarek said. "If he lives in the outside world, he'll be at risk for discovery and far greater dangers."

As much as her runaway emotions made her want to argue, he was right. The rational logic he offered couldn't be denied. The boy belonged where he would be understood and accepted. There he could have a family, something Moriah had never had, outside of Celie.

She whispered to the child, "Sweetness, you need to go with Jarek. He'll find a new family to take care of you."

He shook his head vehemently. "Mommy. I want Mommy!"

Moriah relinquished her hold on the boy and Jarek gently pried him away. Cradling the child against him, he stood and turned to Sabin.

"Thanks for helping out here, Travers. I'm sorry you had to go through this again. I know it was tough."

Again? Sabin had been through a similar experience before? Moriah stared at him, noting his shuttered expression, the starkness in his eyes. He shook his head and clasped Jarek's outstretched hand.

"I'll get by. Take care of that boy. See that he gets with a family who wants him."

Without a word to Moriah, he turned and strode toward the ship. She leaned over to press a kiss against the boy's muddy cheek. "Take good care of him," she told Jarek. She scooped up the weapons and headed after Sabin.

He walked swiftly, his back ramrod-straight. Practically running to catch up, Moriah could think only about him going through such a horrendous experience before. Once was enough to last a lifetime. Had he actually been a victim in a colony that was attacked, or had he only investigated the remains of one?

His reaction today was understandable. With a jolt, she realized Sabin's reaction had started two cycles ago when Jarek contacted him. He'd become withdrawn and moody. She'd been too caught up in her own concerns about the iridon and her irritation at his apparent lack of trust or gratitude to pay much attention.

Out of breath, she reached the ship and stepped through the open hatch. Standing inside, Sabin punched the control, and the hatch lowered. Silent, he went to the weapons vault and pitched in his helmet and weapons. Leaving the vault open, he strode into the cockpit.

Moriah followed more slowly, placing the phaser and blaster inside the vault, then straightening the helmet and weapons Sabin had tossed in. He'd given her a weapon to defend herself. Told her to take his ship and flee if he didn't come back. Stroked her face with startling gentleness.

Just stay safe, okay?

She closed the vault and rested her forehead against it. She didn't like the tender emotions trying to push into her heart. Didn't need this crazy warmth flowing through her veins, accompanying thoughts of Sabin. Didn't need to become involved with any man. She would never place her trust in a man, or ever again allow a man power over her. Never.

The engines roared to life. They were taking off, whether or not she was strapped in. She stumbled her way into the cockpit, bracing herself against the wall as the hoverlifts surged and the ship listed momentarily. Sabin corrected the angle, and she slid into her seat, securing her harness.

They blasted away from the planet in one of the roughest takeoffs Moriah had ever experienced. She didn't object. As far as she was concerned, they couldn't get away from this wasteland fast enough.

Chapter Thirteen

"Get to work, muckworm."

Normally, Radd was a low-key kinda guy, but he was starting to get a little ticked. He dug in his heels, slouching against the ship. "Nope. Don't work when I'm chained."

He knew that would get Lionia's kerani, and it did. Her narrowed eyes sparking like a nova, she clenched her magnasteel dagger so hard, her knuckles turned white. He was getting damn tired of that knife, too.

"You're not in a position to resist, serpent. You're a prisoner, with no rights. I order you to repair this ship."

"I will. When ya remove the chain."

The dagger whipped against his windpipe. "I will not allow a serpent free reign to slither around our camp. You would terrorize the other females."

"Naw, I wouldn't. I've never terrorized a woman in my life. Every female I've ever had dealings with has left with a smile on her face."

She struggled to maintain her composure. He knew she wanted to carve him up bad, but had given her word she wouldn't. He admired her honor—was mighty grateful for it, matter of fact.

"Some of our females are innocent," she growled. "You couldn't be trusted around them."

Best as he could tell, the only carnally innocent females on Risa were Celie and Lionia. Celie's youthful innocence was obvious, and Lionia still wore the Zarian virtue chain around her waist.

"Ya talkin' about Celie? She's just a girl. I prefer women who've filled out some." He took a moment to appreciate the lush form before him, then added, "Like you."

He moved before she could react. An upward chop to her arm jolted the dagger away from his throat. Grabbing her wrist, he gave an efficient twist, loosening her hold on the weapon. He snatched it with his free hand and pressed the point against her throat.

"You're disarmed," he stated calmly. "I claim challenge."

Incredulity chased shock in her eyes. "Only Zarians issue challenge."

Usually only Zarians were brave enough to challenge another Zarian. But Radd was confident he had the situation well in hand. "I possess your weapon," he pointed out. "By Zarian law, I have the right to claim challenge. Unless ya choose to dishonor yer law."

Lionia's face flushed. Fury, then blood lust, darkened her eyes. "A death challenge?" she asked hopefully.

"Naw. Mental challenge."

She was obviously disappointed. Good thing he'd beat her to the challenge, and got to choose the type. He didn't stand a chance in a physical

240

contest, especially one to the death. Taller, and in prime physical condition, Lionia would have pounded the neutrons out of him, then carved him into space debris. He was quick on his feet and knew that invaluable wrist twist, but other than that, he couldn't boast any great strength. He even hated exercise. It was a useless expenditure of energy.

He could hold his own in a battle of wits, however, even though the highly intelligent Zarians spent as much time acquiring knowledge as they did physical strength. Next to mutilating their enemies, they loved nothing better than showing off their impressive intellects.

As the one being challenged, Lionia was entitled to pick the topic and launch the first question. But Radd felt certain he knew what subject she would select. He'd overheard a conversation which had clued him in on her intellectual passion.

"I choose Zarian star system astrophysics."

Yes! Successful strike. Hiding his satisfaction, he nodded in agreement and withdrew the dagger from her throat, slipping it into his utility belt. "All right."

Lionia considered a moment. "How long is Zaria's orbital period around its sun?"

She was a sneaky one. "Zaria's in a binary star system," Radd answered. "Has two suns. Takes 507 standard cycles to orbit 'em."

He heard her sharp intake of breath, knew he had surprised her. His turn to challenge. "What is the spectral class of Zaria's suns?"

She gave him a look that clearly expressed her low opinion of him. "One is an F5, the other a G2. What is the equatorial diameter of Zaria?"

He grinned, enjoying the game. "Hmmm, let's see. I'd guess about 4,921 kilometers."

That seemed to startle her. She jerked her head to acknowledge his correct answer. He contemplated his next question. "What is Zaria's distance from its closest sun?"

"1.2 astronomical units," she answered without hesitation.

He had her. "Nope."

Fire flared in her eyes. "What do you mean by that, serpent? I know more about the Zarian star system than all the knowledge contained in your scrawny brain."

Nonchalantly, he pulled out his pocket scanner. He held it up so she could see it had been off during the challenge, then activated it. It opened in a program on the Zarian star system.

"Cheat!" she spat, stepping forward to see the display.

"Been off the entire time." Radd scrolled to data on the star system's habitable zone. "See? Zaria is 1.25 AU from Marius, not 1.2."

Her chest heaved and color suffused her face. "Slime! Muckworm! You cheated!"

"Did not. Never looked at it. 'Sides, it was off." Radd shrugged. "But if you want to renege, nothin' I can do about it."

She drew herself up, haughty despite the blow to her warrior pride. "I never go back on my word or my obligations."

"As the loser, you must obey all my orders for an entire cycle," he reminded her.

If she clenched her fists any tighter, her palms would bleed. "I'm well aware of the consequences," she growled.

He was gonna enjoy this. "First order—take off this chain."

Her movements jerky, she pulled the sequencer off her belt and slapped it onto the lock plate on his ankle. The mechanism whirred, clicked, and opened. Radd shook his leg free of the shackle and kicked it back toward where it was attached to the side of the ship.

He returned his attention to Lionia, who stood ramrod-stiff. "Now, take your hair down."

"Why?" she snarled.

"I'm not sure you're allowed to question orders, but I'll tell ya why. 'Cause I'm gonna kiss ya. Long and hard and wet."

"What?" Her composure slipped even more, her voice rising above its normal, husky growl. Her sun-bronzed skin paled, incredulity filled her jewel eyes. She probably had no idea how revealing those eyes were. He wasn't gonna tell her, either.

"You heard me. Makin' out. Me. You. Now."

"Zarians don't kiss," she informed him, defiant and beautiful.

"Yeah, well, I like to improvise." He planned to foray far beyond lip alignment, but would never force a female against her will. He was confident he could rev Lionia's thrusters and breach her shields. After all, he knew almost as much about women as he did about spacecraft.

And he was very good with his hands.

"So back to your hair. Take it down."

Her eyes narrowed. "What does that have to do with kissing?"

"It's just part of the routine. Ambience and all that."

She stood there sullenly. "Loser obeys the challenge winner," he reminded her. "Take it down." Glaring at him, she reached up and yanked the clips from her hair. The sumptuous waves fell in twisted coils to her shoulders. Yep, he had her right where he wanted her.

He sauntered closer and combed his fingers through the glossy strands, shaking them out. She was something else with her hair all glorious around her like an aurora. Ignoring her involuntary flinch, he rested his hand over her breast, rubbing the silky strands between his fingers.

"Beautiful," he murmured in awe.

"You mock me."

He looked up, finding wariness and uncertainty in her eyes. Not only did she not trust him, but she'd apparently never been told how exquisite she was. Like a Starcraft MS-6000 fighter in free flight.

"I say what I mean. You *are* beautiful. So's your hair."

Taking her hand, he tugged her toward the ship hatch. She resisted, and he pulled hard, jolting her forward. Practically dragging her to the ramp, he backed up the incline until they were eye level. Sifting his hands through her hair, he cupped her face. She tried to jerk her head away, and he tightened his hold.

"Be still," he ordered, tracing her exotic cheekbones with his thumbs.

Her skin, tanned as golden as an Elysian sunset, was smooth and supple. He moved his thumbs to gently test the texture of her full lips. Then, their gazes locked, he started to lower his mouth to hers.

She hissed and he pulled back. "No bitin'," he warned. "I'll bite back."

Promised retribution kindled in her eyes. She was not a happy spacer. He might have to go into hiding when his cycle was up. It'd be worth it, though.

He again lowered his mouth to hers. Applied light pressure. Teased and nibbled.

Contact. Ignition. Lift-off.

He'd planned to go slow, to let her acclimate to male/female relations. But somehow they had rapidly progressed to major acceleration. Lionia took to kissing like a Shen to secrecy. Once she got the hang of the mechanics, she seized the lead, grabbing his hair and yanking him closer.

They wrestled to the floor just inside the hatch. Moments later, her soft growls of pleasure drifted on the air. "Oh . . . oh, oh, ooooh . . . By the gods! *Your hands!*"

Upon departing Nissar, Sabin immediately broadcast an alert to all his contacts, offering a hefty personal reward to anyone who could lead him to Galen. After that, he stared out the starboard portal, his face hard, his gaze distant. Moriah didn't attempt conversation.

They traveled for hours with an interminable silence heavy between them. She tried to concentrate on her computer screen, but the gruesome images from Nissar invaded her mind. She clenched her hands into fists, willing them away without success.

She suspected Sabin was experiencing the same images. Her stomach churned, thinking about what he must be going through. How could anyone forget such horror even once, much less twice?

Shuddering, Moriah checked her chronometer. It was way past time for the evening meal. She didn't care, having lost all appetite. Thankfully, the time signaled the close of the most awful cycle she'd ever experienced.

She rose from her chair, suspecting she'd never be able to sleep. "Sabin."

Silence met her address, and she wondered if

he'd heard her. "I'm turning in," she continued. "If you—if you need anything, let me know."

He didn't answer, his focus somewhere out in the vast expanse of space. She could find nothing else to say. How could mere words ease the horrors of today? Or the curse of being a Shielder, endlessly hated and hunted? She could only begin to imagine what Sabin's life must be like.

She went to her cabin, her heart heavy. Once there, she stepped out of her flightsuit, realizing for the first time that the stench of smoke and death had infiltrated the fabric. Sickened, she stuffed the suit into the refuse bin. She'd wear the rhapha before she'd ever touch the defiled garment again. Better yet, she'd borrow one of Sabin's flightsuits.

But first she had to get rid of the odor which clung to her skin and hair. She took a lengthy hot shower, ignoring the rules on water and electricity usage. After drying off, she eyed the rhapha draped across the chair. She felt certain Sabin would still be up. She'd ask to borrow a flightsuit now, so she wouldn't have to deal with it tomorrow.

She slipped into the tight rhapha, struggling to fasten the side closure. Then she wrapped the large scarf over her chest and headed for Sabin's cabin. She sounded the tone, getting no answer. He must still be in the cockpit. Perhaps that was for the best. She wouldn't intrude on him tonight; just help herself to a flightsuit and tell him about it tomorrow. Entering the cabin, she halted, surprised.

Sabin was slouched in his massive chair. His clothing appeared clean, and his hair looked damp. He must have showered. The torn, filthy flightsuit, bloodied from the carnage on Nissar, lay in a heap nearby.

"Excuse my intrusion," Moriah said. "You didn't answer the tone and I thought you were still in the cockpit. I just wanted to borrow one of your flight-suits and—" She faltered as Sabin swung his head toward her.

Pain radiated from the dark, despairing pools of his eyes. The stark desperation wound around her heart, squeezing until she couldn't breathe. Drawn like debris to a black hole, she went to him, sinking onto her knees before him. "I'm sorry," she whispered. "I can't imagine how you must feel."

His eyes locked with hers, colder than Atara's glaciers. He jerked his arm toward the recessed storage. "Take a flightsuit, then get out."

His agony pulled at her. She'd always had a soft spot for anyone in pain. Moriah placed her hand on his arm. "Sabin—" He knocked it away.

"You're right. You can't imagine," he rasped hoarsely. "Can't imagine watching your father, sister, mother being murdered; blasted to smithereens at close range. Can't imagine lying beneath the dead weight of your mother, who shielded you with her body, her blood running into your face. Hearing the screams, the pleas for mercy—" He broke off, pivoting away.

Sickened, Moriah leaned forward and slid her arms around him. "I'm sorry," was all she could say. He turned back, probably as stunned by her impulsive action as she was. Her heart pounding, she looked into his tormented eyes. She froze, time suspended, mesmerized by the smoldering emotions in his gaze.

Images—not of death this time, but of Sabin— flashed through her mind. Sabin, carrying the terrified boy in his arms, as carefully as if the child were more precious than gold, his big hands infinitely gentle . . . those same hands stroking her body, bestowing exquisite pleasure. Sabin, handing her the child, anguish pooling in his ebony eyes . . . those same midnight eyes burning with passion as his gaze roamed over her bare skin.

She raised her hand to his face.

His voice raw with torment, he whispered, "Help me, Moriah. Help me. Make me forget."

His need, his suffering, sparked a heated rush through her veins. She was sucked into an emotional maelstrom more powerful than any black hole.

"Sabin—" she began, but his mouth crushed down on hers, halting all words, shattering all barriers.

The universe tilted, and she slid her hands to his powerful biceps, holding on tightly in an effort to keep from free-falling into space. He groaned in need against her mouth, and she opened for him. He laved her tongue again and again. He kissed her with shattering absorption, as if she were the center of the universe, as if he couldn't get enough.

Shimmering sensations, provocative memories, swirled through her. Memories of that night in her cabin. Sabin, covering her body with his, touching her with stunning intimacy. His sexual, provocative whispers. *"Spirit, sweetheart, you're so incredibly responsive."*

Like a flash fire, her body responded to the flowing images, unfurling foreign desires. She couldn't think, couldn't get enough oxygen, twisting and aching and needing—

"Sabin," she gasped. "Please. . . ."

She didn't even know what she was asking for until his hands covered her breasts, stroking, teasing. "Is that better?" he whispered, his mouth hovering over hers.

Yes, oh yes! That's what she needed. "More," she

breathed, sealing her lips to his. With a little moan, she gave herself up to him.

Somehow, they moved to his bunk, entwined and sinking down together. Her scarf was gone and the top of the rhapha had been pushed down around her waist. Drugging her with kisses as he caressed one breast, Sabin slid the other hand along her leg to hike her skirt upward. He raised his head, leaving her bereft and wanting more. She framed his face with her hands, trying to urge him back, but he slid over her, moving down to press his mouth to her breast.

The cool air against her face brought a rush of sobriety. With it came acute awareness of Sabin covering her body, pressing her into the mat—weighing her down—No! Spirit, no! Talons of fear ripped through her. Uncontrollable, irrational terror. All physical arousal disintegrating, Moriah went into a panic.

New images blurred, formed. Pax, pushing her down, covering her mouth to silence her protests. Forcing himself on her. She had to get free. Had to breathe.

"No!" she screamed, struggling against Sabin. "Let me go! Let me up!" He rolled sideways, and she scrambled from the bunk, hampered by her bunched-up rhapha.

"Moriah! Whoa!" He came after her, grabbing her arm and turning her back, while she tried desperately to straighten her clothing. "What's wrong?"

Her heart pounded frantically, attempting to burst through her rib cage. Panic overwhelmed her. She struggled to free her arm, frustrated that the tight rhapha limited her mobility.

"Let me go! I can't do this. I can't!"

Maintaining his grip on her arm, Sabin stared

at her, confusion and frustration reflected in his eyes. His heaving chest and flushed skin, indications of his arousal, agitated her further.

"What—" he started, then stopped, a look of comprehension crossing his face. "Oh, Spirit," he groaned.

They both stood frozen, watching each other. Legs trembling, adrenaline pumping, Moriah waited warily for Sabin's next move.

"Blazing hells," he muttered finally, pulling her against him, enfolding her in his arms. He tightened his hold when she tried to squirm away. "Shhh. Stop it. I'm not going to hurt you. Spirit, I hurt enough for the both of us."

She felt his erection pressing against her. He was very aroused, which was bound to affect his behavior. If he was anything like Pax—

"I'm not Pax, Moriah. I'm not going to force you to do anything you don't want to do."

She couldn't talk about this. "Let me go back to my cabin."

"I will, soon." Resting his chin on top of her head, he released his breath in a heavy sigh.

Still trapped, she groaned her frustration against his chest. "I can't—"

"Hush. Just let me hold you. Please. I need that right now. I think you do, too."

The entreaty in his voice cut through the fear, calming her. He'd suffered as much in his life as she had in hers. His anguish and his need dissolved her resistance.

It did feel good, to have the heat of his body to warm her; the strength of his arms, the sincerity in his words to reassure her. To find a haven, no matter how brief, from the cruel reality of the world.

His large hand stroked her hair over and over in

a soothing rhythm. The panic receded and her breathing evened. As rational thought returned, she acknowledged to herself that he wasn't Pax, that he would not—

She couldn't even think the word. Even now, eight seasons later, she still couldn't say it, couldn't think about it. She wondered despairingly if she would ever be free of it.

"Does the panic occur mainly when you're held down, or when someone is on top of you?" Sabin asked quietly.

Spirit, he wanted to *talk* about it. Wanted to bring the ugliness out into the open. She wanted only to retreat to her cabin and try to reclose the wounds. But she sensed his unyielding perseverance, knew he wouldn't let her go until he got some response.

Reluctantly, she nodded against his chest. He was still aroused; she could feel the evidence against her abdomen. She tried to step back, but he held her captive. Slipping his hand beneath her chin, he raised her face to his.

"Did I hurt you the night you drugged me?"

The question brought back a heated rush of memory and sensation. Trying to ignore her body's response, she shook her head. "No."

His brows drew together, and she wondered if he could sense her physical reaction. "That's a start." His gaze held hers, determination shifting to a masculine intensity she knew well. His fingers captured her chin again, forcing her to maintain eye contact.

"Are my memories of that night correct? Was the encounter pleasurable for you?"

Flustered, she felt the heat creeping up her face. "I don't think anything can be accomplished discussing this. I want to go to my cabin."

"I have a better idea. Kiss me."

Startled, she stared at his sensuous lips, unsettled by the sudden warmth churning inside her. "I don't think that's a good idea."

Still holding her chin captive, he leaned down, his mouth hovering over hers. "Just a kiss, Moriah."

She hesitated, lured by the knowledge she had very much enjoyed his kisses—yet torn by the old fears that would give her no rest.

"Just a kiss," he whispered, his lips so close, he could steal her breath.

Then he did just that—claiming her mouth, laying siege with incredible gentleness, breaching her lips with erotic sweeps of his tongue. Sending her senses into orbit and her heart racing at full throttle.

The assault was teasing, tantalizing, until she was so caught up in his skillful seduction of her mouth, she leaned into the hard curve of his body and kissed him back.

He knew the exact second passion overrode fear—the moment when she pressed her lithe body against his and opened her mouth for him with a husky sigh. Sabin's senses went on full alert, the blood rushing to the lower extremities and leaving him almost incapable of rational thought. He battled for control, knowing he had to prove to Moriah that not all men were beasts.

Her tongue dueled boldly with his, and his blood pounded furiously through his veins. All his baser urges clamored to be satiated; they demanded he strip her down, taste every inch of her satiny skin, then bury himself deep inside her. Okay, so most males *were* beasts. But he'd be damned if he'd lose control—not now. Moriah deserved better than that.

Spirit, she deserved better than him. Period. He shouldn't be doing this. Getting involved with her was *not* a good idea . . . damn, her breasts felt good pressed against the solid wall of his chest.

His breathing was labored, his body overheated, aching for release. This is *not a good idea*, he repeated to himself, even as he explored the texture and taste of her mouth. Even as his hands moved of their own volition, slipping between them to cup the lush fullness of her breasts. Her small moan almost undid him.

Tearing himself away, he gulped in air and leaned back, staring down at her breasts as he stroked them. They swelled at his touch, the nipples pebbling. Then with a little cry, she grabbed his shoulders. To hell with ideas—good or bad. He tried to focus, to think of how they could mate without her feeling threatened.

"Moriah," he gasped. She met his gaze, her eyes reflecting the same desire threatening to incinerate him. Electricity arced between them.

"Take me," he said hoarsely. Ripping open his shirt, he fumbled out of it, tossing it aside. "Do what *you* want, sweetheart. Hold me down, lie on top of me. Whatever you want."

Her eyes widened and amazement swept across her face. *"What?"*

"Do it to me. Throw me on the bunk and have your way with me."

She opened her mouth, closed it. "You're crazy."

He reached for the closure of her rhapha. "Crazy with needing you." He opened it, and the gown slid to the floor. Moriah in all her natural glory took his breath away. She was perfect, firm and shapely in all the right places, her skin smooth and golden.

Before the heat of the moment deserted them and she panicked again, he drew her close, claiming her mouth. He slid his hands over her shoulders and down her graceful back, cupping her rear, feeling her flesh heat beneath his touch. Needing her to touch him the same way, he took her hands and placed them on his chest.

"Your turn," he said huskily.

She stared at him, her eyes burnished gold. Hesitant, she moved her palms down his chest. The feel of her warm hands on him was sweet torture. She traced the swells of muscle, circling one nipple with her finger. He didn't think he could take much more. Pulling away, he quickly discarded his boots and his pants.

He guided Moriah to the bunk. Tumbling down on his back, he pulled her on top of him. He held her face between his hands, locking his gaze with hers. "You call the shots, sweetheart. Touch me wherever you want, however you want. Tell me how you want me to touch you. Do this all your way."

Her eyes were misty, luminous. "Sabin," she whispered.

"Moriah," he whispered back.

Slowly, she lowered her mouth to his, her hair forming a silky curtain around them. Her tongue touched his, tentative at first, then becoming more aggressive. He slid his hands over her body, seeking out curves and contours, claiming and caressing until she was moaning into his mouth.

Hot lava flowed through every vein. He couldn't last much longer. He shifted, intending to end the torture for them both.

A sudden turbulence sent the ship listing sharply, hurling them both to the floor in a tangled heap. Alarm sirens blared from the corridor.

They were under attack.

Chapter Fourteen

"Are you okay?" Sabin asked, grabbing the bunk and scrambling up.

The ship righted itself, and he offered Moriah a hand. She waved him away and got to her feet by herself. "I'm fine."

He whirled toward his discarded clothing. "I'm going to find out what in the blazing hells just happened. Get to the cockpit as soon as you can. We might have to outrun some pirates."

He pulled on his pants and ran through the entry. In the corridor, the blare of the sirens was almost deafening. He shut them down, then entered the cockpit where he quickly activated his weapons control panel. Then he started the navigation unit searching for the nearest hyperspace entry.

There was no way a meteor had caused the impact pitching his ship. More likely a rocket, although he wouldn't know for sure until he assessed the damage. Since no follow-up strike ensued, he hoped it had only been a warning of some kind, not the first volley of an all-out attack. He flipped on the external scanners.

A fully armored Leor battleship cruised about five hundred meters off the port side. His heart almost arrested. By the Abyss! Whirling, Sabin switched off the weapons console. Any appearance of attempting to fire on a Leor ship was usually a fatal error.

They would blow his measly vessel to dust before he could get off a single torpedo. To outrun them, even with a nearby hyperspace entry, would be impossible. But why would Leors be after him? He wasn't anywhere near any of their territories.

The subspace transceiver beeped as Moriah slipped into the cockpit, dressed in one of Sabin's flightsuits. "Take a look," he said, gesturing toward the scanner. He reached for the transceiver. "Sabin Travers here."

There was some static, then an impervious, deep male voice commanded, "Show yourself!"

A Leor! How in the universe had they gotten his personal frequency? Sabin narrowed his eyes. If Galen was behind this—

"*Now*," roared the voice.

He turned on the videoviewer and found himself facing a massive, bare-chested Leor male. Behind him, Moriah gasped. Barely keeping his wits about him, Sabin made direct eye contact with the Leor, but held his silence.

Cold, obsidian eyes observed him for a nerve-wracking moment. Finally, the Leor spoke. "I am Commander Gunnar, Lord of the Dukkair clan. I demand to know the whereabouts of Captain Cameron."

"Captain Cameron?" In disbelief, Sabin turned toward Moriah. "What is going on here?"

Ignoring him, she stepped forward. "I'm here,

your Lordship. May a thousand suns shine favorably on you."

"Captain," Gunnar snapped, his black-ice eyes glittering. "You have not contacted us as agreed. I demand to know the status of—" He stopped, his gaze going to Sabin. "Tell him to leave."

Sabin's anger began to build. This was his ship, under threat from a race with which he'd never had any argument, and now he was being told to leave his own cockpit. He glared at Moriah, who had the audacity to suggest, "You'd better do what Commander Gunnar wishes."

It would be a cold day in the Abyss. No way was he deserting the cockpit. Not with Moriah on the inside, and Leors on the outside. He rose, advancing on her, his fists clenched to keep from throttling her. She held her ground, meeting his murderous glare.

"I'm not going anywhere," he growled, his voice pitched too low for the transceiver to pick up. "I'll be out of sight, but I'll be listening to every word. When this is over, you and I have a *lot* to discuss."

She glanced toward the figure waiting on the screen. "It would be best if you left. This business is private—"

"No!" he snarled. "Every transaction on this ship is my business. I deal harshly with those who deceive me and challenge my authority." He jerked his head toward the communicator. "Now deal with these Leors and get rid of them."

He stepped to the side, out of sight of the viewer. Moriah flipped her tangled hair over her shoulder and slid into his seat. "Okay, Commander," she said, her voice calm. "We can talk now. I assume you want to know about the iridon."

"Absolutely. We agreed that you would stay in contact with us. When you did not, we tracked your ship to this sector. You didn't answer our hails, forcing us to get your attention with a small photon blast."

A *small* blast? Sabin resisted the urge to stalk back to the weapons console and show these arrogant Leors the damage their *small* blast had inflicted. He glared at Moriah.

She glanced askance at him, then hastily looked back at Gunnar. "I'm sorry, Commander," she murmured. "We didn't hear your hail. We were . . . in another part of the ship. The iridon shipment is still on schedule."

The Leors were tracking his ship, asking about an iridon shipment. Sabin suddenly remembered his conversation with Celie in the prison. She had told him then that Moriah was involved in delivering an iridon shipment to the Leors. It had to be an illegal shipment, one which every pirate in the quadrant would be trying to hijack.

Not only was Moriah a fool for attempting such a dangerous deal, but she had managed to drag Sabin and his ship into it. He could just imagine trying to explain this to the Controllers, as they sent him to Alta for torture and execution. His anger threatened to teeter out of control.

"The shipment will be delivered to the sector I mentioned earlier, in about ten cycles," Moriah continued. "I don't know the exact location of the drop yet, but I'll contact you when I have that information."

"See that you do," Gunnar barked. "And answer our hails next time, or suffer more damage to your ship." The viewer went blank.

Sabin seethed. It was *his* ship, damn it! It might be a flying junk heap, but it was his. And he wouldn't tolerate any more of Moriah's shenanigans. First things first, however. Clamping his anger under control, he scanned the computer's damage report.

Fortunately, the destruction was minimal, damaging the side of one hold and causing a power outage there. The panel had automatically sealed to prevent decompression in the rest of the ship. Radd could repair it—if he could ever be found. The Leors had acted leniently.

But Moriah wouldn't get the same from him. He spun toward her.

Moriah rose from the pilot's seat and watched Sabin review the damage. She briefly entertained the thought of fleeing the cockpit and his certain wrath, but knew there was nowhere she could hide.

She was no longer a young girl who could cower in a dark storage unit, hoping to avoid a confrontation with a drunken father. She was no longer an indentured slave, helpless to defend herself or Celie, except with sexual acquiescence.

She'd learned to face adversity head on, to stand and fight. She would never again be a victim. Tensing for battle, she took a step back as Sabin advanced on her, his eyes flashing.

"What in the blazing hells do you think you're doing?" he roared. "This is *my ship*! My ship, which was just attacked and damaged because of *you*. Not to mention stolen by you and used to transport contraband through the quadrant. *My ship!*"

He radiated fury. An image of her father's face, twisted with drink and rage, rose in Moriah's mind. She tried to take another step back, but the wall halted her.

"You didn't give me any choice in the matter. You forced me to stay on *your* ship."

A vein throbbed in Sabin's temple. "Because you stowed away without my permission. All you had to do was ask for help on Calt, and none of this would have happened. No, I take that back. Any involvement with you is disaster."

"I'm just trying to survive."

"Survive? By dealing with the Leors and smuggling iridon? Are you *crazy*? Smuggling illegal goods is not survival—it's suicide."

He pressed both hands to the wall on either side of her head. "Have you ever stopped to consider the consequences should you fail or get caught by the authorities?"

Moriah raised her chin. "I can take care of myself."

He leaned closer, his breath warm on her face. "You may think you're tough, but you're not, lady. Believe me, either failure or capture will result in your death—but not right away. The Leors have been known to torture their enemies for days before execution. So have the Controllers. And if the Anteks ever got their claws on your sweet hide, they'd make Pax's assaults look like an enjoyable interlude in a Pleasure Dome."

He managed to target the very fears which plagued her in the darkest moments of the night. She knew the risks, but she had no choice, Celie and the others on Risa depended on her.

"We all do what we have to."

His jaw clenching, Sabin grabbed her shoulders. "What does it take to get through to you?"

Her chest tightened. Threats, physical force—the old pattern. "You don't need to concern yourself. This has nothing to do with you."

Releasing her abruptly, he stepped back and raked a hand though his hair. "Oh, I see. We're not really together on my ship and a Leor battle cruiser didn't just attack us."

"We weren't attacked. Just contacted."

He rolled his eyes and fell against the wall, banging his head back in abject frustration. Rubbing her arms, Moriah sidled away. The heat of the moment eased, and reality intruded. He knew about the iridon shipment. Even though he didn't know the exact sector in which the drop would be made, he could disrupt her plans considerably.

"What are you going to do now?" she asked.

He sighed heavily and banged his head again. "Damned if I know." He drew several deep breaths. His fists relaxed, and the tension seemed to leave his body.

He swept her with an assessing gaze, then said with some exasperation, "Look, I may be angry, but I'm not going to hit you or force myself on you, if that's what you're worried about."

His blunt words shocked her momentarily, then an amazing realization came to her. She believed him. That knowledge shook her to the core.

She believed him.

He was obnoxious, belligerent, and maddeningly unyielding, but he had yet to hurt her. Not even in the throes of rage—and he had been furious with her on several occasions. Yet not once had he harmed her, although he'd had ample opportunity.

With another jolt, she knew, *really knew*, Sabin Travers was a man of his word.

She was safe with him.

The pressure in her chest eased. Her trepidation dissolved. She felt oddly lighthearted. But the adrenaline remained, heightening her senses, pulsing into an altogether different reaction.

Staring into Sabin's midnight eyes, she remembered the feel of his lips against hers, his touch branding her body. Despite the dire warnings about males from her friends on Risa, despite her own bitterness, she wanted to again experience the passion and pleasure he had shown her.

Her breathing and heart rate accelerated, a molten rush of desire flooding her body. His earlier, heated words echoed in her mind. *"Take me. Do what you want, sweetheart. . . . Whatever you want."*

What she wanted was to be free of Pax's legacy, no longer bound by crippling memories. To find nirvana, no matter how fleeting, in Sabin's arms.

Taking a deep breath, she leaped into the Abyss. "It wouldn't be force," she whispered.

His eyes narrowing, he stepped toward her. "What?"

Placing both hands on his chest, she pushed him against the wall.

He grabbed her wrists. "Moriah—"

The protest died abruptly when she pressed a kiss against his bare chest. His heart thundered beneath her mouth.

"I said," she murmured, running her tongue over his nipple, "it won't be against my will."

He appeared to stop breathing. "I think I'm hallucinating."

She pulled her hands free and slid them to his shoulders, pressing herself against him. "Does this feel real?"

He groaned. "You're making it very hard for me to stay mad."

"Please don't be angry. Doesn't this feel good?"

He raised his arms, hesitated. "Ah, what's the use?" he muttered, wrapping his arms around her. "Feels like I've died and gone to Haven."

"Take me with you," she whispered.

His hands slid up, cupping her face. His jet-black gaze locked with hers, delving into her soul—probing, searching, seeking out her innermost secrets.

"Tell me," he ordered softly. "Tell me exactly what you want."

Her heart hammered in her chest. She had no experience with mating games, didn't know how to communicate with a lover. She bit her lip, wanting this, but daunted by the intimacy Sabin demanded.

"Tell me, Moriah. No games, no secrets, between us."

No, she didn't want anything between them. No barriers, no clothing. Only flesh to flesh.

"I want you to touch me," she whispered. "I want the pleasure you gave me in my cabin. I want to mate with you."

His eyes darkened. "That's good," he murmured hoarsely. "Because I want the same thing."

He ran a finger along the seam of her flightsuit, then beneath it, sliding it open. Slowly, he eased the fabric from her shoulders. Cool air rushed over her, but his heated perusal of her body made her skin feel like it had been seared by a laser. His fingers teased one breast, circling the nipple lightly.

"Sabin," she groaned, trying to press into his hand.

He glanced up, his intense gaze paralyzing her. His hand closed over her breast, kneading, caressing, giving her the contact she craved. But it was her face he watched, passion sparking in his eyes as he observed her reaction.

Cupping the back of her head with his other hand, anchoring his fingers in her hair, he dragged her against him. His mouth settled over hers, deliberate, determined. He kissed her hard, letting her taste his need.

His hand slid from her breast to her back, slipping beneath her flightsuit and cupping her buttocks to mold her tighter against him. Surprisingly, she welcomed his aggression, welcomed the feel of his body. This wasn't the painful hold of force, but the embrace of mutual desire.

Desire that spiraled out of control when his fingers slid between her legs. His intimate touch sent shockwaves through her lower body, sensations so intense, she trembled.

When her legs gave out, he swung her into his arms and carried her to his bunk. He stripped away her suit, then his pants, coming down on the mat beside her.

He launched an all-out seduction then, kissing and caressing his way down her body. His hair trailed over her skin, a silken whisper of sensation. Even in the throes of passion, she sensed the care he took with her, felt the tenderness of his touch.

Parting her thighs, he slid his hands upward with excruciating slowness, causing her breath to hitch in expectation. His fingers found her feminine flesh, claimed her with searing intimacy. Coherent thought fled beneath the onslaught of pleasure.

Need, frantic and sharp, pounded through her veins, filling every cell, sparking in her lower body. She inhaled Sabin's intoxicating, masculine scent. Every sense seemed acutely attuned to him, to the feel of his skin beneath her hands, the taste of his mouth.

She opened herself completely to his touch, tension beginning to coil within her. She was poised on the brink of shattering into a billion atoms, but he refused to give her that experience. He tore his mouth from hers, his breathing harsh.

"Sweetheart, lift yourself over me."

Moriah levered up on her elbow, trying to find equilibrium and a semblance of control. Throwing Sabin a challenging glance, she lowered her mouth to his chest and pressed kisses over it.

"I thought I was calling the shots," she murmured. "You said I was in charge."

"That's fine unless I die first," he groaned.

She laughed, intoxicated by her sensual power, and slid over him.

"Lift up a little," he instructed. "I'll help you."

She poised above him, about to enter territory that had been dark and terrifying the other times she'd been there. She hesitated, uncertainty and fear flaring.

"Moriah. Look at me."

Panic beginning to edge out passion, she met his discerning gaze. Understanding and compassion burned in his eyes. "It's me—Sabin. Focus on me."

This is Sabin.

His hands on her hips gently urged her down. She braced her hands against his shoulders as he slowly pushed upward. Dark memories eclipsed the pleasure. Panic reared and she tensed.

"Stay with me, sweetheart."

She forced air into her lungs, and he filled her completely. Clenching her eyes shut, she tried to push away the memories.

"Look at me, Moriah."

She willed her eyes open, dragged her gaze to his—black, molten orbs which mesmerized, commanded.

This is Sabin. Not Pax. Sabin.

"You're beautiful," he told her hoarsely. "So beautiful. I need you. Stay with me."

His words flowed over her like a healing balm.

The tightness around her heart eased, and she moved with the urging of his hands. She felt no pain. Just fullness and a beckoning twinge of pleasure. His hands slid over her, caressing, comforting, tantalizing. She found herself moving freely now, found her inner muscles tightening, anticipating.

He stroked between her legs, unerringly finding the sensitive nub there. Sensation streaked through her every nerve ending. Her eyes closing, she threw back her head.

"No. Focus on me, Moriah."

Slowly, she opened her eyes again, met his heated gaze. He kept stroking, until the need for completion became overwhelming, until her movements matched his. An exhilarating sense of freedom buoyed her. All else faded except sensation and Sabin's face, his glittering eyes, his husky encouragement.

This is Sabin.

"Let go, Moriah. Fly with me."

Oh, Spirit, she was coming apart, exploding into particles, hurtling through space. She cried out, rocked by tremor after tremor, then felt Sabin surge beneath her with his own hoarse cry. Buffeted until all energy was depleted, every muscle weak, she collapsed on him.

They lay that way awhile, their labored breathing the only sound in the room. Finally he shifted, sliding her to his side. He cradled her against him, tucking her head beneath his chin.

"Are you okay?" he asked quietly.

She felt like she'd been shot with a stunner, although her body tingled with pleasurable aftershocks. An emotional tumult raged within. The dark chains of shame seemed to burst and fall away. She felt joyous, free, somehow cleansed.

She also experienced a deep sense of bonding with Sabin, along with gratitude, and some deeper emotions she didn't want to face. So many feelings, positive yet overwhelming in their intensity. Hot tears overflowed and tracked down her cheeks, despite her effort to keep them contained.

"Ah, sweetheart." Sabin shifted and cradled her face in his hands. "Did I hurt you?"

"No. Of course not." He certainly had to know she had enjoyed it. She'd held back nothing from him. Mortified now, she tried to break free of his grasp, hating for him to see this unusual weakness. She never cried.

Stubborn male that he was, he wouldn't let her hide. "Then what is it?"

She clenched her eyes shut. "It's just that all these thoughts and feelings are jumbled up inside."

He relented and let her take refuge, and she burrowed against him. "I think I understand," he murmured, stroking her hair. "Kind of like an emotional meltdown."

Moriah relaxed, soothed by his touch and the comfort of his body. For the moment, she felt utterly safe. Here, in the security of Sabin's arms, the past, the Leors, all the concerns of being solely responsible for an entire colony, seemed very distant.

She batted at the tears still seeping from beneath her closed lids. "I hate to be like this."

"Hey." He shifted again, leaned close. "It's okay to cry." His lips pressed against her eyelids, then followed the tracks of her tears. "I cried a lot after my family was murdered."

What other way could a young boy deal with such pain? She took his hand and held it tightly.

He paused a moment, then fell back, rolling her

against his side. "Only when I was alone, though. Shielders don't like to show emotion in front of other Shielders. I stayed in so many different homes, I never considered myself a part of any family. So I wouldn't show my feelings around anyone."

"How old were you when your family . . . when it happened?"

"Six seasons. Old enough to know what was going on, but too little to be of any use. I blamed myself for a long time. Thought I'd done something wrong, was being punished by having my family taken away."

Her heart ached for the suffering of a boy, for the pain still reflected in the man's voice. "How horrible for you."

He shrugged. "Others have suffered a lot worse. At least I didn't fall into the hands of slavers. Growing up, I had enough to eat and shelter from the elements. Now, I have this ship. Even though it's old and broken down, it's mine."

He lapsed into silence, and she suspected his thoughts traveled a disturbing path. It was odd how quickly they'd gone from high peaks of wild abandon back to bleak uncertainty. Damn the Controllers, and the Anteks and shadowers who worked for them. Power and greed were all they cared about. They were responsible for the rampant misery and suffering that seemed to rule everywhere.

As far as Moriah knew, the Shielders had never caused any problems. Their only crime was their ability to resist Controller mind domination. For that, they'd been driven from their homes, imprisoned, tortured, and murdered.

The Shielders weren't the only citizens suffering under Controller rule. The high taxes levied on all goods sold and wages earned made it nearly impossible for any average being to survive beyond a minimal existence. Only those providing illegal goods and services, or working directly for the Controllers, could recognize material gains.

With so many dependent on her, Moriah had been forced to enter the dangerous arena of smuggling to make ends meet. And she'd done quite well. But now, if she failed to get the iridon delivered . . . She wouldn't fail—she couldn't. But to ensure her success, she'd have to make sure Sabin didn't interfere.

A deep weariness weighed upon her. At some point, she'd have to deal with what had just transpired between them, but she was too depleted to do so now.

"You're very quiet. What are you thinking about?" he asked.

She pushed herself up, brushing her hair away from her face. Staring down at him, into eyes as black and infinite as space, she felt an alarming surge of tenderness. She wanted to smooth the lines of grief and pain from his face, to run her fingers through the dark tangles of his hair.

This would never do. She couldn't afford involvement with any man. Exhaustion was affecting her judgment. Distance and rest would restore clarity.

"I'm really tired," she said, scooting to the edge of the bunk. "We both need some sleep."

As she swung her legs off the bunk, a strong arm snaked around her waist and dragged her back. "Running away?" Sabin asked softly.

"What?" Indignant, she whirled around. "I never—"

He pulled her down, pinning her with his arm and a well-muscled leg. "I'll attribute your lack of

270

manners to general ignorance of mating etiquette."

"Lack of manners?" she screeched, pulling back her arm to slug him.

He grabbed her wrist with his other hand. She tried to jerk free, but his grip was like a steel vise. Then he had the nerve to grin at her like a Vilana banshee. "We still need to work on them."

Thoroughly irritated, she squirmed beneath him. "No, we do not. Let me up!"

"Moriah, Moriah," he sighed. He lowered his mouth and swirled his tongue over her earlobe. "Relax. Don't take everything so seriously."

She shivered, trying to ignore the sensations the moist heat stirred. "I'd never take you seriously, Travers. Now, if you don't mind, I'd like to go to my cabin."

"Oh, but I do mind. You see, I get highly insulted when I have a beautiful, sexy bed partner who tries to bolt from my bunk."

She pulled back to glare at him, but the mischievous glint in his eyes diffused her indignation. As much as she hated to admit it, she found his roguish behavior charming. But she'd walk barefoot on scalding energy stones before she'd ever admit it to him.

"I'm not bolting from your bunk," she retorted. "I'm exhausted, Travers. I need some rest."

"Oh, yeah?" he gloated, radiating pure male satisfaction. "Wonder how you got so tired?"

"I'm sure I don't know."

He threw his head back and laughed. Her heart considerably lighter, she felt the oppressive, negative energy of the day's events dissipating. Trying not to smile, she shoved against his chest. "Let me up."

"Stay with me tonight, Moriah." His voice

turned serious, and he entwined his fingers with hers. "We're both worn out. I just want to hold you while we sleep."

Spirit, but it sounded tempting. She knew only too well how dark the night hours could get, when all was quiet and there were no distractions to keep fears and doubts, loneliness and painful memories at bay. When there was nothing—or no one—to turn to for reassurance and comfort.

She also knew these moments with Sabin were just fleeting whirlwinds of time which would cease when they reached Elysia. Yet she wanted to hold them close. To savor them to the fullest. *Just for tonight*, she told herself.

Just for tonight.

She allowed him to gather her against his side. Resting her head on his chest, she listened to the reassuring thud of his heart and his deep, even breathing. Cocooned in his warmth and quiet strength, she drifted into a deep, dreamless sleep.

She woke some time later, finding herself curled against Sabin. He lay sprawled on his back, one arm thrown behind his head, the other across his body. The auto lights hadn't turned on, so it was still sleep shift. Drowsy, she watched the rise and fall of his chest, remembering the passion they had shared, her surprising lack of modesty or restraint.

She stared at the strong hand resting against a washboard belly, lifting with each breath. Reaching out, she skimmed her fingers over Sabin's hand. How gently he had touched her, how sensuously. Her caress ventured across his powerful chest, tracing the swells of muscle beneath the taut skin. He was beautifully built, masculine and solid.

A hand cupped her face. Sabin rolled to his side,

his eyes locked with hers. Her breath caught. He didn't speak, but then he didn't have to. The current sparking between them communicated their mutual attraction far better than words.

She tilted up her face. His mouth descended on her lips, warm, firm, demanding. With a small sound of pleasure, she sank back on the mat, pulling him down and deepening the kiss. He shifted, looming over her, but not pressing on her.

His hand slid down her, slow, confident, devastating. All drowsiness vanished, her body awakening in a heated rush. How could mere touch render so much pleasure, she wondered, arching into his caresses. Her breasts swelled beneath his palm, the nipples coaxed into hard nubs by his knowledgeable fingers.

Then he moved lower, and anticipation coiled inside her as his hand smoothed over her abdomen, through the auburn curls, finally claiming her most intimate, sensitive flesh. She gasped, tearing her mouth from his. Breathing raggedly, she stared into his glittering eyes.

"Are you sore?" he asked, his voice low and dark.

"I—I don't think so."

"Good." His finger probed, slipping inside her. "Do you want this, Moriah?" He stroked deeply. Heat and moisture pooled there as her body clenched around his finger. An unfamiliar wildness unleashed inside her, pulsing through her.

"What do you think?" she whispered shakily. She did some touching of her own, exploring the hard planes of his chest and abdomen. Boldly, she wrapped her fingers around his own stiffly aroused flesh.

He sucked in his breath. "Spirit!"

Amazed at the feel of him, she stroked him until

he stopped her. Ignoring her protest, he entwined his fingers with hers and pressed their hands against the mat.

"This is going way too fast," he murmured, lowering his face to press kisses down her neck. "I want to take it slow this time."

She shivered as his lips moved down her breast. "I don't . . . know if I can take it . . . slow."

He laughed. "Let me know when you want me to stop, sweetheart. Until then, I'm all yours."

His mouth covered her nipple and she forgot about everything but the sensations inundating her body. And when he finally lay back on the bunk, allowing her to take control, she knew just what to do.

Chapter Fifteen

Moriah watched as Sabin replicated the morning meal. Odd how putting on clothing seemed to raise barriers. Their conversation had been stilted and awkward since they left his cabin. But in his bunk . . . there had been no holding back. She flushed, remembering her total abandonment. He had given her free rein, allowing her to guide their mating.

More importantly, he'd given her back her soul; freed her from the chains of shame, from the clutches of Pax's degrading legacy. Even so, she had no delusions about a relationship between them. With her responsibilities, that would never be possible. She would always be grateful to him for helping her break free of the past, but she knew their paths must part after they reached Elysia.

As soon as their agreement was met, she must make arrangements to get the iridon—or lose her life. Surely Sabin understood the desperation spurring her to follow such a risky path. He'd told her he carried deliveries for the Controllers. Only an evil or very desperate person would have anything to do with them. Knowing Sabin better now, she chose to assume he had good reasons for his actions. Besides, agents performed a variety of services for the Controllers which weren't necessarily bad—from acting as envoys to other cultures, to carrying supplies to distant outposts, to checking on colonies that had lost touch.

Sabin probably just delivered supplies. She suspected he worked for the Controllers to get money to aid Shielder colonies. He could travel freely throughout the quadrant that way, in relative safety. And unless they performed a special blood test, the Controllers would never know he was one of the very breed they despised. He was hiding out in the open.

Yet, despite her growing respect for him, despite her belief he had good reasons for his actions, she still wondered if she could truly trust Sabin. She wanted to, but old doubts, long ingrained by bitter experience, made her cautious.

Thus her main concern. She still didn't know what Sabin might do to interfere with the iridon delivery. Since he knew about it, she saw no sense in ignoring the issue. It was time to deal with it.

"I have to make that iridon pickup," she stated bluntly.

He pivoted around from the replicator. "It's too dangerous."

"It's far too late to worry about that," she argued. "The deal is already arranged. It's not like this is the first time I've made a delivery to the Leors."

His eyes narrowing, he strode to the table. "Then you're a fool. Smuggling the usual contraband is dangerous enough. It's no business for a woman. Smuggling iridon or dealing with the Leors is incredibly risky. Doing both is downright insane."

"Being a woman has nothing to do with it," Moriah argued. "I can fight and pilot a ship as well as any man. And I can talk my way out of many situations a man couldn't."

"What? Dressed in your rhapha? What happens if you meet up with someone like Pax? Admit it. There are situations where brute strength counts."

He really knew how to hit her where it hurt. She rose from the chair and wheeled away from him. "Pax has nothing to do with this."

He cursed and caught her arm. "I didn't mean to throw that at you."

"Let me go!"

"Not until I talk some sense into that thick head of yours." He pulled her back to the chair. "Sit." She glared at him, and he threw up his hands. "All right. Stand then."

He ran his fingers through his hair. "I apologize for the comment about Pax. But I was trying to make a point. You are a good fighter, Moriah. You're smart and you're brave, but because you're a woman, you're at a physical disadvantage with most men."

She'd been at a physical disadvantage most of her life. She didn't need Sabin to point that out to her. "I have to do what is necessary to survive. If you want to talk about danger, consider what will happen if I *don't* make that delivery."

"I know. I have thought about it. I guess you'll have to follow through on the deal."

"Then you won't tell anyone about the iridon?"

He heaved a sigh, obviously not happy with the situation. "Probably not. Blazing hells, I wish I could go with you. But I have to find Galen." His face hardened into the menacing mask of a predator. "He'll pay for his crimes."

A pall settled over the galley. Images of Nissar resurrected, and Moriah shuddered. The night left behind hadn't banished the horror, simply held it at bay for a few short hours.

"I'm not hungry," she said.

Sabin clenched his hands, his body rigid. "Neither am I." With a violent curse, he whirled and slammed the replicator closed. "Damn Galen's black soul for all eternity!"

They spent the rest of the day in the cockpit, much as they had the evening before—in silence. The only spoken words came from Sabin sending out another broadcast regarding Galen and checking with his contacts. No one had seen the criminal. For now, it seemed, he had vanished like vapor.

As the day passed, Moriah tried to focus on formulating foolproof plans for the pickup, but other thoughts sabotaged her efforts. Nissar, Sabin, images of them entwined in passion. Resolute, she'd force her focus back to the iridon, only to have it wander away again.

Midday came and went, sliding into evening shift. They still hadn't eaten, neither one hungry. Finally, Sabin leaned back, rubbing his eyes wearily. "Spirit, what a day."

Sabin remained silent for several moments, staring straight ahead, and she suspected he was thinking about something. Finally, he got to the point. "Moriah, we need to discuss your deals with the Leors."

Oh, great. Back to that. "No we don't," she responded. "I haven't pried into your business dealings and I expect you to stay out of mine."

"I wouldn't pry if you exhibited good sense.

What you're doing is totally foolhardy."

"Butt out, Travers."

His eyes narrowed, flashed fire. "I want your word that this will be your last deal with the Leors."

"You have no right to dictate how I live my life."

"Someone has to, before you get yourself killed."

She glared at him, seeing the sheer determination etched on his face. He meant to curtail her activities, which she would never allow. What would happen when she left him behind? He might turn her in to the Controllers, though she doubted he would.

He still didn't know the location of the iridon delivery, and the quadrant was huge. He couldn't possibly disrupt the deal. She'd make a break from him after she saw the healer tomorrow. Roanne should already be on her way to Elysia to meet her.

The probability of ever crossing paths again with Sabin was very unlikely. Regret and a jumble of unfamiliar emotions swept through her.

"I can take care of myself," she insisted.

He growled in frustration. "Very few people can hold their own against the Leors. Smuggling is a dangerous business, period. I'm worried about your safety, Moriah. I don't want anything to happen to you."

Sabin's concern touched her more than she liked to admit. Warmth flowed through her veins, thickening her blood. By the fires, he was attractive. And compassionate and honorable and . . . very appealing.

Her body began to feel heavy, languid. Heated yearnings coiled and beckoned. Funny, but she could think of things she'd much rather do than talk about something that was never going to happen.

Her newfound feminine power lent her a startling boldness. She rose and moved to Sabin. "Shut up, Travers." Shoving him back against his chair, she leaned over him. She brushed her lips against his and whispered, "Why don't you use your mouth for something constructive?"

One thing she liked about Sabin Travers—he wasn't one to let opportunities pass him by. She found herself yanked onto his lap, his lips fastened hungrily on hers. He rapidly dispensed with her shirt; she got his partway off.

She couldn't believe how quickly desire had displaced her sexual fears, how quickly passion escalated into an inferno. She'd never known it could be like this, never realized the craving to be touched and possessed grew with each sensual encounter. She'd never known need could be so intense, so urgent. She'd never imagined her skin could become so highly sensitized, burning for Sabin's touch.

With a cry, she arched back, offering herself to his hands and mouth. He took full advantage, fueling the flames. A mating fever possessed her, hot and wild. She straddled him, pressing kisses on his chest, his neck, his face. Her hands slid over him, down his belly, scraping along his thighs. His chest heaved when she caressed the bulge straining against his pants. Undoing the front seam, she slid her hand inside.

"Oh, Spirit," he groaned. "Sweetheart, slow down."

His arousal throbbed against her hand. He needed her as much as she needed him. "I can't," she whispered, stroking him. "I want you inside me—*now*."

"I like a woman who gets straight to the point," he gasped, his breathing labored.

He dragged her to her knees, tugging her pants down, finally ripping them to get them out of the way. She slid over him, and he entered her in one blazing thrust.

She gripped his shoulders, giving herself over to the fever. It was fast, it was frenzied, and she gloried in it. Sabin held her securely, safely, through the tempest.

He held her afterwards, too, as their bodies cooled and their breathing calmed. And later, he held her again, as they lay in his bunk, satiated and tired.

She stayed awake a long time, listening to the steady beat of his heart, to his deep, even breathing. She committed his warmth and strength to memory.

Tomorrow they would reach Elysia. This could well be their last night together.

"That's great news, Nealon," Sabin said. "We'll meet you there in about half an hour."

Only half-listening to the conversation, Moriah stared out the portal. Elysia was as beautiful as always, the sun shining, the palms swaying gently in the breeze. This was it—the end of their journey. One more cycle, and she'd be on her way to pick up the iridon. Away from Sabin. Her chest tightened, but she shoved away all sentiment. She could never allow a man into her life. *Never*.

Sabin's hand on her waist pulled her back from her thoughts. "Ready to go?"

Taking a breath, she nodded. They stepped through the hatch and into a virtual paradise. The balmy breeze caressed them, carrying the mouth-watering smells of food from the nearby marketplace. The sound of chimes floated through the air, along with the babble of hundreds of voices.

Surprising her, Sabin took her hand and tucked it inside his much warmer one. He whistled jauntily as they strolled toward the marketplace. She glanced askance at him. "You're certainly in a good mood."

He inhaled the fragrant air and squeezed her hand. "Yep. I'm debating how much of your mind to have altered. I was thinking of having Darya delete the obstinate, hardheaded parts of your nature."

Moriah tensed. She didn't find him at all amusing. Knowing very little about memory alteration, she was apprehensive about the procedure.

She halted, trying to withdraw her hand. "That's not funny, Travers. I don't want anyone tampering with my mind. Unless you can give me some guarantees, I won't go anywhere near your damn healer!"

He turned toward her, his expression now serious. "You're really nervous about this, aren't you?" He brushed her cheek with his knuckles. "I didn't think you were afraid of anything."

Only a fool would be ignorant of the dangers in the world. She'd seen too many things in the quadrant that inspired fear, or at least a healthy respect. But she had learned admitting fear could be seen as a weakness.

She brushed away Sabin's hand. "I'm not. I just don't know anything about the procedure."

"It's simple and painless. Darya will erase only your knowledge of the colony's location. I'll be there the entire time, and I'll make sure that's all she does."

"*That's* reassuring," Moriah muttered. "How does Darya do this feat?"

"She uses a mild drug, along with a form of hypnosis that mimics psionic brain waves. While you're hypnotized, she'll instruct you to forget the colony and its location. Then she'll give you suggestions which will block any attempt, including Controller probes, to force you to remember."

It sounded simple enough. Moriah had given her word and didn't intend to back down now. "Let's get it over with, then."

"Good idea." Sabin started off again, her hand still clasped in his. "We have one stop to make first."

Suspicion reared. "What?"

He grinned mysteriously. "Show you when we get there."

Rolling her eyes, Moriah gave up on retrieving her hand and decided to enjoy the market. She had traded at Elysia on several occasions, but each time she visited, she was fascinated anew with the masses of people and the amazing store of goods available. This time was no different, and she avidly took in the sights and sounds.

The one area she preferred to avoid was Slavers Square, where the slaves were sold. The sight of the huddled, shackled beings, children included, sickened her, reminding her of her time with Pax.

Sabin appeared to feel the same way, as he took a path that detoured around the square. Or perhaps he liked passing by the Pleasure Domes, which happened to be in the direction they took.

He certainly seemed to enjoy watching the female dancers outside the Domes. Dressed in sheer silks leaving very little to the imagination, they writhed erotically and beckoned passersby to come inside and sample the myriad pleasures available. Undaunted by Moriah's presence, one well-endowed brunette approached Sabin and shimmied up against him. He didn't seem to mind her advances at all.

Moriah narrowed her eyes. Lightning bolts of anger sparked, much to her shock. She wasn't jealous, she told herself. Just irritated with Sabin's behavior. She tried to jerk her hand free and leave the idiot to his dark-haired prostitute. They deserved each other.

Laughing, he extricated himself from the clinging female. His jovial mood was starting to get on Moriah's nerves.

"Jealous?" he asked, tugging her along the path.

"No!" she snapped. "Disgusted."

Still grinning, he swung around and pulled her against him. "You put those females to shame, sweetheart. Especially when you're wearing your rhapha." Lifting her chin, he brushed his lips against hers. Her heart skittered. "Or better yet," he whispered, "when you're wearing nothing at all."

Desire unfurled, sending a firestorm through her body. Her immediate, wanton response to him alarmed her. She didn't want this sensual pull between them, didn't want him to have such power over her. She started to object as he kissed her, but that only granted his tongue entry. Giving in, she kissed him back. She'd be far away by this time tomorrow. Then the ties would be severed, and she'd no longer be affected by him.

Ending the kiss, he raised his head. "Hold that thought," he said, his gaze hot with unspoken promises. Taking her hand again, he strode on.

They left the Domes behind, turning along a path that, according to the direction monitor, led to the shipyard.

Confused, Moriah asked, "Is Darya near here?"

"No, she's on the other side of Slaver's Square."

He quickened his pace, and she struggled to keep up. "Then why are we going this way?"

"To see my new ship."

"Your new ship?" She stopped dead in her tracks, gaping at him.

He beamed, more excited than she'd ever seen him. "Yep. *My new ship*. There it is."

She looked where he pointed. Surely he didn't mean the large Skymaster dead ahead. Skymasters were the finest ships made, the sturdiest, the fastest, top of the line—and extremely expensive.

Sabin strode straight to the craft in question. A man lounging against the side straightened and came forward to greet them. Tall and burly with a shock of red hair, he wore a metallic gold flight-suit with the Skymaster logo imprinted across the front.

He extended his hand. "Sabin!"

Sabin shook the proffered hand. "Nealon. Good to see you." His gaze scanned the ship. "She's beautiful."

Nealon nodded politely to Moriah, then stepped beside Sabin. He folded his arms across his beefy chest as he perused the ship. "Yep, she's a beaut, all right. Wait 'til you see the inside. Built exactly to your specs. Looks great."

This was a custom ship? Amazed, Moriah studied the sleek lines and the royal-blue lettering emblazoned over the silver-blue metal. It was an SC-8400, a long-range cruiser about twice the size of Sabin's old craft.

She followed behind the two men as they walked its perimeter. The vessel was impressive, but Sabin's reaction interested her more. Reaching out to touch different external components, he glowed with pride. Not that she blamed him, considering the junker he'd been flying. But how could he possibly afford a ship such as this?

When they approached the hatch, Nealon drew back. "Go on in and check her out. Take all the time you want. I'll wait for you at the office. We'll settle the final payment after you make sure everything is to your satisfaction."

Moriah followed Sabin aboard, consumed by curiosity. "I didn't know you were getting a new ship. Not that you didn't need one."

"It's been in the works for a while now."

He looked down the long corridor, immense satisfaction etched on his face. Strolling along, he inspected tiles, moldings, and control pads, then stepped inside each of the compartments. She walked behind him, taking it all in.

On the port side, there were two spacious cabins, each with their own lav. The roomy galley had state-of-the-art appliances, including a preprogrammed replicator. "That's a good thing," Moriah teased. "No more protein sticks and amargrain."

Sabin grinned like a Shen who'd stumbled across a hidden treasure, then stepped back out into the corridor. They retraced their steps, examining the starboard side. Three more compartments, much smaller than the other cabins, opened off this side.

"Are these for storage?" she asked.

He hesitated. "Not exactly. I'm going to check out the cockpit." He headed toward the front of the ship.

Curious, she explored one compartment. It had a narrow bunk, but no shelves and no lav. No, wait—recessed hygiene facilities were across from the bunk. An ugly suspicion reared, but she refused to accept it. She walked to the entry and looked for the inside control pad. *There wasn't one.*

Trepidation slithering through her, she stepped into the corridor and studied the control unit there. She pushed one pad, expecting the panel to close. No panel slid out. Instead, a low hum, and faint, greenish waves shimmered in the opening. A force field.

A brig. Moriah stumbled back, her heart pounding. Surely she was wrong. She glanced toward the other two compartments. They had identical control pads. *Three brigs?* No one would have need of brigs, unless . . . they were carrying prisoners.

Only two types of ships regularly carried prisoners—Controller transport ships, taking felons en masse from regional prisons and star bases to the main prison on Alta, or . . . a ship belonging to a shadower.

A shadower. Sabin a shadower? No! Her lungs constricted, and she battled for air. He couldn't be. She sagged against the wall, fighting swiftly rising panic.

Think, Moriah, think. She forced herself to take a breath, forced her mind to calm and sort facts. Sabin had done nothing to indicate he was a shadower. He hadn't transported any prisoners—at least not while she was with him. She hadn't seen any of the familiar offender reports regularly issued from Alta, or a brig on his old ship or— wait . . .

His third cabin didn't have a panel on it. She had assumed it was just open, but Sabin had tried to put her inside, had punched the pad, then declared it broken. It could be a brig. He'd also downloaded reports on his computer in the cockpit, but she'd been unable to see them. He'd admitted he worked for the Controllers. She thought back to the conversation where she'd asked him what he did for a living.

I deliver . . . certain goods, and I get paid for those goods. . . . As a matter of fact, the Controllers approve heartily of the merchandise I deliver.

A shadower. The facts pointed horrifically to that conclusion, but she fought it. Surely Sabin meant he delivered standard everyday supplies to bases. That's what she assumed. A shadower . . . he couldn't be. She needed to be absolutely certain before she reacted. She forced her legs to move, and headed for the cockpit. Just outside, she took a deep breath, then stepped in.

Sabin sat in the captain's seat, checking the various controls. He touched the panels almost reverently, as if each were made of gold. He turned his head when she entered, looking like an excited kid. "Hey. What do you think?"

"Oh . . . it's very nice," she murmured, edging around him toward the weapons console.

"Yeah, it is, isn't it?" Pride reverberated in his voice.

She waited until his attention returned to the navigation and engineering pods, then she pressed the weapons display pad. The console lit up. The display listed available weapons: particle accelerators, lasers, missile launchers, torpedoes— enough firepower to destroy a small planet, or face down virtually any private spacecraft in the quadrant. Weapons a shadower would need for capturing dangerous felons.

Straightening, she stared at Sabin's broad back. "You're a shadower." The words tore out of her, not a question, but an accusation.

He stiffened, slowly turning to look at her. She saw the answer in his eyes before he spoke.

"Yes."

Waves of nausea churned in her stomach. *A shadower.* Just like her father . . . just like Pax. A cold-blooded mercenary who routinely exchanged lives for gold. Spirit help her. She closed her eyes, giving herself time for the panic to subside to a manageable level.

"You said you made deliveries for the Controllers. That's what you told me!" Incredulity made her voice unnaturally high.

He rose. "That's what I do. I deliver criminals."

She grabbed the edge of the weapons console to keep from falling. "That's not how you explained it. You made it sound like you transported goods, not people."

"I never told you that. You assumed it. I didn't lie, Moriah. I just didn't go into detail. It was nothing you needed to know."

Of course he'd lied. He was a shadower. And she was an idiot, for not realizing the truth, which had been right in front of her. Her infatuation with Sabin had blinded her. Never again. Forcing a breath into her constricted lungs, she shoved away from the console.

"Moriah—"

She held up a hand, unable to bear the thoughts whirling through her mind. Desperately, she tried to come to grips with the fact that the man she had lain with so intimately was a shadower—a scum, a lowlife no better than the criminals he hunted.

But he was a Shielder. Why would he . . . ? She gasped. As far as she knew, the only reason a Shielder became a shadower was to turn in fellow Shielders for the bounty offered on them. Now she knew how he'd been able to afford a custom-built Skymaster cruiser. By befriending others of his race, like that Jarek, then betraying them. Had his story of his parents' deaths just been so many lies?

"No need to explain," she gritted out. She had to get away from him. Fast.

He stepped toward her, dark and dangerous. "I want to explain. It's not what you think."

Right. A shadower is a shadower is a shadower— as her father and Pax and others had so aptly proven. "Oh, I'm sure," she said, stalling for time. "But since I'm still nervous about the healer, could we discuss this later?"

He looked like he wanted to force the issue, but he shrugged and nodded. "All right. Later. But we will discuss this, Moriah. There's a lot you don't understand."

"Of course," she agreed, plotting her escape. *There sure is a lot I don't understand. Like why you don't want me to know the location of a Shielder colony you're going to turn in one day.*

This new ship was very much to her benefit, because now she'd be able to take Sabin's old one without guilt. She'd disable the homing device and ditch the ship at the first opportunity. Then he'd never be able to find her. She just had to put him out of commission long enough to get away.

Sabin glanced around the cockpit again. "Everything appears to be in order. Let me settle with Nealon, then we'll go to Darya."

Moriah walked down the corridor, her skin crawling at the thought of him so close behind her. As they passed the first brig, she had an idea. She slowed at the second hold, thinking it over. It might work. Halting at the third chamber, she turned to Sabin.

"You need to tell Nealon there's a big gap in the molding in this compartment." She pointed to the opposite corner in the brig. "I noticed it earlier."

His brows rose. "I didn't see that." He strode

into the brig to investigate, as she had hoped. She activated the force field and ran, ignoring his roar of outrage.

He sounded like the monster he was.

He was alone—again. Hell, who was he kidding? He'd been alone since he was six seasons old. Nothing had changed. Moriah—the sweet, treacherous liar—had just been a diversion. A very costly one at that. Disdaining the use of a glass, Sabin raised the bottle of liquor and drank. It was much faster.

But not fast enough to dull the pain.

He should have known she wouldn't honor her word, shouldn't have allowed himself to be taken in by her seeming vulnerability and lush body. She was just a master con artist, biding her time until she could give him the slip and take his ship. She'd never intended to go to Darya. Thank Spirit Nealon had come looking for him when he didn't show at the office. Otherwise, he might still be in that cursed brig.

Why in the blazing hells had he been so concerned for Moriah's welfare, so worried about her dealing with the Leors? She was about as defenseless as a Zarian army, and more obstinate than an indoctrinated Antek. He felt sorry for anyone who got entangled with her. She and the Leors deserved each other.

He was lucky she was out of his hair. Now he wouldn't have to put up with her treachery. He could get back to tracking Galen. Now he could be . . . alone.

Sabin drained the bottle. Nothing had changed, he told himself again. His life was simply righting itself after *she* had capsized it. He'd lived a solitary life for twenty-four seasons, and he liked it that way. Safer, simpler. He would forget about Moriah.

Actually, he couldn't. Starting to feel a faint buzz, he got another bottle from the console. He never drank like this, but figured numbness was better than the pain, or facing the truth. The truth. . . . What the hell was he going to do about Moriah's knowledge of the Shielder base? She'd clearly demonstrated she couldn't be trusted. What if she sold that information? Besides, she had possession of his old ship. It might be a junk heap, but it had some scrap value, or could be used by fellow Shielders.

He groaned, cursing the liquor's delay in providing oblivion. He had to go after Moriah. Track her like a criminal, which she was. Yeah, she deserved whatever she got.

He'd find her, too. She would have disabled the homing beacon by now—she was too smart to overlook that. But she didn't know about the hidden signal Radd had installed. His vision blurring slightly, Sabin punched a command on his new, state-of-the-art keyboard. Moriah had only been gone half a cycle, so he routed his search through the closest satellite base. And he found her, by Spirit!

He'd located her on the first attempt—she didn't stand a chance. He locked in on the signal and linked it to the navigation pod. Despite his fingers getting tangled more than once, he managed to program the navigator to track her signal and constantly update for directional coordinates to follow it. Damn, this new ship was responsive. Cooperative and trustworthy, unlike the deceitful, bronze-haired woman he wished he'd never met.

He tried to pat the console in approval, but his hand slipped off the edge and he lurched forward.

A welcome numbness was setting in. Just to be sure, he picked up the bottle.

He managed to down another generous portion, right before he collapsed over the console and passed out.

Chapter Sixteen

"Eark informed me the iridon shipment was almost confiscated by Controller agents," Moriah told Lionia. "The delivery has been delayed for several cycles."

"What do you plan to do?"

"I've decided to return to Risa for a few cycles. I had planned to dump this junk heap and ride with Roanne, but I'll fly it home instead. We can either sell the ship for scrap or use the parts from it."

Lionia considered a moment. "That could be dangerous. The ship might be tracked or reported."

"I don't think there's any great risk. I've disconnected the homing beacon, so I can't be tracked. Risa's in a pretty deserted sector of the quadrant. There's little chance of anyone sighting the ship or recognizing it as stolen. It should be safe enough."

Lionia nodded. "It will be good to have you back."

"I'll see you in a few cycles." Moriah turned off the videoviewer.

Risa. Home. She was going home, to the only stable place she'd ever known—one she'd built herself. Celie and the others would be waiting for her. Everything she needed was there. *Everything*.

Even as she told herself that, Sabin's image flashed in her mind. Ebony hair, midnight eyes . . . black heart. *Shadower*. She gripped the console, battling waves of despair and self-derision. *Fool! Fool, fool, fool!* Her father and Pax should have been a sufficient lesson in the cruel ways of men, especially men of the bounty-hunting kind.

No one who willingly hunted people for a living could be a decent person. And a Shielder who betrayed others of his kind to the Controllers was the lowest of lifeforms. Sabin Travers fit that mold. His apparent despair over the destruction on Nissar had probably just been an act.

She'd made the stupendous mistake of being lured by his seeming honor and compassion, by his seductive kisses and erotic touches. He'd taken full advantage of her stupidity.

She had mated with a *shadower*, letting him touch her in shockingly intimate ways, eagerly opening her body for his invasion. At the thought of their heated encounters, her face burned and her stomach threatened to rebel.

Sabin's physical possession of her wasn't the worst thing, though. She'd long ago learned to mentally distance herself from her body. While her father had beaten her, or Pax violated her, she'd retreated to a place in her mind, a mental haven where no one could touch her. That place she'd envisioned was a paradise, green and lush, with deep pools of clear water—a vision she hoped Risa would one day reflect.

She had learned that domination of a body didn't necessarily mean domination of the mind or spirit. Yet Sabin had done just that, not only invading her body, but her soul as well. She'd held nothing back from him, had never really retreated emotionally. She had begun to trust him, to believe he could be different. She had allowed him to creep into her heart.

Shadower.

It apparently was her destiny to attract the most despicable males in the universe, she mused bitterly. But fate could be changed, and she intended to do just that, by holding on to this hard-won lesson with a vengeance. She would never again trust any male.

If Sabin Travers ever recrossed her path, he'd be very, very sorry.

Sabin punched the transceiver com pad. "Travers here."

"Jarek here. How's the new ship?"

Sitting up straighter, Sabin shook his hair back. He turned on the videoviewer. "Hey, san Ranul. The ship's great."

He glanced around the sleek cockpit, with its gleaming equipment panels and computer screens. It seemed sterile . . . empty. Shrugging away the thought, he added, "Running smooth as Saija silk."

"Man, I'd love to fly that baby." A touch of envy echoed in Jarek's voice. As a reconnaissance scout for the Shielders, he flew the fastest ships they had, but their fleets were old and rundown.

"The next time I make a run to Liron, you can give her a spin," Sabin offered.

"Thanks. I'll take you up on that. So, what did

you do with your old ship? Any possibility of donating it to the fleet?"

Sabin felt a twinge of anger. Damn Moriah's worthless hide. She had no business stealing a ship for her own selfish gain, when Shielders were being outmanned and massacred at a horrendous rate. Drawing a deep breath, Sabin forced his anger to recede.

"The ship is on temporary loan to someone right now. But I plan to have it back *very* soon. I'll be glad to contribute it, although it may not be too dependable."

"We'll take what we can get, and we'd be mighty grateful. But that's not the main reason I contacted you."

Thinking of Nissar, Sabin tensed. "What's up?"

"I've got some information on Galen. I understand you were looking for him."

The mention of Galen shot adrenaline through Sabin. He knew Jarek didn't know why he was hunting the felon. He had only requested information on Galen's whereabouts; he hadn't specified a reason. He'd been too distraught and disoriented on Nissar that day to tell Jarek his suspicions.

"Hell, yes, I'm looking for him. I think the bastard was responsible for Nissar."

Jarek went rigid, fury blazing from his dark eyes. "Then he's a dead man."

"Not before he suffers for all he's done," Sabin bit out, bloodlust pounding in his own veins. "He also murdered Aron and stole his ship. Where is he?"

"Damn!" Jarek pounded his console. "I don't have an exact location, although I wish to Spirit I did. I heard he's planning on hijacking an illegal iridon shipment somewhere in the sixth sector."

Not much iridon came into the quadrant, legal or otherwise. This had to be the shipment Moriah was picking up for the Leors. By the Fires! Apparently everyone knew about it, which made the deal even more dangerous.

"What else do you know?" Sabin demanded, refusing to feel concern for Moriah.

Jarek shook his head. "Only that the deal is going down in about six cycles. Damn, now I wish I knew more."

"That might be enough. I just happen to know someone who has information on that iridon shipment." *And I'll get that information, if I have to throttle her.*

"I want to be in on this," Jarek said fiercely. "I intend to watch Galen die."

"I wouldn't mind having some backup. Galen is as slippery as a Trion eel. He's evaded me for over a season."

"He won't get away this time. When will you have more information?"

"Give me a few cycles," Sabin answered. "I'm not sure where my informant is at the moment." *But I'll have my hands on her very soon.*

"Why don't I stay near the sixth sector?" Jarek suggested. "You can contact me as soon as you know the location and date, and I'll meet you there."

"Will do, san Ranul."

"Hey, I heard you were also looking for Pax Blacklock. Is he in with Galen?"

Unbeknownst to Moriah, Sabin had sent out requests for information on Pax's whereabouts. He'd entertained some crazy notion of making Pax pay for what he'd done to her. She didn't need a defender, he reminded himself now. What she really needed was a padded prison cell.

Yet he could still remember the look on her face the day he'd torn her rhapha, the stark terror and pain reflected in her golden eyes. And her deep, gut-wrenching panic when he'd pushed their mating too fast.

She'd only been eighteen seasons old when she fell prey to Pax, far too young to have her innocence brutalized. Hell, no woman deserved the abuse that shadower seemed to enjoy inflicting. Whatever resentment Sabin felt toward Moriah didn't mitigate Pax's evil.

Not only that, but the man had hunted and turned in many Shielders. He was vicious and cruel; he enjoyed his work too much. Like a rabid krat, he needed to be put down. Sabin had just needed a reason.

"Pax isn't in with Galen that I know of," Sabin told Jarek. "But he poses a threat to our people. I also have a personal grievance to settle with him."

"We're well aware of his activities," Jarek replied. "I'll keep a lookout for him."

"Thanks. I'll be in touch." Sabin signed off, his blood still racing from the knowledge he was closing in on Galen.

Silence reverberated in the cockpit, a constant reminder that he was alone. He kept telling himself he didn't care, that he was used to it. And he almost believed it.

Then he would walk through the long, gleaming corridor and empty compartments of his fancy new ship. Until he could no longer stand the loneliness echoing off the barren walls. Then the isolation closed in on him. He'd never felt this way in his old ship, couldn't understand why he felt it now, when he had finally attained the spacecraft he'd always dreamed of having.

This ship was his, and his alone, not some hand-me-down from a ragged military fleet. He owned it, free and clear, and he'd earned every miteron it had cost. It had every amenity, and then some. So why wasn't he happy, damn it?

And why did this reaction always lead to thoughts of Moriah? When it did, a storm of emotions ripped though him, anger and a sense of betrayal. Why he should even care was beyond him. Moriah was a thief and a liar, a smuggler by profession. She'd been true to form.

And he was a shadower—a hunter, a predator.

He would find her. He'd make damn sure her memory got erased this time. But first he'd force her to reveal the rendezvous point for the iridon delivery. If she refused to tell him, he'd loosen her tongue with a truth serum. He could run with the best of them, if he had to.

He *would* be the victor in their next encounter.

Sabin landed on Risa, well away from the settlement his sensors indicated. He wasn't worried about a tracking/alert system, because his ship had stealth capability. But he chose to come in after dark in case Moriah kept a lookout posted, and because his long-range scanners hadn't noted much on this part of the planet which would provide cover. There were no hills or mountains, very few trees, and those were scraggly, desert trees at that. The area appeared as barren as Calt, only without many buildings or people.

With the element of surprise, he could choose his approach to the settlement. Ideally, he'd be able to keep the confrontation to a minimum, abduct Moriah under the cover of darkness, and hightail it out of there.

If it came to an encounter, he wasn't too concerned about being outnumbered. While in prison, Celie had told him only eight women inhabited the colony, and one of those was elderly. Celie didn't pose a threat, and he already knew Moriah's capabilities. She was a good fighter, but he was better. The Zarian might be a problem, and he'd have to watch out for her. The other women were unknown factors, but he was confident he could handle the situation.

He had no intention of harming the women, but he would use the stun guns strapped to his belt if he had to. Even then, the guns would only incapacitate a person temporarily, with no serious side-effects.

Lowering the special loading ramp at the rear of his ship, Sabin brought out a land skimmer. Virtually silent, the vehicle would allow him to approach the settlement without risk of detection, as well as enable a fast retreat once he had Moriah. It was fully equipped with a restraining body harness and sedatives. Standard equipment for tracking felons, and a definite necessity with Moriah.

He jumped into the skimmer and headed across the hard, bare surface of the planet, using the navigator to guide him to the settlement. The night was warm, and sweat pooled inside his flightsuit, but he ignored it. He had traveled about thirty kilometers before he saw the faint glow of torches ahead.

Bringing the skimmer to rest on the ground, he strapped the portable body harness onto his back, slid two sedative-filled hypochambers into a special sheath on his belt, then trekked toward the colony. He wasn't sure how he could approach undetected with no ground cover, but much to his surprise, he saw some trees and underbrush ahead.

He dropped to the ground and crawled silently

to the outcropping, again surprised when he felt a blanket of grass beneath him, beginning at the line of bushes, which sported large, fragrant blossoms. This was obviously an artificial oasis in the midst of natural desolation.

Sabin crawled forward, halting just before he reached the edge of a clearing. The tree line ended, but the lush grass extended onward and beyond a semicircle of crude huts approximately twenty meters ahead. Two solar lanterns positioned on poles in the center of the grass illuminated the area. He looked around, seeing no one. Wondering where the inhabitants might be, he lay still and listened. *There*. Voices—on the other side of the huts.

He worked his way around the clearing, snaking through the encircling undergrowth, following the voices, until he came to the other side. More solar lanterns provided light for a large dirt landing pad. A midsized space cruiser sat on the pad, with a group of people clustered near its hatch.

Sabin edged forward. He saw Celie, two females he didn't recognize, and a very tall woman he assumed was the Zarian. She looked different without her prison uniform and with her blond hair down. Moriah was nowhere in sight.

Celie tried to heft one of the crates stacked by the hatch. "I can't even lift this," she complained. "Tyna, you packed too much in here."

"Begone with you, imp," the stout woman fussed. But she affectionately mussed Celie's hair as she spoke.

"Here," the Zarian said imperiously, stepping forward and lifting the crate. "I will load these. Celie, go pack a change of clothing for your sister." She leveled a steely look at the two older women.

"Tyna, Marna, you check the supplies in the galley."

The women hurried to do her bidding. Celie headed for the huts, and the other two clambered up the ramp to the hatch. The Zarian followed behind with the crate.

Excitement thrummed through Sabin. He'd be willing to bet this ship was being stocked for departure, most likely to pick up the iridon shipment. His timing was perfect. Just then, Moriah strode down the ramp. Blood surged through his veins, and his pulse raced. It was only the thrill of the hunt, he told himself, fixing her in his sights.

She'd rolled up her sleeves, and opened her flightsuit partway down, exposing a generous swell of smooth skin. Her hair was piled in a brilliant jumble on her head. Heat pooled in Sabin's body, particularly the lower half. Damning his body's traitorous reaction, he forced his attention to the immediate goal of abducting Moriah.

He quickly scanned the area to see if anyone else was around. There were other ships beyond the dirt pad. The lighting wasn't as good there, so he couldn't determine the exact number. He saw two smaller ships, built more for speed than capacity. Then another midsized cruiser, then his ship. Right there it sat—*his ship*. Old, cantankerous, undependable, but *his*.

Anger reared and his fingers itched to wrap themselves around Moriah's deceitful neck. One more glance around to be sure the coast was clear and—*Radd?* It couldn't be. Sabin stared at the young man working on the spacecraft to the far right.

It couldn't be!

But . . . it sure looked like Radd. The whistling sure sounded like his. Sabin scrabbled around in the dirt, extracting a small teleglass and studying the man through it.

What the blazing hells is Radd doing here?

Then pain exploded in his head. The mechanic and the ships and the lights went into a whirling kaleidoscope, rapidly fading into darkness.

Spirit, his head hurt. It felt like it had been put in a rocket coil and hurled against a magnasteel wall. Sabin groaned, trying to bring his hand to his throbbing temple, but his arm wouldn't move.

"Open your eyes, *shadower*."

What? He knew that husky female voice. He knew where he was, too. Just needed to clear his mind and get rid of this damn headache, then he'd figure it out.

"Open your eyes."

He forced his eyes open, blinking against the bright light. Another burst of pain shot through his skull. He tried to focus on the two forms before him. They blurred, merged, then blurred again. Ignoring the pain, he concentrated until the images sharpened, unifying into one person. Moriah.

Sabin shook his head, trying to clear it. Big mistake. Shards of agony bombarded him. He gasped, unable to catch his breath. His chest was constricted somehow.

"How does it feel, shadower?"

He stared at her, still confused. "My head feels like it had a bad day in the Abyss. Where are we?"

Her golden eyes narrowed, glimmered. Leaning closer, she flicked at his chest. "I don't care about your head, shadower. I want to know what you think of your body harness."

Body harness? He looked down, realizing he was in a full body restraint. That explained why he couldn't move his arms, couldn't draw a full breath. Coherent thought began returning. He'd followed Moriah, had been watching her, planning on abducting her.

"I wanted you to see what the harness feels like," she continued. "Radd showed me how it works."

Radd? Right. . . . He'd seen Radd. Slowly, painfully, Sabin moved his focus from Moriah, taking in his surroundings, and the people standing behind her.

Celie, her hands twisted together, her face pinched in distress, stood to his left. Next to her was a silver-haired woman brandishing a thick Yarton branch, watching him suspiciously. Nearby hulked the Zarian, radiating hatred, dagger clutched in her hand. Next to her, barely topping her shoulder, stood Radd, his arm casually draped around her waist.

Sabin's gaze fixed on Radd. The mechanic shrugged. "She asked me how to work the harness, so I told her. Didn't figure she planned to use it on ya, especially after Janaye knocked ya out with her stick."

Janaye must be the old crone holding the tree branch. She sure packed a punch. If his current level of pain was any indication, Sabin figured he'd have a headache for a lunar cycle. Forgetting the harness, he tried to move, but again found himself restrained.

"All right, you've had your fun. Let me out of this thing," he demanded.

"Oh, no, shadower," Moriah sneered. "I want you to experience the helplessness your victims feel when you've hunted them, trapped them, and put them in the harness."

Sabin frowned, trying to make sense of everything. "What is going on here?"

305

The Zarian stepped closer, her dagger angled. "Let me have him. *Kamta* is a very effective method of demonstrating pain."

Radd moved to her side, slipping his arm around her. "Naw, don't do that, Lionia. Ya wanted to carve me up, too, and it was kinda good ya didn't."

She growled, her venomous gaze still fixed on Sabin. But she lowered the knife. Astonished, he realized she had not only listened to Radd, but allowed him to touch her. As a rule, Zarians didn't allow *anyone* that intimacy.

Blowing out his breath, Sabin returned his attention to Moriah. "We need to talk. Release me."

"I can't believe Janaye caught you crawling around our camp like the viper you are," she countered. "How did you find me? Why did you follow me here?"

She apparently couldn't comprehend why he might be upset with her. Lying and stealing must mean nothing to her; they were an everyday occurrence.

"You lied to me, Moriah. You gave me your word of honor—swore on Celie's life—that you'd go to a healer and have your memory altered. You broke your word. Then you stole my ship—for the second time."

You left me. Alone.

Angrily brushing away that foolish thought, he snapped, "Why the hell do you think I followed you?"

Her lips curled contemptuously. "I don't keep deals with demons. Why would you care about that junk heap I borrowed? You have a fancy new ship, very efficient for hunting down victims, attacking them, then imprisoning them. It travels fast, too, so you can deliver your victims to your

Controller buddies and collect your precious gold."

Demons? Sabin stared at her, stunned by the unmistakable loathing in her expression. "Is that what this is about? Me delivering criminals to the Controllers? I told you I could explain."

"There's no explanation you could give. You're a shadower. That says it all. Now you're my prisoner."

Remembering Moriah's father and Pax, he groaned inwardly. When she had asked him if he was a shadower, it hadn't occurred to him that she might react this way. He should have told her the truth immediately. "Moriah, listen to me. It's not what you think. I tried to explain on Elysia and—"

"Spare me your lies. I don't want to hear any more." She turned to go. "You'll stay here until I return. Then I'll decide what to do with you."

"Wait! You can't go to that iridon pickup alone."

She whirled, livid. "There's nothing you can do about it, shadower."

"*Listen to me*. I have to go with you. Not only is it dangerous, but Galen is headed that way."

"He's no worse than you are. It's too bad this interferes with your hunt and your gold—not that I give a damn."

Desperate, Sabin looked at Celie. "You have to stop her, Celie. It's too dangerous. Everyone knows about the shipment. Galen, a vicious murderer I was tracking, is headed there as we speak."

"Shut up!" Moriah ordered.

Shaking her head, Celie pressed her hand to her mouth and backed away. Sabin turned toward Radd. "Radd, you know I'm right. You know Galen. You have to tell Moriah how dangerous he is. If she insists on going, then I need to go along."

"I'm going with her," Lionia growled. "As is Kiah. She'll be well protected. Silence your tongue before I cut it out."

Sabin kept his gaze on Radd, who offered another shrug. "I'm outnumbered, Sabin. But don't ya worry. Lionia and Moriah can take care of themselves."

Sabin closed his eyes. His head still pounded, and desperation flooded his soul. Galen was going to get away. After all the crimes the man had committed, the hijackings, the murders—Aron, Nissar—the bastard was going to get away. And, as much as he hated to admit it, real worry for Moriah gnawed at him. Not that she deserved his concern. It had to be the blow to his head making him soft.

"I'm leaving," Moriah muttered.

His eyes snapped open. "Wait!" He made one last attempt, making eye contact with the old woman. "Janaye, right? Won't you listen to reason? Won't *anyone* listen? This shipment is common knowledge. There are highly dangerous criminals planning to hijack it. I can help you. Let me bring my ship and offer my protection."

"That's it," Moriah snapped. She strode back toward him. "He's a liar. He only wants the bounty." Her gaze locked with his, her eyes sparking fury. "I guess I'm going to have to force you to be quiet, before you put everyone in a panic."

She snatched up his sheath from a nearby table and pulled out the hypochambers. "I know what these are, Travers. My father used them. Pax used them. Am I going to have to sedate you?"

Would she really do that to him, after all that had passed between them? Hell, *nothing* had happened between them. Nothing except sex. Anything else was wishful thinking on his part.

Besides, she'd already drugged him once. She was a con artist, and he was a fool. Sabin watched her, refusing to answer.

She whirled toward Radd. "How do these things work?"

"Ya just press this end to the jugular, then push this button here," Radd informed her cheerfully.

He was one dead mechanic, when Sabin got out of here—assuming he ever did. He glared at his former ship mechanic turned traitor, but Radd just smiled back guilelessly.

"It's your choice," Moriah told him. "I'm leaving these with Janaye. If you continue this ranting and raving, or cause *any* trouble, she'll knock you out. Is that clear enough?"

He met her narrowed gaze steadily. Where was the woman who had teased and tantalized him, then made love to him with a stunning passion he would never forget? She wasn't this woman standing here, stiff and angry. This woman was filled with lies and hatred.

The Moriah he thought he knew didn't exist.

"Yeah," he said, cursing himself for being every kind of fool. "You've made yourself perfectly clear."

Without another word, she turned and left. Celie shot an agonized glance his way, then ran after her. The others followed, Radd whistling jauntily. At the entry he turned and gave a farewell salute.

"Night, Sabin. See ya." He took the solar lantern, shutting the door behind him and leaving the room pitch black.

That's one dead mechanic, Sabin thought again. He had the long hours of the night to think about a lot of things as he lay there, strapped in the harness.

In darkness. In pain. Alone.

*   *   *

They released him from the harness the next morning, but chained one leg to a bolt in the wall and shackled his hands. Lionia and a Leor female named Kiah did the honors. Sabin was surprised to see a Leor in Moriah's camp, since they rarely strayed from their own kind. As tall as Lionia, but heftier, Kiah looked fierce and savage, with her bald head and obsidian eyes.

Knowing both women were ruthless warriors who wouldn't hesitate to kill him, he offered no resistance. Nor did he try to convince them to abandon their plans. He did ask to speak with Moriah, several times, but they ignored him.

While he was being chained and shackled, the two other women he'd seen last night—Marna and Tyna—stood guard with activated phasers. Janaye was also present, clutching her Yarton branch like a club. A sixth woman he didn't know, small and dark-haired, hovered nervously outside the doorway.

All the women looked at him as if he were kerani dung. He wasn't sure if it was because he was a shadower or a male, but he suspected his life expectancy in this settlement would be limited.

Not that he'd be here long. He would find a way to escape, but he'd have to bide his time. He was chained and not at his physical best. His head still hurt, and he was nauseous and fatigued from a long night with little sleep.

After the women left him, he went to the window, chain dragging behind him. He was apparently in one of the huts facing the copse of trees and bushes. The sun reflected off the grass, which looked like a large oval carpet of vivid green. It presented an odd contrast to the bare dirt outside its perimeter.

He wondered how the women were getting the grass, as well as the trees and bushes, to grow in this relatively barren environment. He got his answer a moment later, when he spotted two massive drilling irrigators resting at the far end of the compound. The planet must have some underground aquifers. Apparently the women were pumping water from beneath the surface, an arduous undertaking.

Sabin had no doubt Moriah was responsible for this endeavor. She was very ambitious—too much so. He paced the room, ignoring his throbbing head. He needed to talk to her, to pound some sense into that thick head of hers, to convince her she needed his help.

That option terminated when he heard the roar of engines revving and hoverlifts firing. Returning to the window, he saw the same ship which had been loaded last night rising upward. The cabin vibrated as it moved overhead, picking up speed. Blazing hells!

He yanked the chain, chafing at his confinement. Moriah was headed into certain peril, and Galen was slipping through his fingers, while he was chained in a crude cabin in a desolate sector of the quadrant.

Hearing the door open, he whirled to see Radd enter. Fury flared, and Sabin stalked toward the scrawny traitor. "What the hell are you doing on this nowhere planet?" he growled. "I've been looking for you all over the quadrant, and you turn up here, strutting around like you own the place."

"It's a kinda long story. Are ya okay?"

"Do I look okay? That's another thing. Thanks for standing by while I was trussed up like a wild boar." The chain ran out, bringing Sabin up short. Unfortunately, Radd was just outside his reach.

"Sorry 'bout that." Radd leaned against the door frame. "Didn't make much sense to go against the women. They get kinda militant when they're crossed. Figured I could help ya better if I stayed outta it."

Sabin's fingers itched to wrap around the twerp's throat. "Yeah, take the coward's way out."

Radd didn't appear insulted. "Naw. Take the smart way. I coulda objected to ya being tied up, but then the women woulda been mad at me. Lionia woulda been difficult to settle down. See, they're startin' to trust me."

"By the Fires, Radd! You have to help me get out of here." Sabin strained against the chain, but it refused to give. "Moriah has no idea what she's heading into. Galen will go free."

Radd's youthful face took on a serious expression. "I know the danger. And I know Galen. He needs to be taken out."

"Then help me, damn it!"

Radd pulled a sequencer from his pocket, tossed it casually in the air, then caught it. "I was plannin' on it."

"You've had that all along? Give it to me!" Sabin lunged for the sequencer, but Radd retreated a step.

"Not so fast. Ya gotta do this right."

"What the hell do you mean?"

"Well, there's still five women here. If they see ya tryin' to escape, they'll maim ya. So ya have to sneak off the planet."

With Lionia and Kiah gone, Sabin could handle the ones left. "Give me back my stun guns, and I'll take care of the women."

"Naw, don't do that. I like these women. And if ya did stun 'em, they'd still warn Moriah after they came 'round. Ya leave at night, and they'll never know ya got away."

"That will give Moriah too much lead time," Sabin argued, urgency riding him hard.

"I've worked on the ship she's using. Your Skymaster is much faster. I know ya can catch up. But there's another problem."

Sabin groaned in frustration. "What now?"

"Ya don't know where Moriah is headed."

"I expect you'll tell me."

"Uh, I don't know."

"What do you mean, you don't know? You appear to be pretty damn friendly with Lionia. Surely she told you something."

Radd scuffled his feet. "Uh, well, we usually don't do much talkin'."

He'd just bet. The mechanic was proving to be full of surprises. Sabin considered other possibilities for finding Moriah. "I suppose it's useless for me to ask about a homing beacon?"

"I think the Leors insist on Moriah usin' one so they can track her. Only problem is, I don't know the frequency."

"Great. So which woman do I torture the information out of?"

"Celie."

"Celie knows where they're headed? I'm surprised Moriah would tell her."

"She didn't. Celie's been real nervous about this deal, so she broke into Moriah's personal computer logs. I caught her doin' it."

The little scamp. Sabin wanted to hug her. "Then free me and get Celie in here."

"Uh, Sabin, it isn't gonna be that easy. Celie's scared of ya now. Ya got to treat her real gentle and convince her ya really intend to help Moriah."

Ah, hell, he'd forgotten Celie knew he was a

shadower. She would equate him with her father and Pax. She'd probably been influenced by Moriah's opinion of him as well. Worse, every minute it took to convince her was precious time lost.

"All right. See if you can get her to talk to me. I'll try to make her understand the situation. Give me the sequencer."

Radd shook his head. "She'll be too nervous if you're loose. Might even sound the alarm."

Why did he have to be so logical? Sabin seethed, wanting to be free of the shackles, but knowing Radd was right. He strode to the wall and sank to the floor. He'd be less threatening in that position. "Then get her."

"She's right outside. Been frettin' over both you and Moriah all mornin'." Radd leaned out. "Come on in, Celie."

She appeared in the doorway, dark eyes huge in her pale face. Hesitant, she clenched her hands.

"It's okay," Sabin reassured her. Everything depended on him convincing her he could be trusted. "Come in, sweetheart. I won't hurt you. I promise."

She stepped inside slowly, then raised her chin, fixing her gaze on him. "You're a shadower." The tremor in her voice belied the bravado of her stare.

"I am a shadower," he agreed quietly. "But there are special circumstances involved. Moriah didn't give me a chance to explain. Are you willing to hear me out?"

She looked away, a few locks of blond hair partially covering her face. "You lied to her."

He hadn't answered Moriah completely when she asked him what he did for a living, but he hadn't actually lied, either. "No, Celie, I didn't. Moriah didn't ask if I was a shadower until we reached Elysia. When she did, I told her the truth."

She turned toward him, her expression doubtful.

"I can understand how learning I was a shadower upset your sister," he pressed on. "I know it upsets you, too. But it's crucial that you hear me out. Moriah is in great danger."

Fear flared in the girl's eyes. Sabin knew concern for Moriah was the key to obtaining her cooperation.

"I come from a group of people who are very poor." He paused, at an impasse. Very few knew he was a Shielder. Radd didn't know. Sabin's own partner, Chase, didn't know. If that information ever circulated, Sabin's death would be imminent. He was too much in the view of the Controllers.

He drew a deep breath and proceeded carefully. "Our planet has very few resources, and necessities are scarce. Unless we wished to turn to illegal activities—such as smuggling—" He paused to let his innuendo sink in. A flush spread over Celie's face, and he knew he'd found his mark.

"Then we had to find a legitimate way to get the goods we desperately needed. I volunteered to become a shadower and I use the miterons I earn to purchase supplies for my people. But I only track really bad criminals, Celie. I swear it." He leaned forward, his voice fervent.

"I would never turn in someone who had broken one of the minor, stupid ordinances. Nor would I turn in someone who might be innocent. I've always been careful to capture felons I know to be evil. Except for the money I used to purchase my new ship, every single miteron has gone to benefit my people."

He told the truth with genuine sincerity. The only information he didn't disclose was that the money was going to Shielders. Since the gold helped fund ships and weapons for the purpose of battling the Controllers, it was actually a strike against the evil system that perpetuated shadowers and grievous injustices.

Celie took a tentative step forward. "You're a shadower. Like my father. Like Pax. They were liars, both of them. . . ."

"So how do you know I'm telling the truth?" he finished for her.

She nodded, her hands twisting her flightsuit. He could see she wanted to believe him, wanted to help Moriah, but fear and doubt held her back.

"Celie, sometimes all we have to go on are someone's actions and our own instincts. You and I were alone together in a prison cell for almost an entire cycle. You were on my ship for another cycle. During that time, did I threaten you in any way or do anything to harm you?"

She looked down, shook her head. "No."

"Did Moriah ever accuse me of hurting her in any way? Do you know I treated the wound she received from the Jaccians?"

She met his gaze, her teeth worrying her bottom lip. She was a younger version of Moriah, in so many ways. "No, she didn't appear hurt after being with you. I-I don't know much about the Jaccian wound. Moriah doesn't tell me things that might upset me."

Sabin nodded, drawing a deep breath. "Then what does your heart tell you, Celie? Am I a bad person?"

Moisture pooled in her eyes, and her face contorted with indecision. "I don't know!" She whirled, stepped toward the door. "You're a *shadower!*"

He tensed, anxiety spearing through him. "I'm Sabin. *Sabin.* I kept the Anteks away from you,

Celie. I returned you safely to your sister. I defended Moriah against two Jaccians, and treated her wound. I knew she was a smuggler, but I never turned her in. Think about that. I could have gotten a reward, but *I never turned her in*. I don't hurt innocent people."

In desperation, he flung his hand toward Radd. "Ask Radd. He's known me a long time." Then Sabin held his breath. No telling what Radd might say.

Radd placed a reassuring hand on Celie's arm. "He's okay, for a shadower."

She stood there for what seemed an eternity. Finally she nodded. "All right. I'll help you, but you have to promise you'll go straight to Moriah and protect her."

Sabin sagged against the wall in relief. "You have my word. I plan to stop Galen and make certain your sister is safe." What he did with Moriah after that didn't count.

He held out his wrists, and Radd pressed the sequencer on the lock. The shackles came off, then Radd released the chain. Rubbing his wrists, Sabin strode to Celie. He gently cupped her chin, and her eyes widened. Uncertainty still lurked in their brown depths.

"You did the right thing, sweetheart. I'll do my best to keep Moriah and the others safe. But I need to know where they're headed."

She nodded, drew a deep breath. "The iridon will be delivered to Saron in two more cycles."

"Is there a specific location on the planet?"

"I don't know. Moriah's log didn't name one. Eark will probably give her exact coordinates when she gets closer."

"Okay. Don't worry about it. I'll find them."

"I'd better go with ya," Radd said. "Ya might need some help."

"I'll take all the assistance I can get." Sabin clasped Celie's shoulders. "Can you keep the other women distracted until after we're gone?"

She smiled for the first time. "Sure. I'll tell them Radd is bringing your meal. They don't want to come near you anyway."

"Good girl." Sabin turned to Radd. "I'd like my weapons back, if you don't mind. Then let's get the hell out of here."

Chapter Seventeen

They circled Saron twice, running off space scum who had descended on the planet like vultures on a carcass. The rumors of the iridon shipment had flown far and wide. Luckily, Sabin's new ship was impressive enough to convince most of the villains he was indeed a Controller agent, with the authority to arrest or kill anyone who crossed him. At the very least, the pirates weren't about to argue with his firepower. And the two who were foolish enough to challenge him regretted it.

Jarek maintained orbit further out, weapons ready in case Sabin needed him. It proved unnecessary, though, and he flew in behind them. They did one more orbit, this time to scan the planet's surface.

Saron was basically a stopover planet, offering fuel, supplies, and entertainment for space-weary travellers. Situated in a remote part of the quadrant, it wasn't heavily monitored by the Controllers. It also had a hilly, wooded terrain, making it a good location for illegal transactions.

Sabin figured the iridon exchange would take place away from the primary area of activity. About one hundred kilometers from Saron's main landing field, his sensors found what he was seeking—two ships on the ground. More than likely, they were those of Moriah and the smugglers delivering the iridon. A third, lone ship was moored twenty or so kilometers beyond that. Could it be Galen's? Sabin hadn't chased off any ships that appeared to be his.

Anticipation and adrenaline thrumming through him, Sabin brought his craft down near the base of a hill situated between the two groups of ships. Jarek landed on the other side of a thicket of trees. The sun, a fiery orange ball, was beginning its descent. Nightfall was two hours away.

Jarek joined Radd and Sabin outside the ship. "Where's your partner?" he asked Sabin. "Didn't you say he was headed this way?"

"He should be here any time," Sabin answered. "It seems the person delivering the iridon is someone McKnight has been tracking for over a season."

One cycle ago, Chase had learned Dansan was making the iridon delivery, and he'd headed for Saron immediately. Dansan didn't have a bounty on her head, though, and Sabin had no idea why McKnight was so obsessed with finding her. Still, he knew of Dansan's reputation. She was ruthless and lethal. She was one more element of danger in this situation. How could Moriah take so many risks?

"Let's see who's around." Sabin raised infrared binoculars to his eyes and turned slowly, scanning at full range. He picked up seven lifeforms near the two ships. "They must be Moriah, Lionia, and

Kiah, Dansan and her people," he speculated, uneasy that Moriah's group was outnumbered.

He wouldn't put it past Dansan to doublecross Moriah, take the credit disk, and keep the iridon for herself. But as resourceful as Dansan was, she probably knew the Leors were behind the purchase. He hoped the woman had enough sense not to tangle with that race. Galen was another matter. Arrogant and overconfident, he wouldn't hesitate to cross the Leors.

Sabin turned, continuing his surveillance. Five kilometers from the two ships, four lifeforms rapidly approached the first group. Galen, or other marauders?

"There they are, and they're closing in fast. Get the skimmer," he ordered.

They quickly unloaded the land craft and took off toward the two ships, Jarek piloting. Watching through the binocs, Sabin cursed. "The thieves are almost on Moriah's group. How far are we?"

"Six kilometers," Jarek answered.

Damn. They couldn't take the skimmer much faster, because they were weaving through the trees.

Moriah. Concern for her sent Sabin's heart racing. Why had she put herself in this danger? He tried to push away the emotions that kept nagging at him. He'd known at a young age he never wanted to lose a loved one again; never wanted to feel the overwhelming grief and loneliness when that love was ripped away. Moriah didn't even care about him. She'd lied to him, used him, left him. Alone—which was the safest existence.

A rumble caught his attention. He heard the roar of a ship taking off. Up ahead, a large black spacecraft lifted, then arced away. That must be Dansan leaving. Sabin returned to the binocs.

Only one ship now, with three lifeforms beside it. And the four approaching lifeforms had circled around them and were closing in. Blazing hells!

"Go to full speed!" he yelled to Jarek.

The Shielder opened the throttle and the skimmer hurtled toward the converging groups of people.

But Sabin knew it was too late.

Watching Dansan's ship speed across the horizon, Moriah breathed a sigh of relief. The woman gave her the creeps, with those pale eyes devoid of any humanity. Knowing her treacherous reputation, Moriah had been prepared for a trap. She and Lionia and Kiah had all worn protective body suits and blast helmets, and carried extra weapons. But it had all gone down without a hitch.

Now the iridon was safely loaded on the ship, and Dansan was gone. Galen and all the other space scum Sabin had been so worried about hadn't materialized. Or perhaps his dire warnings had just been a ruse to get her to reveal the delivery location.

A wave of pain swept through her. A shadower couldn't be trusted. *Never.* Not even a handsome shadower with a seductive body and bone-melting, husky-voiced promises.

She'd have to deal with Sabin when they returned to Risa. Suddenly tired, Moriah pulled off her helmet and turned toward Lionia and Kiah, who had also removed their helmets. "Come on, let's get out of here."

"Now don't rush off on our account."

She whirled around. A man stepped into the clearing, flanked by three others, all heavily armed. Moriah recognized one of the three immediately. Turlock. He sported his favorite weapon, a long-barreled disrupter. Her gaze shot to the leader. He was the man she'd seen on Sabin's videoviewer. Galen.

He spoke again, his voice soft and well modulated. "Please don't try to be heroic." He patted the laser rifle he carried. "Life is cheap. But I've been known to spare cowards."

Moriah studied him. He was compact but muscular. His neatly trimmed hair and beard were gray. He looked ordinary enough, except for his eyes. They were pale, malevolent, maniacal. She met his chilling gaze. "What do you want, Galen?"

He tilted his head arrogantly. "Ah, you know me. My reputation precedes me." He bowed with a flourish of his hand. "Galen Kane, at your service. No, make that at *my service*." He straightened, a sinister glint in his eyes.

This man had been responsible for the deaths of hundreds of innocent Shielders. Moriah grew cold inside. "What do you want?" she demanded again, refusing to show fear to this madman.

"Please." He rolled his eyes in mock dismay. "I think it should be obvious why I'm here. This iridon delivery has been big news for cycles now."

Spirit, Sabin had been right. "I don't know what you're talking about," she hedged, slowly inching her hand toward her holster.

"Oh, I think you do. No sense playing games. You're outnumbered, outgunned, and out of iridon." Galen raised his hand and snapped his fingers.

Turlock and one of the men moved toward Moriah, while a third strode toward the ship. She reached for her phaser. She was fast, but the men were faster. Their weapons snapped up and discharged. She aimed at Turlock and fired. She heard a cry behind her. Automatically, she whirled.

Kiah! The Leor female lay crumpled on the ground, her magnetic bow clutched in her hands. Blood pooled nearby. Lionia was also sprawled on the ground, two meters from Kiah. Both women must have drawn their weapons when the men moved.

"No!" Moriah screamed. She started toward them, but common sense kicked in. Spirit, what was she thinking? Galen was behind her. She swung around, bringing up her phaser.

A fist crashed into the side of her face, sending her reeling sideways. She staggered, battling to regain her balance. A cruel yank on her hair brought her up short. A hand gripped her arm and dragged her back.

"Drop the weapon," Galen hissed in her ear. "Drop it *now*."

The phaser fell from her nerveless fingers. Kiah. Lionia. *Spirit, let them live.* She tried to turn her head to see them.

"No. Don't look at them. *Look at me.* Always look at me when I'm talking." His smooth voice rising a notch, Galen jerked her hair harder, forcing her head back in a painful arch.

She stared into icy, remorseless eyes. *Kiah, Lionia.* Her body trembled violently. Their deaths were all her fault.

Galen smiled diabolically. "You don't mind if we take your ship, do you? So much easier than transferring the iridon. Besides, you won't be needing it."

Releasing her hair, he stroked her bruised cheek. Her body registered the pain, but her stunned mind ignored it. She could think only of her friends lying on the ground.

"The swelling will go away," Galen crooned, his hand resting against her face. "Now, I can't see any sense in killing you, like those two there. Not when you'll bring a good price at Slaver's Square. Waste not, want not."

She would rather die than ever again be a slave. Hatred swelled, sharp and overwhelming. Moriah forced herself to push away her grief and clear her mind. She had to be levelheaded and ready for the first opportunity to free herself. Then she'd seek revenge against this monster.

"Moriah. We meet again." Turlock's grating voice came from her right. "It looks like I get another one of your ships."

Damn, her shot had missed the bastard. She didn't bother to turn her head. "You can burn in the Abyss."

"Children, children," Galen chided. "We must get along—at least until we sell you, my dear, to the slavers."

Her ship's thrusters roared to life, and she realized Galen's man had managed to override the security codes. Bitter despair pooled in her chest. Her odds of escaping or surviving were growing slimmer by the millisecond. What would happen to Celie?

A sudden whirr of phaser fire burst through the air. Turlock let out a bellow of pain. Galen turned, and Moriah saw her chance. She wrenched away from his arm and dove for the ground. Grabbing her phaser, she rolled, coming up in a crouch.

Turlock writhed on the ground in front of her, clutching his shoulder. Galen aimed his rifle, but before she could raise her phaser and save herself, another blast knocked the rifle from his hands. With a snarl, Galen reached for the disrupter on his belt.

Moriah took cover, hurling herself into the edge of the woods and behind a tree. While she wanted to kill Galen, she didn't know who was shooting at them. Safely out of the open, she readied her phaser.

"Hold it right there."

She froze at the familiar voice, and held her fire. Sabin, along with Jarek and Radd, stepped into the clearing. All three aimed activated phasers toward Galen. Radd must have freed Sabin. But how had they known to come *here?*

Galen raised his hands out by his side. "All right, all right. I'm not foolish enough to try to outshoot three of you."

Keeping his gaze fixed on Galen, Sabin motioned to Radd and Jarek. They quickly surveyed the camp. Turlock and another man were on the ground. Moriah guessed Galen's third man was still on her ship, readying it for takeoff.

Jarek moved to stand guard over the downed men. Radd saw Lionia and ran to her, crouching beside her. She stirred when he touched her. Moriah's heart leaped. Lionia was alive! She crawled over to her.

Radd had located the blaster wound on Lionia's upper chest. Ripping off his shirt, he folded it and placed it over the bleeding, then applied pressure. Red immediately stained the cloth. "Lionia, it's me, Radd," he said. "Everything's gonna be okay." Lionia stirred and groaned. Her eyes fluttered open.

Seeing she was in capable hands, Moriah moved to Kiah. But as she neared, she knew immediately that the Leor was dead. She had taken a direct hit to the head. Grief roared through Moriah, a burning agony. She gathered Kiah's body against her, heedless of the blood.

"You sorry son of a bitch!"

Sabin's furious words cut through Moriah's pain, drawing her attention. She looked up to see him gesture toward them and speak to Galen. "You didn't have to hurt these women. You enjoy killing, don't you?"

The man shrugged. "Self-defense."

She'd show him self-defense. Clutching her phaser, Moriah rose and slipped behind the tree line. She moved sideways, positioning herself and taking aim. She'd never shot anyone in the back, but Galen deserved a coward's death.

A powerful arm snaked around her neck, jerking her backwards against a hard body. Pressure on her windpipe cut off her air. She grabbed the arm choking her and tried to pry it loose. Tried to yank free.

Cold magnasteel pressed against her right temple. "Stop struggling. I'd hate to hurt you, sweet thing. Especially before you and I get to have a little fun. Like old times."

She froze, far more terrified by the low, insidious voice than the thought of death. *Pax*. Spirit, what was he doing here? She thought she'd escaped him forever.

"That's better. I knew you'd be anxious to see me again."

His arm lock on her neck eased. She dragged air into her lungs, her heart racing. *Pax*. Black talons of terror descended, ripping at her sanity. Panic pounded inside her head, swelling to horrendous pressure. Red blanketed her field of vision, and for a moment, she feared she'd pass out. If that happened, she'd be helpless. *Breathe. Breathe!*

"Did you miss me, sweet thing?" he whispered in her ear. "Shouldn't have run off and left me. That made me very unhappy."

Pax. Nausea roiled in her stomach. Spirit help her. She had to think. *Think!*

"Tell you what, Moriah. I'll claim this bounty here, then you and I can take up right where we left off."

"I'd rather die," she hissed, jerking against his arm. "Let me go!"

Pax shoved her forward, tightening his arm when she tried to resist. The metal dug painfully into her temple. "I'd hate to destroy a pretty piece like you. So don't push your luck."

She made herself relax. Tried to fight back the panic. It was foolish to struggle with a weapon against her head. She'd gotten away from Pax before. She could again.

He forced her into the clearing, away from Radd and Lionia. His movement caught Sabin's eye. He looked toward them.

"Hey, Travers," Pax yelled. "Thanks for holding my bounty for me."

Just then, Galen took advantage of Sabin's momentary distraction. Drawing his blaster, he started shooting.

Sabin managed to drop and roll. Galen's shot nicked his thigh, but it didn't slow him. He pressed his shoulder into the ground, aimed, and discharged his own weapon. Galen staggered, a look of shock on his face. A moment later he collapsed, face down, in the dust.

Sabin scrambled up and limped forward, his phaser still fixed on Galen. Moving nearer, he saw a hole gaping in the back of the villain's head. Sabin glanced up to see Jarek standing a few meters away, lowering his weapon. With his foot, Sabin levered Galen onto his back. Blood oozed from a second wound directly above his heart. Two hits, both fatal.

Shielder justice had been served.

Blowing out his breath, Sabin looked across the clearing. Pax had one arm locked around Moriah's throat and a blaster pressed against her head. Her hands were curled around the arm across her neck, fingers dug in.

Her face was battered, her flightsuit bloody. Sabin couldn't tell where the blood was from, but he took some comfort from the fact that she didn't appear seriously injured. But the expression of raw terror on her face wrenched him.

Rage boiled up, but he tamped it down. Pax was a loose cannon, had to be handled carefully. Sabin stared steadily at him. "Let her go."

"Why would I do that? She belongs to me."

"Because I'm going to kill you if you don't."

Pax shook his head. "Now, Travers, that's a little extreme. I've already got the girl. There's nothing you can do about it. This is fate. She was meant to be mine."

Sabin fought for control. He'd have to wait for the right opportunity to take Pax down. "What the hell are you doing here, Blacklock?"

Pax casually waved his blaster toward Galen's body. "I came to get my bounty. Been hunting Galen two seasons now. About time I caught up with him. Nice of you to take him out for me, since he's worth the same, dead or alive." He returned the barrel to Moriah's head. She flinched.

Sabin's gut tightened. *Do not overreact.* He considered Pax's demand. Galen was dead. Justice had been served. The reward meant nothing, compared to Moriah's safety. Sabin knew he couldn't back down, though. Pax would pounce at the first sign of weakness.

"Sorry, Blacklock. But as you can see, I got here first."

Pax's eyes narrowed. "Hate to hear you say that, Travers." He backed toward Moriah's ship. She bucked and tried to dig in her heels. He clamped his arm against her windpipe. "Stop," he hissed, and wrenched her toward Radd and Lionia. He pointed the blaster at them. "Any more resistance from you, and they die. That clear?"

Moriah closed her eyes a moment, then nodded. Sabin clenched his hands into fists, fury almost robbing him of good sense. Pax resumed backing up, positioning himself so he couldn't be attacked from behind. His hostage had effectively become a live body shield.

"You see, Travers, you'll have to go through Moriah to get to me. Now, why don't you hand over Galen, and we'll be going."

"Galen is mine," Sabin insisted, knowing the body was the only bargaining chip he had. "But I might be willing to make a trade. Galen for Moriah."

"I don't know about that." Pax tilted his head sideways, his lecherous gaze scanning over Moriah. "Sweet thing here has some real nice assets." He lowered the blaster and stroked the barrel over her breasts. She jerked and dug her fingers deeper into his arm. Fear and revulsion flared on her pale face.

It took every ounce of control Sabin had to stand still. He wanted to rip out Pax's heart with his bare hands.

Pax looked up, smiling. "No, don't think I want to trade her. She's mine. I won her, fair and square. Though I might share her with you, Travers, if you hand over Galen. Would you like that?"

"Galen for Moriah. Take it or leave it."

330

Pax scowled. "You're beginning to annoy me, Travers. I tracked Galen for two seasons, followed him here. I have the rights to him. Seems clear enough to me."

He thought a moment, then fixed a cunning gaze on Sabin. "Still, I've already sampled everything Moriah has to offer. I suppose I could be persuaded to give her up. For the right price."

"What's your price?"

"I saw that fancy new ship of yours when I landed. I might be willing to trade Moriah . . . for your ship."

Shock pounded Sabin. His ship. He'd worked twelve seasons for that ship. Dreamed it, designed it, made it a reality. He looked at Moriah, who stared back, wide-eyed. A life . . . just a life. *Moriah*. She'd lied to him, stolen from him, deserted him. Yet he still cared for her. A ship . . . for a life.

For Moriah.

He nodded. "Take the ship."

A leering smile spread across Pax's face. "I think I will. I get Galen, too."

It was only a bounty now. "Agreed," Sabin said.

"Good. Give me your override codes."

Sabin hesitated. "Release Moriah."

"Don't think so," Pax smirked. "Codes first."

This scum didn't intend to honor the bargain. But Sabin couldn't take action yet. Seething inside, he stated the codes. Pax repeated them into his wrist comm, then pointed toward Sabin's skimmer. "Load Galen in that skimmer. Use the back seat."

Nodding at Jarek, Sabin leaned down to grasp Galen's arm and leg. Jarek got on the other side and they heaved the body into the land craft.

Pax moved toward the skimmer, keeping Moriah as a shield in front of him. He reached the craft and edged along the far side, staying behind it. Neither Sabin nor Jarek could shoot him from there. He pushed Moriah toward the front seat, blaster still at her head.

"Get in, sweet thing. You can ride with me to my new ship."

"You gave your word, Pax," Sabin growled. "Let her go."

Pax shoved Moriah across the seat and slid in next to her. "I'll turn her loose at the ship."

"Let her go now, or I'll kill you," Sabin promised, blood lust pounding through his body.

"Got to catch me first, Travers. Thanks for the new ship." Pax started the engine.

Helpless rage washed over Sabin. Pax was keeping Moriah between them. He couldn't shoot without risk to her. But then, as Pax lowered the blaster to put the skimmer in gear, a shot came from Moriah's ship.

Sabin and Jarek both reacted, turning their phasers that direction. A man ran down the ramp, firing at them. Guessing he was one of Galen's men, Sabin discharged his phaser. Jarek must have come to the same conclusion. Taking two blasts to the chest, the man rolled off the ramp.

Sabin spun back. Pax, distracted by the shooting, had turned his blaster toward the ship. Moriah heaved herself to the back of her seat. She swung up her legs and kicked him in the head. He dropped the blaster. Cursing, he grabbed for her, but she kicked him again. Then she hurled herself over the side of the skimmer, rolling away as she hit the ground.

Before Sabin could process what had just occurred, Pax roared off at maximum speed. Sabin fired after him, but the shadower skillfully zigzagged the craft, evading the blasts. He disappeared over the hill. Moriah leaped up and ran to Lionia. Seeing that Moriah didn't appear injured, Sabin whirled, looking for Galen's skimmer.

It was gone. So was Turlock. And the bloody trail to where the skimmer had been explained what had happened.

"Blazing hells! I think Turlock is the one who actually gave the Controllers the information on Nissar," he told Jarek.

"Then we have to go after him," Jarek replied. "I picked up the frequency of that lone ship when we did the surface scan. It had to be Galen's craft. If I can get back to my ship, I should be able to track down Turlock."

Sabin thought a minute. "Pax must have left a skimmer around here somewhere."

"Good idea. I'll see if I can find it. Then I'll go after Turlock." Jarek hesitated. "Unless you want to use my ship to go after Pax."

"No. Your craft couldn't catch my new ship. Turlock is more important right now." Sabin glanced at Radd and Moriah huddled over Lionia. "I'll see what I can do here."

Jarek headed in the direction they had first seen Pax, disappearing through the trees. Sabin limped toward Lionia. In the heat of the action, he'd forgotten about his wounded thigh. Now it hurt like the Fires, and blood trickled down his leg. Still, he'd survived worse.

Radd was applying pressure to a blood-soaked cloth over Lionia's chest. Moriah crouched on the other side, holding the wounded woman's hand. "Everything's going to be okay," she crooned. "There's no more danger. We'll get you help. Stay with us, Lionia."

Moriah glanced up as Sabin drew near. One side

of her face was bruised, the eye swollen almost shut. Desolation shone in the other eye. He cursed silently. Her physical bruising would heal, but he didn't know about the emotional battering. He wanted to take her in his arms, warm her soul, make the memories go away.

Yeah, Travers, she'd really like that, especially from you, he thought derisively.

The roar of a descending ship vibrated overhead. He looked up, relieved to see McKnight's ship coming in about fifty meters away. Thank Spirit his partner was here. Not only would McKnight have medical supplies to help Lionia, but he had something else Sabin needed.

A ship fast enough to catch up with Pax Blacklock.

Sabin overtook Pax one hour out. The shadower didn't seem in much of a hurry. Apparently, he hadn't expected anyone to follow him. Sabin stared at the image of his ship reflected on the external viewer.

My ship. Beautiful and sleek, built to offer luxury and speed. His ship—his home, if only for a short time. Now in the hands of Pax Blacklock.

Sabin thought of Pax fondling Moriah, and the terrified look on her face. Anger welled anew. He opened communication. "You can't outrun me, Blacklock. Surrender yourself, you bastard."

"That you, Travers?"

"Yeah, it's me. Didn't think I'd come after you, did you?"

"What do you want? I got your ship in a fair trade."

"Fair, hell. You had no intention of releasing Moriah."

"Sure I would have. Word of honor. You have her now, and I have a new ship. Deal's a deal."

"This isn't about a deal, Blacklock. This is about what you did to Moriah."

"I didn't do anything to her. Took her off her old man's hands when he didn't want her anymore. Saved her from more of his backhanding."

"Yeah, then you raped her."

"I just had some fun with her, Travers. She didn't mind. Women like it when the man shows them who's boss."

Sabin felt sickened to his soul. Pax was no better than the Antek prison guards. Or the Anteks who attacked Shielder colonies, raping the women before they slaughtered them. He knew about that firsthand.

"I intend to make you pay for your actions, Pax."

"How you going to do that?"

"I'm challenging you to a fair fight. You and me, no weapons. We head to the nearest base and see how tough you really are." He was going to enjoy pounding Pax into atoms.

"You're crazy. I'll see you in hell before I let you have a go at me. As a matter of fact, think I'll send you on your way right now."

Pax discharged an accelerator beam. Sabin sent Chase's ship hard to port. Not quite fast enough. The beam grazed it, shaking it hard. Blazing hells. Sabin checked the damage as he switched on his diagnostic panels. The beam had hit the starboard storage bay. The ship's systems were already sealing off the area.

"Consider yourself warned, Blacklock. Don't fire on me again, or I'll retaliate."

"You're a dead man, Travers."

Sabin had another incoming transmission.

Watching for Pax's next move, he disconnected and answered the new hail. "Travers here."

"Hey, Sabin. How's it goin'?"

"Radd! Why are you contacting me? Is it Lionia?"

"Naw. Chase got her all fixed up. Just thought ya could use some information."

"Umm, I'm pretty busy right now, trying to avoid destruction."

"Listen, the 8400s maneuver a lot better to starboard. It's the distribution of the armaments and the—"

"Whoa!" Sabin swerved sharply starboard as Pax discharged another accelerator beam. Radd was right. The ship was more responsive in that direction.

"Ya still there?"

"Barely. Any other advice you'd care to share?"

"Yeah, one more thing. Ya can take him out with your lasers, providin' ya hit the right spot."

"It's great to know my ship has all these weaknesses," Sabin muttered.

"Hit him just forward of the rear thruster. The hydrogen drive is vulnerable right there. A laser hit will cause a major reaction. Blow him to bits."

Blow him to bits. Blow Sabin's ship to bits. But the infrared scan indicated Pax was powering up his torpedoes, and Sabin had limited choices. He could battle it out, risking Chase's ship as well as his own. He could retreat and hope to catch up with Pax at a more opportune time. Or . . . he could end it now.

Destroy his own ship. His dream. He had worked twelve seasons to see his dream realized. Moriah's face flashed in his mind. Her panic, her terror. Her frantic words: *Nobody, ever again, is going to lay a hand on me.*

Just thinking about what she must have suffered at this bastard's hands made his gut clench. If Pax got away, she'd never be free. She'd always know he was out there.

Sabin maneuvered into position to aim at the rear of the ship. He activated the lasers, then locked on target just forward of the rear. His ship. Twelve long seasons. His ship, his home. The only thing that had ever truly belonged to him.

Deep down, he knew the ship was just an inanimate object. It had represented things he'd always craved, but which had been denied him. A family, stability, relationships. His ship would have provided an emotional haven, without the risks.

But Moriah had shaken up his world, made him care, made him want something more, something outside just a spacecraft. He wanted her—just one more thing he couldn't have.

Moriah. Nothing could ever undo what had been done to her, or countless other women. And blowing up this man and his ship couldn't either. Yet Sabin knew he couldn't let Pax's atrocities continue. Blacklock was a rabid krat; he needed to be put down.

Sabin drew a deep breath.

He thought of all the women who had been assaulted, by Anteks, by shadowers, by the low-lifes of the universe. He thought of Moriah. He held the image of her face in his mind . . . in his heart.

"This one's for you, Mori."

He discharged the laser.

The screen indicated a direct hit. Nosing Chase's ship in the opposite direction, he fired the thrusters and hurtled away. He watched the external scanner as he sped to safety. Nothing happened for a moment. Then a huge fireball filled his viewscreen.

Pax would never terrorize anyone again.

Chapter Eighteen

It was dark on Saron, but McKnight was waiting outside when Sabin stepped down off his ship. "Did you get him?" his partner asked.

"He won't bother anyone again."

McKnight raised his brows. "Your ship . . . ?"

Bone-weary, mercifully numb inside, Sabin blew out his breath. "Blacklock's incinerator."

His partner stared at him a long moment. "Sorry."

"Me, too."

McKnight stepped closer to his ship, raising the solar lantern he carried. "Do I see a scorch mark here, Travers?"

One thing Sabin liked about Chase—he knew when to change the subject. "That's nothing compared to the storage bay on the other side. Ought to keep Radd busy for a while." Sabin winced and eased the pressure off his throbbing leg. "How's Lionia?"

McKnight started around his ship. "She's stable.

I'll suture your wound in a moment. Have to see the damage before I decide whether or not to deaden the leg first."

"Hell, I'd better get drunk then," Sabin muttered.

He turned to see Moriah by her ship's ramp, watching him. The night was clear, Saron's massive moon illuminating the area. The light reflected like a halo off her hair. She looked surreal, ethereal, like a vision at an oasis. He felt an inexplicable pull to her, despite her obvious loathing for him. He limped over to deliver the news.

She stood as still as a statue, but Sabin had learned her cool exterior hid a cauldron of emotion and spirit. He knew better than anyone how her experiences with Pax and her father had shaped her.

He also understood that her animosity toward him stemmed from those experiences. Sadly, he didn't think he could overcome her beliefs about shadowers.

In reality, after today, she probably wouldn't want any male getting close to her. Being held hostage by the man who had once terrorized her, feeling his hands groping her body, would have revived the horrible memories and the trauma.

He halted beside her. "You'll never have to worry about Pax again. He's dead."

He hadn't intended to be so blunt. But their relationship had shifted irrevocably, severed by deception and prejudice. There was nothing else for them to say to each other. He started to walk away.

"Sabin."

He halted, waiting.

"Thank you."

Sincerity reverberated in the husky timbre of her voice. He felt an odd catch in his chest.

He turned to face her. "He had it coming," he said gruffly. "Sooner or later, someone would have gotten him."

"But you took care of it," she said softly.

His chest constricted. "Someone had to."

"What—what about your ship?"

The emotions he'd carefully dammed up threatened to burst through. "It's gone." He clenched his fists, went for levity. "Easy come, easy go."

She stared at him, chewing her bottom lip. He had to get out of here. "I'd better let McKnight doctor my leg."

"Wait."

He halted again.

"You need a ship. I think it's only fair to return your old one."

The one she had stolen—twice. All he needed right now a reminder that Moriah was a thief. It would make the separation easier.

"Yeah, I would like my ship back."

"And the least I can do is give you a ride to Risa to get it. Chase said something about heading for Verante as soon as you returned with his ship. That's the opposite direction from Risa, and"— she hesitated, drew a deep breath—"I owe you a ship."

Sabin didn't know if he could stand being in close quarters with Moriah for three cycles. Knowing she despised him, knowing he couldn't touch her, couldn't ever have anything other than a singular, lonely existence. He wasn't even sure he could trust her. As bitter as she was toward shadowers, he might end up in the body harness, or sedated.

But he had obligations to his fellow Shielders. If McKnight was going after Dansan, and headed for Verante, it might be a full lunar cycle before he could take Sabin to Risa. After those fourteen miserable cycles spent with McKnight, Sabin wasn't sure he could stand his partner's company that long.

"I'll take you up on your offer," he said.

He'd retrieve his ship. Then he'd put Moriah behind him for good and get on with his life.

Alone.

She couldn't comprehend why Sabin had gone after Pax, destroying his own ship in the process. She tried to tell herself it was because Pax had cheated Sabin out of the bounty on Galen and had stolen his ship. Perhaps he'd cheated Sabin on other occasions and they had a long-standing vendetta between them. Shadowers were known for their vindictiveness.

Moriah held the Thermaplant between her hands, sharing with it her life force. The plant's waxy fragrance drifted to her. Sabin had given her this beautiful flower. He had replaced her torn rhapha. He had stroked his hands over her body, held back taking his own pleasure until she found her own nirvana. He had destroyed her tormentor. Restored her soul.

Where was the cruelty, the violence—the hallmarks of shadowers? Why, when she looked at this particular shadower, did she see honor and compassion? Painful indecision, conflicting emotions, battled within her. She didn't know what to think or feel anymore. She needed time to regroup, calm the storm within, deal with her grief over Kiah.

The alert sounded a warning of an approaching ship. Probably the Leors, rendezvousing to receive the iridon. Moriah set down the Thermaplant and prepared to greet Commander Gunnar.

The ship slowed and came around to dock as she stepped from her cabin into the corridor. Sabin was in the cockpit, having taken up residence there. Since the ship's only two cabins were occupied, he'd been sleeping in the captain's chair.

Rather than endure his presence, it seemed simpler to turn over the piloting to him. She kept a close watch to be sure they stayed on course to Risa. But she avoided the cockpit—avoided Sabin—for the most part. It was too unsettling to be around him. Not that they spoke much; they maintained a stilted silence most of the time.

Lionia and Radd emerged from their cabin. Lionia's chest was still bandaged and she moved stiffly. Radd made sure she got enough rest and didn't overexert herself. Zarians did not make good patients, but he seemed to be able to deal with Lionia's frustration over her enforced inactivity.

Lionia's acceptance of him into her life still amazed Moriah. Actually, Radd had fit into the camp without upsetting the women. He had the uncanny ability to appear nonthreatening, to smooth ruffled feathers.

The ship thudded. Docking was complete. Moriah drew herself up and strode to the airlock. Commander Gunnar stepped through, two Leor warriors behind him. His intimidating frame towered over her. He wore a cape loosely draped across his bare upper torso, and his bald head glinted beneath the lights. His ice-cold, obsidian gaze swept her, like a probing black hole sucking the soul from her body. Then his perusal moved to Lionia, Radd, and Sabin, who stood outside the cockpit.

He turned back to Moriah. Reminding herself to breathe, she met his chilling stare.

"Captain Cameron."

"Commander. May a thousand suns bestow their warmth upon you."

"I would see the iridon now."

She indicated the bays on each side of the airlock. Gunnar checked every crate, opening the special alloy containers and examining the hunks of ore. Finally he nodded to his men and they began transporting the crates to their ship. Radd and Sabin assisted, while Lionia watched, her hand resting on her dagger.

Moriah and Gunnar moved to the other end of the corridor to complete the transaction and transfer credits into her account.

"Commander, I would request a favor," she ventured when the transfer had been made.

"What?"

"I have a crew member—a valued, cherished crew member—" Her throat clogged. She inhaled, composing herself. "Who died bravely and honorably, defending the iridon. She was a Leor."

"A female Leor was under your command? I find it hard to believe she would leave her clan. Was she mated?"

Moriah clenched her fists against her thighs, pushing back the grief. "Yes, your lordship, she was. Her mate . . . abused her. She chose to live away from him."

Gunnar's expression turned ominous. "You will tell me everything. This matter will be investigated."

"I'll share what I know. I am asking, for Kiah, that you take her back to Raman with you. Bury her with honor among her people. She would want that."

He considered, nodded. "Your actions have been trustworthy, Captain. I will accept your word that Kiah is deserving of a warrior's burial. Where is the body?"

A great heaviness settling in her chest, she showed Gunnar the bay containing Kiah's coffin. Sabin and Radd had fashioned the crude box on Saron. Moriah and Lionia had carefully placed Kiah's body inside, along with her bow and her armor. They had each wished their friend a good journey through the spiritual planes.

Moriah stood back as Gunnar's men took Kiah and carried her to their ship for her final flight. *Good-bye, my friend.* Guilt assailed her. Kiah's death was her fault. She should have listened to Sabin and taken greater precautions. Instead, she'd chosen to believe he was lying for his own selfish purposes. Now it was too late.

She held herself in check while Gunnar and his soldiers departed. Lionia and Radd returned to their cabin. Moriah stood frozen, staring at the airlock. Anguish ripped through her chest. She felt desolate, bereft. Turning to go to her cabin, she saw Sabin, leaning against the wall, arms crossed, observing her.

She could have dealt with his usual nonchalant arrogance. But the concern and compassion reflected on his face crumpled her defenses. She struggled for control. She wouldn't break down in front of him. Gathering her dignity around her, she walked to her cabin, brushing past him.

"Moriah."

His deep voice, filled with sympathy, reverberated somewhere deep inside. *I won't show any weakness. Not to him.*

"Leave me alone, Travers."

She gained the sanctuary of her cabin, her emotional grip slipping perilously.

A hand closed over her shoulder. "I'm sorry about Kiah."

Pain wrenched through her. "Go away." Tears burned her eyelids. "Get out," she gasped, but then the dam burst.

He turned her into him, cradling her head against his chest. She beat at him weakly, but he simply tightened his arms around her. "Don't fight it, Moriah."

"It's you I'm fighting," she bit out, trying to halt the flood.

"Then stop fighting me."

He stroked her hair, and she was lost. Her grief rushed out in a torrent of tears. She sobbed against him, as he held her and soothed her with nonsensical murmurings, his voice pitched low against her ear.

The storm of her fury finally spent, she leaned against his strength, her legs too weak to support her. She realized she was clutching the front of his flightsuit. Spirit, he felt good, warm and solid. No one else had ever offered her comfort, held her through dark moments.

But he was a shadower. Damn him to the Abyss! Why couldn't he leave her alone? Why couldn't he be cold and uncaring, like every other man in her life?

"Not everything is what it appears," he said quietly. "You've never given me a chance to explain, Moriah. I wish you would listen to me."

She hesitated, torn between the increasing evidence exonerating him and her personal experiences. She didn't think she could stand it if he lied to her now.

"How can I know you'll tell me the truth?"

"Just hear me out. I think you owe me that much."

How could she object? He'd saved her and Lionia from Galen; had killed Pax, sacrificing his revered ship in the process. She did owe him. She nodded, staring at his chest. Grasping her chin, he tipped up her face. His serious gaze held her prisoner.

"You know I'm a Shielder. You've seen firsthand how the Controllers deal with us. We've been forced to flee to the outer reaches of the quadrant. To barely exist on barren moons and planets. We have no natural resources, no way to survive.

"Desperate times call for desperate measures. Twelve seasons ago, I made a commitment to do everything I could for my people. I was commissioned as a shadower for the Controllers. But I vowed to myself I would never hunt innocent citizens, or even minor criminals. I track only the most vicious and hardened felons. I hate turning over anyone for execution, but these criminals are preying on others and deserve to die. I've given all my bounty earnings, except those I used to purchase the Skymaster, to Shielder colonies."

He paused, gently stroking his thumb over her cheeks to wipe away her tears. The tenderness of his action sent warmth chasing the chill in her body.

"I don't like what I do, but it's a necessary evil," he said quietly. "I rid the quadrant of ruthless predators, and my people gain a chance to survive. I'm not ashamed of the choices I've made. And I'm not like your father or Pax. Please believe me."

The power of his words reverberated down to her boots. His sincerity flowed into her heart; the plea in his eyes touched her soul. She did believe him.

Realization seeped past her exhausted defenses,

past her stubborn hold on her perceptions about men, shadowers in particular.

Shadower. It was simply a label, a term for someone who worked for the Controllers and tracked felons. The label didn't necessarily encompass the morals, the values, or the actions of the person who bore it.

In reality, the label meant nothing.

It was the heart and the soul of a person that demonstrated true merit. Just as she had looked past her women's physical appearance and emotional handicaps, taking them into her circle because they were good people, she should have looked past Sabin's label. Should have judged him by his actions. Celie had told her as much.

She studied his face. It was a face defined by character; darkened with one cycle's beard growth, laugh lines around the eyes, worry and concern creating a furrow between his dark brows. She couldn't help herself; she reached up and smoothed away his worry. Chemistry sparked between them, potent, electrifying.

Heat flamed in his eyes, and he leaned toward her. She stretched upward, anticipating, welcoming his mouth on hers. She welcomed the feel of his hands sliding through her hair, shaking it loose, then possessively cradling her head; welcomed his tongue into her mouth, the taste, the feel. Desire and need awakened with a fury.

Groaning, Sabin tore his mouth free. He released her and backed away. "I'm sorry. I shouldn't have done that."

She couldn't quite focus, not with her body in such an uproar. "Why?"

He raked his hands through his hair, blew out his breath. "You don't need me pawing at you after all you've been through, with Pax, with Kiah—"

He threw up his hands in a frustrated gesture.

His consideration wrapped around her heart, while his mention of Pax brought a new flash of insight. Seeing Pax again *had* thrown her into a tailspin, resurrected hideous memories, brought back the nightmares these past three nights.

Yet . . . Sabin's touch did not repulse her. Instead, she craved it, like a drug addict craved the powder from an Elysian starflower.

Elation rushed through her as she realized what her reaction to Sabin signified. *She could overcome her demons.* The choice was hers. If she let her basic distrust of men keep her from acknowledging her feelings for Sabin, then Pax and her father would have won.

But as long as she refused to cater to the memories, as long as she refused to allow her experiences to warp her, they would never have the victory.

In that moment, she chose. *To win.*

"I know now that you're not Pax, and you're not my father," she said slowly. "I realize you're nothing like either of them, even if you are a shadower."

Sabin watched her intently. "What are you saying?"

She wanted to tell him how she felt. But he had no reason to trust her, not after everything she'd done. From his viewpoint, he'd be a fool to believe anything she told him.

"My actions around you haven't been very exemplary. You probably think I'm dishonorable, cold, uncaring."

He shook his head. "No, I don't think that at all."

"How could you believe otherwise?"

"Moriah, I realize the things you did were acts of desperation. You had good reason to be upset when you discovered I was a shadower. And you are very caring. I've seen you with Celie. I saw how you held that boy on Nissar, calmed him. I watched you mourn for Kiah."

He paused, his warm gaze melting her. "I've held you in my arms, seen you in the throes of passion. You're definitely not cold. We've had some bad experiences between us, but we've also shared a lot of good things. I want us to focus on the good experiences."

Moriah struggled to assimilate what Sabin was saying, struggled to accept what he offered so freely. After all she'd done to him, after all he'd lost because of her, he was gifting her with understanding and forgiveness.

Spirit, she had underestimated him on so many levels; sadly misjudged the true measure of this man, and his ability to see into her soul. She'd be a fool to let him slip away.

She suddenly felt liberated, unfettered by fear and doubt. Her heart soared and hurtled into free flight, urging her to take a chance, to reach for the stars. She took a deep breath.

"I love you, Sabin Travers."

A stunned expression flashed on his face. "What did you say?"

She'd come this far; she never backed down once negotiations were opened. She stepped forward, grabbed the front of his flightsuit, and pulled him closer. "You heard what I said, Travers."

"I—I think I'd like to hear it again."

"What I'd like," she murmured near his ear, "is for you to take me to bed and make me forget Pax Blacklock ever existed."

His eyes flared, and his body stiffened. His hands framed her face. "I find it hard to believe our conversation brought this on. You hated my guts up until about five minutes ago."

"I never hated you. I hated what you represented," she told him earnestly. "I was letting the past taint my life. But you helped clear the path. Pax can never bother me again. I refuse to give any more power to the past. Only the future."

Myriad emotions swept through his eyes. He stroked her cheek, then dropped his hand lightly over her breast. "My touch doesn't bother you? Doesn't remind you of what Pax did?"

His touch was enough to send her heart racing and her breast aching for more. She placed her hand over his and pressed it closer.

"Yes, it bothers me. It makes me hot and breathless and wanting you. Mate with me, Sabin."

His body responded instantly, springing to life against her abdomen. Desire molded his face into sharp angles.

"Take off your flightsuit," he ordered.

His husky command made her heart pound even faster. She wondered if her rib cage could hold up under the strain. Stepping back, she undressed with shaking fingers. He watched every move, his searing perusal sending molten lava through her veins.

"What about your clothing?" she challenged, when her boots and flightsuit had been shed.

He didn't raise his gaze from her body. "What about it?"

"Take it off, Travers."

She went to him, tugging impatiently at his flightsuit. He had other ideas, like kissing her, and caressing her breasts. By the time she got him undressed, she was almost delirious with desire.

Trapping her against him, Sabin commandeered her mouth. She gave herself over to him, body and soul. He fanned the flames expertly, stretching her out on the bunk, sweeping his hands over her.

"Tell me again what you said earlier," he murmured, his lips tracing her curves, moving lower.

Moriah couldn't think straight, much less utter love words. Words she hadn't returned. "Maybe I don't want to repeat it," she gasped as he kissed her abdomen.

"Oh, I'll make you say it again." He spread her legs and slid his tongue along her thigh, coming precariously close to—

"Sabin!"

He looked up, flashed his devil's smile. "And again."

He lowered his head, kissed her intimately, then delved into her feminine core. *Oh, Spirit!* She twisted beneath him, shocked and stunned and . . . burning. He was merciless, holding her down while he teased and tasted. He hurled her over the precipice, and she shattered into a thousand starbursts.

She was still reeling when he began his seduction anew, flowing up her body like melted caroba. He didn't allow her to drift down, but hurled her back into the fire.

She retaliated, touching and kissing the hard planes of his body, tantalizing and teasing, until his need was as great as hers. When he urged her to slide over him, she resisted.

"No. I want you on top this time."

He touched her face, his eyes searching. "Are you sure?"

She loved him, trusted him totally. "Yes."

He covered her, slid into her gently. She didn't feel any panic. Having Sabin over her, inside her, felt so good, so right.

"Are you okay?"

She gazed into his ebony eyes, so beautiful and caring. "I've never been better."

"I love you," he said softly.

Emotion swelled, filling her heart until she thought it might burst. This was the way it should be between a man and a woman. Give and take. Love and respect.

Sabin moved against her, slow sure strokes that left her gasping. "Stay with me, sweetheart. We're going to the sun."

He proceeded to take her breath away with a possession so hot and fierce, her sun went nova.

Much later, she stretched languorously against him, levering up to press a kiss against his lips.

He groaned. "Sorry, sweetheart, I couldn't possibly do it again."

"Weakling," she teased.

"You're insatiable," he growled, rolling and pinning her beneath him. He kissed her, then rested his forehead against hers. "There is something you can tell me, though. Something I've been wondering about."

"What's that?"

"About that night in your cabin. I have vague memories of you naked, but that's about it. What *really* happened?"

Moriah smiled slowly, fully confident in her feminine power. Should she tell him? Or keep him guessing?

She slid her hand behind his head, urging him down. "Well, it's like this. . . ."

She proceeded to whisper a sultry, suggestive tale into his ear. Truth or fiction? He would never know for sure. But there was one thing she intended him to know with absolute certainty.

That she loved him.

Epilogue

It was a perfect day for a wedding. A small breeze had kicked up, keeping the temperature bearable. Wispy clouds drifted across a vivid turquoise sky, filtering the intense sun's rays.

Sabin and Moriah stood on the embankment of a modest crater which would eventually be a full-fledged lake.

"Isn't it beautiful?" Moriah asked proudly. Already, water flowed up from the underground aquifer, through pipes that had been placed yesterday.

"It's magnificent. When can I go fishing?"

She punched his arm playfully. "You don't have time to fish, Travers. You get today off, then it's back to work for you."

"You're such a slave driver," Sabin complained. But he'd gladly be her slave anytime.

Moriah lifted her face to the sunshine and inhaled the fresh air. She looked stunning in a simple sleeveless gold tunic, with matching leggings

354

that lovingly hugged her shapely legs. He placed a possessive hand over the nape of her neck.

"You know I like your hair down."

"It's too hot to wear it that way." She flashed the smile that always sent his pulse racing. "But you can take it down later."

"Sweetheart, if you can't tolerate *this* heat, you're going to be in serious trouble tonight."

"I think I can handle it," she teased, leaning over to steal a quick kiss. She pulled back before he could deepen the contact, much to his disappointment.

Her gaze scanned down him, radiating pure feminine appreciation. His blood warmed several hundred degrees. "You look very handsome in that tunic," she told him.

Janaye had insisted on making him a new tunic and pants for the wedding. Roanne, who had been a slave in a textile facility, declared solid black silk too severe. She'd spent hours embroidering silver thread into intricate patterns through the shoulders and sleeves.

Sabin had felt uncomfortable with the women fussing over him, but resigned himself. When he'd arrived on Risa, he'd been careful to act nonthreatening. The ladies had been leery and cautious at first, but once they realized he was a permanent part of the colony, that he wouldn't hurt them, they accepted him. Now they seemed at ease around him.

It appeared he had acquired a family of sorts—seven women and one smart-mouthed ship mechanic. That was overwhelming enough, but when Jarek and five other Shielders had shown up seven cycles ago and made camp in the clearing, Risa suddenly seemed like a bustling star base.

The Shielders had come to offer their assistance

in digging the lake and irrigating the land. Jarek explained that they wanted to show their appreciation for everything Sabin had contributed to the Shielder cause.

The women had been extremely apprehensive over the presence of six brawny males in the colony. Kind of like mixing lanraxes and krats together—a volatile situation. But Sabin threatened the men within a millimeter of their lives if they upset the females or acted disrespectful in any way, and they had been great, treating the women with grave courtesy and consideration.

They had also worked very hard, accomplishing an astonishing transformation to Risa in the past seven cycles. A lake was dug, and more grass and trees were planted.

Then today, everyone had gathered to watch Jarek perform the Shielder lifemate ceremony, joining Sabin and Moriah. Of course, they'd all wanted to celebrate the event. They were making good headway, too, if the laughter and singing were any indication.

"Hey, you two. Get over here," Jarek called. "You can be alone later. We're already eating."

"Already drinking is more like it," Sabin commented. Moriah laughed. Holding hands, they strolled toward the tables, which had been placed on the grass and loaded with Elysian delicacies.

He was right. Jarek had filled the glasses with potent Vilana wine. He handed them around, then raised his glass. "A toast, to Sabin and Moriah. May joy be your shadow, happiness your companion. May you live long, in peace and prosperity."

A chorus of male and female voices roared their approval. "Thank you," Moriah said, sipping her drink. She lifted up her glass. "To Jarek and all the men, for working so hard to dig us a lake. And for our expanded greenbelt."

She indicated a large section of land circling outward from the huts. Tiny shoots of morini grass sprouted from the newly irrigated earth in neat rows. A dozen Yarton saplings, brought in from Odera, had been planted at even intervals and would one day provide shade.

Sabin knew better than anyone how much Risa's development meant to Moriah. She had a dream of creating a paradise and a haven for herself and her loved ones. He was committed to helping her, and he had no doubt they'd make that dream a reality.

"You have my thanks as well," he said. "Your time and labor are a very precious gift."

Jarek clasped his shoulder. "No more precious than the twelve seasons you've given to our people, the money and supplies you've provided. We can never repay you."

Emotion clogged Sabin's throat. Uncomfortable, he struggled to find words. Relief swept though him when Moriah broke in, stepping forward to intercept Celie's second glass of wine.

"That's enough, sweetness," she chided her sister gently.

Sabin tried not to smile at Celie's petulant expression. She flounced over to stand beside Jarek, looking at him with adoration shining in her caroba eyes. She had developed a sizable crush on the Shielder commander.

Sabin cleared his throat. "Moriah and I would like to offer our drilling and irrigation equipment for any colonies that can make use of it. We still have some work to do here, but then we're willing to break down the equipment and transport it to a rendezvous point."

Jarek's eyes lit up. "That's great!" He grabbed Sabin's hand and shook it heartily, then kissed Moriah on the cheek. "Thank you. Equipment like that is hard to come by. We can certainly use it, and I'll personally guarantee its safe return."

"We trust you," Moriah replied.

Sabin realized she meant it. The profits from the iridon delivery had financed the new excavating equipment, which was very expensive. The fact that she was willing to loan it out showed how far she'd come from the woman who didn't believe an honorable man existed.

"This calls for another round of drinks." Jarek opened a new bottle of wine and refilled the glasses. "Sorry, pretty lady," he told Celie, skipping the glass she held out. "I can't have your sister mad at me."

Celie glowed at him, totally ensnared by his charm. Smiling, Jarek mussed her hair affectionately. Sabin hoped she wouldn't swoon at his feet. Damn, but she was a looker. He'd have to start brandishing a laser rifle to keep the males at bay.

"So, Travers," Jarek said. "When will I get to meet this mysterious partner of yours? I would think he'd be at your wedding."

Off chasing Dansan again. One of these days, Sabin was going to find out why McKnight was so obsessed with finding the woman. "He was sorry to miss it, but some urgent business came up. He's dropping by for a visit in a few cycles."

Jarek nodded. All Shielders understood urgency and the need to put survival before everything else. "What are your plans now?"

"I'll continue to track felons and contribute the funds to the colonies. Moriah will travel with me and make arrangements to purchase and deliver goods around the quadrant."

On the correct side of the Ordinances this time. Sabin wasn't letting her take any more risks.

"The other women will make most of the deliveries," Moriah interjected. "Lionia will oversee the operations, and Radd will accompany her. He can pick up repair jobs wherever they go."

"I've been thinking about something else," she continued. "I've got an idea that will earn a lot of miterons."

Sabin looked at her sharply. She hadn't discussed any ideas with him. "Do share."

"I want to open a mercantile on Calt." Moriah's eyes shone with excitement. "Right now, the goods are sold directly off the ships. There is no actual store offering merchandise. The mercantile would be easy enough to stock, and we could charge the highest prices in the quadrant."

Calt? The hellhole of the universe? Sabin's eyes narrowed. "Oh, no, you're not going anywhere near Calt. It's too dangerous."

Moriah waved her hand in dismissal. "Don't be so overprotective. I've been to Calt many times."

"Yeah, and look what happened the last time," he growled.

"I met you, didn't I?"

This was going to be an uphill battle all the way. Sabin opened his mouth, intending to lay down the law, but Moriah rushed on. "We could get men from the colonies to take turns running the mercantile. We'd split the profits with the colonists."

Sabin wasn't going for it. He knew Moriah too well. "Now wait a millisecond—"

"That's a great idea!" Jarek exclaimed. "We could make a megaton of gold on Calt. I'm sure I can get plenty of volunteers to man the store. You're a genius, Mori."

Catherine Spangler

Sabin scowled. "Don't encourage her. You don't know her like I do."

"Sweetheart! What a mean thing to say." Moriah turned on the charm, resting her hand on his chest, looking at him with those melted-gold eyes. Blood rushed to his lower extremities. Blazing hells. The woman did not play fair.

"I won't be staffing the mercantile," she assured him, stroking his chest in a very disconcerting way. "Neither will any of the other women. I'll just oversee stocking it and scheduling the men to work there. I'll only fill in from time to time if we're short-handed."

"You won't fill in *ever*," he insisted, feeling his tenuous grip on the situation slipping away.

"We'll see," she murmured.

Sabin realized he couldn't win by arguing the point in front of all these people. They'd finish this discussion in private. Moriah might think she could work around him, but he was learning how to handle her. He hoped.

Conceding for now, he pulled her against him and kissed her thoroughly, amid loud cheers.

"What was that about?" she asked when they came up for air.

"Just taking out my frustration, sweetheart. I've discovered this is a very effective way to deal with it. And with you around, I expect to stay frustrated."

She smiled. "Should be fun."

Grinning, Sabin pulled her against his side. Feeling a deep sense of contentment, he contemplated his oddball family.

Lionia and Radd lounged beneath a mature Yarton tree at the edge of the copse. Radd was stretched out on the grass, his head in the Zarian's lap. She was dipping suman grapes into wine and feeding them to him. She was actually cooing to him. Zarians *never* acted like that. Unbelievable.

Sitting one table over, Roanne stared shyly at her hands, nodding in reply to Ardon, a serious young Shielder who also stuttered. He seemed very taken with Roanne and had sought her company frequently since he'd arrived. That she hadn't bolted like a frightened kerani was another surprise.

It wasn't any more amazing than watching Marna and Tyna fussing over the rest of the men, fixing plates of food for them. Both women were in their middle seasons, and Sabin wondered if they had ever had children of their own. Their maternal instincts certainly seemed intact.

Janaye reposed in a special upholstered chair that had been purchased just for her. The uncontested matriarch, she observed the activities, her discerning gaze everywhere. Her eyes might appear unfocused, or she might doze off from time to time, but she was aware of everything around her. A very astute woman, she knew how to swing her Yarton club pretty hard, too. Sabin still had a small knot on his head to prove it.

Celie trailed behind Jarek like a lovesick lanrax, hanging onto his every word. He treated her kindly, with a gallantry that made her feel special.

Then there was Moriah. Sabin tightened his arm around her. *Moriah*. His wife, beautiful, compassionate—and headstrong. He loved her more than he thought it would ever be possible to love anyone. She had become everything to him. Lover, companion, best friend. She knew all his secrets and his flaws. And she loved him anyway.

She would never get far from him again. Wherever she went, he'd be right beside her. If Risa was her base of operations, then it would be his base, too. The settlement was primitive, and they had a lot of work ahead to mold it to their dreams. But they would.

It certainly wasn't a brand-new, state-of-the-art Skymaster 8400. But it didn't matter, because he had something far better.

He had a home—and a family.

Shielder

Catherine Spangler

Unjustly shunned by her people, Nessa dan Ranul knows she is unlovable—so when an opportunity arises for her to save her world, she leaps at the chance. Setting out for the farthest reaches of the galaxy, she has one goal: to elude capture and deliver her race from destruction. But then she finds herself at the questionable mercy of Chase McKnight, a handsome bounty hunter. Suddenly, Nessa finds that escape is the last thing she wants. In Chase's passionate embrace she finds a nirvana of which she never dared dream—with a man she never dared trust. But as her identity remains a secret and her mission incomplete, each passing day brings her nearer to oblivion.

___52304-3 $5.50 US/$6.50 CAN

THE MAGIC OF TWO
SARANNE DAWSON

Quinn knows he seems mad, deserting everything familiar to sail across the sea to search for a land that probably only existed in his grandfather's imagination. But a chance encounter with a pale-haired beauty erases any doubts he may have had. Jasmine is like no other woman he has known: She is the one he has been searching for, the one who can help him find their lost home. She, too, has heard the tales of a peaceful valley surrounded by tall snow-capped mountains and the two peoples who lived there until they were scattered across the globe. And when she looks into Quinn's soft eyes and feels his strong arms encircle her, she knows that together they can chase away the demons that plague them to find happiness in the valley, if only they can surrender to the magic of two.

_____52308-6 $5.50 US/$6.50 CAN

Dorchester Publishing Co., Inc.
P.O. Box 6640
Wayne, PA 19087-8640

Please add $1.75 for shipping and handling for the first book and $.50 for each book thereafter. NY, NYC, and PA residents, please add appropriate sales tax. No cash, stamps, or C.O.D.s. All orders shipped within 6 weeks via postal service book rate. Canadian orders require $2.00 extra postage and must be paid in U.S. dollars through a U.S. banking facility.

Name_____
Address_____
City_____State_____Zip_____
I have enclosed $_____ in payment for the checked book(s).
Payment <u>must</u> accompany all orders. ☐ Please send a free catalog.
CHECK OUT OUR WEBSITE! www.dorchesterpub.com

THE WHITE SUN
STOBIE PIEL

Sierra of Nirvahda has never known love. But with her long dark tresses and shining eyes she has inspired plenty of it, only to turn away with a tuneless heart. Yet when she finds herself hiding deep within a cavern on the red planet of Tseir, her heart begins to do strange things. For with her in the cave is Arnoth of Valenwood, the sound of his lyre reaching out to her through the dark and winding passageways. His song speaks to her of yearnings, an ache she will come to know when he holds her body close to his, with the rhythm of their hearts beating for the memory and melody of their souls.

___52292-6 $5.50 US/$6.50 CAN

Dorchester Publishing Co., Inc.
P.O. Box 6640
Wayne, PA 19087-8640

Please add $1.75 for shipping and handling for the first book and $.50 for each book thereafter. NY, NYC, and PA residents, please add appropriate sales tax. No cash, stamps, or C.O.D.s. All orders shipped within 6 weeks via postal service book rate. Canadian orders require $2.00 extra postage and must be paid in U.S. dollars through a U.S. banking facility.

Name_____
Address_____
City_____State_____Zip_____
I have enclosed $_____ in payment for the checked book(s).
Payment <u>must</u> accompany all orders. ❑ Please send a free catalog.
    CHECK OUT OUR WEBSITE! www.dorchesterpub.com

A DISTANT STAR

ANNE AVERY

Pride makes her run faster and longer than the others—traveling swiftly to carry her urgent messages. But hard as she tries, Nareen can never subdue her indomitable spirit—the passionate zeal all successful runners learn to suppress. And when she looks into the glittering gaze of the man called Jerrel and feels his searing touch, Nareen fears even more for her ability to maintain self-control. He is searching a distant world for his lost brother when his life is saved by the courageous messenger. Nareen's beauty and daring enchant him, but Jerrel cannot permit anyone to turn him from his mission, not even the proud and passionate woman who offers him a love capable of bridging the stars.

___52335-3 $5.50 US/$6.50 CAN

Starlight, Starbright

Saranne Dawson

Serena has always been curious: insatiable in her quest for knowledge and voracious in her appetite for adventure. No one understands her fascination with the heavens and the wondrous moving stars that trace the vast sky. But when one of those "stars" lands, the biggest, most handsome man she has ever seen steps off the ship and captures her heart.

His mission is simple: Bring Serena to the Sisterhood for training to harness her great mental power. Yet Darian can't stop thinking about the way she looks at him as though he is the only man in the universe. Despite all the forces that conspire to keep them apart, Darian knows that together he and Serena can tap the power of the stars.

___52346-9 $5.50 US/$6.50 CAN

Dorchester Publishing Co., Inc.
P.O. Box 6640
Wayne, PA 19087-8640